Heroes of Thered's Field

Shadows of Ulandir Book One

M. J. Coad

ISBN: 978-1-7635209-0-5 (Paperback)

ISBN: 978-1-7635209-1-2 (E-Book)

Printed by: M. J. Coad

First Printing 2024

<u>Warning</u>

This material contains instances of graphic violence, vulgar language, explicit sexual content, sexual assault, and other such profanities.
It is intended for mature audiences.

Prologue

Selene Amakiir, King John of Estmire

Each tree in the oaken forest stood as a silent sentinel devoid of all emotion. Tall and proud they swayed in a subtle dance with the morning breeze. An unwelcome fog drifted its way from the earth's bowels and still waters, shrouding the underbrush in an impenetrable veil. The sodden ground lay thick with rotting leaves and mud, aftereffects of the previous night's rain. This was a wild forest, encapsulating the term wild in every sense, thick and untamed it stood ignorant to the passage of time.

An occasional rustle of foliage was all that could be heard as the woodland creatures went about their business. Whether it be a return to the eternal quest for food, the rearing of their young or a spontaneous, yet long overdue, home expansion. In short, it was the epitome of tranquillity. Unsurprisingly, as this is a story and an interesting story never stays tranquil for long, the peaceful monotony of the forest was soon broken. Unbidden and unwelcome a cacophony of howls echoed through the trees of the forest.

Selene heard the howls, how could she not, and increased her pace. Her elven grace muted her footfalls to dull slaps against the wet earth. Leaves and ferns smacked her face, her body, and her legs. Still, she ran on ignoring their stinging blows.

I can't stop, mustn't stop.

Even though a pleasant chill hung in the air, Selene's face and body alike were covered in a thin sheen of watery sweat, evidence of her prolonged exertion. The soiled rags that covered her all so barely clung to her slender frame as her chest heaved. Stray strands of golden hair stuck to her damp forehead as the majority of her locks flew freely in her wake. Her eyes, shining ovals of almond, scanned the path before her, constantly seeking the path of least resistance.

At the core of her being burned an ember of desire. She wanted to stop, to lay herself against a tree, or in an earthen hollow and rest. To close her eyes and welcome blessed sleep. She had never wanted anything so badly, but she knew that to surrender to these cravings would be disastrous. Not only for herself, but for all of Ulandir.

There's too much at stake. I can't let them down. I can't stop.

Unexpectantly, a faint buzzing filled her ears. She recognised it for what it was, the precursor to telepathic communication. Reflexively, she steeled her mind, willing a mental wall between herself and whomever sought to encroach upon her.

She gritted her teeth as she felt the tendrils of a malevolent entity probe at the edges of her consciousness. At her best she may have been able to resist, but presently she was far from her best. Despite her efforts her defences crumbled at the first concerted offensive. Pain surged through her head as a vindictive presence entered her mind.

'Well done, Selene. First you escape my clutches and now you resist my powers. Albeit pitifully, ha, ha. Oh, Selene how you amuse me. What an excellent thrall you will make.'

Selene stopped next to a tree and pressed her forehead firmly against its bark. Squeezing her eyes tightly shut she pushed the pain she felt from focus and closed her mind to all distraction. Uttering a prayer to Freyr, she willed an image of his sacred symbol to fill the entirety of her mind. Enamoured by her faith she gathered what little remained of her strength and pushed back against the presence invading her thoughts.

'My mind is my own fiend. I will not suffer your trespass.'

Selene winced as a symphony of cackling laughter reverberated around her mind. Freyr's symbol fading to nothingness, replaced by the mocking visage of Antrayus, her once captor.

'Oh, how strong willed you are, ha, ha. No matter, you will soon be dead and we will be reunited evermore. Ha, ha, ha.'

As quickly as he had entered, Selene felt Antrayus's projection leave her mind. She shook her head clear of the final vestiges of his tainting presence and sighed as her pain receded. As she regained her composure, she noted with growing concern another series of howls fill the air. This time they were noticeably closer. Cursing Antrayus and his distraction, she began to run once more.

As Selene ran her mind was a tangle of troubled thoughts. She pondered Antrayus's motivations and the source of his unnatural powers. She knew his name and his appearance, but nothing more. She feared for the Oldeen Woods and the creatures which dwelled there. She dreaded what would happen to her kin in the Taoiseach Spire if Antrayus's shadowy influence was permitted to spread. But, most of all she wondered as to the fate of her companion, and fellow prisoner, Ronar.

Oh, Ronar. Where are you?

They had planned to escape together, but Ronar, ever true to form, took it upon himself to escape first and lure the majority of Antrayus's guards away from Selene. Sure, it worked, after his escapade Selene found escape to be a trivial endeavour, but she worried for the safety of her friend.

As she thought of Ronar, and the potential peril he was in, her stomach grew queasy. He had been her companion for almost thirty years and in her own way she loved him. Not romantically of course, as a banished goliath he was incapable of providing the physical gratification she needed from a lover, but as kin, as the dearest of brothers. As far as she was concerned there could be no life worth living without him. She had to find him.

Initially, she had just ran blindly from Antrayus's encampment, seeking nothing more than to put distance between him and herself, but now she had to think, *how am I going to find Ronar?* As she lacked any real woodsman skills, tracking him through mundane means was not an option.

Deciding to risk it, Selene stopped by a particularly large tree and muttered a prayer. White waves of divine energy emanated from her hands and pulsed in every direction. Selene could see every living thing that was struck by these pulses clearly as they themselves began to glow. Birds, rabbits, deer and even the smallest of insects were now visible to her.

Not sensing Ronar, Selene expanded the range of the pulses further and further and although the magic she drew upon was not her own, the act of channelling these divine energies was beginning to strain her already depleted stamina. She felt her muscles tighten, her breath shallow and fresh beads of sweat form upon her brow. More and more living creatures become visible to her and although she knew the Oldeen Woods to be ecologically diverse, she was astounded at just how much life these woods contained.

To think that there are those who would see such a place destroyed, the very notion sickens me.

Sensing something unusual, Selene cocked her head and focused upon one white light in particular. Unlike everything else she saw it was immobile and prone. It was also large, as large as an adult goliath. Certain that it was Ronar, Selene marked the white glow's direction and cancelled her channel. She muttered a prayer of thanks to Freyr as the white lights around her blinked from existence. Even more tired than before, but now with a path set before her, Selene headed onwards.

Selene felt as though she had never run as fast as she did now and yet it seemed like an eternity before she broke through the final thicket baring her from Ronar. As she emerged into a small clearing, she immediately saw Ronar laying unmoving at its centre. Weaving her way through the gnarled remains of three wolf corpses, she ran to the goliath's side, gently raised his head, and whispered into his ear.

'Ronar. Wake up Ronar. It's me.'

The large man, easily twice the size of Selene, didn't respond. A flash of panic flew through her mind and her stomach knotted as thoughts of the worst kind surfaced within her. Placing her fingers upon Ronar's throat she felt for a pulse, it was there, steady, but weak. Calmed by the presence of a heartbeat, Selene also noted the slow rise and fall of Ronar's entire torso.

As beat up as he is, he's alive, just unconscious. Thank the gods, thank Freyr.

Sighing in relief, she placed the palm of her hand against Ronar's forehead and muttered another prayer to Freyr. Pulsating waves of green light enveloped the goliath's entire body. Slowly, his visible wounds knitted together and healed. Selene's head spun from the exertion, but she was rewarded for her efforts. As the divine light faded, marking the completion of the ritual, she heard Ronar inhale deeply and splutter confusedly.

'Mm, what's going on? Did I win?'

As Ronar began to rise Selene wrapped her arms around the goliath's chest and planted a passionate kiss on his cheek.

'It sure does look like it my friend, but no doubt there are more on the way.' As if foretold, another series of howls echoed loudly around them. 'And by the sounds of it they'll be here soon. We need to move and now.'

Ronar gave Selene the most impressive eye roll in the history of all eye rolls and responded with his usual sass.

'Bah, I suppose you're right, but damn girl I literally just woke up. Oh, and before we get too busy fleeing for our lives and all that, thank the gods you did wake me up. Having a snooze on nasty ass ground like this does horrendous things to my lumbago, mm hm.'

Despite it all, Selene couldn't help but to smile.

'Anytime Ronar. You're just lucky I really like having you around.'

As the pair began to move off, a sudden snap of a twig alerted them to another's presence. In unison their heads snapped towards the source of the sound. From the shrubs a dire wolf leapt into the clearing. Its fangs were exposed in a vicious snarl as droplets of saliva dribbled slowly from the corners of its maw.

Reacting in the nick of time, Selene managed to roll deftly to one side, barely dodging the creature's assault. Similarly forewarned by the snapping twig, Ronar scrambled to one side, letting the wolf pass him by, but also avoiding an almost certain disembowelment.

The beast circled to face the pair and it was in that moment that Selene noticed this to be no ordinary wolf. Its fur was nothing more than a series of ragged clumps that did little to cover a patchwork of underlying bone and sinew. However, the most disturbing feature was the creature's eyes, or rather lack thereof. In both of the wolf's eye sockets flickered as flame wisps of pure shadow. They danced with the ferocity of one affronted by the very world itself and although Selene was appalled, she was also transfixed.

It's so wrong, unnatural, but the way the shadow moves, contrasted against the light, it's also beautiful. Hauntingly so.

Sensing the imminent danger Selene was in, Ronar knelt, placing his hand upon the ground, and summoned forth his sacred blade. The earth beneath his palm crumbled and roiled upwards as the sod encrusted hilt of a great sword rose from the sundered dirt. Ronar took the hilt in both hands and stood, spinning the obsidian blade towards the wolf. Devoid of any hesitation, Ronar unleashed a primal cry and charged headlong towards the beast.

The creature stood firm, the only indication that it had heard the Goliath's roar was a small twitch in one of its ears. Still focussing on Selene, the wolf waited till the latest of moments and then, bare seconds before decapitation, leapt nimbly over Ronar's would be killing stroke. No longer held in the wolf's gaze, Selene shook her head as she returned to the moment. Ashamed at allowing herself to become so vulnerable, but also enraged by the indignity of it, she glowered at the wolf.

Alright you rotting maggot sack, let's see how you like this.

Selene spun her arms in a circle as she chanted an elvish prayer. Her hands first darkened, tendrils of wispy smoke coiling around her fingertips, and then ignited in a spontaneous burst of white-hot flame. Bending the holy fire to her will, she sculpted the flames into a trio of small motes which danced in small circles as they orbited her palms.

With a shout, Selene threw the divine fireflies towards the wolf with a shout. Guided by her will they spiralled through the air, tails of superheated gas trailing behind. A wave of fatigue washed over Selene and for a moment she lost control. One of the projectiles spun wildly into a nearby tree and exploded in a fiery flash, scorching the ancient bark. Fortunately, she recovered her composure before the other missiles were lost and with a strained grimace guided them successfully to their mark.

The wolf whined in pain as two fiery explosions erupted from its flank. What little fur the creature had smouldered to ash and what was once sun-bleached bone was now charred black. Clearly hurt, the beast faltered. It had lost the element of surprise and now had the unenviable task of fighting two prepared warriors head on. Knowing that it was outmatched, the creature arched its neck into the sky and howled with all its might.

Intense waves of sound poured from the beast, pulsating violently throughout the clearing and beyond. Both Selene and Ronar cupped their ears in an attempt to lessen the noise assaulting their senses, but it did little. Blood began to trickle from their ears and Selene cursed inwardly as she saw the edges of her vision recede as unconsciousness threatened.

Too much, it's too much. Oh gods.

Selene fell to her knees as agony overcame her. In that moment she thought that this would be her end, but somehow, she held on to life. Just as her sight surrendered to darkness, blessed relief replaced the pain as the wolf stopped its devilish wail.

Thank Freyr.

Her vision was slow to return, but in her periphery, she noticed another two wolves emerge from the underbrush behind Ronar. He was too dazed to notice their approach, and, Selene worried, unable to hear them as surely his ears rang as much as hers did. She waved her arms and shouted as loudly as she could, trying everything she could think of to get her friend's attention, to warn him of the danger he was in. Alas her warnings were not heeded.

Sensing his vulnerability, the newcomers attacked Ronar. One of the wolves leapt and clamped its jaws over Ronar's left shoulder. In a coordinated manoeuvre, the second wolf simultaneously latched onto Ronar's leg, shredding his calf, and tearing muscle from bone as it shook its head vigorously. Ronar let loose a pain fuelled scream, but still he stood, defiant towards those who would see him felled.

In response to this fresh offensive, he grabbed the wolf on his shoulder and threw it off, tearing his shoulder muscles further in the process. Now deep in the throes of rage he ignored the pain.

Utilising the momentum of his throw, he swung his fist down and punched the second wolf directly in its muzzle. Startled, the wolf released its grip with a shake of its head and backed off two paces. Now able to move more freely Ronar adjusted his grip on his sword, taking it in both hands, shuffled his feet to properly align his stance and then swung his blade as hard as he could at the second wolf.

An almost unperceivable swish was all that could be heard as Ronar's sword cleaved through the beast. Utter sundered, two disparate pieces fell to the ground. Gore and entrails gushed equally from both halves, plopping onto the ground in a cascade of wet splashes.

Seeing Ronar so hurt saddened Selene beyond measure, but there was no way she could heal him while they were still in immediate danger.

Hang in their big fella, I'll get to you in a minute.

So, instead she focussed her attention to destroying the remaining wolves. Without fanfare she raised her hand towards the wolf Ronar had just seconds ago thrown from his shoulder. Under her breath she beseeched Freyr and with a flash a bolt of white fire shot outwards. Just as she had intended it to, the bolt struck the wolf's face and exploded with a dull thud. Both the creature's fur and skin burned away to nothing in an instant. Now lifeless, the wolf fell, scorched skull grinning at some unknown joke.

Sensing Ronar's weakness and unperturbed by the failure of its fellows, the original wolf charged headlong at Ronar. With a powerful thrust of its hind legs the wolf leapt with jaws open wide, decayed morsels of meat clinging from its tainted teeth. With little time to react, all Ronar could do was raise the point of his sword towards the oncoming wolf and brace himself for impact. His sword took the wolf in the chest, its momentum plunging it deep, and for a moment Selene thought it to be dead. However, it was not yet so.

Ronar's legs buckled under the weight of the beast and giant man collapsed to his knees. Furiously, the beast gnashed its maw trying to edge itself closer to Ronar, to reach his throat and land a killing blow. Even if Ronar was aware of this danger, he could do nothing as his sword slid deeper and deeper into the wolf's chest, bringing the pair ever closer.

Ultimately, the wolf reached a point where it had slid down Ronar's blade enough to be in range of the goliath's throat. Without hesitation the beast struck. Ronar's eyes bulged as the wolf sunk its fangs into his neck. Before Ronar could fight it off, or even cry out for help, the wolf gave its head a single violent shake.

Ronar's throat was torn from his body. Larynx, oesophagus, trachea, and jugular, they were all sundered. In a crimson spray of viscera, blood spurted violently from the wound and it was in this shower that the wolf, painted red by gore, finally succumbed to death.

A primeval scream of pure grief filled the clearing as Selene saw Ronar fall. Without thinking, she ran to him and smothered his body with hers. With her hands pressed firmly against his cheeks and her eyes locked unflinchingly on his, she begged Freyr for his aid. Magical power surged into Selene and, contrary to all reason, she poured it all into Ronar, hoping beyond all hope that he could be saved. An arcane light illuminated the clearing in an ethereal blue glow as divine energy bathed Ronar. If not for the circumstances it would have been a truly beautiful sight.

Selene's head swam as her vision blurred and though nausea threatened, but she carried on. Alas, it was to no avail. On the verge on unconsciousness, the light faded and still Ronar was not healed. Confused, Selene looked to the heavens and screamed a pain fuelled question.

'Why Freyr? Why won't you let me save him?'

Her god gave no answer, as ever was his way, but in her heart, Selene felt as though she already knew the answer.

I'm too weak, I wouldn't be able to cope with the power needed to heal him. He's going to die and it's all my fault.

Unable to abandon her friend, Selene stayed with Ronar, weeping freely as she watched him struggle for breath as he slowly drowned in his own blood. A small mercy it was, that his suffering was not long endured, for scant seconds later the spark that she loved left Ronar's eyes as his soul departed to the next realm. Broken, Selene was overcome by racking sobs.

More howls filled the morning air, disturbing her sorrow. At first, she ignored them, not wanting to leave Ronar, not wanting to face the world without him. But eventually common sense prevailed. Bleary eyed, she swivelled her head, scanning for the source of those who would interrupt her grieving. She saw no one, but knew they had to be close.

With a final kiss on Ronar's forehead, Selene said goodbye and stood.

Fair well my friend. Till me meet again in the next life may your soul know no burden.

As hard as it was to leave Ronar, she had no choice. So, with a heart full of regret and sorrow, she left Ronar's side and sprinted out of the clearing.

As she ran, more growls sounded beside her. Peering to her sides she saw another two wolves emerge from the forest around her. They both kept pace with her, but strangely, neither attacked.

They have me at a disadvantage, why aren't they charging?

Soon the forest thinned and then cleared up entirely as the forest canopy gave way to open sky. Immediately, Selene understood the reason for the wolves' hesitation. Directly ahead of her was a cliff and a sheer drop to gods only know where.

Selene skidded to a stop by the edge of the precipice and spun to face her pursuers. Her mind raced as she tried to think of a way out, any possible avenue for escape. The two wolves before her had her flanked, so she couldn't run past them. The chase, and her extensive channelling, had left her energy reserves utterly spent, so she couldn't fight her way out. There was only one way out and when Selene realised this fact she smiled.

I choose to leave this realm on my own terms.

Resigned to her fate, but happy that Freyr had blessed her with one final modicum of agency at the end, Selene leaned backwards and surrendered herself to the empty air.

*   *   *

It was well past midnight in the Estmirian capital of Estania. Sporadic beams of light from a crescent moon shone down through the cloud cover, casting a faint glow wherever they touched. The city was quiet as all its citizens, save for the resident scoundrels and ne'er do wells, had long since retired for the evening. A sweet-smelling damp hung in the air, the precursor to an unwelcome, but necessary, deluge. Watching over it all was the Grand Keep, largest castle in all Estania, seat of the Royal Council and primary residence of Estania's ruler, King John.

Late nights were common for the Estmirian regent, but even he was normally long asleep by now. As he strode down one of the Grand Keep's many hallways his footfalls echoed around him, grumbling in heavy protestations to his conscious state.

The flickering of light from dancing lamp-flames casted a myriad of deep shadows across his quintessentially handsome face, serving to only accentuate the uncharacteristic scowl that defined his stern look. His electric blue eyes still shone as brightly as they ever head, but were now wearied by the stress he bore.

Much weighed heavily upon him, chief amongst them were the Empire's ceaseless machinations and the impending birth of his firstborn. The latter he could do nothing about, save pray to the gods for a swift and uncomplicated delivery, but the former, well that was the reason for his late-night stroll and why he had left his belaboured wife's side.

Gods be dammed Ronald, this had better be damned important. I should be with my wife, not scurrying about because the Emperor is up to his usual bullshit.

As these cantankerous thoughts welled their way to the forefront of the King's mind, he turned one final corner and reached his destination. Maintaining his brisk pace, he nodded a curt greeting to the pair of guards standing by the entrance and pushed open the door to the war room.

He was immediately greeted by a thick wall of smoke. This concerned the King, in part due to the negative impact breathing in such copious amounts of burnt tobacco would have on his lungs, but mostly for he knew the habits of his advisors well. They were always prone to the casual puff every now and again, that had never bothered the King, but every time the political intrigues of court became too stressful their consumption of the leaf skyrocketed. In short, the more worried his advisors were the more they smoked. There was a lot of smoke in the room.

Bloody hell, this shit reeks. Sometimes I wish their vices were whores or gambling, like most other men, and not this vile weed they insist on smoking.

Trying as hard as he could to limit how much smoke he breathed in, and failing miserably, the King stifled an undignified cough and waded his way through the tobacco haze. As the room was not particularly large, the King was soon met by his senior advisor, Ronald.

The man had clearly seen better days as his hair had thinned to an almost non-existent amount, his belly had grown proportionately to his receding hair line and the wrinkles on his face belonged to a man thirty years his senior. However, and these were the reasons the King held him in such high regard, his mind was impossibly sharp and he singlehandedly managed the best spy network on the peninsula.

Seeing his liege Ronald took the still smouldering pipe from his mouth and bowed deeply.

'Your Majesty, thank you for coming at such a gods' cursed hour. Suffice it to say I'm also deeply apologetic for drawing you from the Queen's side at her most vulnerable time, but we have received grave reports from our spies in The Empire and require your counsel.'

Inwardly the King cursed, but outwardly remained stoic.

'Ronald, I have heard many a rumour, either fanciful or obvious the lot of them. Tell it to me plainly, what exactly is going on?'

Sighing heavily, Ronald sat his pipe on a nearby table and gestured towards a gaggle of lesser advisors clustered around the map that occupied the entirety of the back wall.

'It would be much easier to explain if we referred to the map while doing so Your Majesty.'

Wordlessly, the King gestured for Ronald to take the lead. He did so and together the pair moved towards the back of the room. Up until this point none of the junior advisors had noticed the King's presence, but now, as he neared them, he was discovered. Immediately they stopped their intense discussion and in turn bowed and exclaimed formal greetings towards the King.

Gods. Sometimes I wish I was born a farmer, then I wouldn't have to deal with this incessant pleasantry obsessed pageantry.

Having endured the formal greetings his position demanded the King redirected proceedings back to the matter at hand.

'All right then gentlemen I'll ask one more time, why in blazes am I here?'

Ronald coughed, clearing his throat from habit more than necessity, grabbed a nearby cane, inhaled deeply and, without any further ado, began to explain.

'In short, your Majesty we have received confirmation that an Imperial invasion of the Southlands is imminent. We have received several separate reports, each of which has been verified, of considerable troop movements within the Empire. This is by no means an unusual occurrence, but in this instance a large number of these troops have been drawn from key Imperial garrisons. The emptying of these strongholds has in the past, in every instance I might add, been a precursor to invasion.'

Pausing to gather his thoughts, Ronald pointed to the map with his cane and continued.

'Another key part of information that lends credibility to the idea of the Southlands being the target of Imperial aggression is the fact that all troop movements are directed towards the south. Specifically, along these three major roads.'

Before Ronald could continue with the finer intricacies of the briefing, of which the King knew there would be many, the Estmirian ruler raised his hand.

'How many?'

Ronald stuttered mid-speech, but recovered quickly.

'We are currently unaware of their exact numbers, but we believe it to be in the tens of thousands.'

Deep in contemplation the King started to stroke his goatee absentmindedly. Staring intensely at the map he considered the strategic ramifications of an Imperial annexation of the Southlands.

We'd lose access to the only free deep-water port in the region. We'd be cut off from the world. We'd be the next to fall. If they fall, then we do too. Shit. And gods know you're already aware of this reality you shifty bastard.

Sighing with a heavy resignation to his fated path, the King turned to Ronald and looked his advisor in the eye.

'Have we sent warning to the Southlands Government?'

'Yes, Your Majesty. We sent a squad of riders as soon as the reports were validated, but I'd be surprised if they didn't already know. Their spies are almost as good as our own after all.'

'Good, at least we now know for certain that they're aware.'

A single question burned in the King's mind, and though he believed to already know its answer, he felt compelled to ask it anyway. After hesitating momentarily, the King asked solemnly.

'In your opinion Ronald, what chance do they have?'

'It's not good Your Majesty. As you know the Southlands maintains a small military, relying on almost entirely on mercenaries. I doubt they'd be a match for Imperial troops, and that's even if they decided to fight. In addition, now that The Empire's conquest of Khull has concluded they are free to shift their entire military might, most of which is comprised of seasoned troops I might add, towards the conflict.'

Growing impatient of the in-depth analysis of the situation, the King narrowed his eyes into the most intimidating stare he could manage. As socially inept as Ronald was prone to be, even he recognised the meaning behind the King's glowering gaze.

'Well, yes, um. In short, without significant aid they will fall. And they will fall quickly.'

Just as I thought.

The King exhaled deeply as he tried to rub the stress from his knotted brow. Alas, he could find no relief. He knew what had to be done, what he had to do. But the ramifications for his people weighed heavily upon his soul.

'We cannot allow that to occur Ronald, for if we do the same fate will befall us. It pains me that I have been forced to this, but it must be done. Raise the banners and muster our armies.'

As soon as the King uttered the final word of this edict, a small group of advisors scurried hastily from the room, no doubt to do as the King had just bid. Ronald, however, remained by the King's side as his liege continued to issue more commands.

'Once they are assembled send our knights as a vanguard force, we need them to bolster the frontline as soon as possible. As for our infantry, send them to Súthburh directly, I have a feeling that we'll inevitably be forced to withdraw to the city anyway.'

'Very prudent Your Majesty.'

Ignoring Ronald's interjection, the King continued.

'As for the home front, begin conscription immediately. Anyone, man, woman, or child, who is of able body is to be trained to take up arms. We won't be able to spare the men to train them, so reinstate all retired knights who are to elderly for the frontlines to act as instructors. It is unlikely that The Empire will send forces through the Oldeen Wood, but if they do I want our people to be prepared.'

More importantly I'd like to give them a choice, to die free rather than to die as slaves. By the gods I hope it doesn't come to that.

'Finally, notify our allies of our plight and our intentions. Appeal to them for support. I doubt the elves will be of any use, but the dwarves may just aid us.'

Ronald's face was grim, but determined. Bowing, he gave the King a nod of understanding and turned to leave.

'It will be done at once Your Majesty.'

'Wait Ronald.'

'Yes, Your Majesty?'

'Leave it till morning. It's far too late in the day to worry about it now. Get some sleep and start afresh on the morn.'

Ronald let out a deep sigh that betrayed just how fatigued he was. He turned to the King, his lips curled into a warm smile, but whatever the aged advisor was about to say died as an unspoken thought as he was interrupted by a knock on the door. Curtly the King called out 'enter.'

At his call one of his wife's handmaidens hurried into the room. She addressed him with a reverential curtsy and, driven by rushed purpose, ignored all social decorum by breathlessly blurting out unbidden the message she had come to deliver.

'Your Majesty. It's the Queen. The baby is on its way it is.'

Instantly all thoughts of war vanished from the King's mind as all he could think about was his wife. Overcome by a primal need to be there for her, to help and protect her, he ran from the room, leaving his wife's handmaiden and Ronald forgotten behind him.

As he hurtled along the castle's corridors his robe behind him and his sheathed sword banged annoyingly against his thigh, but he paid neither no heed. The scant few servants and the occasional guard he encountered jumped from his path, lest they be bowled over by the veritable force of nature that the King had become.

As the King skidded through the door of his wife's antechamber, he heard a series of muffled cries and gurgles from the room beyond. Immediately he felt different.

Gods. It's here already. I'm a father.

Before entering the Queen's chambers proper, the King swallowed nervously as he tried to compose himself. Though he already knew it to be the case he found himself standing on the precipice of fatherhood. As of now it was an abstract notion, but as soon as he entered that room it would become a reality. This fact both scared and excited him.

Heart pounding in his chest, the King exhaled slowly, opened the door, and eased himself into the room. Before him was the most beautiful sight he had ever seen. His wife, haggard, yet clearly ecstatic, was gazing lovingly down at their new born, a wide smile fixed firmly upon her face. Clearly, she had heard the King enter as she looked up towards the awestruck monarch, smile growing twice as wide, and whispered.

'John, it's a girl.'

Wordlessly the King moved to stand beside his wife and child. The Queen's joy was infectious and unconsciously the King matched her smile with one of his own. Tenderly, afraid of hurting that which he found so fragile and precious, he placed his hand on his daughter's brow and muttered softly.

'By the Gods, she is beautiful.'

Upon hearing his voice, the child turned her head to face the King. She opened her eyes to look up at him and the King felt a conflux of emotions as two bright green beacons, alive with intelligence and mirth, bore into his soul. It was in equal measures the most beautiful and most terrifying sight he had ever seen.

Oh, Lady Fate you fickle bitch. Why did you choose my child to curse with such a poisoned chalice?

The happiness within him shrivelled, replaced by a deep fear. Too strong to be contained the monarch's face twisted to mirror the growing knot of concern lodged firmly in the core of his chest. Unsurprisingly, the Queen noted her husband's transformation.

'John? What's wrong? You're starting to scare me.'

Unable to tear his attention away from his child, the King stammered a response, his usual bravado overridden by a newfound doubt.

'Her eyes. Have you not seen her eyes?'

'Of course, what of them?'

'It's the mark. The mark of a true sorcerer. She has, will have, power. Beyond all reckoning, beyond all measure. Power to create and power to destroy, power to mend and power to break, it will all be hers.'

'John. Look at me.'

Though it took much effort to do so, the King broke the trance-like hold his daughter's eyes held him in and looked up to his wife.

'Be that as it may, right now she's just a baby and well, if we raise her to be a good person and shower her with love, how could she possibly grow to become evil? The power she has, will have, well, she'll choose to be a force for good.'

Despite his mood, the King found his wife's optimism infectious and reflexively smiled.

'Of that I have no doubt.'

'Then what's the problem?'

The King sighed a heavy sigh.

'That's not what I fear. There are those that will hunt her for what she is. They would rather kill her than risk her turning to darkness. Similarly, those that abhor the light will seek her demise, lest she become a force of righteousness.'

He paused. Gathering his thoughts. The queen, knowing the difficulty he faced when tasked with expressing his innermost emotions, waited patiently for him to continue.

'I can't lose her.'

The Queen took the King's hand in her own and squeezed it reassuringly.

'We won't let that happen.'

'I know.'

Gods do I love this woman.

The King raised his wife's hand and kissed it.

'We'll talk more on it later, make plans and the like, but for now let's move on. So, have you a name in mind for her?'

The Queen looked down and gazed lovingly at her child.

'I would name her Esmerelda, if that pleases you, my love.'

Taking the name and rolling it around in his mind, the King considered its suitability for his daughter. Reaching over to his child he tickled the baby's chin.

'How about that sprite, how do you like the name Esmerelda?'

In response the child gurgled melodically, clearly pleased.

'Esmerelda it is then.'

The Queen just smiled, radiating joy. In a physical manifestation of the love he was feeling, the King embraced his wife and kissed her passionately.

It was during their enraptured embrace that an intruder slipped unnoticed into the room. Having scaled the sheer stone of the castle tower, a feat believed to be impossible, a lone halfling vaulted silently over the balcony railing. Crouching low to the ground and moving with deliberate care, the halfling stalked soundlessly towards the royal family.

As he drew near to the rear of the King, he drew a short sword from a muffled sheath and plunged the blade into the monarch's back. Meeting no tangible resistance, the sword sunk deep and with a wet crunch speared its way through the entirety of the King's body and out of his chest.

The King stifled a groan as blood oozed from his mouth and the protruding sword blade in his torso. As quickly as it had entered the blade withdrew from the King's body. Fresh drawn blood sprayed over the Queen as the King collapsed motionless to the floor. Overcome by a swath of emotions, the Queen screamed a primal scream and, though her child knew not for what reason her mother had begun to shriek so wildly, Esmerelda joined suit, wailing as hard as she could.

The assassin took a single step towards the Queen and her baby. In a single fluid movement, he raised his sword, still slick with the King's blood, and prepared to strike. Without hesitation the halfling swung his blade down towards the Queen's head.

In that moment the Queen sat immobile, thinking not of herself, for she knew herself to already be dead, but of her child's welfare and the injustice of robbing one so young of a life not yet lived. However, Lady Fate, as cruel as she could be, was equally prone to acts of kindness. The assassin's blade stopped mid-stroke as his attention was draw to a bright green light radiating from the floor beside him.

Still prone, the King lay at the epicentre of the light. The blood that had pooled onto the floor beside him dissipated slowly as it was reabsorbed through the wound from which it had been spilt.

Overcoming his initial shock, and determining the King to be an immediate threat, the halfling twisted his body and swung his sword at the seemingly resurrected monarch. From the ground, the King mumbled a hurried arcane verse and outstretched his arm. Instantly, the assassin froze mid-swing, held in place by the magical forces the King bore.

As the Estmirian monarch stood, still immersed in an eldritch green glow, his wound rapidly healed. Torn flesh and ruptured organs alike knitted together and were made new in mere moments. It was only once he was fully restored that the light dissipated and though his clothes were ruined his skin was completely unblemished.

Well, that was a surprising turn of events.

While he held the halfling in place the King studied his would-be murderer. Save for his height, which was average for a halfling, the majority of his features were obscured by the nondescript leather that covered him from head to toe. The lower portion of his face was concealed by a mask and a hood was pulled low over his head. The assassin's only discernible feature were his eyes, or rather his lack thereof. In lieu of eyeballs small black flames flickered in their place.

Good gods.

Stunned, the King lost focus and the halfling broke free of his spell. Immediately, the assassin continued his attack, thrusting his sword at the King's throat.

As the blade shot towards his neck, the King barely reacted in time. Stepping back to give himself more space, the King thrusted out his hand in response. A pulse of magical energy bore into the halfling's body, striking him with such force that it propelled him across the room. Landing heavily on the floor, he slid across its surface until the far wall arrested his momentum.

Seeing his foe drop his sword, the King drew his own weapon and advanced. As swiftly as a sparrow the halfling pulled a pair of daggers from his boots and threw them at the King. Fuelled by the adrenaline that surged through his veins, a hyper-focussed King John deflected one of the daggers with his sword and with a dexterous roll he dodged the second.

Continuing his charge, an angry growl escaped the King's mouth as he swung his sword with an expert finesse. As the halfling had no means to mitigate the attack, the King's blade carved a deep gash along the assassin's chest. A thin mist of blood sprayed into the air, but the assassin made no sound.

Not yet dead, the halfling scrambled frantically across the ground in a desperate gambit to retrieve his sword. Before the King's next strike could find its mark, the assassin scooped up his short sword, rolled onto his back and parried the blow that would have surely ended him.

In desperation the halfling lunged out at the King, but it was a foolish endeavour. With ease the King patted the blow aside, stepped into the attack and ran the halfling through. As he stood above his defeated quarry, waiting for him to expire, the King noted with profound bemusement the moment when, simultaneously, the assassin's chest moving and the flames in his eye sockets blinked out, extinguished.

By all that is holy, what in the thirteen realms just happened?

Concerned for their welfare, the King turned to face his wife and child. The Queen's was visibly shaken, her face streaked wet from tears and spattered with specks of the King's blood, and Esmerelda was in a state, far beyond consoling, but at least they were both unhurt. The King sighed in relief, knowing that it could have been far worse, but was deeply troubled by the danger his family had just been exposed to.

In that moment of reflection, the King's mind was awhirl with questions and awash with doubt fuelled by the elusiveness of answers. Only a single realisation burned clearly amongst the chaotic storm of unknowns, both he and his family were no longer safe in their own home. Rightly, or perhaps it was in error, this led the King to a single conclusion.

They need to leave my side. Until this matter, whatever it may be, is resolved I cannot be with them, lest more attempts on my life claim theirs. As much as it pains me to do so, I must send them away. It seems that I have plans to make.

Chapter 1

Neesa

It was the middle of summer and the air was dry and hot. Harsh sunrays beamed down, mercilessly burning all they touched. The earth was hard and parched from the lack of rain and many of the dams were running on empty, having sacrificed themselves to nourish the nearby crops and those that tended them. Clusters of livestock lay sprawled in their fields, too lethargic to move from the sparse shade they coveted. Amongst it all was a carpet of burgeoning wheat in dire need of harvest and those unfortunate sods tasked with the job.

Slaves chained in pairs dotted the fields working as hard as they were able, lest they fail to reach their quota and incur the wrath of the slave driver's lash. As was the way in the Empire, there were no men amongst them. In a society driven by an almost perpetual war, male slaves were the fuel that drove the Imperial military machine. Agricultural endeavours were the realm of women.

As with most slaves, these indentured women did only what they had to and no more. As far as they were concerned there was no point in exceeding their physical limit for no reward. For those fated to a life of servitude knew that by doing such they would only serve to shorten their lifespan. However, amongst these particular slaves there was one who believed differently.

She was an infernati, a rarity in this part of the world, and was currently attacking the wheat before her with a supernatural gusto. Twirling in a blur of perpetual motion, she wielded her scythe with a graceful fury, felling swathes of wheat stalks with every stroke. Her midnight blue muscles rippled and glistened with sweat as she danced. She was lost in a blissful revelry, gone to a place where she forgot all her worries and woes. Unfortunately, she also forgot the length of the chain fastened around her leg.

With a ta-ting the chain pulled taught, arresting her momentum. Caught off balance, the infernati collapsed gracelessly into the dirt. As she lay there, oblivious to any embarrassment and immune to pain, her chest rose and fell rapidly. A seething anger, the fuel that drove her, burned in her chest and her eyes glowered with fury. Her mind was occupied by a single concept, not at all complex, but profound in its power. Rage. Nothing but rage and an accompanying endless scream.

'Fur gods' sake Neesa, take some bloody care.'

Words from her periphery, barely recognisable, but sill understood, pierced the veil of red clouding her consciousness. Slowly the rage faded and she returned to a state of calm.

Damn it. Well done, Neesa. Good to see you're in control of your emotions. Bah.

Groaning, Neesa picked herself up off of the ground. Turning to her partner, whilst dusting the dirt from her shirt the best she could, she responded meekly.

'Sorry Joan, I just got lost in the moment. You know.'

Joan, a dwarf nearing her golden years, just sighed heavily.

'Tis all reit dearie, but I dae no' know how ye bother wi' all 'at training, building yerself up and all. It's no' lek yer goin' tae get free. Nae Wan ever does.'

For a moment an ember of rage returned, smouldering in Neesa's eyes. Stoked by Joan's dismissive attitude and fuelled by her own self-doubt, it threatened to engulf her in a raging inferno. But, in this instance she just blinked it away before it could become anything more than an idle thought.

'That's where you're wrong Joan, I *will* get free. I've done it before and I'll do it again. You'll see.'

'Oh, I will, will I? Weel wee miss escape artist, how dae ye expect tae dae 'at then? Sprout some wings an' fly away? Turn yerself tae smoke an' drift unnoticed in the wee hours when there's nary a soul looking? Ha, ha, dream oan girlie. Oh gods, here nary a week an' already chompin' at the bit tae leave. Ha, ha.'

Neesa ignored her companion and glanced furtively around, making sure there were no guards within earshot.

'No. I'll kill them. I'll kill them all.'

At Neesa's words Joan visibly paled, her face etched deeply with fear.

'Shush! Shut ye blasted mouth girl, hev ye lost yer mind. Ye cannae dae 'at, ye jus' cannae. An' even if ye cuid it'd be the rest o' us that'd get the noose fur yer troubles. Gods be merciful, how is it 'at I always get paired wi' the mad ones.'

Joan continued to rant under her breath as she returned to work, gathering the stalks of wheat Neesa had just felled. Conversation clearly over, Neesa just shrugged and joined her partner.

Well, it seems like a reasonable plan to me. I mean, it's worked before.

Several hours later, when the sun was low in the sky and the working day almost over, a noble's carriage, rosewood with murals of inlaid gold, rolled down a nearby road. Initially, Neesa thought nothing of it, after all it was common for their master to entertain guests, but as it rattled by the whiff of a familiar scent caught her attention. At first it was strange, as recognition hid somewhere just out of reach, so instinctually she breathed in deep, seeking clarification. At once her nose burned with the familiar smell of cherry blossoms and in that instant, she was taken back to the day when she lost it all.

*   *   *

It was early spring and the cherry blossoms had just begun to bloom. Their scent wafted gently through the air, carried by whisps of wind as gentle as a new lamb's wool. Flocks of starlings flew impossibly complex patterns overhead, each individual in perfect synchronicity with the others. Fields of wheat, freshly planted and still young, rippled in the breeze, an ocean of green. New born calves bleated cries of victory in their meadows as they mastered the art of walking and their proud mothers mooed deeply in satisfaction.

At the centre of this picturesque perfection was a young infernati girl of no more than five years old. Dark blue in complexion with a mass of wild purple locks she smiled with glee as she tiptoed along a stonework fence. Coming to a particularly large break in the wall, the girl took a deep breath and steeled herself.

With her arms outstretched and tongue poked out of her mouth concentration wracked her tiny face. As her tail sung lazily behind her, she bent her knees and pushed off as hard as she could. With ease she sprang over the crevice and landed deftly on the other side. Feeling an intense surge of pride, the girl gave a curt bow to a pair of onlooking bovines and continued forward.

Off in the distance, from somewhere behind her, she heard her mother call out.

'Neesa, darling, don't run off too far please.'

Instead of heeding her mother's plea, Neesa giggled mischievously and increased her pace.

Let's go!

A blur of movement from the base of the wall caught the girl's attention, so she bent over to see what it was. Below her there fluttered a flight of butterflies, weaving their way amongst a thicket of wildflowers. Captivated by the intricate patterns on their wings, she stared in wonder and gasped a single word, 'pretty.'

Wanting to see them closer, she extended her hand and tried to grab one. With ease, the butterflies danced around Neesa's hand, always just beyond of reach. Frustrated, the young infernati stretched out her arm even further and flailed it in desperation. Stretching herself just a little too far, Neesa lost her balance and fell. With a small thump she tumbled into the wildflower bush. Fortunately, the flowers softened her landing and she was completely unharmed, if not a little flustered.

Standing up, Neesa brushed the dirt from her coat. Her mother didn't like it when she got dirty and Neesa hated getting into trouble. Midway through cleaning herself she absentmindedly wondered what had become of the butterflies. Instantly she abandoned her current task and looked around for them. Alas, her fall must has scared them off because none were to be seen. Sighing with disappointment she clambered back onto the wall and continued her adventure.

It wasn't long before she was stopped again. Ahead of her the wall separated into two divergent paths, one that went left and one that went right. Indecision gripped Neesa. She wanted to continue her journey but didn't know which way to go. The last thing she wanted was for her to go the wrong way and get separated from her mother.

'Go to the left please sweetheart.'

Filled with new purpose, Neesa turned to the left and started marching, a wild grin dominating her face.

Not two minutes later the wall ended as it came to a small dirt road. Somewhat disappointed that her jaunt had come to an end, Neesa stopped and waited for her mother to catch up, alleviating her bored mind by spinning in erratic circles.

When she did Neesa hopped off of the wall with a stomp of her feet and took her mother's hand. Together they continued along the road.

The tell-tale sound of hoofbeats on dirt foretold the approach of horsemen. Hastily, Neesa's mother dragged her from the road, not out of respect for the riders, but for fear of being trampled. As the riders approached her mother bowed her head and kept her eyes downcast. It was common for infernati, colloquially referred to as hellsborn, to be persecuted for simply being who they were. Not knowing how these strangers would treat her, or more importantly her daughter, she hoped to avoid attention, lest she inadvertently draw the ire of the riders.

Neesa however knew nothing of racism or hatred, so as the riders approached, she looked on with a wide-eyed intensity. She thought the riders to be unkempt, with scruffy beards and dirty clothes.

Wait till their mothers see how messy they are. They're going to be in a lot of trouble.

Their horses on the other hand were in pristine condition, well fed, well-groomed and expertly shod. These men obviously knew the value of a good and well-kept horse. Neesa didn't understand any of this, all she saw were horses, the same as any other. And she liked horses very much. So, unabashed Neesa greeted the riders cheerfully.

'Hello misters. Your horses are very pretty.'

Quickly her mother tried to shush Neesa, but the horsemen's attention was already roused. In unison they stopped, turning to the one who had addressed them. Cold eyes, wearied by what they had seen, bore into Neesa's soul, scrutinising every aspect of her and her mother. In that moment, Neesa felt an unease, the likes of which she had never felt before.

Scary men. I don't like them.

The lead rider bent low in his saddle and smiled at Neesa, his brown and cracked teeth adding to the menace of his stare.

'Why 'ello little one, not often do we see your kind around 'ere.'

One of the riders at the back nudged his nearby compatriot, and though he obviously tried to whisper, Neesa heard him clearly.

'cor 'ow much ya reckon they'd fetch Earl.'

Just as quietly, Earl whispered back.

'Mm, the youngling would be worth quite a bit, I think. The mother not as much, but still more than enough to bother with.'

Hearing the conversation behind him, the lead rider looked back over his shoulder, silencing his fellows with a stern word and a glare.

'Quiet ya muppets or they'll scarper.'

Knowing little of the world she lived in, Neesa had no idea of the danger she was in. Her mother understood it full well. Realising what was about to happen, she hissed as quietly as she could manage to Neesa, desperate to hide her comprehension from the riders.

'Neesa. Please run. Now.'

Run? To where? Why?

Clearly confused Neesa stood idle. Not to be ignored, Neesa's mother begged her child for a second time, desperation saturating her tone.

'Dammit girl, flee.'

Shocked at hearing her mother curse, Neesa complied. Devoid of any forethought, she ran in a random direction, her little arms swinging furiously as she peddled her legs as fast as she could.

'Shit! Get em lads.'

Not to be denied their prize, one of the horsemen spurred the flank of his horse, driving it to intercept Neesa. However, with a fury and desperation only a mother protecting her child could embody, Neesa's mother leapt into the path of the rider and blocked his way. His horse, catching the scent of danger from the infernati before it, reared backwards, trying to escape. The rider was caught unawares and thrown from his mount. With a string of curses and a heavy thump, he thudded heavily into the dirt.

Without hesitation Neesa's mother rushed at a second rider. With one powerful bound she leapt onto the man's horse and began clawing viciously at his face. Her eyes shone with a supernatural fury as she swung her arm over and over. Screams of pain filled the air as ribbons of flesh flew from the man's rapidly diminishing face. The rider's shrieks petered out to pitiful gurgles as Neesa's mother jammed her claws into the rider's throat and with one sickening jerk ripped out the man's gullet. The man fell from his horse, a discarded sack of meat that's blood now soaked the road beneath it.

The remaining horsemen, having recovered from their initial shock, moved quickly to surround the infernati. Each drew a black club from their saddlebags and began to swing wildly at the woman. Many of the strikes swung wide and missed their mark, or were deflected by the infernati's defensive stance, but enough connected to seriously injure her.

Her head throbbed and her vision blurred. It was becoming increasingly difficult to fend off her attackers, more and more blows were landing. Several hit her in the head, each rattling her skull and threatening to knock her unconscious, but still she held on. The thought of her daughter driving her to persist.

A myriad of cuts and gashes covered the Infernati's arms and face. Her balance was failing and it was becoming harder to remain on the horse. In her heart she knew that it was over for her, but that didn't matter. As long as Neesa had gotten far enough away, as long as she escaped the riders, then her sacrifice would maintain its meaning.

Finally, a particularly vicious blow struck the infernati in the back of her head. Instantly, her eyes rolled into the back of skull and she collapsed unconscious onto the road. But still the clubs kept coming.

Though she could see none of this, Neesa ran to the backdrop of screams and shouts, of cries and chaos. She tried to ignore them, to push them from her mind and focus on the task her mother had given her, but she couldn't. Knowing that some of the screams she heard were those of her mother, tore at her insides. Despite wanting to be strong, she began to sob, she simply couldn't help herself.

As her eyes stung with unwelcome tears, Neesa reached a field of corn. For a brief moment she stopped and turned around, trying to see if her mother had escaped. She saw nothing but a ring of horsemen and the rise and fall of clubs.

Mummy?

Powerless to help, Neesa did the only thing that came to mind. She did just as her mother had bidden her to and ran into the corn.

Leaves of corn whipped her face. They stung so Neesa raised her arms to protect her face. However, when coupled with her tear blurred eyes, she failed to see a large rock directly in her path. At full speed she collided with the rock, stubbing her toe, losing her balance, and tumbling heavily to the ground. Her tears intensified as a throbbing pain pulsed in her foot. In that moment she wanted nothing more than to stop running, to curl up into a ball and simply surrender, but she stood anyway. She had to get away. Slower this time, Neesa continued through the corn.

Within the corn, Neesa had no sense of time or direction. Every cornstalk she passed appeared identical to the last and though she knew she was moving she felt no sense of progression. However, eventually she made it to the other side of the field. She pushed aside the final stalk of corn and her stomach knotted as she was greeted by three of the horsemen. One of which was holding a blade to her mother's throat.

'Now, now sweetheart don't go runnin' off again we wouldn't want your mum to hav' and accident, eh?'

Neesa barely recognised her mother. Her face was a mottled collection of cuts, gashes, and bruises. One of her eyes was fused shut, all puffy and swollen. Blood, both her own and others, drenched the front of her tunic and stained her hands. Her normally straight hair was naught but a dishevelled, tangled mess.

Seeing her mother in such a state was the worst thing she had ever seen. It hurt her very soul. It tore at her insides knowing that she was practically powerless, but despite this she had to help her mother. Or at least try to. Mustering the courage to speak Neesa stammered.

'Please mister, don't hurt my mother anymore.'

'Hm. How about this sweetheart. I won't hurt her anymore, if you come with me and my friends.'

Though she didn't trust the man, Neesa felt as though she had no choice. She couldn't leave her mother again. Giving a little nod, she moved out of the cornfield towards the riders. Two of the men rode forward, blocking any escape Neesa may have had, but Neesa didn't care, her attention was fixated firmly upon her mother and the man that held her.

Seeing that Neesa could no longer escape, a wicked grin spread across the face of the rider holding her mother. Neesa faltered in her advance, as she sensed the maliciousness behind that smile. Slowly, the man slid his blade across the infernati's throat. A thick spray of blood spurted from her throat as the rider pushed her from his saddle.

'I said I wouldn't hurt her, said nuttin' about not killin' her. Bitch was too much trouble to bother with.'

In that instant, Neesa's world collapsed. Time slowed to a crawl as her mother's corpse fell to the ground. Neesa dropped to her knees, utterly shocked, an uncontrollable wailing poured from her mouth as snot-tinged tears cascaded down her face.

'Quit yer whining ya brat.'

Neesa heard one of the riders exclaim as rough hands picked her up from the ground. Half-heartedly she tried to fend the man off, but her heart wasn't really in it. She was broken.

*   *   *

'Neesa, stop daydreaming and get back tae work!'

Drawn back from the past, Neesa shook the final remnants of that memory from her mind and turned to face her friend.

'Sorry. I was just. Damn. It's the smell of cherry blossoms, they always seem to take me back. You know, to a place I'd rather forget. Sorry.'

Her voice was weak and shaky, the product of an old sorrow refreshed to inflict new trauma. If her dwarven companion noticed Neesa's downturn in mood, she chose not to address it.

'Be tha' as it may Neesa, I don't want tae get the lash oan account of yer reminiscing. We've all got traumas lassie, part o' the territory I suppose, best ye learn tae deal wi' it.'

Begrudgingly, Neesa returned to her work, but while doing so her mind raced with rebellious machinations.

I will escape. I will kill them all. There's only a week left before harvest's end. There'll be a feast, a festival, most guards will be drunk or tangled in a whore's skirt. Those on duty will be distracted. Hm, if I'm ever going to escape it will be on that night.

Her course decided upon, Neesa mouthed a silent prayer to the gods and began to plan.

Chapter 2

Neesa

Over the course of the next week Neesa spent as much time as she could observing the habits of the guards. Instead of moving with purpose between tasks, she dawdled from place to place, making sure to learn as much as she could. This earnt her more than a few lashings, but as far as she was concerned the knowledge she gained was worth the price.

By the eve of harvests end she knew where the guards liked to post themselves when on watch and she knew the routes they favoured when on patrol. Despite what she knew, Neesa was well aware that all of her intelligence was gathered during daylight hours. She knew that it was entirely possible that the nights watch differed in their habits and that all her efforts would prove to be pointless.

A small kernel of doubt sat heavily in her stomach as she lay in her cot, yearning for sleep and the expeditious arrival of the new day. Alas, a whirring mind fraught with the worries of possibility kept her from slumber. To still the thoughts raging in her head Neesa focused on her breathing, just as she had been taught. A deep breath in, a count to five and then a slow exhale. Her heartbeat slowed and the doubt faded to an immaterial nothingness. Serenity, absolute in its depth, enveloped her and without realisation of time's passage she opened her eyes to the cockerel's morning chorus.

This is it, harvest's end. Today I take my freedom or die in the attempt.

For the most part the day went as any other would have. An early rise, a simple breakfast, a morning shit, and long hours working in the fields. However, on this day Neesa deliberately worked less intensively than usual, wishing to conserve energy for the evening's bloody escapade. Fortunately for Neesa, the guards failed to notice her lethargy, thus saving her from the whip. Joan however, did notice, but chose to comment only once the day's work was completed.

'Ur ye alright lassie? Ye seem tae be a bit mair restrained than usual, no' coming doon wi' an illness I hope.'

'No, no, it's nothing like that. I just feel like taking it easy. You know pace myself and all that.'

I hate to lie, but I can't be overheard by the guards. Not now. You'll see the real reason soon enough.

Joan slapped her on the back, an awkwardly delivered, and uncomfortably received, gesture of encouragement.

'Ha, ha. Good tae see yer starting tae come to yer senses.'

Neesa said nothing, just smiled and nodded. Her mind was elsewhere and she had no real intention of partaking in small talk. Joan didn't push the issue and joined Neesa in her silence. Together they left the freshly harvested fields behind, walking inseparably bound by chains, and joined the rest of the slaves, a meandering column of despondent souls.

Soon they reached the wooden palisade that girthed their master's estate. Neesa knew that it was small in comparison to most fortifications within the Empire, but to many of the slaves it was considered impressive.

The gates swung outwards as if possessed by a poltergeist, compelled to open by some unseen mechanism. Unceremoniously, slaves and guards alike trudged through the open portal. Once they were all inside the gates thumped heavily shut behind them.

Within the wall there were an odd collection of wooden buildings, a barracks for the guards, the slave pens, a simple kitchen, a rudimentary smithy, a shed for storage and a handful of shacks that housed the domesticated livestock. Each of the buildings, though functional in their construction, was composed from a myriad of mismatched materials, giving them all a rundown, shanty town like feel.

A second smaller wall, nothing more than a tall fence, separated the slaves, and those freemen considered to be of low station, from the remainder of their master's estate. It loomed over them, an oppressive allegory for the societal boundaries they could never cross. The upper echelons of their master's manor could be seen peaking from the top of the fence. In contrast to their humble abodes, it served as a constant reminder of their impoverishment. Simply put, it was not an environment conducive to happiness and, slavery aside, Neesa hated the place.

By the gods, what a shit hole.

Even at this late hour oven fires burned strong, as the need for cooked meals was never ending. Pungent aromas of baked goods drifted through the air, but were fouled by the stench of animal muck and human excrement. Smithies continued to toil, an incessant cacophony of banging and clanking, as they mended broken tools and forged ones anew.

As Neesa walked through the gates, she paid no attention to any of this. She was already intimately familiar with the buildings and inner workings of the compound, none of it held any interest for her. Instead, she focused intently on the positions and paths of the guards. As always, two remained stationed by the gate, one on either side. Similarly, another pair of guardsmen stood watch by the only gateway to her master's mansion.

I wonder if there's ever a change of guard? I suppose there must be, but I've never seen it. Oh well, that's not important.

Atop the parapet pairs of guards patrolled constantly, walking in endless circles they looked more bored than alert. More often than not their attention, despite being thoroughly lacklustre, was directed outside of the compound.

Taking out two guards at once might present a challenge, but if I do it from behind, and quickly, I should be able to manage.

Other solitary guardsmen patrolled the interior of the main palisade, winding their way through the outbuildings in a seemingly random fashion. A casual observer would have noted the distinct disinterest their faces radiated, the hallmark of those unfulfilled by their occupation, but not Neesa. She only saw another foe to be overcome.

They'll be the easiest to deal with. As long as I don't allow myself to be taken unawares.

As the slaves marched through the compound a trio of guards took the farming implements from them, scribbling notes in thick tome as they were placed back into storage. If a slave returned what was given to them that morning, then all as well, they received a bowl of gruel and the procession continued. However, if an implement was broken, or worse, missing, then the slave incurred the immediate wrath of the guards and was beaten. Severely. For good measure the offending slave's partner would also be beaten. Suffice it to say, the pair of slaves went hungry as well.

Wordlessly, Neesa handed her scythe to a guard. He checked the ledger. All was well. Silently, he handed her a bowl of thin broth, a lump of stale bread already floating in the soup. Neesa moved on, eating her dinner as fast as she could manage, but her eyes lingered on the shed where her scythe had been stored.

Could be some decent weapons in there. I'd prefer a sword. Hm, I'll aim for a sword, it should be easy enough to take one from a guard's corpse.

After every slave had finished their meal, and those who needed to had relieved themselves, they were herded into their quarters. Whereby they were unshackled from their partners and re-shackled to their cots. That was, all save for one.

Most nights one of the women was taken and raped repeatedly by the guards. A despicable practice to be sure, but one that was condoned by their master. It both kept his employees happy and earnt him a tidy sum of coin from the sale of any offspring, so as long as the guards didn't get too rough, almost anything went. The only rule that was strictly adhered to, and that their master brutally enforced, was that no slave was ever taken before she was the age of sixteen.

Today it so happened to be the sixteenth birthday of one of the slaves, a petite half-elf. Tonight, it would be her turn to 'entertain' the guards.

The girl had heard all the stories from those taken before her and knew what she was about to endure. She resisted briefly, struggling at her bonds, and screaming elvish profanities at the guards. However, a quick slap across her face was all it took for her to realise the futility of her resistance. Breaking down, wracking sobs overcame her as she resigned herself to her fate. Head bowed, she allowed herself to be dragged off to the guards' barracks.

Each of the slaves, save for Neesa and those not yet sixteen, had been taken many times. Each of them, irrespective of history, remembered vividly the first time that they were raped, for who could ever forget such a trauma? At seeing another of their number be taken for the first time many of the younger slaves, whose ordeals were more recent, wept quietly, their tears soaking faces and cots alike. Desensitised to the realities of their existence, the older slaves ignored the entire situation and tried as hard as they could to find sleep, seeking the only escape they knew.

While Neesa had never been taken by these guards, she knew well what her counterpart was about to endure. Long ago she had endured it herself. In that moment she was enraged. Every fibre of her being wanted to scream, to tear reality apart and erase all injustices from existence. Instead, she lay on her cot and waited, breathing hard, but doing nothing.

I'm sorry. It's too early. I have to wait, give them more time to get drunk, fall asleep and lower their defences. Gods be damned. I'm sorry.

Time passed and the world outside grew quiet. The last remnants of sunlight faded, giving way to darkness. All around her the snores of the exhausted echoed, but still she waited.

Hours went by, how many Neesa did not know, but then, at last, she heard it. It was nothing more than a faint whisper carried on the wind, the steady beat of drums and joyous shouts of glee, the hints of unbridled merriment. It was exactly what she had been waiting for.

Breathing out slowly, Neesa muttered a prayer to the gods. At once a tranquil peace born of purpose and determination washed over her. With no further hesitation she sprang into action. Moving quickly, Neesa sat upright and began to pick the lock of her shackles with her claws. Most of the other slaves were already asleep, so didn't react. Joan, however, was still awake and saw exactly what her partner was up to. Her face incredulous, she hissed at Neesa vehemently.

'Gods be damned lassie. Quit with yer messing aboot, ye cannae be doing 'is.'

Neesa kept her attention fixated upon the lock in her hands, she wanted to stay silent, to ignore Joan, but she knew that the dwarf would only pester her further. After sighing deeply, Neesa whispered back to her friend.

'Look, I'm sorry Joan, I really am, but I have to do this. I need to do this. I will not stop.'

'Fur fuck's sake Neesa, ye'll get us all killed.'

'I won't. I'll get the keys, the guard outside has a set, I've seen him with them. Then I'll unlock all your chains.' Thinking of the guard outside, Neesa paused, making sure that they had not been overheard. She strained her ears, but heard no cry of alarm or sound of movement from outside. 'When I've cleared the way, you can escape with everyone else. Or you could just stay here, it's your choice.'

In the short time that Joan had known Neesa, she had gotten to know that once she was set upon something, there was no way she would be persuaded to do otherwise. She knew that Neesa would not be swayed from her course.

'Bah, there be nary a choice tae be had lassie. Any who stay will catch the blame fur yer bullshit and likely hung jus' out o' spite. And it's no' lek we could stop ye, we aint nae fighters. Ye've backed us into a corner weel and good ye hev.'

Joan stopped. Neesa didn't press, she knew that her friend was considering her next words carefully.

'Ye took all choice from us Neesa. We must flee and chances ur we'll all die in the attempt anyhow. I can promise 'at none o' us will stand in yer way, but we shan't help ye either.'

Neesa looked up to her friend and, with sympathetic eyes, gave her a nod of respect. She knew full well the challenges that they all would soon face. She also knew that most of them would soon die.

I'm sorry.

With a loud click, the lock of Neesa's manacles sprang open. Immediately, the chain around her leg fell into a slack heap on her bed. Smiling in triumph, she leapt from her bed and tiptoed to the doorway as quietly as she could. For now, she ignored the door, deciding to instead peak furtively out of the nearby window.

Standing outside of the slave pen was a single guard, whom Neesa did not recognise. He was obviously frustrated that he as missing the current revelries as he continually gazed longingly towards their master's manor and frequently danced from one foot to the other, a physical manifestation of his anxiety.

Perfect there's only one. I always thought there'd be two. No matter.

Neesa gave the door a quick rap with her fingers. As the faint, but audible, tapping rang out into the air, she quickly dove into the corner, out of sight from the window.

Hearing a noise, the guard spun around and stared at the door. Confusion was etched all over his face as he tried desperately to reconcile the mental disconnect between what he knew to be true, that no one could have made that noise, and what he knew had occurred, that someone had knocked on the door next to him. After some brief cognitive gymnastics, the lazy temperament of the guard won out over his curiosity and he turned away from the door, concluding that he had just imagined a sound.

Begrudgingly, Neesa darted from the corner, knocked on the door for a second time, this time a little louder, and then scurried back into the corner.

The guard spun around again, even faster than what he did before. This time he knew he had to investigate, lest he be blamed for something going wrong on his watch. Pulling a ring of keys from his pocket, he unlocked the door and pushed it open. Cautiously, he stepped into the building, spearpoint first.

As he checked the building for anything untoward, his spear swung from side to side, following the gaze of his eyes. Cloaked in shadow and unseen by the man, Neesa bided her time, waiting for the right moment to strike.

The guard took another step, moving deeper in the slave pen. His senses were strained to their limits, as he tired as hard as he could to find whoever, or whatever, had knocked on the door. Seeing nothing, the man stammered nervously into the darkness, his voice suffused with the fear he felt.

'Uh, hello? Who... who's there?'

Neither Neesa, the sleeping slaves, nor the night-born darkness replied.

Swallowing nervously, the guard took a third step. Now his back was to Neesa. This was the moment she had been waiting for.

You're mine.

With a startling turn of speed, Neesa burst from the shadows and rushed towards the guard with a low hiss. To his credit, the guard sensed the displacement of air as she moved and swung his spear towards his attacker. However, Neesa was too fast.

Stepping inside the blow, she grabbed the spear's shaft with her left hand. With a vicious fury she swung out her main hand, tearing the guard's face with her claws. Several droplets of gore splattered against the wall as a quintet of bloody gashes opened upon the guard's face.

The guard growled in pain, eyes seething with anger, but he held fast to his weapon. With a spin and a hard push, he shoved Neesa off of the spear and away from him. She thumped heavily into the wall, gasping in shock as the air was forced from her lungs. Hissing wildly, a manic glee in her eyes, Neesa crouched low in preparation for the guard's next attack.

Yes. Come at me.

Blinded by both the blood that was streaking down his face and indignation, the guard thrust his spear at Neesa. Had the blow struck home, Neesa would have been completely skewered and no doubt slain. Fortunately, her reflexes saved her. With a powerful spring, she leapt gracefully over the spear-thrust. Mid-flight she lashed out with her foot, breaking the nose of the guard with her heel. The guard groaned as more blood spurted from his face and tears welled up in his eyes.

Neesa landed by the guard's side, too close for him to bring his spear to bear against her. Instead, he lunged at her with his forehead. Too close to avoid the guard's cranium completely, Neesa braced herself in preparation for the blow. His head impacted hers and her brain rattled in her skull. Reflexive tears brimmed at the corner of her eyes, but despite the pain she smiled a toothy smirk as she saw her victory.

With the speed of a viper, Neesa thrust her hand to the guard's throat. His eyes went wide as she squeezed and blood dribbled from her claws as they bit into the man's flesh. Desperately, he tried to swat Neesa away, but she would not be denied. Uncontrollable spasms shook his body as he tried futilely to breath. The spear fell to the floor forgotten as the primal dread of one witnessing their own final moments took over the guard. Face twisted in terror, the guard gave one final wheeze and expired.

Searching the guard's corpse, Neesa found a set of keys and a small pouch of gold. She ignored the coin, it was useless to her, but she did take the keys.

Shame he didn't have a sword. I've nothing against spears, but they're just not for me. Hm, might be good if Joan took it though.

Neesa scooped the guard's spear off of the ground and moved quickly across the room to her partner.

'Here take these.' Neesa said as she handed Joan the keys. 'Free yourself, then free the others. Also take this.' Neesa leant the spear against Joan's cot. 'You'll need it more than me, and besides, I can just get another weapon.'

Joan sat immobile, clearly in shock.

'Joan? Are you alright?'

Perhaps it was hearing her name, perhaps it was just time, whatever the case, Joan broke free from her stupor and mumbled meekly.

'Nay. No' even close.'

Neesa took a hold of Joan's shoulders and stared directly into her eyes.

'Listen to me Joan, you need to be strong. Now. Free the others. Wait here for at least an hour before you leave. I'll make sure the path is clear. Take the guard's spear for protection and stick together as much as you can.'

Eying the spear with more than a hint of trepidation Joan remarked.

'I've never held a spear afore in ma life Neesa, I dannae ken how tae use it.'

Neesa pointed to the tip of the weapon.

'It's easy just put this in whatever you want dead.'

At the prospect of having to fight someone, yet alone killing them, Joan visibly balked. Neesa reassured her friend with a smile and a gentle touch.

'If all goes well you won't have to use it. Just make for the Southlands, stay off the roads, travel only at night and don't light any fires. Leave this damned Empire behind.'

Nodding in understanding, Joan replied.

'I'll dae as ye say, but it'll be a fucking miracle if we mek it. An even if we dae I cannae thank ye fur whit ye've done.'

'That's okay. I don't expect you too.'

With a curt dip of her head Neesa bade her friend farewell. As she reached the door, she hesitated briefly and looked back over her shoulder. She saw Joan beginning to release the other slaves and within her she felt a storm of mixed emotions. She was glad that they would be free, but regretted having to farewell another person she cared for. Weighed down by this bittersweet melancholy, Neesa left the slaves behind, hellsbent on completing her bloody vengeance.

Chapter 3

Baron Victor von Grumanhieser III

The last thing the Baron remembered was lying down in his bed to go to sleep. So, he thought, logically speaking he must now be dreaming. If he were to extend this logic further, everything that he was currently witnessing and experiencing wasn't real. In actuality, it couldn't be real. Observing his surroundings further, the Baron surmised that this must be the case, for at that moment he was flying. That was definitely not normal.

As he soared through a sea of darkness, tiny motes of light, akin to distant stars, blurred past his face. They were the only features in an otherwise empty void, but to the Baron they were as vividly beautiful as a peacock's train.

My words, what an absolutely marvellous sight.

So enthralled by the kaleidoscopic brilliance that surrounded him, the Baron barely noticed that his breath was held. Inevitably, realisation dawned upon him and he went to take a breath, as he had become want to do after some sixty-four years of life. However, his lungs would not fill.

Suffering a mild panic, the Baron gasped for air, mouth gaping as a freshly plucked fish from water. Devoid of rational though and driven by desperation he clawed at his throat, trying to clear it of any obstructions. Nothing. In that moment the Baron felt the most afraid he had ever felt before. He believed that he was going to die. He didn't. In fact, his inability to breathe caused him no ill effects at all. It appeared that here, wherever 'here' was, breathing was not a necessity.

My, oh my. Not having to breathe? That's stranger than being able to fly in my opinion. No contest. What in the seven hells is going on?

Regaining his composure, the Baron returned his attention to his surroundings. As he flew, a small dot, a different hue to the others he had seen thus far, appeared directly in front of him. It grew larger and larger as he approached, from inconsequentially small to incomprehensibly large. He was going to hit it. There was no way he could avoid it.

As troubling as this revelation was, another thought, sparked in his mind. He wondered to what extent was it possible to be consciously aware of one's environment, and physical requirements, when dreaming. He asked himself the question, if this were a dream, then how would I be able to cognise my need, and inability, to breathe?

I'm not sure I would be able to.

His answer led the Baron to ask a second, and perhaps more important, question. If this were a dream, wouldn't the fear of being unable to breathe be enough of a shock to cause me to wake?

It should have.

As the dot before him continued to grow larger, the Baron pondered these questions. As a man of logic and science, he believed in rational explanations. Perhaps, he thought, this was not merely a dream.

The dot, now an impossibly large roiling mass, filled the entirety of the Baron's vision. But, as large as it was, he could discern none of its finer details. To the Baron it was nothing more than a wall of luminescence, that constantly blurred and rippled as its surface perpetually moved and shifted.

What in blazes is going on and what in the seven hells is that thing?

Just before he collided with the enigma, it parted slightly and a small hole of blinding white light opened in front of him. Knowing not what lay ahead, the Baron's chest tightened with fear. He wanted nothing more than to awaken, to leave this impossible space behind and return to the comfort of his manor. But he was powerless. Unable to avoid it, he floated into the opening.

Losing the entirety of his vision as the brightness overwhelmed him, the Baron felt his body lose all of its momentum. Floating motionless, the Baron hung, suspended in nothingness. He spun his head trying to ascertain his surroundings, but sill blind he saw nothing, save for an endless expanse of white.

Immobilised, the Baron waited for a change, for a sign as to the purpose of this place and his being there. Nothing. Eternities passed in mere moments. Time was reduced to nothing more than an abstract concept, functionally and realistically meaningless.

Boom. Instantaneously, an almost imperceptible black speck sparked into existence beneath the Baron. Rapidly, it grew into a wave of pure darkness that washed over the Baron. His vision shifted from white to black and he fell. Straight as a pin he plummeted, his chest clenched tightly in fear's grasp. The Baron screamed, or at least he thought he did, for no sound left his mouth.

As quickly as his descent begun, it ended. His momentum arrested in an instant as his feet contacted a solid surface beneath him. The Baron knew that his legs should have shattered from the impact, but he felt no pain, he was in fact fine. Realising that his eyes had been clenched in terror, he opened them. Thankfully, the endless expanse of black was banished, replaced by a land of wondrous oddity.

Things around here, wherever that is, are going from strange to stranger.

Looking down, the Baron appeared to be standing on some translucent material. By its feel, he thought it akin to crystal, but he instinctively knew that it was in fact a completely alien material. How he knew this he could not explain.

The material stretched outwards in every direction, disappearing with the horizon. Beneath the crystal was an infinite mass of brass wheels and cogs. Of varying sizes, they whirled and spun as an ocean of seemingly chaotic motion. A resounding cacophony of clicks and clunks resonated through the crystal, overwhelming the Baron's senses.

Good gods, I can barely hear myself think.

Gazing upwards, the Baron expected to see some semblance of sky. This was not to be, instead he saw a ceiling. At its centre was an impossibly large clock face girt by a series of massive runes, the meaning of which was unknown to the Baron. Similar to those below the crystal floor, the remainder of the ceiling was a collage of wheels and cogs, albeit of a far larger size. They moved at a slower pace than those under the floor, but the constant movement still managed to nauseate the Baron.

Best not look up if I can help it.

A pair of lanterns floated in the air, bobbing gently on their own accord, and emanating a soft yellow glow that somehow comforted the Baron. On the horizon beyond them, a collection of twisted clockwork spires jutted upwards haphazardly. Seeing nothing else of any interest, the Baron set off in their direction, but as he passed by the lanterns their light blinked out, leaving the Baron in darkness.

Blind again. Drat.

Mere seconds later they relit, but the Baron was momentarily confused as he now stood at the base of the spires. It seemed to the Baron that there was a measure of magic in this realm, but he was still unsure of its exact nature. Was he in the realm of a god, or perhaps some other ancient creature? Had he descended into the hells? He knew not, but he was certain that any wrong move could spell his doom.

Well Victor, you had best be careful.

Before him, a pair of large doors barred the Baron's path. It was inlaid with countless runes and pictographs of rose-tinted gold, that the Baron guessed told at least one story, but probably more, relating to the occupants of this realm. Fascinated, the Baron took a single step towards the doors and without word or force they slowly swung silently inwards, revealing an entrance hallway of which the mightiest of kings would be envious of.

Ornately carved pillars of copper and brass stretched from floor to ceiling, their girth more than thrice that of any column the Baron had ever seen before. A thin strip of plush carpet welcomed him inside and led him towards the shadow cloaked rear of the building. It was made from some unknown material of the deepest purple, embroidered with golden vines and flowers. As the Baron walked upon it, he felt as though he was treading upon the clouds themselves.

To either side multi-tiered fountains spurted water in all directions. Pristine water churned chaotically, emitting a fine misty spray that, as it drifted around the room, cooled and refreshed the Baron. Clockwork statues danced around each rim spinning tiny parasols jovially.

Light filtered through a stained window, yellow and resplendent with a depiction of the God of Time, Chronos, harvesting the souls of every possible creature. Beautifully macabre, it caused the very air to glow, warm and soft. The light mixed with the water droplets from the fountain, resulting in a parade of miniature rainbows floating gently in the air.

As the Baron continued along the carpet, he gazed around, awestruck. Never before had he seen such a lavish abode.

Wonderous indeed. Just whom could live in such a place I wonder?

At the carpets end was an embossed face set in the floor surrounded by a circle of brass. Seeing nowhere else to go, the Baron stepped hesitantly onto the plate. At his touch, clockwork whirred to life, first slowly then faster. The plate rose into the air, propelled by some unseen force, carrying the Baron with it.

When it reached its zenith, a pair of giant torches ignited, dispelling the shadows around them to reveal their secrets. In front of the Baron was a colossal head made entirely of clockwork mechanisms, save its eyes, which were pale discs of ivory. The Baron peered below, looking at the statue. It continued into darkness, neck, and then body, stretching downwards to depths unfathomable.

What an amazing oddity this is.

Looking back to the statue's head, the Baron felt, rather than heard, a presence begin to communicate with him.

'*Welcome.*'

That single word boomed into the core of the Baron's mind, reverberating around the inside of his skull. Though not painful, he winced at the surprise of it, clutching his hands to his ears.

'Um, why hello there. So, just to clarify I am talking to a giant clockwork statue, aren't I?'

'*Yes.*'

The Baron grimaced again, but not as violently as before.

'Jolly good, just making sure. Now what in buggery, no offense, am I doing here exactly? Come to think of it where is here?'

'*Knowledge. Learn. Home.*'

Somehow, the Baron knew exactly what the statue meant without any further elaboration. It was as though the statue, whatever it truly was, could impart not only information, but true understanding, directly into the Baron's brain.

Fascinating.

'Alright. Just to be completely sure, you're going to give me some kind of knowledge. Then you're going to get me to learn something. And we're currently standing in your house. Does that about cover it?'

'*Yes. Have Knowledge.*'

A barrage of images rushed into the Baron's mind. Diagrams and blueprints of machinery, the likes of which he had never seen, or even had heard of, before, the inner workings of machines, simple and then complex mechanical concepts, all of this became known to him. Overwhelmed by the instantaneous influx of information, the Baron fell to his knees clutching his head as he struggled to cope.

There was no pain, rather it was the enormity of it all, straining his cognitive functions to their utter limits.

Argh, too much. Too much.

In the passing of a breath, the pressure in his head faded and the Baron stood, now feeling as normal as he could in a place such as this. And although this new knowledge had faded from the forefront of his mind, the Baron instinctively knew that it was simply buried. At any moment, if he was in specific need of it, he knew, he could recall specific elements of that knowledge.

'By the gods, that was a whole lot of information. Thanks for that by the way, it will definitely come in handy. Now what is it do you want me to learn?'

'*Everything.*'

The Baron was flummoxed. He was well aware of what the concept of everything entailed, but he knew that the notion of learning 'everything' fulfilled the definition of impossible perfectly.

'Um, alright then. Do you mean everything in the absolute sense or do you mean everything in relation to a specific topic?'

'*Everything.*'

'Well. I'll tell you what. I, no matter how hard I try, will not be able to learn everything. Even a god would find that beyond them. So, what I will do, is learn absolutely everything that I can. Will that suffice?'

Initially, the head did not respond. Seconds, and then minutes, passed by as it considered the Baron's compromise.

'*Yes.*'

'Brilliant, I will…'

The Baron began to respond, but was silenced as the torches were extinguished and darkness consumed the head. The disc slowly descended and as it clanked into the floor, the entire hallway went dark. Devoid of all light, and unable to see anything, the Baron stood motionless, afraid to wander blindly, and waited for something to happen.

Well, that was a tad rude.

A shock of energy flowed up the Baron's legs. He chest started to burn, pain searing his flesh. Screaming in agony, the Baron collapsed to the floor, his eyes clenched shut. On his side he lay, eyes still closed tightly, ever fearful of more torment.

Moments passed slowly, but eventually the pain receded. Cautiously, the Baron eased his eyes open. The remaining pain vanished instantly as he found himself back in his own bed, just as the first rooster crows greeted the new dawn.

What in the seven hells?

Questioning the reality of what he had just experienced, the Baron looked around his bedchambers frantically. Everything was just as it should have been. Still unsatisfied, the Baron lifted his bedsheets, peering under them. He was wearing his nightclothes, just as he always did when he slept. As far as he could tell, everything was normal.

Perplexing.

Yet, something nagged at the corner of his mind. He remembered everything from his dream and it all felt real. Inexplicably, he parted the top of his nightshirt, undoing the top three buttons, and examined his chest. At its centre was a burn, akin to a bull's brand, in the shape of two intertwined cogs. Expressing his surprise, the Baron gasped and exclaimed softly.

'That was definitely not there yesterday.'

Chapter 4

Baron Victor von Grumanhieser III

Over the next few days, the Baron searched for any mention of the symbol now tattooed on his chest. His personal library, though extensive, held nothing of note. Knowing that it was a long shot at best, he also took a trip to the nearby town's meagre Hall of Knowledge. Unsurprisingly, he found even less there.

After the totality of his research, all he discovered was that his 'brand,' as he liked to refer to it, was a Godmark and that its purpose was to demonstrate a formal bond between a mortal and a god. As to the nature of his bond, the Baron guessed it had something to do with knowledge, but the specifics of his contract were an unknown. From which god the mark was given, the Baron had no idea. How it could be removed, or even if that was possible, he had not a clue.

Perturbed by just how little he knew; the Baron considered his options. He could travel south to the capital, Súthburh. The Peoples Depository of Knowledge, a key feature of the city, was the largest single collection of information in all of Ulandir. If there was anywhere where answers could be found, it would surely be there. Plus, the Baron was already quite familiar with the Depository, having spent many blissful hours wandering its halls and perusing its tomes.

Gods, I haven't been to the Depository for years. I really must get back there. It truly is a splendid place.

However, if he were to go the Súthburh, then he would inevitably have to take part in a plethora of political intrigues, each of which he found simply ghastly. There would also be the obligatory trip to his parents' estate, an insufferable ritual that afforded his parents the opportunity to constantly criticise his life of self-imposed bachelorhood. Visiting his sister would be nice, but alas, her husband was an absolute ass.

Well then. That explains why I haven't been to the Depository for so long. Let's cross Súthburh off of the list. For now, at least.

The possibility also existed for him to travel north into the Empire. While information was not as centralised as in Súthburh, every Imperial city contained at least one library and many of its nobles' owned collections of books that rivalled the Baron's. From a purely numerical standpoint, the sheer number of tomes that resided within the Empire meant that success was a mathematical probability. The Baron was also certain that an excursion into the Empire would broaden his cultural and intellectual horizons, something he was always keen to do.

The Empire. It's so close, yet I've never ventured there. The weather is nice this time of year, perhaps a holiday is in order?

However, as Imperial nobles took little stock in foreign titles, the Baron doubted that many would be willing to share their collections with a veritable nobody. It was possible that a large enough purse of coin could ease any reluctance, but the Baron would never choose to pay for something he could get for free. There was also the fact that the rumblings of war were growing on the horizon. If the Empire invaded the Southlands, which everyone thought was an inevitability, the Baron would rather not find himself entangled in such an occurrence.

By the gods, why can't it ever just be easy? Why are there always pros and cons to everything? Bugger it all.

As the Baron sat in his most comfortable armchair, stroking his scraggly beard, a plan began to formulate in his mind. Logic dictated that he reach a measure of compromise and hedge his bets, so that was exactly what he was going to do. Thinking it over he tried to find flaw in its design, finding none, he resolved himself to set it in motion.

Shouting at the top of his voice he called his butler to attention.

'Jeeves!'

After the briefest of moments, an aged man of at least eighty years old shuffled through the door to the Baron's study.

'Yes, My Lord?'

Even after a lifetime of being served by the man, it always surprised the Baron just how quickly the butler could reach his side. Whenever questioned directly about it, Jeeves would always feign ignorance, but secretly the Baron thought that Jeeves did nothing all day, save for hide close by and lie in wait for his call. On several occasions the Baron had tried to prove his hypothesis by catching the ancient butler in the act, but had failed every time.

Wily bugger. One day I shall learn your secrets. Just you wait.

'Ah, Jeeves. Good to see you're as punctual as ever, just as I like it.'

The butler bowed deeply, but said nothing as he waited for the Baron to make his requirements known.

'I came across this symbol the other day while doing some research.'

The Baron handed Jeeves a piece of folded paper. Immediately, he opened the note, revealing the symbol that was tattooed upon the Baron's chest. Jeeves said nothing, but his eyebrows raised in surprise.

'The book I found it in held no explanation of its meaning and for some reason I find myself intrigued by it. Although I've already looked everywhere, I haven't been able to find any other mentions of it anywhere. By the gods Jeeves, am I frustrated.'

As if to punctuate his emotions, the Baron leapt from his chair and strode purposefully to the window, his hands behind his back and his fingers a blur of motion as they drummed against his palms. Knowing that the Baron never summoned him for idle conversation, Jeeves waited for his master to continue and give him a task.

'Therefore, I need to search even further abroad. As such, I would like you to send a likeness of this image to the Peoples Depository of Knowledge, you know that fancy place in Súthburh, to find out if they know anything about it. In addition, you should send an identical message to each of the larger libraries in the Empire and to each of their Lords. Hopefully someone somewhere will be able to tell me what in the blazes it means.'

'Of course, it will be done at once My Lord. But, before I depart, is there anything else you require?'

The Baron pondered his butler's question for a moment, till a look of remembrance sprang over his face.

'Yes, by my ancestors there is. Oh, what would I do without you Jeeves. Just let me find that list.'

Moving to his work desk, the Baron began to scrounge around his desk, shuffling papers and moving other assorted curios around. An errant elbow knocked over an ink well, sending its contents cascading all over the Baron's desk. While the Baron attempted to save as much as he could, much was lost, a tsunami of ink the ruination of many a document and half-eaten sandwich.

'Blast it to damnation. Jeeves! Fetch something to soak up this mess while I search for that list. Hopefully it isn't buggered. I'm in no mood to make another.'

Before the words had left the Baron's mouth, Jeeves had already started mopping up the spilt ink with a rag, pulled seemingly from nowhere. For the second time in as many minutes, the Baron was flabbergasted by his butler's abilities.

Bloody bastard must be a sorcerer or something.

Shaking the preposterous notion from his mind, the Baron continued his task.

'Good work as always Jeeves. Ah, here it is. Luckily, it's undamaged. Here you go my good man, take this and purchase everything on it. Once you've bought it all, have it delivered to my basement workshop. Should you have need of me, I will be there.'

With another deep bow, Jeeves turned from the Baron and left, intent on seeing his latest task completed.

*   *   *

Almost two weeks had passed since the strange symbol had been placed on the Baron's chest, and he had sent missives seeking information of its meaning, yet, still there had been no word. No one had responded to him. However, the Baron believed that it was simply a matter of time before they did. As soon as he knew more, he would be ready.

It was on the morning of the thirteenth day, the sun was about to dawn and still the Baron had not slept, but still he worked. His masterpiece, revealed to him in a dream, was nearing completion and he refused to rest before it was finished.

With a curse, 'bugger it,' the Baron slipped, driving his screwdriver into his thumb. No blood was drawn, but it smarted something fierce.

Blast and damnations, curse my clumsiness.

Suppressing the urge to flip over his worktable in frustration, the Baron clenched his jaw as his thumb throbbed, doing what he could to remain focussed. With a care that comes from experiential failure, the Baron screwed in the final screw. It was now complete. With a triumphant shout, 'huzzah,' the man held his creation aloft.

It was relatively small and to the unfamiliar eye most unremarkable. A thin tube of hexagonal steel extruded from the main body of the contraption by precisely six inches. It had one central cylinder framed by more steel which tapered off to a leather-bound handle. Directly in front of the handle was a small curved spike of metal encompassed by a thin ring of steel.

Completely engrossed in his triumph, and deeply fatigued, the Baron failed to notice his butler enter the room. After several minutes of waiting the butler gave a low cough to get his Lord's attention. Having failed to hear Jeeves, the Baron continued to ignore his butler. Jeeves coughed again, this time louder, but still his Lord failed to notice. Deciding to change tack the butler raised his voice.

'Very good my Lord. But if I may, what is it?'

Startled, the Baron turned towards the sound of Jeeves's voice, and more forcefully than intended, exclaimed.

'Blast it Jeeves! How many times have I told you not to sneak up on me. It's no small wonder you haven't given me a heart attack yet.'

Jeeves bowed as deeply as he could.

'Apologies my Lord.'

Emphatically waving his hand, the Baron dismissed his butler's expression of regret.

'Never mind Jeeves, you'd think I would be used to it by now. As to what this is, it is my magnum opus, my defining creation, my legacy. I call it a gun, specifically, Peacemaker.'

'Very good my Lord, but what does it do?'

For a second a look of confusion crossed the Baron's face, but he quickly recovered his wits. Turning back to his desk, he scrounged around amongst the copious piles of debris and trinkets. Finding what he sought, he snatched it up triumphantly and held it towards to his butler.

'It's all about this really, I've named it a bullet. You see, the gun is really just a simple mechanical device that fires bullets. When the gun is triggered, it, or more specifically the hammer and firing pin, strikes the rear of the bullet, right here, you see.'

The Baron pointed at the rear of the bullet, towards it centre. Jeeves was completely at a loss as to what he was looking at and had no real idea of what the Baron was talking about, but nodded politely in understanding anyway.

'When struck, the primer that is, not the case, it causes a tiny explosion in the back that ignites the power, the gun powder, in the shell. That causes a bigger explosion, there's a whole bunch of science stuff to do with pressure and rapid expansion, but in essence that explosion propels the front lead portion of the bullet, that's the projectile, at a tremendous velocity down the tube in a highly accurate and deadly manner.'

Jeeves was still confused and his face showed it. However, before the Baron could notice, he regained his composure.

'That sounds utterly remarkable my Lord. Why, and I ask this with the uttermost respect to your accomplishment, is it necessary?'

'Hm, to be honest, I'm not entirely sure. I was just, sort of compelled to make it. It was as though an idea had entered my mind and it wouldn't leave me alone until I had made it a reality. Quite annoying actually.'

The Baron paused and considered the mark on his chest, the god's directive, and his own inadequacies.

'That said, now that it's done, I'm thankful. Have you seen me try and fight with a sword or, heavens forbid, a bow? Anyone worth a pinch of salt would do me in instantly. With this I can kill the buggers before they got anywhere near me. Normally combat isn't something I'd be worried about, but when I'm sent word of that blasted symbol, I plan to go wherever the information can be found. Best to see the source material myself, rather than rely on third hand accounts as it were. I still need to test the blasted thing, but I'm damn well certain it'll work just fine. Now, what was it you were after?'

Jeeves pulled a letter from his breast pocket and handed it to the Baron.

'Word has arrived from the Empire, My Lord. Apparently, a private collector, of some renown if I'm not mistaken, has the information you seek regarding that symbol. There are no specific details in his letter, but he has extended an invitation for you to visit his estate at your earliest convenience. Shall I send a reply with your intentions My Lord?'

Upon finishing reading the letter for himself, the Baron set it down on his desk, his face flooded with triumph.

Finally. I can get some bloody answers.

'Don't bother Jeeves. Instead, make ready for the journey. We'll be off as soon as we're ready. An invitation has been extended and we will be expected. In all probability, we would arrive before any reply, rendering it pointless.'

'As you wish My Lord.'

With a bow Jeeves turned and left the Baron to his ruminations and continued tinkerings.

Chapter 5

Thoron

It was a new day and the sun was just beginning to poke its head above the horizon. The five peaks of Iuga Quinque were the first to be greeted by its rays, their touch slowly warming the snow-capped summits. Beams of light entered the mirrored tubes of the sky pillars, reflecting them down into the bowels of Summa Antemurale, lighting the subterranean fortress of the dwarves and beckoning its inhabitants to awaken from their slumber.

One such beam of light shone directly into the face of a dwarf named Thoron. Roused from his rest, yet still drowsy, he waved his arms at the sunlight willing it to go away.

Ach, how cannae ye jus' leave meh be, ye bloody bahookie.

Immune to his protests, the sun continued to shine. Sighing, Thoron relented to the inevitable and wiped the sleep from his eyes with a yawn. Taking stock of his surroundings, as he was not yet certain of where it was that he slept, he was immediately pleased to find himself indoors, and in a bed no less. A simple thing perhaps, but for Thoron whenever alcohol was involved it was no small accomplishment.

Even though he was not yet fifty years of age, which was considered to be young for a dwarf, his bones and muscles ached from last night's debaucheries He couldn't recall exactly what had transpired, but from the way he now felt, it must have been a good night. Stretching his arms as high as he could, his back gave a satisfying crack. Unable to help himself, he sighed in pleasure. The pounding in his head was not so easily remedied.

Shifting as he moved, his bedsheets lifted to reveal the naked forms of two snoozing women. Voluptuously endowed, yet thin waisted, their nudity aroused a carnal desire within Thoron's loins. A memory of last night emerged in his head, of tangled limbs and shared ecstasy, and he smiled at the remembrance. Alas, despite his longing to reinitiate the trio's passionate lovemaking, he had not the time for such indulgences. He was already running late.

Oh, whit a shame it is ladies. I'd love to go another round wi' the pair of ye, but it is no' tae be.

Careful not to wake them, Thoron extricated himself from the women's interwoven limbs and stumbled from the bed. Barely upon the precipice of wakefulness, he noted that the bedchamber he occupied was his own. That was a surprise but, not altogether welcome.

Shite, letting the wenches I bed ken where I live never ends well. They'll be around at every hour wanting attention, gifts and, gods forbid, commitment. Bah. At's a problem fur future Thoron. Oan the bright side though, I dae no' hev tae walk home.

Strewn upon the floor lay yesterday's clothes, a mess of linen and leather. Ignoring the garments of his latest conquests, he found his trousers and quickly donned them. Tentatively, he lifted an arm and gave his armpit a sniff. It was not pleasant. Grimacing, he shook his head, this would not do. He needed a bath. Desperately.

Usually by this hour his uncle's forge would be lit, rendering the task of heating a tub full of water trivial, however, as he exited his room, he was met by a forge both cold and dormant. This just would not do. Hurriedly, he gathered some kindling and began preparing the forge for lighting. Halfway through his task Thoron's uncle emerged from his bed chamber and with a joviality that exacerbated Thoron's discomfort, boomed a happy welcome.

'Ho hum, how ur ye ta smorin' laddie?'

Thoron groaned.

'By Borun's hairy arsehole, me heid's a poundin' like an elephant 'as jus' sat on me face and me bones ur aching as though I've spent the last week hammerin' steel. But, an' 'is is by far the worst o' it, I smell lek a moond of goat's shite an' thir nary be a fire to heat me bath.'

Staring daggers at his uncle, to make it abundantly clear who he blamed for this greatest of travesties, Thoron struck a match and set the tinder ablaze.

'Bah. Never mind me mood. I'll be fine after I've had meself a wee dram of whiskey and a soak.'

'Ha, ha. Bless me beard ye wee scunner. It be true ye stink tae high heaven, but ye not be needin' any drink. Yer problem is ye drink too much. Ye cannae be solvin' it by havin' more.'

'Ach, whit wood ye ken ye old bastard. Yer problem is ye dinna drink enough, if ye did ye wanne be sooch a grumpy coot. An' besides, ah may be dead tomorrow, an' a'll be buggered if ah dinnae live a wee bit beforehand.'

Thoron's uncle shoved his nephew's chest playfully.

'By the sounds o it ye did plenty of livin' las' night. Yer hootin' and hollerin' kept me up half the night it did. Ha, ha, an' a grump ah may be, but ah'm still yer elder an ye'll show me the respect ah'm due. Noo, pick if ye wan' tae take a cold bath or bugger aff tae work. If ye wait for te water ta geet hot ye'll be late fur rollcall and ah'll no' be hav'in ye flogged fer bein' tardy. Nor will ah hav' ye cluttering me workshop in nary but a pair o soiled trousers.'

'Fine hev it yer own way ye old bugger, but if anyone says nary a word aboot me stank a'll be certain tae pay ye back fur it.'

At this Thoron stormed back into his room to fetch his uniform, his uncle's laughter biting at his heels. No longer caring if he woke the pair of women in his bed, absentmindedly remembering that they were twins, he dressed as quickly as he could. A steel cuirass fastened tightly over a cloth gambeson, a pair of hardened leather bracers and some iron shod boots. Atop his head he placed his galea, standard to all legionaries, and slapped it three times, positioning it to where he found it most comfortable. Content, he completed the ensemble with a tartan sash, encircled over his left shoulder, denoting him as a clansman. Nodding in satisfaction, he gathered his weapons from their storage chest, two throwing axes, a gladius, and a tower scutum. Properly equipped, he left his uncle's house, not bothering to say goodbye to anyone.

Walking briskly through the labyrinthian streets of Lower Summa Antemurale, Thoron breathed deeply the pungent aromas of freshly cooked breakfasts. Bread, bacon, sausage, and eggs. Each on their own appetising, but combined they presented a veritable smorgasbord of deliciousness that made his stomach growl and his mouth water.

Whores, both cheap and expensive, heckled him for his patronage as he passed them by, but he paid them no heed. He had not the time for their company and even if he did, he never paid coin for the intimacy of others.

Orphans and gutter rats danced around his feet, pestering him incessantly for scraps of food or spare change. Thoron gave them neither, but paid extra attention to their sticky fingers, ensuring that they didn't pilfer his belongings.

I feel fur the cheeky buggers, but if they take any o ma stuff, a'll chop aff their hands.

In good time, Thoron arrived at the mighty stairwell. Colloquially dubbed Borun's Stair, but officially known as Haldar's Way, it served as the exit from Lower Summa Antemurale or, depending upon your perspective, its entrance. Three hundred steps curved upwards in a gentle spiral, flanked by intermittent guard towers, and raised portcullises.

Climbing the stairs, the claustrophobically oppressive nature of the slums soon gave way to an open expanse as Thoron emerged on to the Grand Concourse. Standing no less than thirty feet tall, the carved likenesses of those the city deemed important enough to immortalise, flanked the Concourse, their emotionless expressions standing constant vigil over the citizens of Summa Antemurale. Sunlight, originating from the sky pillars, shone through stained windows at the statues rear, illuminating their immaculately carved bodies in soft hues of blue and green. It was an utterly astonishing sight, but Its beauty was lost on Thoron, who now regarded the spectacle as the norm.

However, the purpose of the Grand Concourse was not to be aesthetically pleasing, that was just a happy biproduct of dwarven craftmanship, rather its intended use case was purely functional. Firstly, it served the people of Summa Antemurale as an ample promenade that afforded them access to each of the city's many districts. And secondly, it provided the city with a series of strategic defences.

Spanning almost fourteen miles in total, the Concourse curved upwards within the mountain range like a corkscrew, originating from deep under its base and ending near the highest mountain's peak. Every mile the Concourse was bisected by a fortress that housed one of the city's legions. The gates of which were always open to allow free movement within the city, but, if the need arose, could be closed at a moment's notice to act as bulwarks against any invading force.

Exactly half-way between each of these fortresses there existed a pair of great stairways, one on either side of the Concourse. They always corkscrewed downwards from the Concourse and each of them always led to a specialised district, whether it be residential, commercial, political, industrial, or martial. Borun's Stair was one such great stairway.

Fortunately for Thoron, the fortress his legion was currently stationed in was located at the bottom of the Concourse, meaning that the remainder of his journey would be downhill. Additionally, it was equally fortunate for Thoron that his home district, Lower Summa Antemurale, was the deepest residential district in the city and neighbour to his fortress. He only had half a mile to go. Even so, he felt that at his current pace he would be late.

Ah, bugger me.

Breaking into an easy jog, Thoron soon found himself alone on the Concourse. No one, save for legionaries stationed alongside him, had reason to delve this far into Summa Antemurale's bowels. There was simply nothing down here.

Upon reaching his destination, Thoron was met by a wall of solid stone. Stretching from roof to ceiling it stood some fifty feet tall. Not a single window or tower faced the Concourse, for it was not from within that the dwarves felt threatened. The only deviation from perfectly smooth stone was a single massive archway, the cityside entrance to the fort. As usual its gates were open wide, as if beckoning Thoron to enter.

Known by most as the Deep Redoubt, although its official title was Isca Ianua, this fortress housed the entirety of the Seventh Legion. Standing between the city and the underway, the tunnels that linked Summa Antemurale to all the surrounding dwarven outposts, and by extension the outside world, it was the dwarves first line of defence against invasion and the city's greatest bastion.

As he walked through the fort's gate Thoron noticed an unfamiliar Centurion standing in the centre of the parade ground, the red plume atop his helmet a clear indication of rank. There was another by the Centurion's side, someone else Thoron didn't recognise. However, whatever their business together was, Thoron wanted no part in it as the mess hall was beckoning his hungry belly. So, averting his gaze, Thoron quickened his step.

Please gods, I'm nary in a mood for bullshit. Let me pass freely.

Whether through a blur in his periphery or by the sound of Thoron's steps, the Centurion spotted Thoron and immediately accosted him.

'Legionary! Front and centre.'

Groaning inwardly, Thoron responded to the order without a second thought, running over to the Centurion and slapping his chest in salute as he reached the officer.

'Mornin' Centurion, whit can ah be doin' fur ye?'

The irregularly informal nature of Thoron's greeting obviously riled the Centurion, for his face immediately darkened to a deep shade of crimson.

'How dare you! I am your superior officer, and you will refer to me as *sir*. Failure to do so will result in disciplinary action.'

Thoron merely shrugged.

'Weel, the way I sees it, Centurion, I called ye by yer title an' 'at wuid be as much respect as ye'll be getting, no' tae mention deserving, from me. If ye dae no' lek it, go an' see the Clan Chief an' take it up wi' him.'

If he was mad before, now the Centurion was incensed. Trembling with rage, he bellowed at Thoron.

'Hill-born scum! You may slap your chest, but your disrespectful tone betrays your contempt for your betters!'

With a steel-clad fist, the Centurion slapped Thoron across his face. His head rang from the impact and a wet warmth filled his mouth. Rubbing his cheek, Thoron spat a thick globule of blood onto the floor.

'You *will* show me respect!'

Ignoring the Centurion, a sly grin spread over Thoron's face and his eyes glinted with a mischievous twinkle. Seeing the onlooking legionary cowering nearby, his face aghast, Thoron gestured to the youngster.

'Good mornin' tae ye laddie. If I cuid jus' ask ye tae hold 'is fer a moment, I'd be reit grateful. A'll be nary a moment.'

Thoron held out his scutum towards the legionary. Reluctantly, the dwarf shuffled over to Thoron and, with shaking hands, took it from him.

'Much obliged laddie.'

Jumping three times as he limbered up, shaking his arms and cracking his neck, Thoron locked eyes with those of the Centurion.

'Weel, *sir*, ye really shouldn't have hit me. Tha' wis a mistake.'

As quick as lightning Thoron squared his shoulders and threw a blistering jab at the Centurion's head. Just in time the Centurion ducked, and Thoron's fist sailed over the officer's head. With no pause, Thoron launched a heavy left hook at the Centurion's face. Still off balance from barely avoiding the first attack, the Centurion was unable to avoid the blow.

The courtyard echoed with a resounding crack as Thoron's fist smashed into the Centurion's face. His flesh rippled, indented with knuckles, and his neck snapped to one side, blood and spittle spraying from his mouth. Dropping to one knee, the Centurion's chest heaved as he laboured for breath. Giving his opponent no time to recover, Thoron grabbed the back of the Centurion's head and thrust it down towards his rising knee. In an instant the Centurion's face was pulverised and broken by the impact he fell to the ground unconscious, air wheezing from shattered nose and gore filled mouth.

Fear was evident on the other legionary's face as he looked between Thoron and the fallen Centurion. As he cowered behind Thoron's shield, he stammered, his voice contorted by worry.

'What in the Seven Hells compelled you to do that for? He's our superior officer for Borun's sake, you'll be reprimanded for sure and knowing my luck they'll throw a charge at me too. Shit. It's my first fucking day.'

'Ha, ha. I wouldn't be worried aboot him. He's nothing mair than a wee shite who thinks he's all 'at. If the higher ups knew 'at he struck me first, then the Clan Chief wuid see 'at he's the wan to get reprimanded. Bloody scunner shuid have known better than tae hit a clansman. Noo gi' me back ma shield an' a'll get ye squared away.'

With more than a hint of trepidation, the newly sworn legionary passed the scutum back to Thoron. Giving the young dwarf a nod of thanks, Thoron started to give him a simple tour of the fortress.

'Alrighty then, ye already ken aboot the cityside gate, having used it tae enter, but the wan opposite is the entrance tae the underway. Dae no' worry aboot it though, ye'll only ever go out 'at way when ye're oan patrol an' ye'll never be patrolling alone. 'At building over thir is the mess. We cannae all fit into it, so the mealtimes ur staggered. Which century ye're in will determine when ye'll eat. The three big buildings oan the far end o' the yard, over 'at way past the stables, ur the sleeping quarters. Each cohort has a floor tae themselves an' the officers sleep at the tap. The armouries ur in the basements o' each building, again divided by cohort, but ye cannae get in without a pass or an officer present. Noo the final building, 'at wee wan opposite the stable, is the admin office, that's where ye need ae be going tae noo, they'll assign ye tae yer century.'

The tour ended quickly, despite its size there wasn't much to the fort.

'Um, thanks.'

'Any time mate. Ah, shite. Wi' all the excitement I completely forgot tae ask ye yer name, no' tae mention gi' ye mine. It's Thoron by the by.'

Thoron extended his arm to the young dwarf, who in equal measures respect and fear, graciously accepted the invitation.

'I'm Uthgárt. It's a pleasure to make your acquaintance, even if the meeting was a tad on the unconventional side.'

'Ha, welcome tae the legion.'

Thoron had barely seen the back of Uthgárt when the call to muster was issued. A single horn blared three times, one short toot, then a protracted blare and finally another short blast.

Bugger. I've jus' returned tae duty and already am back in the shite.

Legionaries poured from their sleeping quarters, sleep still lingering on their faces. Yet more streamed from the mess hall, their unfinished breakfasts forgotten. All joined Thoron on the parade ground and, as well versed in drill as they were, they formed perfect squares, arranged first by century and then by cohort. In a scant few moments some five thousand dwarfs, the entirety of the Seventh Legion, stood at attention, silent and immobile, ready for whatever that was about to be asked of them.

Time passed slowly as the air hung thick with anticipation, but even so they didn't have to wait long. Their commander, Legate Valens, marched onto the grounds with a purposeful stride. His tribunes following swiftly at his heels. Even from his distant vantage, Thoron could clearly see the concern painted on his face.

Am starting tae get a bad feeling aboot 'is.

Placing his hand onto his throat, the Legate spoke normally, but even so his voice thundered around the mustering field.

'Seventh! At ease!'

Simultaneously, the entirety of the Seventh Legion parted their feet to be in line with their shoulders, dropped their shields to the ground, so they rested easily against their legs, and folded their arms behind their backs. With a resounding 'Hu rah,' they awaited their Legate's direction.

Pacing in front of his assembled troops, the Legate continued to project his magically enhanced voice so all could hear him.

'I have just received word that one of our outer outposts has gone dark. The Senate has decreed that this must be investigated. Communication *must* be restored. In the unlikely event that the outpost has been overrun by the enemy then it *will* be retaken. And it *will* be the Seventh that retakes it.'

The Legate paused, looking each of those in the front row directly in their eyes. Unflinchingly, they returned his stare with a wealth of determination and pride in equal measures. Nodding to them he continued his address.

'Isca Ianua cannot be abandoned, for the safety of our people depends on those that man its mighty walls, so it will not be. For this mission I will lead the entirety of the first, second and third cohorts. The rest of the Seventh will remain and garrison the fort. In our absence the Legate of the Ninth will assume command of the garrison. Show him why the Seventh is widely regarded as one of the best.'

The Legate paused for a second time, not because he chose to, but because circumstance dictated that he had to. Their pride could no longer be contained and unbidden the Seventh broke out in chant.

'*Hu, Hu, Hu.*'

The Legate raised his hand for silence and the Seventh abided, immediately ceasing their cries.

'We leave immediately. Ad victoriam!'

In unison, those of the first, second and third cohorts lifted their shields and directed by their Centurions, pivoted to their right. In step the trio of cohorts, of which Thoron was a part, marched towards the Plutonic gate and the underway beyond it.

Bugger me. How couldn't I come back tomorrow?

Chapter 6

Máher

Awash with a sea of tiny pricks of light, stars both distant and close, the night sky shone like a brilliant tapestry of the purest majesty. The three moons of Térrtha circled above, casting their borrowed glow upon the water. Free from all worldly concerns distant meteors and comets streaked through the void, hell-bent on the completion of their journey.

In stark contrast to the heavens above, the glass like water lay devoid of any life or motion. Sails empty, slack and impotent, the *Vanity's Pride* bobbed lazily upon its surface, a singular entity alone in a vast and empty expanse. They had now been becalmed for three days. Superstitious as always, the sailors had prayed continuously, some of the livestock had even been sacrificed. Still the wind would not blow.

Invisible to all, black belly merging with the night sky, Beher circled the sloop as he kept watch on his master and horizon alike. His draconic eyes discerned all, even the smallest detail, but the horizon offered nothing of interest as it was void of anything or anyone. A school of fish swimming just below the water's surface caught his attention briefly, but they were too large for him to catch safely and he didn't fancy getting wet. Interest in the fish gone, Beher turned his attention back to his master.

The man, known by most as Máher, normally stood close to seven feet tall, but was no less imposing as he bent over the ship's portside banister. Save for his head, the entirety of his body was covered by a motely assembly of furs and leathers. Thick and well-worn, they served to pad out his already bulky frame to achieve truly herculean proportions.

His ashen complexion was starkly contrasted by his amber eyes and flame red hair. Protruding from either side of his head he bore a pair of curved horns which spiralled and swept gracefully behind him. From a distance most would fail to discern his true heritage, mistakenly believing him to be a hellsborn or some other devil-spawn. However, Máher was in fact almost an entirely purebred Elementarian of the Scorched Lands. His physical abnormalities were the product of a dalliance his mother had undertook with an elder fire dragon, Beher's father.

Finding the solace in solitude, Máher would have preferred to remain alone, but the ship's captain had other ideas. Emerging from the lower decks, the ageing half-orc limped over to Máher, wooden stump clunking on the deck with every step as he approached.

'Hail stranger. We've not had the pleasure of speaking as of yet and I seek to remedy that. I have this bad habit you see, I need to know everyone, personally like, who sails on my vessel. Just took me a bit longer than usual in your case, been busy with an issue with some of the cargo. Bah, there's no need to be bothering you with that, so let's get to it. I'm Captain Silventooth.'

The man outstretched his hand, with the obvious intent of it being shook, and waited for Máher to reciprocate his advance. He did not. Rather, Máher responded with a curt nod and spoke as quietly as a firefly dancing upon the breeze.

'Greetings captain. It is indeed a prudent man who knows his own house well. But tell me, how far do you make out or destination to be?'

If the captain was affronted by Máher's less-than-cordial response he did not show it. Withdrawing his ignored hand with a shrug, the captain replied as jovially as his initial greeting.

'I'd wager that it'll only take two days of good sailing to reach Súthburh. Assuming that blasted old prick Poseidon decides to turn the wind back on. Devious bastard probably stuck us here on purpose, hoping that we'd sacrifice all our rations to him. Ha, ha. Well, the jokes on him, I've got a bottle of prime single malt in my quarters and I won't let him have it. No matter what. Ha, ha.'

Máher gave no outward indication that he had heard the captain's response. He simply turned away from the half-orc and resumed his silent vigil over the still ocean. Seeing a flicker of movement from the corner of his eye, Máher looked up and noticed his brother circling above the vessel.

Concentrating, he extended his consciousness towards his sibling. He met the usual resistance, a mental wall intended to block psychic intrusions, but as he was recognised by Beher, the drake lowered his guard and let Máher enter his mind.

'What do you see?'

In his head, Máher felt Beher answer.

'Beher sees much. Many fish in a vast ocean. A ship covered in bipedal beings, stuck, not moving. Stars in the night sky. Máher knows, the usual.'

'What of the horizon?'

Dutifully, Beher scanned the horizon. For the most part it was exactly as it had been for the previous three days, devoid of anything. However, at the very edge of his sight he noticed an oddity. The tips of two ship masts had just begun to crest into view, emerging from the other side of Térrtha's curvature. Cocking his head in concentration, Beher stared at the oncoming vessels, examining their every detail. Idly, he wondered how they moved, as there was still no wind, but quickly dismissed the thought. Such questions were Máher's domain.

Deciding that his brother should know of what he had seen, Beher circled and dove towards Máher. With supreme grace, the young dragonling flared his wings as he neared the ship's railing. His momentum slowed rapidly and with the lightest of touches he landed upon the sun-bleached oak. Skittering along the wood, Beher made for his brother. Hearing Beher's approach, Máher turned to face his brother.

'What have you seen young one?'

'Beher has seen two of your manling vessels, same but different, crest the horizon. They're heading this way, approaching as swiftly as the fox chases the hare, from aft. Beher knows not how.'

A sense of dread built up in the pit of Máher's stomach. It was possible that he knew who pursued them. All he needed was one final piece of information to confirm it.

'What of their colours?'

'Purple and gold, with a redden eye.'

It was them. Akkadians. Máher swallowed heavily, supressing the urge to vomit, and turned to face the captain, who still stood nearby. In contrast to how he felt, Máher whispered to the half-orc, an impossibly calm whisper, and made the news know.

'Captain. There are two vessels approaching from aft. They are approaching with speed and will be upon us shortly. They hail from the Akkadian Empire. What are your orders?'

The captain barely heard Máher speak, and it took him a moment to process what Máher had just said, but once he had, he visibly paled. He stood for the briefest of moments, fingers drumming nervously on his sword hilt as he assessed the situation.

'Are you certain?'

'There is no doubt.'

The captain sighed heavily and for an instant Máher thought him resigned to hopelessness, but with a firm nod that punctuated his decisiveness, the captain began barking commands.

'Bosun! Sound the beat to quarters. All hands prepare to repel borders! I will not be taken as a fucking slave. Archers, take to the rigging, get as high as you can. Polearms, to the railings, keep those Nergal loving cunts off my ship. Give none of those fuckers any quarter and expect none in return, for you shalt get any. We fight to the death!'

Each crewmember scurried to their station with a purposeful intent, eager to do as their captain commanded. Still facing the captain, Máher murmured.

'Is there anything in particular you would have us do captain?'

The captain directed his attention to Máher. After inspecting the stranger, stroking his chin as if in thought, a glimmer of hope shone in the captain's eyes and it was as though he had seen Máher for the first time. Several seconds passed and then he replied.

'I encountered a fellow, bit like yourself, a few years back. Quiet bugger, and more than a little bit creepy, but he was one hell of a sorcerer, geomancer to be specific. Now, I think I already know the answer, but would you happen to be a sorcerer then?'

Máher gave a single curt nod.

'Pyromancer.'

'Ha, knew it. If you can do half of what that other fellow could do then I reckon we'll be in for a hell of a show. Might even stand a chance. Just kill as many of those shitheads as you can.'

Máher gave the captain another curt nod and turned to go, but a call from the captain stopped him before he could take a single step.

'Hey Máher! If you set my ship on fire, I'll fucking kill you myself. Assuming, of course, that either of us are still alive after this bullshit is over with. Ha, ha.'

Ignoring the captain Máher continued along his way, the poop deck his destination.

'*Beher.*'

'*Yes Máher?*'

'*The men on the ships you saw, they mean us harm. There will be a fight, a skirmish. When it starts try and stay out of the way. Pick some off if they're alone, by all means, but do not engage them head on. Even if there's just one of them. You will be killed.*'

'*Bah, Beher thinks Máher worries too much. Beher is a good fighter, fast and strong. But, more importantly Beher is not stupid. Beher will stay out of it, in the air where Beher belongs.*'

'*Good enough.*'

Upon reaching the poop deck the Akkadian long ships were clearly visible. Although they were half the size of *Vanity's Pride*, they were armed for war. The flanks of each were lined by a row of round shields, gold with a red eye at their centre. One had a loaded ballista mounted on its prow, the other a platform for archers. Both were propelled by a single sail, purple inlaid with intricately woven gold thread, surrounding a similar, but much larger, red eye.

Knuckles white from gripping the ship's banister, Máher looked to the heavens cursing his ill fortune.

Just my luck. Akkadians claim at best one in thirty transports bound for Súthburh and that one just has to be the one I'm on. Fucking bullshit.

Beside Máher, one of the ship's archers stood anxiously tapping his feet upon the deck while muttering an indistinct prayer under his breath. Unbidden, he turned to Máher, eyes pleading expectantly for some form of reassurance. Máher offered him none. Not perturbed in the slightest, the archer attempted to strike up a conversation.

'We're going to be alright aren't we mate?'

Máher offered no response other than a shrug of his shoulders, but he noticed, from the corner of his eye, that this crewmember was barely more than a boy. Still in his teens and new to life on the sea. Nerves driving him onwards, the archer kept talking.

'I mean ours is the bigger ship, must mean we have more crew, right? Surely that has to count for something?'

Sighing, Máher decided, even though he would have preferred to remain silent, to humour the boy and converse with him. So, with little more than a whisper, Máher responded.

'Not necessarily. Theirs are war ships, ours is not. And no. It does not. They are Akkadian. Have you never heard of them?'

'Sure, I have. What sailor hasn't? But what I've heard are just stories, they can't be true.'

'They are. If anything, they understate just how dangerous Akkadians are. Against two of their longships, we don't stand a chance.'

The young archer gulped heavily, clearly perturbed by Máher's remarks. More nervous than ever the pace of his tapping feet increased.

'By the by, how they moving? They're travelling at speed and we're dead in the water.'

'Areomancers. They travel using areomancers.'

Perhaps his curiosity was sated, or perhaps Máher's prickly exterior had finally discouraged the boy from making any more comments, whatever the reason, the archer shuffled away from Máher. Máher was glad for the silence.

Now. It's time.

As the Akkadian's drew ever nearer, Máher closed his eyes and turned his mind inward. Past the surface thoughts and emotions, past the secrets dark and deep, to the core of his very being. Like a burrowing beetle emerging from underground, his consciousness exploded from the dark into the chamber wherein his very soul, an ocean of eternal flame, resided. His consciousness bathed in the fiery light of his innermost being as it flickered in pace with his own heartbeat. An intense heat emanated from his soul, but it pained him not, rather he found comfort in the inferno's grasp. Smiling, he dived into the fire.

Eyes still shut, Máher's mouth curled up into a self-assured grin as his consciousness returned to reality. He opened his eyes. Previously a deep amber, they now shone as brightly as a bonfire, an intensely yellow flecked with a hint of orange. Similarly, his hair had changed, from a fiery red to literal flame. It flickered just as a log fire would, exuding an aura of welcoming warmth. He was now ready, but by no means eager, for combat.

Behind the *Vanity's Pride*, the Akkadian warships broke formation, splitting apart in preparation to pincer their prey. Máher knew this to be a standard tactic of the Akkadian navy and why they almost always sailed in pairs.

One to port. One to starboard. We can't afford to be engaged on two fronts.

Gauging the distance of the approaching vessels, Máher drew upon the inferno at his core, focussing his energy. Slowly, his hair and eyes grew brighter and brighter, as he drew upon more and more energy. Before long they had eclipsed all but the brightest of lights, beacons of daylight in the darkness that rivalled the sun.

Raising his arms to his chest, Máher held his hands an inch apart. A small ball of flame flickered into existence between his palms. Gradually, Máher channelled his energy into the fireball, moving his hands apart as it grew.

Undeterred by the strange light emanating from the stern of the *Vanity's Pride*, the Akkadian longships continued to approach.

The ball of flame between Máher's hands now spanned two feet wide. Pinpricks of black speckled Máher's vision and his head swam as unconsciousness threatened.

Not yet. Almost there.

From somewhere below him, a thunderous crash rocked the *Vanity's Pride*. Sailors from belowdecks cried out, screaming in pain, and begging for aid.

The ballista.

The edges of Máher's vision receded and all feeling in his legs faded. Unbalanced, he fell to his knees, hands held high above him, straining to keep the ever-growing fireball within his control.

'*Beher. Which side is the ship with the ballista on?*'

'*Beher sees ship. It's on what you would call, the port-side.*'

Lifting his downturned head, Máher turned his fading gaze towards the Akkadian longship approaching the portside of the *Vanity's Pride*.

Now.

Mustering the final vestiges of his strength, Máher pushed himself to his feet. Snarling under the strain, he unleashed an uncharacteristically loud roar and launched the ball of fire into the sky.

Utterly spent, Máher collapsed, breathing heavy, but remaining conscious. The missile soared towards the heavens, a thick streak of flame trailing in its wake. Upon reaching its zenith, the fireball began its descent, curving downwards in a smooth arc and then scooting mere feet above the ocean as it rocketed towards the Akkadian vessel.

Striking its target amidships, the ball of fire exploded with a truly mighty sca-doosh. Noise, pure and overwhelming, gushed into everyone's ears aboard the *Vanity's Pride*. Máher Clasped his hands to his ears, trying to deaden the sound, even if just a little, but it was futile. Overwhelmed by the deafening clarion, he screamed unheard as his ears bled.

Men, metal, and splinters were thrown into the air as the vessel's spine was completely severed, rending the vessel in two. Water quickly flooded into the longship's lower decks and almost immediately it was dragged downwards, a once regal vessel destined for the ocean depths. Likewise, its crew. For a while they resisted the pull of the sea, but their bronzed armour, designed as protection, heralded their doom.

Energy spent, Máher's fiery visage diminished, but his eyes still glowed and his hair still burned. As he stood, leaning heavily of the ship's railings for support, he looked out towards the destruction he had just wrought. He displayed no outward emotions, but inwardly he felt his soul darken at the death he had just caused. He knew that he had little choice, that it was either kill or be killed, but it still pained him to take lives. What he found to be worse, was that if he wanted to survive, he knew that he would have to take more.

At the back of his mind, he felt an itch, a subtle whisper presenting him a solution. Absentmindedly, he massaged the ring on his left hand. Jet black and cold to the touch, it resisted all attempts to move it. If he could have, Máher would have torn it from his body and thrown it into the ocean. Angrily, he pushed the urge to change from his mind, this fight was his and he would see it through.

Not this time Dolos. I will not cede control.

The spectacle that was their enemy's demise, resulted in a cheer from half of the *Vanity's Pride's* crew. The remainder eyed Máher with a mixture of awe and wonderment. But the day was far from won, and knowing this, Captain Silventooth focused his crew with a shout.

'Alright lads, that'll do. There's still be plenty of cockheads to deal with in the other boat and those fuckers won't die as easy as the others, so look lively.'

The captain's words calmed his crew's revelry instantly and with steely eyes borne from determination, they each turned their focus to the oncoming Akkadians. Archers knocked arrows, readying themselves to fire. Those with polearms lowered their weapons, preparing to repel all who would board their vessel uninvited.

Chapter 7

Máher

Not perturbed by their ally's demise, or perhaps because of it, the second Akkadian longship closed quickly on the *Vanity's Pride*. Captain Silventooth looked expectantly towards Máher, his face expressing a single silent question, can you stop them as well? Dejectedly, Máher shook his head. The remaining vestiges of hope drained from the captain's face, but in defiance, he held his head high. Clear in his expression, a nervous energy danced in his eyes, and with an impetus born from duty rather than any real belief of success, he shouted more instructions to his crew.

'Archers! Don't fire blind. Pick your shots, aim for the gaps in their armour. You won't pierce their shields so don't fucking try. Polearms! Don't let them get within your reach. If you do then your fucking dead, you're no good to me dead! You won't be able to pierce their shields either, so just push the cunts into the ocean and let Poseidon deal with them.'

Captain Silventooth paused, swallowing nervously. In the air Máher could feel an expectant energy emanating from the crew. They wanted more from their captain, some inspirational words to push them towards heroism, to fend off the fear that they all felt, and they sensed that was what they were about to receive. Máher awaited the captain, as keenly as the rest.

'I am not one for fancy words or grand speeches. I shall not promise any of you victory. That's not a promise I can keep. But, and I say this with every fibre of my being, we will make those fuckers bleed.'

As one, the crew cheered.

'We may all be destined for Poseidon's Hall this day, but we shan't be the only ones. For I guarantee you, there will be more than a few Akkadians that share our fate. We shall not go quietly!'

The deck of the *Vanity's Pride* erupted in a cacophony of noise. Men shouted and clapped. Those that had them, pounded the butts of their pikes upon the deck. Máher just gave the captain a respectful nod.

Not bad. I've heard worse.

Now directly off of their starboard side, the Akkadians begun loosing volley after volley of arrows at the *Vanity's Pride*. Focussing his energy, Máher projected a shield of flame around his person. His muscles strained with the exertion, but every arrow that struck the barrier disintegrated harmlessly before it reached him. He was thankful, a shower of ash was preferrable to a body full of holes.

Unable to protect themselves magically, the rest of the *Vanity's Pride's* crew took shelter the best that they could. Most on deck were fine, as the height advantage of their ship limited the line of sight of the Akkadian archers, but those in the rigging fared poorly. With little to no cover, they were almost all felled with ease. Filled with arrows, they fell to the deck, or into the ocean, dead or dying.

Standing alone on the poop deck, Máher witnessed the Akkadian longship change heading. Instead of passing the *Vanity's Pride* by, it swung, with incredible skill and grace, towards it. However, it did not slow.

They intend to ram us.

'Brace for impact!'

A thunderous crash filled the air and the *Vanity's Pride* shuddered violently, creaking, and groaning in protest. Many of the crew, having heeded Máher's warning, stood firm, but there were several who lost their footing and fell to the deck. For the most part they recovered quickly, but the disruption was all the Akkadians needed to breach the defenders' line.

From below, a wave of men, aided by their areomancer, jumped aboard the *Vanity's Pride*. Each stood at least six feet tall, was tanned in complexion and clad in bronze breastplates and bracers. Angry eyes leered from within their Corinthian helms as they peeked over the rim of their large round shields. Each held the signature weapon of the Akkadian, a spear, pointing menacingly out in front of them, ready to fulfil their murderous purpose.

Defenders fell, their polearms ineffectual, as their chests were pierced by spearpoints. Blood poured from their wounds as they died, coating the deck with a slick of gore. Those few archers still alive, loosed arrows towards the Akkadians, but all bounced harmlessly off of their shields and helmets. Just as Silventooth had predicted they would.

Scowling towards the Akkadians, Máher dropped his shield. Descending the stairs to the main deck, he began muttering ancient draconic curses under his breath. Focussing upon the energy that still hummed at the edge of his consciousness, he willed it to move. The fingers of his right hand started to glow. He held it for a second and then, as he thrust out his hand, a single bolt of flame shot from each of his fingers. Curving through the air, they flew behind a group of four Akkadians. In an instant they reversed direction and slammed into their backs, one bolt impacting each Akkadian. Defenceless against Máher's magic, they each fell, writhing in agony as they burned from the inside, slowly dying upon the deck.

At the heart of the main deck, Captain Silventooth was holding his own against the professional soldiers that assailed him. He swung his great axe with a poise and grace most uncharacteristically to the way most wielded such a heavy weapon. With every one of his strokes, Akkadian shields were shattered or heads sundered.

Alas, despite his skill, he was only one man. Inevitably, he was overwhelmed. Unable to cover every attack angle, one spear pierced his side. He screamed in pain, but claimed his revenge. The hoplite that struck him was the next to die, disembowelled by the blade of a sweeping great axe.

He has excellent form and more than a little skill.

Mid-stride, Máher shot another volley of magical bolts into the crowd of Akkadians that assaulted Silventooth. Two dropped smoking to the deck, heads cleanly removed. His vision blurred at the effort, but he recovered with nothing more than a shake of his head.

Thankful for the aid, the captain waved in appreciation to Máher before lopping off an arm of a careless Akkadian. However, now wounded, his movements were impaired. Soon after, a second spear thrust found its mark and then a third. Still the captain fought, claiming the lives of two more Akkadians, but the fourth blow he suffered proved to be fatal. His jugular impaled, Silventooth fell into a pool of gore as his own blood sprayed around him.

Shame. It's a shame I couldn't save him. That I couldn't save them all.

As Máher's foot left the final stair and contacted the main deck, he clapped his hands together. Drawing them apart slowly, focussing his power as he did so, he formed a staff of fiery energy. When his arms were fully widened, he ceased channelling and dropped the staff. Released from its bonds, the weapon fell towards the deck, but before it landed Máher kicked it with the top of his foot, propelling the staff upwards into his awaiting hand. Thusly armed, he waded into the turmoil of the melee around him.

The staff spun around Máher's body in blur of liquid red flame. Scorching hot, it burnt all it touched, save for its master, Máher. Effortlessly, he batted away enemy spears and crushed Akkadian skulls. He was, while lost in the flow of combat, an untouchable embodiment of death. However, despite his efforts the crew of the *Vanity's Pride* were losing the fight. All around him his compatriots fell, slain, he knew that it was just a matter of time before he would be overwhelmed, just as captain Silventooth had been.

I need an escape plan.

As this realisation crossed Máher's mind, the *Vanity's Pride* lurched. Gripping a handrail to steady himself, Máher looked below him. The Akkadian longship had freed itself from the hull of the *Vanity's Pride* and was backing away slowly. The *Vanity's Pride* lurched again as seawater started to pour into its lower decks.

I really need an escape plan.

Slapping an oncoming Akkadian overboard with his staff, Máher withdrew back to the poop deck and started to think.

The ship is lost. Even if we could defeat the Akkadians, there are too few of us left to sail it effectively. Swimming? Idiotic. I'd drown, die from exposure, or die from dehydration. Not an option. An escape raft? Maybe, but I'd have to destroy that longship, it'll catch me otherwise. What of the longship itself? That could work, but I'd have to take the areomancer alive. There's no way I could sail it without one.

Máher was torn from his ruminations as an Akkadian charged onto the poop deck. The hoplite thrust his spear at Máher's face. Barely in time, Máher deflected the blow with his arm. The spear edge cut into Máher's furs, slicing them easily, but scraped harmlessly along his scaled forearm. Consternation clouded the hoplite's eyes, for as far as he was concerned, his strike should have cut Máher at the very least.

Taking advantage of the hoplite's surprise, Máher retaliated, thrusting his staff at the Akkadian's exposed flank. Deftly, the hoplite blocked the blow with his shield and launched another attack. Máher stepped backwards, trying to doge the thrust, but this time the spear tip caught him in the abdomen, where there were no scales to protect him. Luckily, the blade failed to bite deeply and it was only a minor wound. Máher knew that it, if given enough time, would heal well enough on its own

That was too close for my liking.

Stepping further backwards, Máher feinted a lefthanded strike. The hoplite took the bait, dodging the blow and counterattacking towards Máher's exposed side. Expecting the attack, Máher easily evaded the Akkadian's spear and launched a counterattack of his own. His staff smacked into the side of the hoplite's face, shattering the Akkadian's jaw despite his helmet. Woozy, the Akkadian attempted to strike Máher again, but missed. All it took was a second blow to the hoplite's head, for Máher to put the man down for good.

Breathing heavy, Máher looked to the main deck. A second's respite was all he had to assess the situation as more Akkadians were marching towards his position. As far as he could tell, all of the *Vanity's Pride's* crew were either dead or captured and there were more Akkadians left alive than he could foreseeably deal with. From all that Máher could see, only a single glimmer of hope remained, it was a long shot, but undoubtedly better than death. Plan set in his mind, Máher started to run.

Sprinting towards the portside, he started launching bolts of fire into the rigging. With little coaxing, the sails quickly started to burn. Reaching the banister, Máher leapt onto it, ducking under an errantly thrown spear, and kept running. Shooting more fiery balls at the *Vanity's Pride*, aiming to ignite both rope and wood, Máher dropped down to the quarter deck. Black specs were beginning to encroach upon the periphery of his vision, but he continued his magical bombardment, just as he continued to run. The *Vanity's Pride* was now well alight.

It has long been claimed amongst seafaring folk that fire is a sailor's greatest foe. The Akkadians, having not only had heard this sentiment before, but believing in it, did everything they could to stop Máher. Spear after spear was thrown at him. Some missed, others he blocked with magic and yet more were deflected by his staff. Whatever the reason, none found their mark, nothing could stop Máher.

Nearing his objective, a partially lowered skiff, Máher focused his energy, conjuring a thin disc of flame into his hand. Without breaking stride, he threw the disc at the pair of ropes holding the skiff over the water. Without issue the disc sliced through the first rope and then the second. Released from its bonds, the row boat fell into the ocean with a heavy splash. Beside him, the *Vanity's Pride* was now an inferno, but Máher felt none of the scorching heat it exuded.

Without hesitation, Máher leapt off of the railing and dove into the ocean after the skiff. Swimming to the skiff, Máher clambered aboard. It was a struggle, as his drenched furs were far more weighty than usual, but he managed it.

Time to get out of here.

Looking around the boat, Máher searched for some oars. There were none.

Shit. Looks like it's plan B.

Extending his consciousness, Máher searched for Beher. Finding him circling above the fray, he eased his mind into his brother's.

'Beher, I need you to push this boat for me. Please.'

Beher's response was immediate.

'Beher wonders why Máher can't push his own boat, but Beher will do as much as able.'

The young dragon dived through the air and splashed into the water. Surfacing moments later, he swam up to the rear of the skiff and placing his head upon the rear of the vessel. Beher pushed as hard as he could, tail swinging madly from side to side in the water behind him. Slowly the skiff began to move.

'Thank you young one.'

'Máher owes Beher.'

Gradually the skiff increased its pace and in no time at all it was at a safe distance from the *Vanity's Pride*. However, Máher was not yet out of the woods. The remaining Akkadian longship was off of his starboard bow and it's heading had it on an intercept course.

Instantly, Máher started launching firebolts at the longship. Most hit their mark, but each in turn failed to deal any lasting damage, only managing to singe the ship's hull. Unperturbed, Máher kept firing, even though his vision blurred and his head grew light. More balls of fire slammed into the Akkadian vessel, but the ship refused to catch fire. Cursing his misfortune, Máher's mind started racing.

Limited options. Only one course of action left. Bugger. Plan C anyone?

'*Beher, I am going to jump from this boat and board the longship. When I do, push this boat from their path, I might still need it and can't have it getting crushed. Should I fall, live happy and free.*'

'*Bah, Máher asks much of Beher this day, very needy Máher is. Máher had better get Beher a present for Beher's dutiful service. Beher wishes Máher to know that Beher likes piglets.*'

'*Noted.*'

Gauging velocities, Máher jumped from the skiff when he judged the time to be right. For the second that night the air rushed from his lungs as he was embraced by the icy cold of the ocean.

All in all, this has been a shitty night.

As he swam towards the longship, keeping his head above water, Máher waited until he was close enough to the enemy vessel. Channelling his arcane power, he sent a wave of sustained energy downwards. He shot from the ocean like a cork from a bottle and landed, somewhat less than gracefully, on the deck of the Akkadian longship. Stumbling to regain his balance, Máher looked around the vessel's deck, gauging his opposition.

Beneath the ship's only mast was a man, clothed in resplendent blue robes, chanting indistinctly, and directing an obviously magical force towards the sail.

He must be the ship's areomancer. Good. I'll keep that one alive.

A second man, a hoplite in full dress regalia, stood beside the tiller at the far end of the vessel. This hoplite was unlike the others Máher had already seen, he was more importantly dressed and his helmet plume was significantly grander.

The captain? He needs to go.

Strangely, or perhaps fortuitously, there appeared to be no other people on board.

That was all Máher was able to cognise before the hoplite threw his spear at him. As it hurtled towards him, Máher held up his hand and projected a wall of fiery energy in front of him. When it hit the barrier, the spear, from tip to butt, turned to ash, vanishing in an explosion of dust. Thwarted, the hoplite screamed a primal war cry, drew the short sword from his hip and charged at Máher.

In response, Máher fired a pair of firebolts towards the captain. The first exploded harmlessly upon the Akkadian's shield, leaving nothing more than a circle of soot where it impacted. The second hit the hoplite on his relatively unprotected thigh. Forcefully, the Akkadian's leg was knocked out from under him. Mid-stride, the hoplite lost his footing and tumbled into a heap upon the deck. Smells of burning flesh, along with the sounds of pained torment, filled the air.

Gingerly, the captain regained his footing, keeping as much weight as he could off of his injured leg. His heart still set upon dealing with the interloper aboard his vessel, he hobbled towards Máher.

Not wanting to contend with the hoplite in close quarters, Máher channelled more magical energy. His hair and eyes glowed brilliantly as a molten spear, an eldritch imitation of the hoplite's own doru, formed between his hands. Without moving, Máher willed the spear to rotate, to face the oncoming Akkadian. Then, with a shout, and a surge of power, he launched the weapon at the hoplite.

Seeing this, the Akkadian held up his shield to block the projectile, but it was futile. The molten spear impacted the hoplite's shield dead centre, piercing its hardened bronze exterior like it was naught but butter. Barely slowed, it seared its way through the Akkadians arm and continued into the captain's chest. It only stopped once the tip of the blade protruded six inches out of the hoplite's back. Thusly impaled, the captain sunk to the ship's deck, already dead.

Not moving from where he stood, Máher directed his attention to the areomancer. At witnessing his captain's demise, the man had stopped channelling energy into the ship's sail and was now quivering in fear at the base of its mast. Sensing that the man would not be a threat, Máher moved over to him, addressing him with a consoling whisper.

'It's going to be fine. There's no need to worry, I will not hurt you without cause.'

The areomancer visibly calmed. His breathing eased and his body ceased shaking.

'You're not going to kill me?'

'That was never my intention, but I would ask of you one thing. I am in the need of passage.'

As if to add meaning to this statement, Máher paused and looked towards the bonfire that was once the *Vanity's Pride*.

'So, I wonder, would you mind sailing this vessel, and by extension me, to Súthburh? I would look upon such a favour most kindly. Refusal, however, would be most unwise.'

Upon Máher's final word, Beher descended from the sky and landed onto the longship's railing. Staring hungrily at the areomancer, he opened his mouth and ran his purple tongue over his teeth. The areomancer squeaked as he jumped in both fear and surprise.

'Good timing.'

'Beher thought so too.'

Quickly seeing that his only choice was compliance or death, the areomancer nodded to Máher.

'I will do as you ask, but I can't steer the ship. You'll have to do that. Don't worry, you won't have to worry about the heading, I know the way and will tell you when and where to turn.'

Máher shrugged.

'Acceptable.'

Máher's flaming visage cooled, his hair returned to its normal red and his eyes to their deep amber. His task clear, Máher moved to the rear of the vessel and prepared to direct its movements. However, as he passed the areomancer the man faced Máher and blurted out a question.

'Begging your pardon sir, but what will you do with me once we've reached our destination?'

'Simple. I will let you leave. With the ship no less.'

Thankful that his continued existence was somewhat guaranteed, the areomancer sighed in relief.

'Thank you.'

'Beher wonders why Máher got him to push little boat if we were going to just take big boat, makes no sense to Beher. Beher also thinks master should let him eat that human, pushing little boat made Beher hungry.'

'*Contingencies. No eating, yet. We need him to get us to Súthburh. Once we are there feel free. Search the lower decks if you want. Eat whatever you find.*'

Oblivious to the telepathic conversation between Máher and Beher, the areomancer resumed his chanting. The sail filled with wind and the longship began to move. Despite what had occurred, Máher was happy to be moving once more. He only hoped that he could find what he sought.

Chapter 8

Eris

Elongating shadows crept over the city of Súthburh as the long summer day slowly gave way to the night. As the stars blinked on, one by one, the sounds of daytime ceded their eminence to the evening harmony of the city.

Carefree children who played in the streets were called indoors by their mothers for supper and sleep, their gleeful merriment silenced for the moment. All life fled the market square as the merchants' ceased trade for the day, all hustle and bustle stilled. The incessant clanging din from forges and foundries alike was finally hushed as exhausted workers trudged towards either home or libations.

Like the calm before the storm the city of Súthburh paused as it took a deep breath. For a time, as the city sat mid-metamorphosis, Súthburh was utterly becalmed. Half an hour passed and the city exhaled, displacing the awkward quiet with the unbridled revelry of a populace at play.

A myriad of beats and melodies emanated from each of the city's many taverns as musicians played, bards sang and patrons chattered vigorously, intent on sharing even the smallest of gossips. Cacophonies of pleasured moans spilled unabashedly from houses of ill repute. Clusters of drunken men sang, in a manner equal to the loosest meaning of the word, as they wandered from alehouse to alehouse, courting an unpleasant awakening on the morrow.

As the last vestiges of daylight faded Eris awoke. She rolled sleepily from her bed, arching her back and stretching her arms skyward. Pale skin, as unblemished as the finest porcelain, stretched taught over her slender abdomen. Fiery red hair flowed from her scalp, doing little to cover her naked bosom as it draped over her shoulders. Two pointed ears poked shyly from her locks, extenuating her obviously elven features.

Wiping the final remains of sleep from her eyes, Eris approached a pile of dishevelled clothes, hastily discarded the morning before. A rustle of sheets drew her attention as her partner, Mikael, also began to stir. Turning back towards the bed, its displaced linens revealed the equally naked form of her lover, she paused, inspecting his impeccable physique. Eris felt a stirring in the pit of her stomach and her heart increased in tempo.

Mm, delicious.

Lost in a sea of emotions, Eris failed to notice Mikael open his eyes, but was instantly roused by his husky voice.

'I hope you're enjoying the view, because I most certainly am.'

Without even the slightest trace of abashment, Eris met her man's eyes, cocked her head to one side and smiled.

'I can think of no better sight in all of Térrtha. It is my only disappointment that I am forced to view it from such a distance.'

'That is easily remedied my love.'

Mikael threw the remaining sheets from his body and leapt from the bed. Crossing the room in an instant, he gathered Eris in his well-tanned arms. Caressing her back gently, he stared into her eyes.

'By all the gods, I love you.'

Leaning in to Eris, Mikael kissed her passionately, slowly moving his hand down her back until it rested upon her butt. Eris returned Mikael's passion with her own, fingertips tracing the outline of his chiselled musculature while her tongue wrestled with his. Mikael gave her bum a gentle squeeze and at that moment she wanted nothing more than to let him have his way with her. But she could not. Fighting every fibre of her being, Eris broke free of Mikael's grasp, his impassioned eyes begging for an explanation to balm his scorned affections.

Equally exasperated Eris sighed and offered justification.

'I want nothing more than to stay forever in your arms, but tonight I cannot. There is a job that I must complete, lest those more powerful than we wrest us apart permanently.'

Disappointed understanding washed over Mikael's face.

'That I well understand, but I would not have you do such things, the risks being as they are. I implore you Eris, make tonight's venture your final one, lest we be torn asunder despite our intentions towards the opposite.'

'I would have it so my dear, but fellowship with those who I am employed by is not so easily sundered. I fear that my skills will shackle me to them for a while longer. Unless I fail them, then my bonds would be broken in death.'

'Such a fate I would avoid at any cost. But this cannot continue. I would not have the woman whom I love above all others, put herself, or our unborn child, at undue risk.'

Mikael moved his hand, resting it on Eris's belly.

'If I were to lose either of you, I would die. My world would cease, all hopes of happiness lost.'

'I know. The same emotions are branded upon my soul. But my pregnancy is still young and the risks no greater than usual. I will work with them a while longer while we endeavour to find a feasible escape. For now, we have little choice.'

With her words, Eris's eyes glistened with tears, the roiling emotions in her heart threatening release. Seeing her turmoil, Mikael drew Eris close to his breast and with the gentlest of caresses stroked her cheek. At his touch unbridled passion welled within Eris's chest and she embraced the man she loved with a hungry desire. Their lips met and their tongues intertwined. Several blissful moments passed until at last the clam of reason regained dominance and they parted.

'I think it would be best if you depart presently. For I fear that if you do not, I will soon be unable to let you leave, consequences be damned.'

'Mm, your fears are well justified as I do not believe myself capable of wresting my person from such a palatable captivity.'

Deep and hearty laughter echoed from Mikael's chest as he moved to dress.

'Palatable, am I?'

A mischievous grin crossed Eris's face as she followed suit and gathered her own clothing.

'Absolutely. Not just, in fact. You are easily the most delectable cuisine I have ever sampled.'

Eris quickly pulled on a pair of dark leather trousers, tight as to extenuate her natural curves, and on a more practical level, to prevent the ruffling of fabric when she moved. Over her head she pulled a cotton shirt, long of sleeve, dark of colour and also form fitted. As she drew it down over her waist, Mikael made his appreciation of her fashion known.

'By the Gods, those pants are positively, exquisite.'

'Are you sure it's the clothing? Or is it what lies beneath?'

With this Eris bent over slightly, exaggerating her already shapely figure, and gave her behind a playful slap. Mikael's only response was a pleasured mumbling and Eris knew that her actions had resulted in the desired effect. The grin, still upon her face, grew into a fully-fledged smile.

Oh, just you wait till I get home.

Over her shirt she placed a hooded leather jacket, also black, replete with numerous pockets and knife sheaths. Fetching her daggers from her bedside dresser she placed each of them in their respective sheaths. Similarly, she gathered her thief's kit, an assortment of lockpicks and glass cutters, and placed it in its designated pocket.

The final component of the ensemble was a pair of black, knee-high leather boots. Of all her possessions these were her most favoured. Once her mother's, they were all that Eris had left of her, save for the fleeting memories of childhood. Ruggedly simple, yet well made, they were both aesthetically pleasing and functionally sound. Not to mention more than just a little magical.

Once she was fully dressed Eris turned to face Mikael and with a bow of her head addressed her partner.

'Till we next meet my love, know that for me there is only you.'

Mikael bowed his head in return and replied.

'As for me there will only ever be you.'

Farewells made, Eris climbed the ladder to the roof and greeted the warm night air of Súthburh with purposeful intent.

With a grace born of both experience and bloodline, Eris flew across the rooftops, leaping from building to building with wanton abandon. As she arrived at each new landing she tucked and rolled, both to muffle the impact and maintain her momentum. Never once did she falter or stumble and her mouth was turned upward in a perpetual smile, a reflection of her primal revelry.

Eris soon arrived at the appointed rendezvous, and despite her tardiness, her contact was nowhere to be seen. Fearing betrayal, she kept to the shadows and glanced around nervously. Seeing no one her anxiety rose. A cold sweat formed on her brow and her heart raced.

By all that it holy Asher, where in the seven hells are you?

More time passed, a scant few minutes, but for Eris it was torturous. Then, just as Eris was thinking that she'd have to flee, her contact slinked silently from a nearby alley.

'Well, it's good to see that your man, or should I say half-breed squeeze. Oh, what was his name? Ah, that's right, Mikael. Didn't delay you too long. Our esteemed leader would have been most vexed had you not fulfilled your obligations this night. And to be honest, I was beginning to worry that this was going to be so. Need I remind you, Eris, of the consequences that will greet you, and Mikael for that matter, should you displease him?'

Eris spun towards the halfling, addressing him with a vehement hiss.

'Stow your threats Asher. I have come to complete my duties as required and it was you who were late. Now. What would you have of me, worm?'

'Oh my, there's no need to be so hostile. And I would have nothing from you, save for your deference towards and obedience to our esteemed leader.'

At this non-answer Eris's frustration grew, but before she could form her ire into words, Asher stilled her with a raised hand and a high-pitched giggle.

'Ha, ha. I know what you seek answered, elf. I merely wished to remind you of your place. The pleasure I gain from enticing anger and confusion from those of inferior intellect to my own is simply a happy bi-product.'

Never have I met anyone as arrogant as you. Little shit.

'Now then. To what you need to know for tonight's task. You are to burgle the villa of a prominent merchant, Mercurius. You are permitted to take whatever you can carry, but we want it to hurt Mercurius's financials, a lot, so you'll need to lift only that which is most valuable. Of course, you'll still receive the standard thirty percent cut. However, and this is critical, under no circumstances are you to kill Mercurius or any of his family. The guild wishes to punish him, but we still require his business. Bah, I digress. So, let me make this clear, if you do, or if you're captured, you, and your man, will be marked for death.'

Eris scoffed.

'Don't kill. Okay Asher. Answer me this, when have I ever killed a mark?'

'Hm. To my knowledge, never. But that's not the point. Mercurius is dangerous, he will defend himself if provoked and he is well guarded. Combat is likely and when one's blood is up, mistakes are commonplace.'

Eris scoffed again.

'Not from me they're not.'

'Hm. We shall see.'

Asher paused and, as if in thought, peered furtively around. For what purpose Eris knew not, as she was certain that they were alone. In any case, she suppressed her growing impatience and waited for the halfling to continue.

'Oh. You're still here? Do you need directions then?'

'Shove off halfling. I well know where the merchant resides, I was simply waiting for you to give me your leave. Shall I surmise that it has been given?'

'Yes, yes. I give you, my leave. Now, get to work and hurry back to the Burrow once finished.'

Eris bowed in the most flamboyant manner she could manage, not in deference to the halfling, but to rather mock his false assumptions of superiority.

'It will be done with all speed and care.'

Asher said nothing in response as he turned and departed down the same alleyway he had arrived from. As he left, Eris hacked up a globule of phlegm and spat it in his direction.

By the gods, do I hate that swine.

Eschewing the rooftops in favour of the streets, Eris left for the Merchant's villa. There were a few groups of city watch patrolling major boulevards, but as no curfew was currently in effect, they paid her no heed. In seemingly no time at all, she arrived at her destination and without breaking stride, she assessed the environment before her. Instantly, she regretted her path of travel.

Chapter 9

Eris

The villa before her was girted by a stone wall of no less than fifteen feet tall. A single wrought iron gate, undoubtedly locked, afforded entry to the estate's interior. Usually, this would have done nothing to stop her, but in this instance, and unfortunately for Eris, two Khullite tribesmen also barred her way.

Strange. Khullite's don't usually venture from their oases. Imperial oppression must be worse than the rumours, either that or Mercurius pays phenomenally well.

Quickly, Eris dismissed an attempt at bluffing her way through. She knew Khullite's to be an exceptionally logical people, who would no doubt detect any of her deceptions. Fighting them openly would have also been foolish, infiltration was the intent, not combat.

I'm not getting in this way. Another route is needed.

Turning on her heels, Eris ducked into a nearby alley before she aroused the suspicion of the Khullites. Glancing around quickly, Eris inspected her surroundings, seeing if anyone was paying her any attention. Failing to see anyone, she tapped the heels of her boots together three times. Simultaneously, she mumbled an incomprehensible verse of ancient elvish. With the third click, her boots emanated a faint eldritch glow and she sprang into action.

Running full tilt at an alley wall, Eris leapt off of the cobbles, summersaulting through the air. Landing feet-first upon the wall, in defiance to gravity, she maintained her momentum and continued to sprint up the side of the wall. At the pinnacle of her ascent, Eris kicked off of the wall, summersaulting and corkscrewing through the air. She landed on the opposite rooftop with a roll, and without pause, stood and continued sprinting towards Mercurius's villa.

The edge of the rooftop rushed ever nearer, but Eris did not slow, in fact she pushed herself to increase her pace. Reaching the precipice, she inhaled as deeply as she could and thrust off of as hard as she could. Stretching her arms out in front of her, Eris speared through the air.

In the seconds that she had before landfall, Eris analysed as much of the Merchant's villa as she could. Three stories of polished stone sat as a vain monument to Mercurius's success. Far larger than the standard Súthburh townhouse, it dwarfed each its surrounding buildings, both in terms of height and girth. A lavish veranda, replete with potted plants and expensive furniture, protruded from the villa's side and, despite that space in central Súthburh was premium, a large garden graced the rear of the building.

As quickly as her flight had begun, Eris soon started to descend. Knowing that her boots were about to become once again dormant, the magic within them temporarily expired, she judged the necessary vector. Then, using her feet to angle her body towards the ground, she allowed herself to descend. Falling even faster, her momentum drove air past her face with an ever-increasing force. Her hood blew back from her head, setting her hair loose in a wild tangle of fluttering red.

The villa's outer wall loomed into Eris's vision and she knew with a cold certainty that she was not going to make it. Summoning the entirety of her strength, Eris tucked her legs into her chest and strained her core, flipping herself over. At the exact moment her legs faced away from the wall, Eris kicked outwards, pushing herself off of the very air itself.

It's going to be close.

This final nudge was all she needed. With the barest of margins, Eris cleared the top of the wall, leather scuffed against stone as her legs scraped the partition's upper edge.

Too close.

Still falling, Eris spun herself around, legs facing towards the ground, impact fast approaching. Focussing her mind upon her boot's enchantment, she willed the air beneath her to partially solidify. Her momentum slowed, but not enough. At the final moment, and using the last ounce of magic remaining in her boots, she jumped off of the hardened air.

Her fall had been slowed, but still Eris struck the earth of the Merchant's yard with force. Doing all she could, Eris bent her knees to dampen the impact and rolled into the landing. However, her legs were still jarred by the impact and stumbling, she lost her footing. Her chest thudded into the ground and her lungs expunged all the air they held as a pained gasp escaped her mouth. Overcome by pain, Eris curled into a foetal ball, all thoughts of subtlety and stealth fled.

Ow, that was a long way from my finest performance. Hopefully no one saw.

Several moments passed, the pain slowly subsiding to manageable levels. Groaning, she raised her head and assessed the situation. In her heart Eris felt as though she had already failed. She believed, with all certainty, that her incursion had been detected and that at any moment a bevy of guards would be there, swarming over her, to arrest or even kill her. But there was nothing. No sound of alarm. No onrushing guards. She had not been discovered.

Praise be to Laverna. There still exists a chance of success.

Gritting her teeth, she staggered to her feet. Staying as low as she could, Eris moved towards the villa. As she reached the veranda, she placed her hands upon the oaken floorboards and pushed herself onto it. Tuck and rolling, she took cover behind a marble pillar and scanned the vicinity for patrolling guards. A lone Khullite was meandering along the veranda towards her. He was clearly bored for eyes that should have been scanning his surroundings in an alert and constant pattern were instead fixated upon the floor not three feet in front of him.

A life of mediocracy has dulled his edge.

As she waited for the guard, Eris slowed her breathing in preparation. Silently, she drew one of her daggers, her ears ringing with every step the Khullite took. Despite her efforts to remain calm, her heart pounded in her chest as adrenaline surged through her system.

The Khullite passed Eris's position without even a cursory glance in her direction. He had not seen her. Standing slowly, Eris rose from her crouch and fell in behind the guard, her feet falling silently upon the wooden floorboards. The guard did not react, he had not heard her. With three steps Eris had reached striking distance. She wrapped her left hand around the guard's mouth, muffling any cries he would have made, and with her right, she thrust the blade of her dagger between his ribs. Without hesitation, she struck again and then again, a flurry of blows eviscerating the Khullite's internal organs. Eris felt the guard's body slacken. He was now dead.

With care, as to minimise the sound she made, Eris pushed the guard's corpse onto the ground below. Stepping down after it, she rolled the body under the veranda, in the hope that it would not be discovered for some time. Once her victim was hidden, she hopped back onto the veranda, keeping both her ears and eyes peeled as she searched for a point of ingress.

It didn't take her long to find a doorway into the villa. Glancing around for any nearby guards, and spotting none, Eris moved to the door and tried the handle. Unsurprisingly, it was locked.

You never know.

Furtively, Eris scanned her surroundings a second time, just in case, but there were still no guards. With a deftness that only comes from years of practice, she extricated her tools from her breast pocket and began to work on the lock. In a scant few seconds, and with minimal effort, there was a barely audible click as the lock capitulated to Eris's efforts. As swiftly as she could, while remaining silent, Eris opened the door, entered the building, and shut the door behind her.

Even though it was the middle of the night, numerous lanterns lit the villa's interior, revealing all. Eris was immediately taken aback. As opulent as the building's exterior was, it paled in comparison to the interior. Lavish tapestries and masterwork paintings filled the room, barely an inch of the plastered wall behind was evident. The floor was similarly covered, but differed as it was occupied by only a single rug. Gargantuan and impossibly intricate, it would have taken thousands of hours to complete. She had no doubt that such a piece would cost as much as a small house. Eris was repulsed by the extravagance.

I wonder Mercurius. What evils did you commit to acquire such wealth?

Busts of the famous, infamous, and influential were displayed with pride. Eris recognised them as Bernini's work, and each was amongst his best. Each was worth a small fortune, but alas Eris needed to find things that were of a more portable nature. Inwardly, she lamented her ill-preparedness, if only Asher had given her a bag of holding, or maybe two.

Incompetent bastard.

The room, which appeared to be some kind of sitting room, also held an assortment of luxurious chairs and couches, intricately carved tables, and dark-wooded bookcases replete with countless tomes. However, Eris paid them little attention as, while undoubtedly valuable, she knew that far greater treasures abounded elsewhere. So, for the moment empty handed, Eris left the room and delved deeper into the villa.

She encountered no one as she moved through the building. First to a kitchen, then to a dining room and finally to the main entrance way. Each was as equally lavish as the sitting room and far grander than strictly necessary, by comparison the humble loft Eris called home would have fitted in the dining room three times over. Eris felt her disdain for the Merchant grow, in her opinion such extravagance only served to distance one's self from what they truly required. For her that was Mikael.

In the entrance way Eris encountered a staircase of speckled marble, black, grey and white, angled gently upwards bridging the first and second floors in an appealing and inviting manner. Surmising that the villa's bedrooms, and particularly the master bedroom, would be on the second floor Eris embraced the architectural welcome and proceeded upwards.

Before she had made it halfway up, Eris heard a muffled footfall and the quietest of sneezes from the base of the stairs. Reacting with pure instinct, and in one fluid motion, she drew one of her daggers from its sheath, spun to face the noise and then threw her blade. The dagger spun through the air with a subtle whirling sound and even though Eris knew not the exact location of her target, she knew her blade flew true. But to late she realised her mistake. Her target was naught but a child.

With a wet thunk, the dagger sunk deeply into the child's chest. Stunned, the boy staggered briefly as blood spluttered from his mouth. The cup he was holding fell to the ground, shattering on the floorboards and spilling water everywhere. Wide-eyed, he collapsed face first onto the lower stairs.

Eris could barely register what was happening as the pool of blood beneath the boy grew and shock set in. Standing motionless, she knew in her heart of hearts that the boy was dead, she knew that her dagger had pierced his heart. But, some irrational part of her brain questioned this reality, maybe he was alive and maybe everything was going to be fine?

As if in a trance, Eris shuffled over to the boy. Laying utterly immobile, he made not a trace of sound. He was not breathing. Yet, despite all evidence to the contrary, a part of Eris still did not want to face reality. Turning the boy over, she checked his neck for a pulse. She did not find one. He was dead.

Oh gods, what have I done?

She had killed a child. She had robbed another of the most precious of things, what she herself had always desired above all else. What she had up until very recently believed she would never produce.

In that moment of realisation, Eris lost all semblance of composure and sunk to her knees beside the child. Instantly, nausea overcame her and she vomited uncontrollably onto the floor. Even once her stomach was utterly voided, she continued to dry retch as tears streamed unfettered from their ducts and fell to the floor as rain.

All notions of purpose fled. Eris sat weeping, overcame with grief and shame, unable and unwilling to act. She no longer cared if she were discovered, if she were captured, or even if she were killed. As far as she was concerned her life was forfeit, she deserved to be punished.

Eventually, the rational part of her brain was able to be heard over the impossibly loud cacophony of sorrow plaguing her mind. It asked the question, what of Mikael? She deserved to be penalised, in a way most severe, but he did not. He had done nothing wrong.

They don't care. It doesn't matter. They'll kill him for my mistake.

This realisation jolted Eris from her stupor. She had to get to him with all haste and together they had to flee Súthburh.

But before she could move, Eris heard the pattering of footsteps from the top of the stairs. Her reflexes slowed from grief, she did nothing. She did not attempt to hide, nor did she ready another dagger. She simply sat there helplessly, staring up the stairwell, waiting for her to be discovered.

A girl of no more than twelve, whom Eris could only presume to be the dead boy's older sister, crested the top of the stairway. She wore a cotton nightgown, three sizes too big, and striped woollen socks. Rubbing the sleep from her eyes the girl failed to notice Eris, or the corpse of her brother. As she descended the stairs the child hissed out in muffled tones.

'Jackson, where are you? What are you doing? You know how angry father gets when you sneak around at night. Jackson?'

Halfway down the stairs the girl spotted Eris. With a calm that only comes from a life of power and safety she addressed Eris.

'Who are you and what are you doing in my house?'

Eris stammered, shocked, unable to say anything of tangible meaning. Before she could articulate even the simplest of responses, the girl's gaze drifted down to that of her sibling's body. It took her a moment to register what she was seeing, but when realisation dawned her face crumbled and a howl of anguish erupted from her mouth.

Knowing it was too late to calm the child and that everyone in the villa would now be alerted to her presence, Eris took the only option she had. She ran.

Turning around, Eris sprinted back into the dining room. All around her the house echoed with cries of alarm, of men shouting calls to action. From above her, from below her and every direction otherwise.

I'm in trouble. Big trouble.

By the time Eris entered the kitchen two Khullite mercenaries had arrived in response to the ruckus. They now blocked her way. Without slowing down, Eris drew a pair of daggers and threw them at the guards. The first dagger hit its mark, the forehead of one of the mercenaries, and with a crack of splintering bone the man collapsed dead. The second missed. Its target, a scrawny Khullite, ducked under the flying blade.

Seeing that her attack had failed, Eris palmed another dagger, but before she could throw it, the Khullite drew his scimitar and slashed it violently towards Eris's face. Without breaking stride, Eris stepped into the sword's arc and blocked the blow, catching the guard's forearm with her own. Within her foe's defences, Eris thrust her dagger at the mercenary's chest. The strike hit home, but was unable to penetrate the man's hide armour.

Curses.

Sensing an imminent victory, the Khullite snarled as he thrust his head towards Eris's face. Unable to avoid the blow, the man's forehead slammed into Eris's nose. With a loud crack her nasal bone shattered and blood spurted from her nostrils. Wincing with pain, her eyes watered unbidden, blurring her vision, yet, despite this handicap, she slashed her dagger towards the mercenary for a second time. Arterial blood sprayed from the man's throat as her blade severed his carotid artery. Wracking for breath, and rapidly bleeding out, the Khullite collapsed to the floor and died.

Angry shouts from behind her spurred Eris to even greater speeds. She began to pant from the exertion, but she did not slow. The sitting room, from which she had entered the villa by, flashed by in a blur as she dashed through it with no opposition. More yells filled her ears, from closer than before.

Out into the cool night air she emerged, a relief for her near exhausted body, but by no means the freedom she sought. Unable to slow, let alone stop, Eris clapped the heels of her boots together as she ran, an began to recite the words which would activate their charm. The ancient magic started to stir, the outer wall looming nearer and nearer. With no room to spare, the boots sprang to life and Eris started to run upwards, on nothing but the air.

As Eris crested the top of the wall, her back was struck by a heavy impact. Agony exploded through her body as a crossbow bolt drove itself deeply into the rear of her shoulder. A scream of pure anguish erupted from her mouth, yet even so she maintained her concentration and remained airborne. Within her, she could feel the bolt's head shred and tear her flesh as she moved, but she couldn't stop, to do so would be to die. She kept running.

This is bad. Really bad.

Once over the wall, and close enough to the ground, Eris dropped the incantation powering her boots and fell to the cobbles. Upon landing, she stumbled, the pain that throbbed throughout her entire body affecting her coordination. Staggering into a nearby alley, Eris heard a clearly tormented voice yell in her direction.

'I will kill you. You fucking bitch! By my honour and the honour of my son's departed soul, you will suffer!'

Mercurius.

The voice continued to rant in her direction, but it quickly faded to nothing as Eris continued to run.

I was ordered to return to the Barrow, but to do so would mean my death. Vejovis would offer me up to the merchant as appeasement in an instant. There is only one option, I need to get home. Mikael can help.

All around her she could hear the frenzied cries and shouts of her pursuers. They were close. Too close. Eris tried to increase her pace, but she was already at her limits.

A fresh wave of pain surged through her body as the shaft of the bolt struck the side of a building. She gritted her teeth and did all she could to remain silent, she could not afford a scream revealing her position.

I have to do something about this bolt. But, to pull it out would be foolish, especially if it has pierced an artery. I'd bleed out. Perhaps breaking the shaft would help? Then, at least, it wouldn't wiggle around as much.

Steadying herself against a nearby wall, Eris gripped the bolt's shaft and attempted to snap it. Pain erupted in her shoulder and she stifled a growl as more of her blood oozed onto the ground below. Clenching her jaw, she tried and tried, but to no avail, the shaft would not break. It was too thick and she was too exhausted. Giving up she ran on.

So much for that.

She didn't get far. Eris knew that her pace was flagging and the voices around her were as close as ever. She wasn't going to make it, she had to hide. Ducking into an even smaller side alley, Eris found a small nook between two buildings. She squeezed in the best she could, ever mindful of the bolt protruding from her shoulder, and prayed to Laverna once more. Her final thoughts before the darkness took her were of Mikael and how she had failed him.

*   *   *

The inky void that had taken Eris slowly began to recede. All her senses fuzzy, she noticed small things at first through a thick haze. Voices, muffled and distant, yet nearby. Heavy footsteps, with purpose and vigour, echoed off of the stone around her. It was dark, too dark for it to be daytime, was it the same night or the next? She did not know, for no time passes for the mind when in the thrall of unconsciousness.

Voices once fuzzy slowly became clearer. She also noticed the barking of dogs. Eris hated dogs. They always impeded her work.

'This way boys, the hounds have, caught the sent for sure.'

'Woof, woof.'

Eris attempted to stand, to try and flee, but the agony was too much. Her legs, stiff and sore from the exertion, collapsed under her. More pain, by the gods did she hate the pain.

A low growl pierced through her tormented stupor and she turned to face the source. Eris's heart skipped a beat as a stake of primal fear thrust itself into her chest. There before her, was a massive pit dog, bred for war, an expert at killing. Thick, viscous drool oozed from its mouth as it licked its chops with anticipation. It lowered itself onto its haunches, in preparation for the leap that it so wanted to take, hunger clearly evident in its eyes. Resigned to her fate, Eris whispered a prayer to the gods, hoping that the afterlife would be kind.

Chapter 10

Neesa

As Neesa exited the slaves' quarters the dirt beneath her feet crunched, barely audible above the echoes of revelry that wafted gently around her. Glancing furtively to either side, she checked to see if any guards were in the vicinity. Seeing, nor hearing, no one, she crouched low against the wall of the slaves' quarters, hugging it as she moved towards the palisade.

I should clear the wall first. Deny my foe the high ground, lest they spot me as I move between the compound's buildings.

Neesa doubted that that there would be as many guards on patrol as normal, but she knew that discretion would be the epitome of prudence. Reaching the corner of the slaves' quarters, she scanned to her left and then to the right. Still there was no one.

Before her was the inner wall of the palisade. She assessed its height and within moments one fact became inescapably obvious. It was unassailable. However, this conclusion was not new to Neesa. Knowing from the beginning that she would have to scale the palisade, she had discovered this truth almost immediately after resolving herself to escape. So, over the past weeks, as those replete with idle time are wont to do, she thought the problem over and devised the simplest of solutions.

A series of small steps will get you as far as a single bound.

With a powerful leap, Neesa jumped upwards, her arms extended above her head. The tips of her fingers found purchase on the edge of the slaves' quarters roof. Her claws dug into the aged wood, but Neesa knew that her hold was precarious. As quickly as she could manage, Neesa pushed herself and began to swing back and forth, slowly building her momentum. At her peak, Neesa released her grip on the roof, while pushing off of it as hard as she could.

With an acrobatic grace, far in excess of what would be considered possible for a simple slave girl, Neesa summersaulted backwards through the air. It was a truly masterful manoeuvre and, just as Neesa had intended, once her flight was completed, she landed silently onto the smithy's roof.

That's the first step taken.

From her newfound height, Neesa knew that the palisade would be far easier to reach. Backing away from the wall to give herself some room, she ran, rapidly picking up speed. Her feet slapped audibly against the roof shingles. Internally, she worried that there might be someone nearby, an auditory witness to her passing, but committed to her course, she pushed these concerns aside.

Reaching the end of the roof, she jumped, her legs pushing her forward as hard as they could. There was little panache to her flight, as distance, rather than style, was the intent, but it served to achieve the desired outcome.

Her outstretched hands barely managed to grasp the edge of the palisade, splinters speared into her fingers, tearing at her flesh. Her body impacted heavily against the wall and the air in her lungs rushed from her body as she gasped in both pain and shock. But somehow, she managed to hang on. Barely.

Oh gods. That was most unpleasant. And not at all how I envisioned that would go.

Through gritted teeth, Neesa pulled herself onto the top of the palisade. Crouching low, she cocked her head to one side, straining her ears as she tried to ascertain if she had been discovered or not. Hearing no cries of alarm, Neesa breathed a sigh of relief and, still in a crouch, began to move along the top of the wall.

Scanning ahead, Neesa saw a pair of guards walking towards her. Instantly, Neesa dropped to her belly and lay flat. As of yet they hadn't seen her, but her heart pounded in her chest as she considered her options.

To do nothing would be idiotic beyond belief and tantamount to suicide. A frontal assault would be similarly foolish. Overpowering the guards was not the issue, she knew that she could do that. The problem lay in the approach, for if they were to see her coming then they would no doubt raise the alarm before she could silence them. Perhaps, she thought, it would be prudent to withdraw. Just for now.

As the guards came ever closer, the window for Neesa's escape closed. If she were to stand now, she would be seen.

Fucking shit balls.

Knowing that she had to act, Neesa took the only avenue open to her. Remaining prone, she rolled, off of the palisade. However, rather than surrendering entirely to gravity's embrace, she latched onto the edge of the walkway and hung there, hoping she would go unnoticed.

Okay. Once these arsehole pass, I'll ambush them from behind.

'Damn Ricardo, that lucky bastard. He gets the best post every time he does. Jus' happens to work in the Master's mansion when a party's goin' on. Cor, I wish I was him with all those lovely ladies around.'

'Bah, you're a sour bastard mate, it's not like he'll be able to do anything with them.'

'I don't know about that. I heard from Mikey that las' harvest he copped a blowie from some noble lass.'

'Ha, Mikey's full of shite. More likely he got caught jerking off in a corner.'

'Ha, ha, too right. The fucker's still lucky though. I'd be happy to jus' enjoy the view, if you catch my drift.'

'I sure do mate. Hey, do you see that?'

'What?'

'That. On the floor over there.'

Shit.

Neesa knew what it was the guard had seen. Clearly, he had spotted her hands. Knowing that they would inevitably come and investigate, Neesa readied herself and prayed that they wouldn't have their blades pointed low towards her.

'No idea. It's probably nothin,' but we'd better check it out.'

Listening intently to the guards' footsteps, Neesa waited. Despite the cool air, beads of sweat formed upon her brow. Rapidly, they pooled by the bridge of her nose, threatening to stream into her eyes and blind her. She wanted to wipe them away, to clear her face of their unwelcome presence, but she could not. She dared not move. Soon enough she judged the guards to be close enough to strike.

Straining her muscles, she propelled her body upwards. Shooting high above the palisade and the dumbstruck guards. Neesa summersaulted mid-flight, her tail lashing out as she spun. The spear that one of the guard's held was knocked cleanly from his hands, falling uselessly onto the ground below.

Landing directly in front of the guards, Neesa thrust out a palm, smashing the disarmed guard in the throat. The hapless man was spun around by the force of the blow and to the floor he fell, struggling to breathe as his crushed larynx slowly choked him to death.

The second guard could barely react before a clenched fist slammed into his face. His jaw cracked loudly as bone broke. Despite the fact that he was in serious pain, the guard slashed his spear towards Neesa. The attack lacked any real finesse, as it was born from desperation rather than skill, so Neesa back-flipped away from the oncoming spear-blade with ease.

As soon as her feet contacted the walkway, Neesa propelled herself forward, summersaulting over the outstretched spear. Mid-flight, she unleashed a powerful kick. The guard's head snapped back as the heel of Neesa's foot careened into his already broken jaw. Overwhelmed by the pain, he fell to the floor unconscious.

Well, that went remarkably well.

Spending no time to admire her handiwork, Neesa bent down, checking on the first guard. He was dead. A quick rummage through his pockets revealed nothing of worth, so she picked him up and unceremoniously threw him outside the compound.

The second guard was only unconscious, so Neesa covered his mouth with a hand and pinched his nose closed. His body twitched and spasmed as it desperately fought for air, but Neesa didn't let go. Eventually, as the man perished, the struggling stopped. Just as she had done with the first, Neesa threw his corpse over the wall, to join his comrade below.

Returning to her low crouch, Neesa continued along the wall. She soon came upon a second pair of guards chatting idly, seemingly oblivious to the fracas that had occurred some one hundred feet from their station.

'Hey, did you 'appen to catch a gander at that fancy noble bird that came round last week.'

'Can't say that I did, but I heard tell that she was proper creepy.'

'Yeah, I got a glimpse of her and she was at that. It was her eyes, they chilled me to the bone they did. Not an ounce of life in 'em.'

Concerned only with their conversation, and not expecting any real trouble, the guards failed to notice Neesa approach from their rear.

'Now, I'm not a picky man, normally I'd take the company of any willing lass and count me blessings. But as fine as that lady was, I'd never…'

As soon as Neesa reached striking range, she stood and wrapped her arm around the throat of the talking guard. His speech stopped mid-sentence, replaced by raspy croaks, as he struggled to breath. The second guard reacted, but far too slowly. With mouth agape from surprise, he began to draw the short sword from his hip. Causally, Neesa wrenched the first guard's neck and with a sickening snap he fell to the walkway, dead.

Steel hissed from its scabbard and swung through the air towards Neesa's head. The guard's attack was sloppy and openly telegraphed. With ease, Neesa stepped backwards and the blade met nothing but air.

In counter, Neesa lunged for the guard's throat with a clenched fist. Had it connected the man would have died, a slow drawn-out death, but he was able to avoid injury by sidestepping the blow. Continuing to press her offensive, Neesa threw another punch. Unlike her last strike, this blow struck home, but for the most part was absorbed by the guard's leather jerkin.

Grunting at the blow to his ribs, the guard snarled in anger and launched a vicious thrust towards Neesa. Had the blade struck, Neesa would have been skewered and no doubt slain. Fortunately for Neesa, the guard lost his footing mid-thrust, tripping on the corpse of his deceased companion. With a heavy thump, and a string of curses, he fell arse first onto the walkway.

Not one to forgo such an opportunity, Neesa pounced. Rage fuelled blow after blow rained down onto the head of the hapless man. His sword fell to the floor beside him, forgotten, as he was forced from consciousness. Ceasing her tirade, Neesa picked up the guard's sword and at first slowly, but then faster, she slid its blade into the man's jaw. It met a modicum of resistance, but with a final thrust Neesa drove it deep into the guard's brain.

As the man expired with a final twitch, Neesa once again strained herself to determine if she had been discovered. At hearing nothing but the usual sounds of the night and the faint melodic waves of music, she allowed herself a moment to slow her rapid breathing, reassured by the absence of any alarm.

Thank the gods that last one didn't scream out for help. If he had, I'd be in a bit of strife right now. Idiot.

Thinking it pertinent, Neesa quickly searched the corpses of the guards for anything useful. All she found were a small assortment of coins, which for her were worthless, and a duplicate set of keys to the ones she already had, equally useless. So, over the wall they went.

In her hands she still held the guard's short sword. She swung it once, to test its balance, and after the briefest of considerations, decided to keep it. Unbuckling the belt of its previous owner, Neesa took the leather and looped it over one of her shoulders. Fastening it tightly, she angled the scabbard across her back so she could reach the sword's hilt easily and not have it restrict her movement.

Well, it's a tad on the unconventional side, but it should work. And I imagine it makes me look cool. Bonus.

Just as it was with the previous pair of guards, Neesa didn't want these bodies to be discovered. So, they were also tossed over the wall. Once all the evidence of her altercation was cleared, save for the blood-soaked timber, Neesa crouched low and once more continued with her mission.

While she walked, Neesa observed the occasional guard below. Some stood idly, smoking tobacco filled pipes. Others paced in erratic circles as they attempted to stave off boredom and the eventual slumber it would bring. Each in turn failed to notice her passing, so she took note of their positions and resolved herself to dealing with them later.

The entrance to the compound lay before her and Neesa noticed two guards, one stationed on either side. Unlike the others she had witnessed, Neesa knew that she would have to deal with these two now. It would be impossible for her to pass them undetected and they blocked the only escape route of her fellow slaves.

If they're still here when the others leave, they'll kill them all. Or worse. I can't have that.

Looking ahead, Neesa noted how the palisade's walkway continued over the guards' heads. A plan, albeit a flimsy one, formulated in her mind. Perching herself above one of the sentries, she pointed her sword downwards.

Okay then, here goes nothing.

Blade first, she stepped off of the palisade. Neither of the guards saw the attack coming.

Gore crusted steel plunged deep into the shoulder of her target. In an instant, his internal organs were lacerated. Blood spluttered from the guard's mouth as his lungs filled with blood and he struggle to breath. Neesa pulled her blade from the soon to be corpse, a fresh fountain of gore erupted from the man's wound, and rolled towards the second guard.

Just in time. A spear blade thrust over her tumbling form, penetrating naught but the empty space she had just vacated.

Gods, that was close.

Rising from her roll, Neesa swung her sword in a vicious swing. The blade bit deep into the torso of the guard, eviscerating his mid-section. In equal measure, the man's face twisted in surprise and shock as his entrails spilled to the ground. Mere moments later his lifeless body followed silently behind them.

Palisade now completely clear of guards, Neesa turned her attention towards the interior of the compound. Amongst the buildings she stalked, using the shadows as her shield. One by one, with an efficiency far removed from the warmth of humanity, she exterminated the remaining guards. Slit throats and broken necks the just desserts for those she viewed as guilty of, or complicit in, the crimes she both bore and witnessed.

In barely any time at all the entire compound was clear of guards, their bodies hidden beyond the sight of a casual observer.

Well, that was fun. What's next?

All it took was a moment of thought and her next objective became clear. Neesa knew that the next changing of the guard would reveal her butchery and that the alarm would surely be raised in response. She also knew that this would occur regardless, discovery was an inevitability, but she wanted to delay it for as long as possible, to improve the odds of a successful escape.

It seems to me that the barracks is my next destination.

No one stood in her way as Neesa weaved her way through the compound. As she reached the exterior of the guards' barracks, Neesa peeked through one of its windows. Inside, most of the bunks lay bare, only a lousy few were occupied by sleeping men.

Good. As long as I'm quiet they'll be easy to deal with.

Moving to the next window, Neesa snuck another glance inside the building. Scattered cups and plates, still soiled from the evening's meal, were strewn over the handful of tables dispersed chaotically throughout the room. The space was almost devoid of life, save for a lone man. Over one of the tables he stood, bare from the waist down, buttocks jiggling wildly as he violated the spread-legged form of the half-elf girl.

An intense pain stabbed into Neesa's chest and nausea threatened as memories of her own, similar past threatened to overwhelm her. Closing her eyes, she focussed on her breathing, just as she had been taught to do, and tried to regain clarity. To no avail. Disjointed images of a tavern, a bedroom, poorly lit and heavy with stale air, of a noble man, heavyset and sweaty, assaulted her mind. Feelings of shame and memories of physical trauma bore down upon her already fractured soul.

Though these memories were never truly forgotten, they were normally buried deep, far beyond casual reach. Now that they had surfaced, Neesa felt what she had never wanted to feel again, a pain and sorrow beyond all words. Her only recourse, lest she shatter to a million pieces, was to take refuge in the rage.

It went beyond mere anger, which is manageable and who's nature is in comparison timid. This was instead akin to the fury of the tempest. A tumultuous ocean of the purest obsidian, continuously roiling against the constraints of the shore, destroying, and consuming all that dared to encroach upon its dominion.

Neesa's conscious mind returned to the present in a jarring instant as her memories were banished back to the past. Her heart pounded and her chest heaved. Oxygen rich blood surged through her veins. Her senses heightened, she felt the world around her like no other, she felt truly alive. No longer would pain threaten her, in fact she would welcome it, for pain was now the fuel that drove her. She was lost in the revelry that was her rage, a drug most treacherous, but within its walls she felt safe.

Incensed beyond all notions of subtlety, Neesa charged to the entrance of the barracks. With one almighty kick she shattered the door from its hinges. Unbound, the aged pine collided with the wall, denting it horrendously. Snarling viciously, Neesa strode through the open portal, scanning the building's interior for her prey.

Lost in the heat of his debaucheries, the guard failed to hear Neesa's ingress, just as he failed to notice her approach.

Must kill. Must kill him now!

Running up behind the guard, Neesa wrapped her hand around his mouth, stifling his grotesques moans. Momentarily, his eyes bulged in anger at this unexpected transgression. He fought to free himself, both from Neesa's hold and the inside of the half-elf girl, but Neesa held him firm. But he was soon becalmed as Neesa struck. A clenched fist thrust into the back of the man's neck. Vertebrae were driven from their alignment, instantly severing his spinal cord. His head bent unnaturally backwards, Neesa released the guard and allowed him to fall to the floor, where he lay twitching sporadically.

All vestiges of rage evaporated, replaced by sadness and pity, as the snow-white form of the half-elf girl occupied the entirety of Neesa's focus. Now free from the guard's intrusions, she had curled herself into a ball. Not to hide what remained of her shattered dignity, but rather to seek shelter from the cruelties of an imperfect world within the sanctity of her imagination.

Having been in the girl's position, Neesa knew what it was that she was going through. Kneeling down beside the girl, Neesa caressed the half-elf's shoulder reassuringly. Initially, the girl recoiled at the touch, but calmed as soon as she realised that Neesa meant her no harm. Whispering gently into the girl's ear, Neesa tried to console the half-elf.

'I know that no words can undo, or make right, what has happened to you and I know that you won't believe me, but I do understand. I know how you feel, I've felt it too. And. Well, the pain, the shame, the anger, none of it really goes away, but it will get easier to live with. I promise, it will get better.'

The girl turned her head to face Neesa. Her eyes, devoid of all mirth, bore into Neesa's soul, challenging the validity of her claim. Within them Neesa saw a resignation, a surrendering of all care and any possible redemption. In the face of this, Neesa's conviction, well intentioned as it was, rang hollow, even to herself. It crushed her conviction and left her at a loss as to what she should do. Awkwardly, she stroked the girl's face, further trying to calm and reassure her.

'I'll fix this I swear. Now, there's something I need to do, but I'll be right back, ok?'

The girl showed no evidence of having heard, or even understanding, Neesa. She just lay, in her immobile ball, silently staring into the distance. Torn, Neesa left the girl's side and ventured into the guard's sleeping quarters.

I'll make them all pay.

Still unaware of Neesa's presence, the remaining guards slept on. As silent as a shadow, she moved between each of the bunks, stifling their cries with her hand as she slit each of their throats in turn. Once all the men had been dealt with, she expected to feel some sense of accomplishment, some sense of pride in having righted a wrong most egregious. Instead, she felt just as she had before, violated and incensed.

These men are but the product of another. I'll never be satisfied until I've killed our master.

A noise from behind her, drew Neesa's attention from her thoughts. Spinning around she saw a young man, still in his teens, stagger into the room, rubbing sleep from his bleary eyes. Before the boy could react to her presence, Neesa dashed across the room and took his throat in her hands. She squeezed tightly, not enough to render him mute, but enough to highlight the peril he was in.

'Plea... please. Don't, hu... hurt me.'

Her fury rekindled shone in Neesa's eyes and she glowered at the boy, her stare rich with contempt.

'Why not? Did you stop when she begged you too? Did you not take what you wanted, despite it never being offered? Why shouldn't I end your life?'

The front of the boy's pants grew dark as he relieved himself unbidden.

'I... I, didn't. I ne... never. I wouldn't.'

'And yet here you are. In the company of those who would, of those who did. Answer me this why didn't you stop them? Did you even try?'

'How co... could I?'

Neesa's eyes narrowed.

'Not good enough.'

Whatever the boy was about to say, no doubt a plea for mercy or a protestation of innocence, was lost as Neesa increased her pressure upon the boy's neck. His eyes bulged and his face turned red as blood vessels burst. In an attempt to win his freedom, he flailed wildly at Neesa, initially with some force, but as he gradually weakened, they lost all potency. Inevitably, he died and disgusted, Neesa discarded the boy's remains as she would have an irreparable utensil.

Bah, you received no less than what you deserved. Now, back to more important things. I can't have the girl walk about naked. I need to cover her with something.

Giving the room a cursory once over, Neesa could see nothing of any use, save for a relatively clean bedsheet.

It's less than ideal, but it will have to do.

When Neesa re-entered the mess area she was met with a most horrid sight. Stunned, she stood idle, momentarily frozen. An impromptu gasp escaped her mouth and she dropped the bedsheet as her hand shot to her mouth.

Before her hung the half-elf girl, suspended from the rafters by the guard's belt she had used to hang herself. As the girl swayed, still naked as a new born, Neesa felt her legs give way from beneath her. Collapsing to the floor, she lamented the cruelty of fate and choked back the lump of anger that rose in her throat, incensed at the senseless waste of such potential.

Gathering herself, Neesa determined that the girl would not be left like this, so exposed to the world's cruel judgements. Climbing onto the table, Neesa unfastened the belt and lowered the girl as gently as she could. In her heart Neesa wished that she could give the elf a proper burial, to grant her the respects she deserved, but she knew that time and circumstance rendered this impossible. Instead, Neesa cleared the table and laid the elf upon it. Picking up the bedsheet from the floor, she draped it over the child's lifeless form and bowed her head in respect.

I'm so sorry. But know this, my promise still stands. I will fix this.

Chapter 11

Neesa

A kaleidoscope of stars shone above Neesa as she exited the barracks, but their beauty, intrinsic and undeniable, was lost to her. Deep in the throes of purpose, which was by far preferrable to the alternative of remorse, they barely registered as present. Stalking her way through the compound, she met no resistance, as any that would have opposed her were already dead.

Arriving at the fence that surrounded her master's villa, Neesa wasted no time and scrambled deftly up its sun-bleached façade. Once at the top, she held herself there and assessed the interior.

Two guards were stationed by the main entrance to the house. They were obviously displeased with their situation, as they greeted each passer-by with a scowl. Music they couldn't dance to reverberated alluringly around them. The enticing scent of food, of which they couldn't eat, tempted their eager bellies. Beautiful women, they were unable to seduce, frolicked gleefully in the flickering torch light.

They'll be easy to avoid, distracted as they are. Undoubtedly, there are more guards than them, but I have no idea where they'd be. Damn. Regardless, there's nothing for it.

When she judged the way to be as clear as it was going to get, Neesa threw her body over the fence. Dropping to the other side, she landed in a roll, maintaining her momentum while simultaneously dampening the impact of her landfall. Keeping as low as she could, she wasted no time and sprinted across the luscious grass. Reaching the nearest column of the house, Neesa took cover behind it and paused, both to catch her breath and determine if her passing had been detected. It had been.

Having seen a blur of motion from the corner of his eye, one of the guards tore his attention from the well-dressed lass dancing provocatively before him. Without turning, he spoke to his companion from the corner of his mouth.

'Oi, did you happen to see that?'

Well, so much for being easy to avoid. Hopefully they'll lose interest and ignore me.

'Nah. What was it?'

The man took a step towards the pillar Neesa was hiding behind, his spear lowered in her direction.

'Dunno, but it looked like someone running across the lawn.'

Shit. I can't move. They'll see me.

'Bah, it's probably just a guest who's had too much wine and is looking for a private place to piss.'

The first guard took another step towards Neesa.

'Yeah, you're probably right, but we should check it out.'

The second guard just shrugged.

'Alright.'

Looks like we're doing this then.

No longer talking to his compatriot, the first guard shouted angrily into the dark.

'Who goes there? Get out here and show yourself.'

Remaining silent, Neesa stilled her breathing and drew the sword from her back as silently as she could. Upon hearing no response, the first guard gestured for his companion to advance.

'Come on, quit playing silly buggers. If you come out now, we won't punish you too badly.'

As the guards kept advancing slowly, wary of whatever may be hidden in the darkness of shadow, Neesa waited, listening to their subtle footsteps, biding her time. At last, she judged them to be close enough. Exhaling slowly, she struck.

Neesa rolled out from behind the marble pillar, grabbing the spear shaft of the first guard with her off hand and thrusting out her sword. The blade bit deep into the chest of the unprepared man and with a rapid twist, Neesa yanked her sword free from the flesh that clung to its edge. A shower of blood, now unrestrained, flowed freely onto the grass below. Yet, still the man stood.

To his credit, the guard uttered no cry of pain in response to this attack upon his person. Instead, he dropped his spear, recognising the tactical disadvantage it presented in such close quarters to his quarry, and drew his own short sword. He swung the blade desperately, but weakened by his wound, failed to contact the infernati woman dancing wildly before him.

As Neesa dodged another errant sword-stroke, the second guard thrust his own spear towards her, striking her in the shoulder. Cold steel plunged deep, lacerating tissue, and skidding over bone. Pain, searing hot, surged through her, awakening the rage that slumbered in her core.

Argh!

Her teeth bared in fury, Neesa dropped the first guard's spear and grabbed the one sticking from her shoulder. She pulled on it as hard as she could, the blade eased itself deeper inside her, but she felt nothing of it. Caught off balance, the second guard stumbled forward, into range of Neesa's blade. Imbued with rage, she swung her sword. The strike, borne from a wild fury, was devoid of any skill, and yet muscle and sinew alike were cleaved in twain as the man's head was sundered from his body.

Seeing his friend's head thump softly to the ground beside him, followed soon after by that of his body, the first guard began to scream for assistance. The cry died in his throat as soon as it had begun as Neesa encircled her hand around the man's throat. Squeezing tightly, her claws dug deep into flesh and in an instant were soaking in crimson. Yanking hard, Neesa tore the guard's throat apart. Deceased, he fell to the ground air whistling from his perforated trachea.

Guards dealt with Neesa stood over their corpses breathing hard. Her shoulder throbbed as it haemorrhaged slowly, her blood joining that of the slain men by her feet. Gradually her heartbeat slowed and the rage faded, her mind returning to normal.

Good grief, he got me good. Sloppy Neesa, very sloppy.

To Neesa it appeared that no one had noticed her tussle, as no screams, nor cries of alarm, could be heard.

By all that is holy, how in the seven hells did that not go unnoticed? No matter.

Bracing herself for more pain, Neesa pulled the spear from her shoulder. An animalistic snarl almost escaped her lips, but she managed to muffle it so it was nothing more than a low growl. The bleeding from her shoulder intensified.

I'll need to deal with that.

Stooping low, Neesa tore off a sleeve from one of the guard's shirts. It was a little grubby, and not at all sterile, but it would have to do. Taking care to cover the entirety of her injury, encompassing both the entry and exit wound, she wrapped it around her shoulder, pulled it tight and tied it off. It hurt her to do so, and she grimaced at the pain, but at least the bleeding was staunched.

Not wishing the bodies of her victims to be discovered, but knowing that they eventually would be, Neesa dragged the guards' remains behind a nearby pillar and dumped them into a particularly voluptuous shrub. There was no way her deception would stand up to serious scrutiny, but for now, it would have to suffice.

Aware that haste was now a necessity, Neesa looked around for a way to get inside her master's villa. The best, and most obvious, point of ingress was the balcony above her, but there was no easy way for her to climb the sheer walls and columns. Neither afforded her any handholds or purchase. She would have to look elsewhere for another means of entry.

Damn.

Wishing to draw as little attention to herself as possible, Neesa hugged the wall of the house, kept low and stalked towards the rear of the building.

Surely a house this large has a back door. And probably some side doors. Well, it probably has a lot of doors. Maybe there's a way in that's not being watched.

Ahead of Neesa, two giggling women, clearly inebriated, stumbled from the side of the house, spilling their already depleted drinks. Neesa froze, worry causing her heart to race, and waited for them to leave, hoping that they wouldn't see her and that she wouldn't be forced to kill them.

'Oh, my gods, can you believe that guy? I mean like seriously, as if someone as highborn as me would been seen dancing with such a nobody like him. And don't get me started on his face, totally gross.'

'Oh, my gods, you're totally right. The gall. Anyways, we better get back to Sha'ni, I'm sure someone is trying to weasel their way into her skirts and we both know how mad her father will get if she's knocked up before her wedding. He would totally blame us.'

'He totally would. Arsehole. Just wait a minute, I need to pee.'

Neesa watched on, enthralled, disgusted and somewhat bemusedly, as one of the women lifted the hem of her dress to her waist, squatted over the grass and then relieved herself.

'Taylah! You disgusting retch, have you no shame?'

'Oh, quit your whining. You've seen me do worse and it's not like anyone else is here watching.'

I am. Though I wish I wasn't.

'Gods did I need that. Okay then, let's find Sha'ni. And another drink. And some handsome men to make out with.'

A fresh chorus of high-pitched giggling pierced Neesa's ears as the pair of wayward guests stumbled towards the rear of the building. For the briefest of instants, Neesa considered their conversation and almost regretted not ending their existence, but quickly dismissed this violent notion as impractical and unnecessary.

As painful as that was to witness, at least they revealed a way inside.

Neesa emerged from her hiding place and ran to the door. Thankfully, it was not locked and it opened easily and silently. Looking around before she crossed the threshold proper, she saw no one to oppose her entrance. To her left, and to her right, there were doors that no doubt lead deeper into the bowels of the mansion.

To enter the fox's warren with no semblance of a plan seems like a bad idea to me.

From her perspective, a more promising prospect lay directly in front of her. A simple staircase, most probably used by the servants, spiralled both upwards and downwards. With the briefest of hesitations, Neesa moved swiftly to the stairs and began to climb up. A plan quickly formulating in her mind.

Okay, find the Master's room, break in unnoticed, hide, wait for him to retire for the evening and ambush him in his sleep. Perfect. What could go wrong?

At the stair's zenith, Neesa was met by a long hallway, either side lined by doors. Encountering no one, she continued along the corridor, both as quickly and as quietly as she could manage. Half-way down the hallway, she stopped as the right side of the corridor gave way to a grand staircase that swept gracefully from this floor to the building's main entrance below. Peeking carefully around the corner, Neesa noted a pair of guards standing sentry by the base of the stairs.

Not wanting to alert them to her presence, Neesa considered her options. She could easily continue along the hallway and avoid the guards. She could also turn back, but that seemed pointless. A third, more appealing option, presented itself as she regarded the door to her left. This door was easily twice the size of the others around it and was framed with ornate carvings and gold inlaid fil de gre. It was by far too fancy to be the entrance to just another room, Neesa thought. In all probability this was the entrance to her master's chambers.

Well, that sure is convenient.

Ignoring the guards below, Neesa moved to the door and tried to open it. Surprisingly, it opened. She was momentarily taken aback that it wasn't locked, but quickly pushed her confoundment aside and entered the room. Not wishing to be taken unawares from behind, and thinking it prudent to do so, she closed the door behind her.

The space before her was dimly lit, even though two oil lamps burned strongly by the entrance to the room. Light, glowing softly in the dark, pulsated as the flames that drove it forward danced erratically in their cages. Wild and powerful the light fought against the night, but the chamber was just too large for the flames to illuminate. No matter how hard they tried, the room was still mostly cloaked in shadow. Squinting into the darkness, Neesa took a lamp from the wall and began to search the room.

She was greeted by a complete ensemble of extravagant furniture, each constructed from deep walnuts and mahoganies, and upholstered in cashmere and suede. Lavish rugs, while hideously garish, comforted her weary feet as their soft and welcoming fibres encapsulated her toes. Grandiose paintings of elves, dwarves, and men of old, each trying a little too hard to be regal, dotted the walls. Numerous pedestals, each supporting a unique ceramic, circled the room and while Neesa knew not their value, they appeared to her to be expensive. A four-post bed, easily the largest Neesa had ever seen, covered in a veritable ocean of pillows and cushions, sat as a dominant statement, a proclamation of her master's wealth.

Over compensating much?

As she walked around the Master's chamber's, Neesa tried to open each of the chests, dressers, and drawers she encountered in turn. Each was locked, and beyond her skills to open, save for one. Only the main wardrobe was unlocked. Its stained doors opened with nothing more than a subtle creak from its hinges. Neesa gasped. Before her was a plethora of fine garments. Most were made from exotic fabrics, of which she recognised few, and tailored in a way that sacrificed function for the sake of form.

Looking down at what she was wearing, a simple shirt, length extended to her knees, bloodstained, and torn, it was clear to Neesa that her modesty was covered by nothing more than rags.

Oh. This will not do. Time for an upgrade.

Placing the lantern on a nearby table, Neesa dove into the ocean of fabric before her and began her search. She soon found a pair of slim fitting, black cotton trousers.

Hm, comfortable and practical. They will do nicely.

She also found and considered several shirts, most were several sizes too large, or altogether too frilly, but finally she settled on a plain button up shirt, long sleeved and charcoal grey.

Shouldn't be too tight, won't restrict my movement. But also, not too large, so it won't make me look exceedingly comical. It'll do.

Even though these two garments were, strictly speaking, enough to cover Neesa from head to toe, her eyes caught the glimmer of a silken item, buried deep underneath a pile of nondescript trousers. Intrigued, she couldn't help but to retrieve the mystery piece from its cotton walled mausoleum. Holding the garment up to the light, Neesa was immediately taken aback by its beauty.

It was a kimono of the finest silk, as black as obsidian and irresistibly smooth. Dragons of fiery red flew circles around cherry blossoms of the softest pink. It was hemmed by bands of the purest white, stark contrast to both the rest of the piece and her skin. Golden, the central sash shone and glimmered in the torchlight.

Gods. There are no words that could do your beauty justice.

Hastily, Neesa removed the belt from her around her should and threw it onto the bed. Just as quickly she tore off her shirt, discarding it unceremoniously into a heap on the floor. She had to alter her new pants, cutting a slit in their back for her tail, but once this was done, she pulled them on and was pleased to find that they fitted phenomenally well. Next was the shirt, and while it was a little on the spacious side, Neesa saw this a good thing. This way it wouldn't rip when she fought. Finally, she donned the silk kimono. It was by far the least practical aspect of her ensemble, but she simply adored it and would not be parted from it. Tying the sash firmly around her waist, she moved to the mirror and inspected her appearance.

Wow, this makes me look like a butterfly. A beautiful, badass butterfly. I approve.

'My, oh my. I must say that particular article of clothing actually suits you rather well. Who would have thought that from all my collection a slave girl would have had the audacity to choose something so positively fabulous?'

Startled, Neesa spun to face the now open doorway. A thin man was nursing a glass of red wine as he slouched nonchalantly against the door frame. His eyes, fixated firmly upon her, sparkled with a malicious intensity that Neesa found deeply disturbing. His hair, of long platinum blonde, combined with his hawkish features marked him clearly to be of elvish descent.

Oh gods, could this be the Master? Even if it isn't there goes my plan of laying an ambush for him.

'Come on darling. No witty comments or fancy retorts. I must say I am terribly disappointed for clearly you lack the wit to match your taste in fashion.'

Neesa said nothing, her only response was to stare at this fancily dressed man, her distrust and malice obvious, as she assessed this new threat.

'Tsk, tsk, there's no need to be so rude. I mean, seriously, I clothe and feed you. Give you something to do with your otherwise, worthless time. I give you purpose and meaning. The least you could do is be civil.'

With one long pull the Master drained his glass of wine.

While Neesa had started to suspect that this man was her master as soon as he had begun to speak, it was this final statement that cemented her surety. He was her master. All the hardships she had endured in the past few weeks, and the transgressions she had witnessed, it was all of it at the behest of this man. It was all his fault.

Sense gave way to madness as anger surged within her. Without thinking she ran towards her master, bloody intentions consuming her mind utterly. However, before she could reach her foe, he raised his hand and muttered an incomprehensible phrase under his breath.

Neesa stumbled as a wave of pain shot through her skull. Usually, she welcomed pain, she drew strength from it as it fuelled her rage, but this was different, this was unbearable. Gasping, she clutched at her temples as the torment amplified. She felt like her brain was going to burst from her cranium, but still the pressure increased. Falling to her knees, she screamed as her agony reached its bitter crescendo.

Her vision blurred as unconsciousness threatened, but then as quickly as it had started, it ended. Her pain vanished, leaving behind a void. She felt no pleasure in it, but in comparison to what she had just experienced it was bliss. Growling, Neesa rose to her feet her face marred by the tiny rivulets of blood streaking from her eyes, ears, and nose.

Smirking, as only one who believed himself to be utterly superior could, the Master goaded Neesa with what he believed to be a witty quip.

'Good heavens my dear. I truly did not expect you to get up from that. Colour me impressed.'

In an instant the emotional void within Neesa filled with a torrent of rage and she went berserk. Crossing the room in a single bound, she swung a massive right hook at her master's face. Had it have connected his head would have been turned to nothing more than pulp, but he had anticipated the strike and dodged it with ease.

Lost in a haze of red, Neesa followed up with a lightning-fast left jab. Her master lost all composure as his nose shattered with a sickening cack. As torrents of hot blood gushed freely from his broken nose, her master drew an ornate rapier from his side.

'You hells borned bitch, no one strikes me. I will destroy you!'

Still lost in the throes of fury, Neesa failed to perceive her master's threat and paid his blade no heed.

His calm now shattered; the Master thrust his sword-point recklessly at Neesa's throat. Sensing, more than seeing, the oncoming attack, Neesa bent backwards and the blade stabbed harmlessly over her face. Planting her hands firmly on the floor behind her, Neesa pushed off of the floor with all her strength, propelling herself towards her master.

To close to avoid her attack, the Master could do nothing as Neesa's knee slammed into his chin. Pain blasted through him as his head was flung backwards, rattling his brain against the inside of his skull.

Neesa landed gracefully beside a staggered master and continued her offensive. Simultaneously, she drove both of her palms into her master's chest, snapping his ribs as easily as dry twigs, puncturing his lungs. From the force of Neesa's blow, the Master was knocked from his feet and slid across the well-lacquered floorboards.

He tried to stand, as fresh blood drooled from the corner of his mouth, but Neesa wouldn't allow him to. She pounced on top of his prone form, expunging what little air was left in his lungs, and took his head in her hands. Her eyes burned with a hellsborn fury, terror inducing, blood chilling, but it was her words, barely audible and forced through toothy snarl, that broke the final remnants of the Master's resolve.

'No. I will destroy you.'

Driven by rage, Neesa pounded her master's head against the wall behind him. *Thump.* Her master's eyes rolled back into his head as he faded from conscious thought. He was no longer a threat, but the monster inside of her was not satisfied. It wanted more.

So, completely consumed, Neesa took the Master's head and drove it into the wall again. *Thump.* And again. *Tump.* Body long since limp and breathing long since stopped, Neesa continued beating her master against the wall, inescapably lost in the depths of her rage. Finally, the Master's skull exploded in a shower of splintered bone, gore, and grey matter. It was only then, that the darkness within her released its hold and the anger began to fade.

As Neesa sat on her master's still chest, she breathed hard and deep. The final vestiges of red tainting her vision faded from view. Her heart rate slowed and rational thought returned to the forefront of her mind.

Discovery is imminent. I must flee.

Moving quickly, she gathered her sword from the Master's bed, strapping it back across her shoulders. A glimmer from the hilt of her master's rapier drew her attention, and even though she was short on time, she crossed the room and picked it up.

The rapier's blade was steel, unblemished, but nothing particularly special. Its hilt however, was far from ordinary. Wrought from finely crafted gold intertwined with silver and platinum, it bore as its pommel a single large gem, of which Neesa could only guess to be an emerald. It was a masterful piece that caught the light in a truly spectacular fashion.

Giving the sword a swing to test its balance, Neesa quickly judged the blade to be ill suited for her fighting style. For a moment she considered leaving it behind, as it would only serve as dead weight, but then opted to instead keep it.

It looks like it'd be worth a lot of coin. Even if I don't use it, I can always sell it.

Thus, she fastened it to her belt, beside her short sword, and moved towards the balcony, her exit of choice.

It was at that moment when an ear-spitting scream echoed throughout the estate. Rolling her eyes, Neesa cursed her luck. As assuredly as the sun rose in the east, someone had just discovered the body of one of the dead guards.

Why is it that whenever anyone discovers a body, someone always screams? I mean seriously.

It was definitely time for her to leave.

Chapter 12

Thoron

As the column of dwarven centuries marched in perfect unison, the clanking of steel shod boots echoed from the tunnel's stone walls like thunderous booms. Thoron moved at the heart of his own century, the third of three and last in the column, and pondered what this sortie would entail. He knew such thoughts were irrelevant, he would follow orders regardless, but he couldn't help it. A part of him liked to dream of the tales of old, of the slaying of evil and the triumph of heroes, and wonder if he could ever achieve such feats, or simply play a part in such a story.

Turning to his fellows, Thoron wondered how many of them would die, how many of them would survive, how many would live on maimed or crippled. Idly, he questioned if he would survive. He was not overly pessimistic by nature and he knew the strength of the Legion, but still these thoughts persisted. He thought the same things on every mission.

Thoron was torn from his ponderings as a pair of outriders rode past, their rockclimbers bounding by, joyous at being free from their pens.

They're scouts. Thir must be a cavern ahead. It cannae be the outpost. We heveny bin marching fur long enough.

The centurion of the first century raised his fist to stop his men. The centurions of the second and third centuries followed suit straight after and the entire column ground to a halt. One of Legate Valens' tribunes rode down the column atop his own rockclimber, voice booming as he issued directives to each of the centuries.

'Cavern ahead! First century moves to the left, as far as able. Second century will hold the centre. Third century will take the right flank. Scouts were sent in and they have not returned. Form up into battle formations and prepare for combat. Give no quarter.'

At the tribune's final word, the dwarves pounded their right fists against their chests in unison, while simultaneously shouting, 'huh.' One resounding wave of sound boomed through the tunnel as steel fists impacted steel breastplates, complimented by the deep grunts of the dwarves. Another wave of noise shuddered through the passageway as the dwarves thumped their chests for the second time. A third and final pulse of sound rocked the tunnel with its force. Thoron felt each soundwave shake his bones to his core. Thoron's heart surged in tempo, his chest pounding, as a rush of adrenaline poured into his bloodstream.

'Is is it.

The reverberations from the dwarven battle chant had barely eased when, as one, each of the centurions raised a fist and then dropped it bare seconds later. A second metallic noise filled the passageway as every dwarf present drew their gladius form its scabbard in perfect unison. Without further ado, the column resumed its march into the unknow and the rhythmic clanking of steel shod boots began once more.

Just as they had been ordered, the first century wheeled to the left as it entered the cavern, widening to fill the third of the battleline it was tasked to hold. The second century followed immediately after and did as the first, stretching itself out to fill the centre. Thoron's century brought up the rear and took the right flank.

As he entered the cavern, Thoron tried to assess as much of his surroundings as possible, but it was hard. Their torches, that only a few of the dwarves carried, did little to light the otherwise pitch-black cavern and the bodies of his comrades obscured most of his line of sight. What was easily apparent however, was that the cavern was wide and their line was thin. In his short time with the Legion, Thoron has experienced several skirmishes and a handful of battles. He had quickly learned that a thin line was never good.

Ah, 'is is a fine bit o' shite fur sure.

From somewhere behind him, Thoron heard either the Legate or one of his tribune's, he knew not which, call out an order. Six balls of light shot from the hand of a Legion cleric and soared towards the roof of the cavern. Spreading themselves evenly across the width of the cavern, they stopped when they contacted the ceiling. There they hung, emanating a warm golden glow that extended from themselves to the cavern floor below.

Newly lit, Thoron examined the chamber again. All was not as it should have been. The light from the magic glow balls did not extend as far into the cavern as it should have. Rather than fading slowly as it diminished in strength, the light simply stopped, met by a wall of impenetrable darkness. Thoron felt, even though he had never experienced anything of this nature before, that something was horribly wrong. The Legate must have felt the same, as with a frantic shout, he issued the centuries new orders.

'All centuries form testudo now!'

Without even a thought to as why, each of the centurions moved to obey. A cacophony of noise filled the cavern as the dwarves at the front of the line slammed their shields onto the ground, interweaving them with the shields of those beside them, their gladius's pointed menacingly outwards. The dwarves in the remaining lines, of which Thoron was one, raised their shields above their heads, providing a protective ceiling to the entire formation.

No sooner than the testudo had been completed, a cloud of arrows burst from the wall of shadow. As they streaked towards the dwarves an eerie whistle screeched from their shafts, but the dwarves stood firm, immobile.

Like the water from a storm slashing the side of a mountain, the arrows smashed into dwarven shields, shattering against that impenetrable bulwark. Thoron both heard and felt their ineffectual sting against his shield and, just as his comrades did, he stood fast. Not a single dwarf fell.

Soon after the first, another volley of arrows flew across the cavern, just as ineffectual as the last. More followed suit, volley after volley of arrows shattered uselessly upon dwarven steel. Until at last they stopped.

Thoron stood waiting, his heart the only thing disrupting the silence, for something to happen. For an order to be given or for the foe to attack. Anything. He hated the waiting, for that was when his mind gravitated towards the unknown, the what ifs and the maybes.

In Thoron's mind questions raced. What if there was too many of them? What if he was going to be killed or worse, captured, and tortured? What if they were all going to die? What if their defeat lead to the final collapsed of dwarf kind and the extinction of their race? There was no rational basis for these thoughts and he knew that to dwell upon them would bring about his own demise as certainly as a storm cloud brings about the rain. But, the darkness of an idle mind in tumultuous environs is far from rational.

Focus. Calm yourself. You've been through worse. You'll be fine.

The horrors of maybes were soon interrupted by the terrors of certainty. One of the magic globes above them blinked out, its light instantly swallowed by nothingness. Behind him, Thoron could hear the frantic movement of rockclimbers and the muffled conversations of his commanders. He couldn't make out exactly what they were saying, but whatever it was, it was said in worried tones. He dared not turn around, instead he stood motionless, staring ahead, sweat soaking his brow, waiting in trepidation for whatever was out there to attack. Nothing did, but two more lights went out.

In a momentary lapse of discipline, Thoron snuck a glance to his rear. A rockclimber of one of the outrider's whinnied as its rider dug his spurred heels into its flank. The beast spun and then accelerated out of the cavern, back towards Summa Antemurale. A dagger of fear thrust itself into Thoron's heart as he began to fear the worst, but he quickly calmed as rationality regained dominance.

Jus' a messenger reporting oor progress. Nothing tae fear.

Another light went out. Only two remained.

Thoron's head snapped back towards the front as a horn rang out. It was no dwarf horn. Emanating from the shadow, a low and mournful thrum, it chilled Thoron's soul, the epitome of ominous. For an unnaturally long span the note persisted. Before it died three more of its ilk joined in the chorus. Thoron felt a crushing pain in his head, tiny pinpricks of black dotted his vision, threatening unconsciousness. But he stood firm, as did each of the other legionaries. As the blaring of horns ceased, Thoron's head cleared and he felt his constitution improve. However, when the horns died so did the last two lights.

Plunged into almost complete darkness, the cavern took on a new level of horror. Shadows danced from the dwarven torches, mocking in their merriment. The slightest of noises, source indeterminate, seemed to be amplified beyond reason, a pebble fall seeming to be that of a boulder. The unknown extended its tendrils of influence into the legionaries' minds, seeding insecurities born from doubt and uncertainty. Inexplicitly, the dwarven torches were blown out by an impossible wind.

In that moment the waiting ended as a wave of chitters and chatters erupted from the darkness. Followed immediately by an immeasurable discordance of pattering feet. Thoron knew what was to come.

Shite. Goblins. Lots o' goblins.

With a confidence that only comes from experience, the Legate did not hesitate and began issuing more commands at the top of his lungs.

'Form shield wall. Swords down. Axes up. Prepare to loose. Clerics, give me some damned light!'

As bidden, each century moved from testudo to a shield wall formation. Each legionary, save for those in the first rank, sheathed their sword and drew one of their throwing axes in its place. Ready, they cocked their arms back, prepared to throw their weapons with everything they had.

Originating from somewhere behind him, Thoron saw six more balls of light shoot over his head. However, after not yet travelling thirty feet from the front of the line, they blinked from existence, dispelled. Dismayed, Thoron couldn't help but swear under his breath.

Amidst his fellow legionaries Thoron waited, ears and arms straining. One for a command, the other for release. Beads of sweat rolled down his forehead leaving thin trails of moisture across his face. One meandered into his eye, thick with salt it stung, but there was nothing he could do about it, so he ignored it.

Louder and louder the goblins grew as they came ever closer. Before long, their steps had grown to a deafening chorus. Thoron knew that they would have to loose their axes soon, lest their foes charge them at full force.

Come oan, gi' the order. Gi' it noo dammit.

As if reading Thoron's thoughts, the Legate barked a series of orders in rapid succession, his voice booming over the goblins din.

'Loose. Draw. Loose. Swords. Give me some fucking light!'

With a snarl, Thoron let his axe fly, just as all the other legionaries did. A deluge of steel spun through the cavern, thrumming as they carved the air in twain. Without seeing or hearing the effects of his attack, Thoron drew his second throwing axe and sent it into the void after the first. He paused briefly, not yet drawing his sword, idly wondering as to the effectiveness of their attack. He couldn't see anything so he strained his ears and listened.

Others had not been as fast as Thoron, so he heard their axes impact goblin flesh with heavy thunks as they bit deep into their chests. The avalanche of skittering had stopped, replaced by the high-pitched screams and wails of wounded goblins that lay dying upon the cavern ground. Noticing that many of his comrades around him had their swords in their hands, Thoron followed suit and pulled his from its scabbard. Planting his shield firmly into the ground, he braced himself for the inevitable impact of the goblin advance.

Alright, come at me ye scunners.

Flesh and steel collided with astounding force as a wave of goblins struck the dwarven shield wall. The power of the blow drove the dwarves back a step, but they dug in their heels and stood their ground. Goblins snarled at their foe, swinging their motley collection of blades and cudgels in rage. Most failed to do any real harm, bouncing harmlessly off of the dwarves' heavy plate. However, every now and again a lucky blow struck home, felling, or rendering infirm one of the dwarves.

In response, the dwarves thrust their swords over their shields. Blades bit deep into goblin flesh, puncturing skulls and severing arteries. With a powerful 'hah' the entire dwarven line shoved their shields against the goblin horde, forcing them back. In unison, each dwarf took a step forward with another 'hah,' jabbing their swords before them. Those goblins who had fallen, were crushed beneath them as they advanced. Like a harvestman felling wheat, the dwarves slew their foe.

The air hung thick with the stench of gore and voided bowels. The ground ran thick with green-skin blood. Thoron advanced with his kin through the muck and the mire, executing any foe that had till then escaped the slaughter.

For the third time the cleric tried to illuminate the cavern. Six more globes of light speed towards the centre of the cave, but just as before, they dissipated before they could reach their destination.

Atop his rockclimber the Legate swore and issued another directive.

'For fuck's sake. Tribunes use the bloody flares we need those gods damned lights!'

Three of his tribunes reached into pouches on their belts, each withdrawing a single cylindrical object. The tribunes aimed these objects towards the roof and with a twist and a pull they exploded with a small pop. Each emitted a bright red ball of sparkling light that flew, and adhered, to the cavern ceiling, illuminating the chamber.

Taking a moment from the fray, Thoron looked around, examining the cavern. All around him lay a field of broken and mangled bodies, mostly goblin, but speckled amongst the green was a handful of black clad dwarves. At the far end of the cave the wall of darkness remained as ominous and ineffable as ever.

'At cannot be natural. Whit in the names o' the gods is going oan?

The legionaries had stopped pushing forwards as the last vestiges of the goblin force were annihilated. As the final goblin fell the cave reverberated with ecstasy as each of the legionaries slapped their shields with their swords and shouted, 'huh, huh, huh.' Thoron did not take part in the revelry. He still felt as though something was wrong. Normally, the goblins would have retreated long before being completely destroyed.

Something wicked is afoot.

The Legate must have shared Thoron's suspicions as he did not participate in the celebrations either. Instead, he sat atop his rockclimber, thinking, assessing the situation. He must have come to some form of conclusion, as Thoron heard him begin to issue a warning, but movement from the darkness quelled the notion before it had left his lips.

The centre of the wall began to move. Ripples permeating from its centre, just as a pond that had been struck would have. A massive globule of darkness rose from the ripples, larger and larger it grew, from thirty and then to sixty feet in diameter. All revelries stopped as the dwarves stared at this phenomenon, not knowing its purpose, or meaning. Upon reaching eighty feet in diameter, the sphere snapped free from the black umbilical that had held it to the wall and floated freely above the cavern floor.

The ripples upon the wall grew in frequency and intensity. Thoron looked on equally entranced and dismayed. Quicker than what could be easily perceived the globe accelerated, moving from a standstill to the speed of lightning in an instant. It flew into the passageway where the dwarves had come from, its wake sending chills down Thoron's spine as it passed by. One hundred feet into the hallway it exploded.

A pulse wave of black eldritch energy expanded from the blast, shattering, and cracking the surrounding stone. As it sped into the cavern, it carried rocks and boulders in its wake, shooting them from the tunnel's mouth.

Thoron braced himself behind his shield just as the shockwave hit him. As to what use to him this was, he had no notion, for even so, he was thrown roughly onto his back. In that moment, Thoron thought with all certainty that he was about to die. His muscles shook like slapped jelly and his bones felt as though they had been shattered into innumerable shards, each of which dug into his insides. If it were possible to feel one's internal organs, Thoron would have sworn that his were slopping around his chest cavity like soup in a pot.

Oh shite, 'is is bad.

Though he fought it, Thoron drifted from consciousness, succumbing to the darkness.

Chapter 13

Thoron

Dust hung heavy in the cavern's air. Silence, unnaturally still, prevailed over the sounds of life.

Returning to the realm of the living, yet still dazed, Thoron staggered to his feet, ears ringing and head pounding. Cognition clearly impaired, he looked around confused, trying as hard as he could to gain even an iota of understanding. Thoughts moved through his mind as slowly as molasses rolling down hill on a winter's morning. He had no notion of what had just happened. He saw a mountain of rocks and rubble and wondered where they had come from, he couldn't remember them being there before. He wondered where the tunnel back to Summa Antemurale was, it would be hard to get home without it.

A great deal of his comrades still lay on the ground. Some started to rise as he did, sluggishly and with obvious difficulty. Others did not try to stand. Even in his confuddled state Thoron knew that they were dead. Normally, he would have felt some grief or remorse, but impaired as he was, he felt nothing. He should have felt something, why didn't he? Before he could descend too deeply into that cognitive rabbit hole, he felt a hand grasp his shoulder.

Thoron turned to greet whomever it was, not for a second thinking it could be anyone other than a friend. It was one of the Legate's tribunes. That was odd, he thought. What could a tribune want with him? The tribune started to shake Thoron, his mouth was moving, but Thoron couldn't hear what he was saying. Strange. Thoron strained his ears, trying to understand what the tribune was saying, but it didn't help, a profound ringing was all he could hear. Well, that wasn't normal. Thoron gestured to his ears and shook his head.

'I cannae hear ye. Whit dae ye want?'

The tribune didn't bother to respond, instead he simply held up a potion bottle and mimicked a drinking motion. He gave the bottle to Thoron, intention clear. Without thinking, Thoron drank the potion. Immediately he felt better. The ringing in his ears ceased, the pain diminished and his mind started to clear. Now he could understand what the tribune was saying.

'Legionnaire! Where in blazes is the Legate? We're cut off and need some damned orders.'

Thoron thought for a moment, trying to remember the last place he had seen the Legate. Turning, he looked over the battlefield and tried to get his bearings. It looked completely different to what it had only three minutes before, but he knew roughly how far he had been thrown by the explosion and roughly where the Legate was relative to his original position. So, after doing some mental geometry he pointed to a particularly large pile of rubble.

'From whit I remember, I think 'at before the blast he wis over there. Gods, ye dae no' think he wis crushed, dae ye?'

The tribune's face paled and he swore under his breath. For a moment he paced around in circles muttering undiscernible nonsenses, clearly perturbed. He cursed under his breath for a second time and ran off to convene with the other surviving tribunes, leaving Thoron to his own devices.

Directionless, Thoron stood where he was, gazing over the battlefield. His mind was now clear of the fog that had previously dulled his cognition and he felt the full emotional impact of the scene before him. The mangled bodies of his comrades, those he knew well and those he didn't know at all, lay torn and rent on the ground. Sightless eyes stared into oblivion; their souls departed for the afterlife.

Dear gods.

A pang of intense sadness stabbed at his heart, the boy, Uthgárt, was one of the fallen. His head had been caved in, by the force of the explosion or an errant stone, Thoron knew not which. It mattered not. In either case he was gone. Thoron lamented that the boy's hopes and dreams would be ever unfulfilled, lost to circumstance, and his potential unrecognised. He had known loss before, of those close and those distant, but for some reason this loss affected Thoron like none had ever done so before. In that moment he cried hot tears of sorrow that scorched a path through the grime on his face, clear as the midday sun their streaks marked his cheeks. He did nothing to hide them for he felt no shame in feeling what he did for what had just been taken from the world.

His pain burned his insides, a torment most horrendous, but he knew that it would hurt worse for the families of the lost. That enraged him. Rising from the pit of his stomach, Thoron felt an anger, nay a hatred, towards those who had assaulted his home and slaughtered his kin. Tears stopped and his mouth turned down into a wicked snarl. The very core of his being seared with a fury, the likes of which he had never felt before. Turning towards the wall of darkness, and his unseen foe, he raised his sword in challenge. The anger would be contained no more. Unbidden, Thoron unleashed an unholy scream.

All of the other dwarves turned to look at Thoron. They all felt the same emotions as he, the pain, sorrow, and anger. Roused by the authenticity of Thoron's display, they each joined him in his emotive battle cry. The cavern resounded with the loss-fuelled fury of the dwarf-kin.

Chest heaving, Thoron took a single step towards the darkness, and then a second. Slowly he increased his stride, from a slow walk to a full-blown sprint. One by one his kin joined him, until they all ran by his side.

The wall of darkness began to roil once more. Thoron slowed for a moment, cautious of more hostile magic, but quickly dismissed any notions of hesitation and pushed himself even harder than before.

Three separate sets of ripples grew upon the face of the darkness, equidistantly spread across its surface and roughly the size of a man. Thoron didn't know what their appearance entailed, but currently he didn't care. No matter what, he would see his enemies slain. He continued to run, the other dwarves keeping pace.

The ripples reached a crescendo, vibrating rapidly, but then slowed as three figures stepped through the wall. An elderly orc emerged at its centre, his wispy white hair cascading wildly from his head, framing a crooked grin. In his hands he held a twisted staff of bleached bone, topped with a baby steer's skull. On either side of the orc, a goblin, both obviously shamans, also emerged from the wall. Clad in tattered black robes, they both held identical, albeit smaller, versions of the orc's staff.

Upon seeing these figures, Thoron felt his chest tighten with fear and doubt. It was not for the orc, even though he stood at least eight feet tall and was as wide as two adult dwarves, it was for the goblins. Though small, their faces alluded to some unnatural powers. It was their eyes, or rather the lack there of. In their stead, two smouldering flames of obsidian burned, dancing in the windless cave to their own tune.

Thoron kept on running forwards, anger overcoming all traces of fear and honour quelling any hint of uncertainty. His kin did not abandon him.

Finding the stubbornness of the dwarven forces amusing, the orc started to laugh. A foul racking cackle that grated the nerves and sent shivers down the spine. Thoron felt a presence tickle the frontier of his mind. He tried to focus, to keep it at bay, but he could not. Thoron grimaced as a foul presence bit into his consciousness and a rasping whisper echo around the confines of his head.

'*Foolish, stunted creatures. Run. Run as fast as you can towards your death and an eternity of servitude. You will serve me. You will all serve me.*'

Every fibre of his being wanted him to stop. His soul screamed at him, urging him to cease his futile protestations, but he would not. Despite it all, Thoron kept running. However, half of his fellow legionaries did not. Overcame, they fell to their knees, clutching their heads, screaming in pained terror.

The orc raised his staff in the direction of the dwarves, his goblin minions following suit. A conflux of eldritch energy spewed from the skull atop each of their staffs and started circling around them. Forks of dark matter arced from the wall of darkness, crackling with power, and joined with the conflux. Raising his other hand, the orc spoke some unfathomable arcane words, his eyes clouded over with shadow and bolts of jet-black lightning shot from the spinning conflux across the cavern.

Thinking the projectiles meant for him, Thoron held his shield high and ducked behind it as he ran. They weren't. Each of the bolts, first ten, then one hundred, then more than could easily be counted, flew into the corpses of both dwarf and goblin alike.

Surprised, Thoron watched on aghast as the corpses sprang into motion. Their bodies twitching and spasming, moving at angles far from being naturally possible. A poor facsimile of life, they shambled and groaned, their eyes burning with shadowy fire.

Thoron knew not the exact nature of these abominations, but he was certain that they served his enemy. As such they needed to be destroyed. One of the creatures was scrambling to its feet directly in Thoron's path. As he passed by, he swung his sword, separating its head from its torso with ease.

They may look frightful, but they're easily vanquished.

Three more of the creatures leapt to their feet and assaulted Thoron. One bumped harmlessly off of his shield, Thoron cut another down with a swipe of his sword, but the third grappled Thoron around his legs. Instantly, he fell, his forward momentum working against him. As his face rushed to meet the cavern floor, he tried to soften the blow with his hands, but couldn't react in time. His chin smashed against stone, shaking his entire head with the impact. Blood filled his mouth and his vision blurred out of focus.

Argh, bloody scunner. I better not hev lost a tooth.

Sounds of scratching and snarling, emanating from his legs, snapped Thoron from his thoughts. There was still a goblin wrapped around his legs. Kicking with all his might, Thoron tried to free himself from this unwelcome bondage. However, try as he might he couldn't break loose of the undead goblin's hold. Swearing at the fiend, he rolled onto his back and thrust the point of his sword through the creature's open mouth. Gore spurted from the back of the goblin's head as it was skewered. Once again dead, the goblin fell to the ground limp, blood oozing from its mouth.

An' stay dead, ye fucker.

As he lay on the ground panting, Thoron looked around. Countless more of the dead were rising, bogging the advancing dwarves down in an inexorable meat grinder. Surrounded and vastly outnumbered, the dwarves tried to continue their advance, and for a time they did, slaying countless of these shadow-eyed-ones while staggering onwards. However, their foes numbers were endless. Every time one would fall, another was immediately reanimated in its place. Inevitably, each of the dwarves was overwhelmed, tackled to the ground, and bludgeoned to death. Once they died, they rose again as puppets of the orc.

Ah shite. As long as 'at orc is alive, victory is an impossibility. But we cannae get tae him.

At that realisation, Thoron's anger dissipated, destroyed by the hopelessness of the situation. He knew that he was going to die, that they all were. As more tears welled in his eyes, he bowed his head and prayed silently to Rivalitas. He apologised for his inability to do what was needed of him and he pleaded with her. If he couldn't have vengeance then he wished for another to claim retribution for those who had fallen this day.

Once he had completed his prayer, Thoron felt a calmness born from acceptance wash over him. Resolute, he picked himself up off of the ground and waded into the nearest group of risen. Despite the futility of his actions, he refused to go quietly. He swung his blade to the left and to the right. He thrust it into shadow goblin and shadow dwarf alike, felling enemies with every blow. They rose again and again, but he kept on fighting.

Inevitably, fatigue started to wear heavily upon his body, diminishing the power and finesse of his attacks. Thoron felt a stabbing pain in his side as a dagger slipped between his armour plates and pierced his flesh. He roared in pain, but did not fall. A fresh surge of adrenaline coursed into his bloodstream, granting him a second wind. He struck with renewed vigour, more of the risen were temporarily slain, but it was of little use. A second blade dug deep into his side and a third lacerated the back of his leg, severing his Achilles' tendon. Unable to move, Thoron crumpled to his knees, dropping his sword and shield to the ground as he fell. With eyes closed, he stretched his arms to his side and welcomed death to take him.

Alright. Am done.

Nothing. He felt nothing. His body suffered no more hostile ingresses, there was no new pain. Thoron opened his eyes. As statues, all of the undead around him were frozen in place, weapons and fists stuck mid-swing. Further afield, the few remaining legionaries were also motionless, as were the orc and his two goblin cronies. Everyone was frozen, save for Thoron.

Looking down, he noticed for the first time a soft red glow illuminating the ground around him. Cautiously, he placed his hand upon the glowing stone. A warmth that tingled his skin swept over his entire body. Shocked, he gasped in surprise as his pain ceased and his wounds healed before his very eyes.

By the gods. It's a miracle.

Sensing, rather than hearing, movement behind him, Thoron stood and turned around slowly, uncertain of what he would find. There before him floated a woman of the most serene beauty imaginable. Two wings of the purest white extended from her back and flapped gently. A cloth wrapped around her alabaster face, screening her eyes. She wore naught but a sleek white dress, pulled tight against her voluptuous frame, that fell lop-sided and tattered below her knees. In her left hand she held a set of balancing scales, in her right she grasped a flaming sword. Rivalitas had come.

Thoron took to his knees and bowed his head in deference.

'Ma Lady. It's truly an honour fur ye tae grace me wi' yer presence. If thir's anything I can dae fur ye, I will endeavour tae dae it. But I doubt I can dae much, since I'm aboot tae die and all 'at.'

Rivalitas smiled. It was the kindest grin you could possibly imagine, shinning with the radiance of a star and alluding to a hope forgotten.

'My dearest Thoron, you will not be dying today, unless you choose too, for I have a use for you. The courage and determination you have shown in the name of vengeance has moved me to intercede on your behalf. All I ask in return is that hence forth you embody vengeance in all its forms and grant it swiftly to those deserving of it whenever able. Should you refuse this charge then I will leave you to your fate. What say you?'

Thoron made his decision instantly.

'Ma Lady, it seems tae me 'at thir's nae choice at all. I hev tae accept. I can think o' a few 'at need killing and I'd love tae be the one who did it.'

'Know that there is always a choice and that oft times it is easier to pass from this realm than to stay. In any case, I now ask that you swear some oaths. I will hold you to them and should you break them you will wish you had died this day. Now repeat after me. I do hereby swear to always combat the greater evil, even if that means foregoing challenge to a lesser evil that I have vested interests in. I do hereby swear to grant no mercy for the wicked, the only justice for the wicked is death. I do hereby swear to use any and all means at my disposal to exterminate my foes. Finally, I do hereby swear that I shall assist any and all that have been harmed by my foes in any way I can.'

Thoron did as he was bidden and repeated the oaths. As he spoke the final word, he felt a change within him. He couldn't explain why or how, but for some reason he felt glad at this new direction, this new purpose for being, somehow it felt right.

Rivalitas dipped her head in respect towards Thoron.

'Very well, it is done, you are now mine. Go forth and find those who aspire to wickedness and show them the error of their ways. Seek out just causes and help those wishing them completed. Focus not too intently on the plight of your kin, there is far more at stake.'

Rivalitas raised her scales and tapped them with the hilt of her sword. A metallic ting, as clear as the purest crystal, filled Thoron's ears and reverberated around his skull. To his side a blue portal popped audibly into existence. Rivalitas gestured for Thoron to step into the swirling vortex. He complied.

Chapter 14

Máher

Despite what captain Silventooth had said, it only took Máher and the 'liberated' longship a single day to reach Súthburh. It had been a great many years since he had been in the city, but upon seeing it again, Máher was reminded why he simultaneously loved and hated the city. Its beauty and grandeur could not be denied, simply put it was an architectural masterpiece. However, for all its wealth there hid at its underbelly a patent contempt for any whom society deemed as undesirable.

Sailing into the walled port, two colossi greeted Máher, one whose hand was outstretched in welcome, the other sword raised in warning. Just as he always remembered it to be, the harbour was filled with a myriad of ships, each hailing from every corner of Térrtha, from simple fishing skiffs to ornately decorated junks and everything in between.

Atop the hill which the city occupied, large towers and cathedral spires dominated the skyline, each jutting skyward ever higher in an eternal competition for dominance. However, each of them was easily bested by the grandeur of Súthburh's Government House, known colloquially as the grand jewel of the Republic. Its tallest minaret stood one hundred feet higher than the next largest tower. Three golden domes, the largest in Térrtha, crowned the thousands upon thousands of square feet of carved stone and intricate murals that the building was comprised of.

Beneath the crème de la crème of the city, a veritable sea of town houses dwelt, residences to the city's elite. Each was far larger than their counterparts in other cities and even though they were crammed together it was possible to see the green of trees and other smaller plants from the harbour.

Nevertheless, despite its opulence and prosperity, the city also had a darker, less appealing side. Those less fortunate were forced to live in shanty houses at the Western base of Súthburh Hill, where the law barely ventured and survival of the fittest was king. Very few, save for the morally dubious, ever ventured willingly into the slums and no one lived there by choice.

From the industrial quarter a continuous stream of smoke poured into the sky as the foundries and forges attempted to meet the incessant demands of the consumer. Depending upon the direction of the wind, it was common for those in the lower districts to be covered in soot and smog. Amongst the poor and homeless, lung conditions were common and the mortality rate high.

Súthburh was the preeminent trading port in Ulandir and it showed. Even at this late hour each of the seven port districts were bustling with activity. No one tarried for long, for time was money and inactivity costly.

Their turn to dock, the longship pulled up to an empty jetty and Máher stepped off of the vessel, onto the pier. Turning back for a moment, he gave a nod to Beher. Before the ship had stopped moving the young dragon leapt off of his perch and dove upon the areomancer. The hapless man was unable to scream as Beher wrapped his jaw around his throat and bit down hard. As Beher gorged himself on the Akkadian's blood he repeatedly thrust his tail into the man's chest, killing him quickly. Once dead, Beher sunk his fangs into the areomancer's belly, revelling in the consumption of his flesh.

'Mm, tasty. Not as good as a baby pig, but Beher thinks that it will do for now. Beher can only survive on fish for so long.'

Máher paid no attention to his brother's debauchery as he was intercepted by one of the harbourmasters, a scrawny little gnome, and quickly questioned.

'Hold. Hold a moment if you please sir. I will be needing some information from you for the dock ledger.'

Máher offered the gnome no response, but stared into his eyes as he waited expectantly for the harbourmaster to ask his questions. However, before any questions could be asked, there was a gentle bump from the long ship as it softly impacted the jetty Both Máher and the gnome turned to towards the ship. Neither said a word as it slowly started drifting away from the pier and into the harbour.

Perhaps I should have moored it to the dock? Nah.

After a silent moment, the pair turned back to face each other. The gnome continued to speak, all the while running his wrinkled fingers across the ledger in his hands, as if reading by touch as much as by sight.

'Well. This is most irregular, most irregular indeed. In any case the ledger must be filled in, it's the law you know. So first off, what's the name of your ship?'

Máher answered with a shrug.

'Mm, less than helpful. Okay then, let's just put in *A Long Ship* for that one. Next. What is the name of the captain, slash master, of said ship and what is the name of the said ship's first officer?'

In his signature whisper Máher replied cryptically.

'My name is my own. The name of this ship's captain is unknown for that ship has no known master.'

Initially Máher thought that the gnome hadn't heard him, as the elderly man just squinted his eyes at him, face locked in a lopsided scowl, saying nothing. Máher waited. After a minute of awkward silence, the gnome's face returned to normal and, completely oblivious to Máher's witticism, he continued the conversation without even a break in his stride.

'Okay then, for ship's master we have Unknown and for first officer we have My Own. Well, I've got to tell you friend these are some strange names, but they're by no means the strangest I've come across. I remember, a few years back, there was this boat from only the gods know where and the crew only spoke in clicks and clacks, you know with their tongues.'

Although Máher didn't ask him to, and definitely didn't want him to, the gnome demonstrated what he was referring to by clicking his tongue. It was not a good impression.

By the gods, kill me now.

'It sounded just like that it did, very odd indeed. And don't get me started on how hard it was to fill in the ledger, I mean how do you write words that aren't words? They're just sounds after all. That one had me stumped for literally hours that did.'

Stopping to catch a breath, the gnome looked up to Máher, noticing his impatient gaze. Flustered, the gnome offered a rambling apology.

'Oh, blast I've done it again haven't I. I'm so sorry to have kept you waiting My Own. This mouth of mine runs away from me sometimes and it just won't stop. Now, where were we up to? Ah, here we go, only one question left. How long do you plan on being docked here?'

Glancing to his side, Máher looked towards the longship. It was no longer beside the jetty. Sensing his interest, the gnome followed Máher's gaze and together the pair watched as the longship, captured by the outgoing tide, drifted slowly out to sea.

'I would have to say my good gnome that my ship was never truly docked here at all and that the ship that was has already gone.'

If the gnome was confused by this answer he did not show it.

'Blast me down. That was easily the most efficient docking and undocking manoeuvre I have ever witnessed, straight in and then straight out again. Very nice. Well, let's just put a one in the ledger. No need to specify what quantity the one relates to, and then we'll say that your docking fees for today's visit will be, um, one silver. That sounds about right to me.'

Remaining silent, Máher tossed the gnome a single gold piece as he walked past the elderly, and clearly stupid, harbourmaster. The gnome caught the coin, barely, and was surprised to see the glint of gold rather than that of silver.

'Goodness me. The city thanks you for your kindness mister My Own.'

Máher paid him no heed.

Walking along the cobbled streets of Súthburh docks, Máher ignored everyone around him. Most, being accustomed to the unusual, paid him no heed, just as he liked. It was only a handful that gave him the occasional sideways glance, finding him to be odder than most.

Sensing Beher above him, Máher reached out.

'I hope you found your meal satisfactory.'

'Beher thought the man was a little sinewy for Beher's liking, but is mostly satisfied for now. Beher wonders why Máher allowed Beher to eat the human, that is most unlike Máher. Anyway, Beher still wants piglets, just as Máher promised. Beher will not forget.'

Máher grinned in amusement, his pointed teeth protruding from between his lips.

'Of course.'

Turning off the main thoroughfare, Máher started to climb uphill. Distant sounds of yelling, accompanied by the exited barks of dogs, drifted over the rooftops. To Máher it sounded just as fox hunt would, albeit a residential one. Absentmindedly, Máher wondered what some poor soul had done, or been accused of doing, to become the victim of such a game.

He did not care for the pursued, that was their bad luck. Nor did he blame the pursuers, it was likely that they only participated in this twisted sport for the chance of a reward. All in all, he barely cared at all, and in fact would never have normally even given the matter a second of consideration. However, this ruckus, whatever its cause was, had the potential to interfere with his plans. That simply would not do. He needed to know more.

Seeking answers, Máher sought out the nearest person he could see. He didn't have to look far, the streets of Súthburh never truly emptied. It was an old man, currently enjoying a bowl of steaming broth, whose long-frazzled beard compensated for his completely bald head. Máher walked over to the man and as quiet as always, he addressed the elderly man.

'Excuse me. Do you know what's the cause of all this commotion.'

The man looked up from soup and was initially taken aback by Máher's appearance. Once his preliminary surprise had passed, he responded with gusto, delighted by the opportunity to spread some gossip.

'There was a murder there was. Some brigand broke into the Grand Merchant's villa and killed his only son. Right nasty bit of business it was, he was only a wee lad. Made the Grand Merchant, Mercurius his name is, right mad it did, he put a bounty on the Elven lass that did it, a real big one mind you, so everyone's out to get her.'

Máher pondered this information. Extra people on the streets would make it harder to pass by unnoticed, but they were actively looking for another.

This could be advantageous.

'Where did the murder happen? Was it close to the Peoples Depository of Knowledge?'

'In Mercurius's villa I assume, up near the top of the hill it is, So, obviously it's pretty close to the Archives, but it's not like its right next door to them or nothing. Anyway, what's your interest in the Archives? It's not like they're open at night.'

As the man asked of Máher's intent, suspicion was clearly evident in the old man's eyes. Knowing that the absolute truth would not serve his purpose at all, Máher decided to give the man a half-truth and hope that it nullified the man's inquisitiveness.

'It has been a long time since I have been in this city and my memories of the Archives are strongest. I simply sought to use their location as a reference point for the relative location of the incident, nothing more. In any case what was the elf doing in the merchant's house, what reason did she have for the murder?'

The man's suspicions did not seem to be alleviated by Máher's explanation, as upon hearing it, distrust still burned in his eyes. However, it was soon forgotten as he was given another opportunity to spread rumours.

'No one knows for sure, but I did hear some say she was in there thieving and the boy got in her way. So, she killed him, she's a right bloodthirsty bitch I hear. If you be asking me, it'll be the best for everyone when she gets caught it will. Then they'll hang her, publicly and all, it'll be quite the show it will be. Unless she gets killed beforehand, I do hate it when that happens.'

Having found all that he needed to, Máher turned and left the old man. The man failed to notice and continued to ramble into the empty night air.

'*Beher, try and find this elf everyone is looking for. She could be easy to manipulate and may serve our needs, a thief will make breaking into the Repository easier. Do all that you can to make sure she stays alive until I can talk to her.*'

'*Beher will try for Máher, but Beher thinks Máher had best find some gold for more piglets. Máher will need a lot of piglets.*'

'*You're lucky that we're kin and that you're useful, but once I am able, I will get you your damned piglets.*'

Increasing his pace, from a leisurely walk to a sprint, Máher tore along the cobbles, strands of various furs and leathers streaking behind him. Above him, Beher soared ahead of him, his head moving from side to side as he scanned the ground for the elf.

'Beher thinks that Beher has found the elf girl. Turn left down the next alley, then take the third right. The elf girl is tucked in a little nook half way down. Beher thinks that the elf girl must be injured, elf girl smells of blood, much blood.'

Almost overshooting the alley, Máher skidded along the stones, using a corner wall to arrest his momentum. Grunting from the impact, Máher resumed his rapid pace, lungs heaving and heart thumping and as he passed the first alley Beher contacted him again.

'Máher needs to run faster, others have almost found the girl. As amazing as Beher is, Beher can't fight them all by himself. Beher thinks we could always give up and let elf get taken, but Beher knows that Máher is a stubborn one.'

Defying the impossible, Máher increased his pace, pushing his body to the extreme. But he knew that it wouldn't be enough. He looked to his centre, concentrating on the magical wellspring at his core. He willed the power at his heart, raw and unrefined, to flow throughout his body. His hair and eyes lit up as torches in the dark. All fatigue vanished and he felt himself reinvigorated. Time seemed to slow at an ever-increasing rate, and while he still ran, he now moved at a truly inhuman pace, the world passing him by as a blur.

In an instant Máher passed the second alley and in another he had reached the third. Turning the corner, he saw every detail of the scene as if it were a still life drawing. He saw the elf sitting on the ground. He saw the crossbow bolt protruding from her shoulder. He saw her eyes wide in fear as a dog, large with teeth bared snarling, inched its way through the air, already having pounced upon its prey.

Not slowing, Máher charged at the dog, covering the distance almost instantaneously. Lowering his shoulder Máher crashed into the hound. As it was struck, the beast's flesh undulated violently and bone was shattered. Upon contact, Máher's vast pool of kinetic energy transferred into the dog, propelling the hound at a tremendous velocity into the brick wall opposite. It slumped to the ground, unquestionably dead, body mangled beyond recognition.

As Máher let the magic fade, and his physical form reverted to normal, a bout of uncontrollable lethargy overcame him. The price for his earlier speed, he was now stuck looking at the elf, to slow to look away. Frozen in time, she looked back at him, not for a second averting her gaze.

Initially, he was taken aback by her beauty. In no uncertain terms she was stunning. Peeking out from her hood hair of the brightest crimson complimented her chocolate eyes perfectly. The handful of freckles that dotted her face did nothing to diminish her loveliness, as far as Máher was concerned they instead added to it.

Staring into her eyes for even the briefest of moments, Máher saw something special. He couldn't explain what it was exactly, perhaps it was the shadow of some greater strength, as of yet untapped. Or perhaps it was the mark of a person who had found what, or who, it was that completed them. He knew not what it was, but as he looked at her, he found himself intrigued to no end.

However, mixed with the profound positivity within her, there was something else, something far more nefarious of nature. It was fear. He saw the fear that Beher had mentioned, it was a fear replete with pain and regret, of sorrow and shame. He knew, with barely any doubts, that her soul was damaged. But he also knew, with even more certainty, that her soul could be healed, that she could be redeemed.

As Máher returned to normal speed, the elf's eyes rolled back into her head and she keeled over, passed out. Máher rushed to her side and supported her limp frame, carful of the crossbow bolt protruding from her back. Examining the wound, he knew that it was bad, exactly how bad he did not know, but he was certain that she needed help that he was unable to provide.

'Beher. Have you heard of The Sisters? Do you know where they reside? We have a need for their healing abilities.'

Beher, who was currently consuming the corpse of the dog that Máher had just slain, stopped gnawing on one of its bones and turned his head to face Máher.

'Beher does not. How could Beher know? Beher has never been to this human city before.'

Máher sighed, worry for the elf exacerbated by his inability to assist her.

'Okay then. I'm going to need you to look into my mind. I am going to show you what their house looks like and the area around it. Once you are familiar with this information, I am going to need you to guide me past those that are hunting the elf, along the safest possible path.'

'Beher worries for Máher. If Beher ever left Máher's side, Máher would be helpless. Beher to the rescue again. So many little juicy piglets for Beher.'

In his mind Máher concentrated on The Sisters house, projecting the scene to Beher. It was small and rickety, with a distinct leftwards lean, and although it was three stories tall, it was far thinner than usual. The weatherboards that clad the house were in many places bent and peeling, as if they were trying desperately to escape the side of the building. Its roof was in fact more holes than ceiling and its windows, all two of them, were clouded with grime and grit. This was a house that was in every way far removed from any dwelling of good repute.

As if from a bird's eye view, Máher's perspective shifted as the house grew smaller, revealing more clearly its surrounds. The house was situated in the heart of the city's slums, a myriad of other hovels its neighbours. Ever so slowly his perspective shifted ever further, gradually showing Beher the central district, the market quarter, the docks, the government district, and the industrial zone. Until at last, Beher had an accurate picture of the entirety of Súthburh etched in his mind. He could now guide Máher to where they needed to go.

'Beher sees The Sisters house. Beher sees how to get there.'

'Good. Guide us there.'

Beher didn't bother to respond to Máher's directive. The young drake simply flapped his wings once, twice, and then thrice, taking to the sky.

Crouching beside the elf, Máher placed her body gently over his shoulder and stood. Supporting her slender frame, the best he could, he readied himself for the journey as the sounds of shouts and dog barks echoed throughout the alleyways.

Chapter 15

Dolos

Several tense moments passed for Máher as he waited for Beher. Sweat formed on his brow, his breathing shallow and pulse erratic. Normally, he wouldn't have been so affected by his current predicament, as he was more than accustomed to stressful situations, but this time it was different. Not only could he not afford to be captured, the thought of the elf that he carried dying pained him, unusually so.

From the darkest corners of his mind, Máher felt an itch, subtle, barely present. He knew what it foretold and steeled himself, trying to supress it, to force it back to the shadows whence it came. But this time it would not be denied. Growing to a raging force it swelled within him, the urge, the desire, the need to change. Though he fought it, his hand moved on its own accord, shaking as it hovered over the ring he wore. Internally Máher surrendered as the final remnants of his defiance died. He placed his index finger upon the roughly cut sapphire at the ring's centre. A voice from within, foreign and ancient, spoke an indecipherable phrase, harsh and guttural. At its end, the gemstone glowed a pale blue in the moonlight.

Máher's form shimmered and shifted, contorted, and twisted. Then, with a snap, reality shifted and in place of Máher stood another. He was a human man, slender with raven hair, a matching goatee, and indigo eyes. In lieu of furs and leathers, this new man wore a black velvet suit that clung snugly to his lean frame. A cape of the darkest jet flowed carefree from his shoulders, its bright purple lining occasionally flittering into sight, hinting at some metaphorical duality. This was far from a simple illusion, Máher was now essentially gone. In his place stood another entity entirely, one that went by the name of Dolos.

My oh my, what a mess. It's just like that buffoon to dump me into the thick of it. Oh well, I shouldn't look poorly on an opportunity to stretch one's legs I suppose.

Dolos felt Beher's presence probe the edges of his consciousness. For a moment he contemplated blocking the dragon, but then decided that he couldn't be bothered. So, reluctantly he let Beher into his mind.

'Hello?'

'Oh great, Beher thinks, it's Dolos the demented. Why Máher ever lets Dolos out is a mystery to Beher. Bah. Feel lucky Dolos should, that Máher will die if Dolos does. Otherwise Beher would let Dolos die, or maybe Beher would kill Dolos himself.'

'No greeting. Not even a hello? Well, go and suck eggs you glorified iguana.'

'No. No time for Dolos's usual craziness. Dolos has important job to do. Beher helps.'

'Oh, stow it lizard breath. You're forgetting that I know what he knows. I'm already up to speed, so could you please get a move on with those directions already?'

Cutting off their telepathic jousting, angry voices echoed throughout the labyrinth of streets and alleyways. Dolos listened to them as they drew closer.

'Where in the seven hells did Ripper get to, blasted mutt better not be chasing stray tabbies again.'

'Fucked if I know mate, but he should be bloody close, I saw him turn right just here only a few seconds ago. Ripper! Get back here boy.'

'How's it going up there, scaly boy? The local rabble are, how is it put, hot on my heels and I'd rather like to be running away from them. Like now please.'

'Blah, blah, blah. Dolos needed patience, Beher ready now. Do as Beher says.'

At last, Beher started giving Dolos directions. With gusto, he started running, the sounds of his pursuers fading into nothing behind him. As he whizzed past closed doorways and alley entrances, the elf bounced vigorously upon Dolos's shoulder. Despite the situation, and the impropriety of it, Dolos, unable to stop himself, glanced at the woman's jiggling arse.

Not bad, not bad at all. If I wasn't currently running for my life, I'd love to stop and get better acquainted with you darling. I'm starting to see why Máher wanted you saved. Cheeky devil.

A left turn then a right. His feet slapped harshly against the cobblestones. His lungs burned from the exertion. Unseen watchers yelled abuse from their shuttered windows, others shouted inspirational quips. Dolos ignored them all.

A desperate shout emanating from the depths of his mind shook his consciousness.

'*Stop! Beher sees many people in front of Dolos.*'

Panic rushed through Dolos's head and his heart skipped a beat. Barely reacting in time, he skidded to a stop scant few moments before leaving the alley and revealing himself to those beyond. Sweat coated, his hand slipped on the taught leather the elf wore, almost dropping her. For the second time in as many seconds, his heart skipped a beat.

Goodness gracious, that was close.

Peering from the alleyway, taking as much care as he could to not be seen, Dolos assessed the courtyard in front of him. A small group of men, numbering three in total, stood in a loose group near the square's centre. They chatted idly, but were clearly highly strung and alert, their heads moved constantly, gazes never lingering. At their feet were two large war hounds, practically identical to the one that Máher had already killed, drooling from their open maws as they too scanned their surroundings for prey.

Dogs. That's a hard no.

Thinking that discretion would be the best course of action, Dolos slowly started to back away, trying his best to be silent. He failed. Inadvertently, he scrapped one of the elf's boots against the alley wall. It was only a small sound and normally it would have gone unheard, Dolos only barely registered it himself, but the war hounds were on high alert. Both dogs swivelled in the direction of the sound and started growling intensely. Picking up on their dogs' demeanour, the men followed suit and stared intently in Dolos's direction. They saw him.

'Oi! Who's there, watch ya doin' skulkin about when there be a hunt on? If ya wan' ta join ya can, bu' be open abou' it or you'll end up shot.'

As he finished his sentence the man patted the crossbow he held for emphasis. It was a large, heavy thing, simple yet effective. Dolos thought that to be shot by it would be worse than bad.

'Ya hear me? We knows' ya in there, now come out nice an' slow like or me an' me boys here will show ya wot for.'

The other three men each raised their crossbows, each a carbon copy to the one that the first man held, and pointed them in Dolos's direction. Their eyes never wavering from the mouth of the alleyway.

Okay then. Gift of the gab, do not fail me now.

Dolos raised one of his hands in surrender, the other remained firmly wrapped around the waist of the elf, and slowly moved into the square. In stark contrast to Máher, Dolos's voice was both firm and resounding.

'Now, now friends. There is no need for hostilities, we are all out tonight for the same thing after all. My name is Dolos, hello everyone.'

Dolos waved to the men. They did not return his greeting.

'You see, I heard about all that nasty business that befell Mercurius, poor devil, and I thought to myself, gosh, something must be done about it. So, I went looking for the harpy that killed his son, and do you know what, in no time at all I found the wretch. I was just on my way to collect the bounty when I ran into you good folks.'

Two of the men started to lower their weapons, clearly convinced by Dolos's deception. However, the one who had addressed him previously wasn't swayed, his crossbow remained fixed on Dolos's chest and his eyes narrowed in suspicion. A sideways glance from him was all it took for his companions to re-elevate their weapons towards Dolos.

'There be something off about ya, an' while I don' know exactly wha' it may be, I don' like it.'

Frozen, the man lost himself in his thoughts, as if trying to decide what the best course of action would be, but he couldn't quite decide. Gaze never wavering from Dolos, and after a metaphorical infinity of deliberation, he nodded in affirmation.

'I think it would be for the better if ya jus' gave us that there woman an' we claim the reward for ourselves. It's yar choice if it goes easy or if it goes hard.'

Each of the men steeled themselves in anticipation of conflict, their eyes bold with the expectancy of an easy victory. The leader held his ground as his two underlings advanced slowly, dogs growling viciously by their sides.

I'm losing them.

'My dear fellows, there is no need for such vulgarity. I'd be more than happy to give you a share of the bounty, a lion's share in fact. Perhaps, and this is just a humble suggestion, we join in partnership. I carry the woman, which as far as I am concerned is the most strenuous part, and you fine fellows escort me to

Mercurius's house, ensuring that I, and our prize, remain unmolested. I mean, I would be ever so grateful if you agreed.'

Dolos's words fell on deaf ears and the men continued their approach.

'Nah, I think we'll jus' be takin' the lass. We don' wan' ta have to share our spoils with no uppity prick like ya self an' I don' reckon you'd be able to stop us anyhow.'

Dolos let out a frustrated sigh.

'Well then. I must say that I am disappointed, if not completely surprised, with this turn of events. Just so you all know I gave you a chance and you squandered it. I am not at all sorry for what is about to transpire. You lot have proved yourselves to be quite a bunch of ignoramuses and foul ne'er do wells that I shall not be troubled to remove from this fine, alright, somewhat acceptable, city.'

Dolos's sly grin vanished, twisting into a malevolent snarl. The joviality, almost a kindness, left his eyes, replaced with a deranged viciousness.

'Plus, and for me this is the most important factor, I haven't any real fun for ages. Thank you for obliging me.'

Tightening his grasp on the elf, Dolos focused his mind and extended his consciousness outwards. His eyes glowed with an unnatural brightness, a vivid violet hue, as, unseen to all except Dolos, tendrils of psychic energies snaked from his fingertips. Driven by Dolos's will, they wound their way towards each of the men and dogs. As they reached their heads the tendrils darted at them excitedly, penetrating any orifice they could find, ears, nose, or mouth.

Dolos's consciousness entered the minds of his adversaries and they stopped, frozen, unable to move. They fought against Dolos's will, their bodies spasming and convulsing under the strain, teeth chattering to the point of almost breaking. One by one they each in turn succumbed to Dolos's dominion, their eyes glazed over and their breathing slowed. They were now Dolos's to control as he willed.

Mine. Mine. Mine. They're all mine, ha, ha, ha.

Only one of the men resisted. Shaking off Dolos's influence, he stared aghast at the state of his friends. For the time being he forgot Dolos and stammering wildly, he tried to rouse his compatriots.

'W… w… Wilhelm, snap out of it mate. Fr… f… Fredrich what's got into ya.'

There was no response from his friends, they didn't react at all. Terror holding him in his place, the man watched on helplessly as both Wilhelm and Fredrich turned their crossbows towards themselves, pointing them directly at their own faces. Without a moment of hesitation, they both pulled their triggers.

Heavy bolts shot from their bows, instantaneously piercing the men's skulls as easily as they were naught but overripened fruit. Bone shattered into tiny fragments and brain tissue was turned into pulp, both of which exploded from the rear of the men's heads as the bolts tore clean through. Simultaneously, they both collapsed to the cobbles, dead.

Hideously twisted laughter burst from Dolos's mouth, echoing eerily off of the courtyard's walls.

'Ha, ha, ha. The way their heads exploded was beautiful. Let's do it again! let's do it again! Ha, ha, ha.'

A scream borne from both fear and anger surged from the mouth of the last remaining man. Overcoming his terror fuelled stupor, he raised his bow and loosened a shot towards Dolos. His aim was poor and the bolt flew wildly off to the side, clattering harmlessly off of a stone wall. With feverous intent borne from desperation, the man clumsily started to draw the bowstring back.

Dolos's grin returned as he wiggled a finger at the man.

'Tsk, tsk, tsk, that just won't do. I'm having fun here and you go and try to ruin it. Unacceptable. Oh my. I've just thought of something. You like dogs. I wonder? Do dogs like you? Let's find out. Ha, ha, ha.'

Without moving, Dolos focused his mind on those of the dogs. It was not a pleasant experience. The consciousnesses of lesser beasts were almost exclusively a frothing cauldron of raw emotions and base desires, difficult to decipher and even harder to endure. But, endure it he did.

Into the minds of the dogs Dolos projected the image of the man. He presented the man as food, like a street vendor would his freshly cooked produce, tasty and to be desired. Dolos stoked the fire of hunger in the beasts' bellies, they were hungry, they felt hungry. Drool pooled on the ground at their feet as it oozed from their maws. Low growls emanated from deep within their chests as Dolos directed them towards the man, towards their next meal.

The string of his crossbow was at full draw when the man noticed the hounds stalking slowly towards him. His eyes never leaving the beasts, he fumbled with the quiver at his hip. A bolt dropped from his shaking hands, clattering onto the stone ground. Panic rising in his chest the man tried a second time, another bolt slipped from his sweat ridden palm. More steel clattered on the cobbles. The man took his attention off of the hounds for a second. He turned towards Dolos with a pleading look in his eyes, still trying to extricate a bolt from his quiver.

'Pl… Please.'

In that moment the dogs attacked. A myriad of deep barks rumbled from their mouths as they both leapt at the man. One went for the throat and the other for the groin. At the last second the man tried to fend off the hounds, but to no avail. His arms flailed helplessly, crossbow dropped and forgotten, as rabid teeth bit deep into his fleshy parts. He fell to the ground silently as blood poured from his neck and genitals. Although his death was quick, it was replete with the agonising pain and primal terror of being eaten alive.

Dolos watched on as the dogs consumed their prey with a ravenous hunger. He felt no pity for the men who had just died, he felt no remorse. He felt nothing, but an overwhelming joy at being alive and free.

'Well. It appears that dogs do in fact like you. Ha, ha, ha. Oh my. I did not think that was going to go that well.'

'And Dolos wonders why Dolos is despised by Beher. It's obvious. Dolos is crazy.'

'Beher! Hey there. Fat lot of good you were. Didn't help at all. Oh well, more fun for me I suppose. Let's get on with it then. Lead on my scaly friend adjacent.'

Guided by Beher, Dolos jogged cheerfully away from the hounds as they continued to enjoy their meal.

Chapter 16

Eris

Standing on the precipice of death, Eris saw everything in vivid detail. The dog's fur stood on end as it growled at her. Its ears lay flat upon its head and the muscles of its haunches quivered as they tensed. A low growl morphed into a deep bark as the beast released the tension in its legs and it leapt. Eris blinked. Her eyes reopened and as if in slow motion she saw the hound drift slowly through the air, its eyes fixated upon her, nefarious intent clear.

Now I die.

Her mind barely registered a blur of fiery motion, originating somewhere from her periphery, as it smashed into the hound. In an instant the dog was gone, thrust away from her with tremendous speed and force. Eris glanced towards the dog's broken corpse in astonishment, incapable of comprehending what had just occurred.

Eris's entire body started to shake and convulse. Perhaps from the blood loss, maybe from the emotional tole of being spared a gruesome demise, she did not know. In either case she felt a fresh wave of panic wash over her as a new shadow loomed over her. Eris turned to face its source.

The blur that had saved her had solidified into a man. He stood motionless, frozen in place and barely breathing. An assortment of scuffed leather and ragged furs clad his imposing frame, but his face was what Eris found most striking. Two horns curved sleekly towards the back of his head, his skin was unnaturally grey, his hair was not as vivid as her own, but was in her opinion the perfect simile for a raging flame, and his eyes glowed a deep amber. Without question he was the most striking man Eris had ever seen.

Her vision lost focus and her head swam in an ocean of dizziness. Eris was met by darkness as she passed out again.

Several times she regained her senses, but every time she lost herself to the void after mere moments. In her lucidity she saw a river of blurry stone rushing past her face. Her body bounced and swayed, seemingly floating on its own accord. She passed various house fronts, their windows glowing at her like the eyes of a wild beast. Startled, but too tired to move, let alone care, Eris surrendered herself to her fate. She blacked out.

*   *   *

The first thing that Eris noticed was the rhythmic beat of a clock, *tic, tock, tick tock*. Keeping her eyes closed, she controlled her breathing, holding it as steady as possible.

Best to let them think that I'm still sleeping. Maybe I can surprise them and escape.

Straining her ears, she tried to ascertain whatever she could regarding her current location, but apart from the clock, she heard nothing.

At least I'm comfortable. Firm pillow, soft mattress and, by the feeling of it, fresh sheets. Could be worse.

As subtlety as she could, Eris sniffed the air. Her nose picked up the scent of several herbs, and although she didn't recognise them all, the tell-tale aromas of cloves and nutmeg were distinctly familiar.

Both are common in most cuisines, but they're also used in herbal disinfectants. Whoever captured me has also healed me. Intriguing.

Thinking it time that she examined her location visually, Eris opened her eye, just a smidge. Seeing nothing of worth, she decided to risk it and open them fully. However, before she could, a soft voice spoke.

'Hello. It's good to see you're finally awake. The Sisters did a good job with your wound, their talents never fail to amaze. I'm Máher, by the way.'

Eris, chagrined at having her deception discovered, surrendered all notions of subterfuge. Opening her eyes, she turned to where she had heard the voice. No one was there.

'Though I don't know how, it appears your ordeal has affected your audio perception. I'm sure it will recover presently.'

Eris rolled over in the bed as fast as she could, sitting up to better see whomever it was that was speaking to her. In the far corner of the room, sitting casually in a chair, was the horned man that had stopped the war hound from chewing her face off. Though she had many questions, Eris found herself lost for words. She felt herself staring at the man, he was just so entrancingly strange, she couldn't bring herself to look away.

The man, Máher he had called himself, looked away from Eris, shielded his face with one of his hands and gestured towards her chest with the other.

'I may be mistaken, but I believe in this instance that your promiscuity is not intentional.'

Eris looked down. The bedsheets had fallen to reveal her naked bosom. Immediately, she felt her face warm with a blush. Though she was far from ashamed of her figure, this man was a stranger to her. What would Mikael think? Quickly, she hoisted the sheets to cover herself, glaring daggers at Máher. Wondering as to the extent of her undress, Eris lifted the sheet and peered under it. She was completely nude.

'I do hope it wasn't you who has violated me so, by rendering me naked without prior consent. I'm Eris, by the way.'

'No. I would never take such liberties with a woman.'

'That's good to hear. Oh, and you can lower your arm, I'm covered.'

Máher did as Eris bid, lowering his arm he turned to face her and looked her squarely in the eye.

'It was the Sisters that removed your garments. They didn't want them further spoiled as they mended your wound. In fact, they also repaired and cleaned them.'

Memories of last night flooded into the forefront of her mind and Eris remembered.

I failed, I killed a child, I was shot, Mikael.

Panic and unease bit deep into her stomach. Her heart pounded in her chest and she found herself struggling to breathe. Head bent, she gasped for breath, trying desperately to fill her lungs, yet she found no relief even once she had accomplished this simple goal.

Oh gods.

Lost in her anxiety, the first Eris noticed of Máher was his hand upon her shoulder. His touch was gentle and through it Eris felt reassured. Looking up to him, she saw the care in his eyes and she knew, despite it all, that everything was going to be okay. Her breathing eased and her pulsed slowed.

'Thank you. I needed that.'

Verbally, Máher said nothing in response, but his smile conveyed everything it needed too.

'And, perhaps more importantly, I thank you for saving me. However, I must leave There are things I need to see to. Um, so, where are my clothes?'

'They are on the chest at the foot of the bed. But I think it would be best if you stayed here, just for a little while.'

'I can't. I must leave.'

'Look. It's the middle of the day and your face is plastered on wanted posters all over the city. If you go now, you will be captured. I didn't save you just to have you end up being caught the very next day.'

Eris turned to Máher, a quizzical look on her face.

'Then it begs the question, Máher, why did you save me? I am no one to you. Why do you care?'

'True. It would have been easy for me to ignore you. But I have my own agenda. The intricacies of which, I will not admit to you now, but I thought you could be of use.'

Eris scoffed.

'For what?'

'You are a thief. I wish to steal something, but have no expertise in burglary. That's where you come in. Obviously.'

Eris's eyes narrowed.

'What do you wish to steal and from whom?'

'Information. From the Peoples Depository of Knowledge.'

'Um, why?'

'Because I want it.'

'Okay. That's not what I meant. Information from the Depository is free for everybody. Anyone can access it. You can just walk in and ask for whatever you want, there's no need to steal it.'

'Really?'

'Yes.'

'Oh.'

Máher leaned back, stoking his chin in thought.

'How strange. When I was last here the Depository was only open to citizens, and only those who had coin. When did that change?'

'Almost fifteen years ago.'

Máher frowned, a confused look on his face. Slowly, he stood, leaving Eris's side, and walked to the room's corner. There, he turned away from Eris and looked out the window.

'Well then. It looks like I don't need a thief. Be that as it may, when I rescued you, I saw something. Something in you. I can't explain it, but it made me believe that you may be able to help me achieve my goals. What they are I cannot tell you, yet, but in return for your aid, I will assist you in any way you need, within reason of course. I just need to know one thing.'

Máher paused briefly, turning back to face Eris. His eyes scanned her face, meeting hers, and she felt his gaze burn into her very soul. It was like he saw everything she was, and everything she could be, all at once. It was one of the most uncomfortable things Eris had ever experienced, but she did not look away.

'Did you kill a child?'

Eris swallowed nervously, but did not avert her gaze.

'Yes.'

'Did you intend too?'

'No. It was a mistake.'

Máher bowed his head and Eris watched on silently, her eyes never leaving Máher, as he walked to the door. Upon reaching the threshold, he turned back to her, meeting her eyes once more.

'Very well. I cannot force you to stay, I wouldn't even try to, but I implore you to consider your position before acting rashly. Also, I bid you stay for lunch. I can hear your belly rumbling from here.'

As if on que, her stomach growled, announcing her hunger to the world with no thought of discretion. For the second time that day Eris felt her face glow with embarrassment. Máher chuckled playfully and left Eris to herself.

Scowling, Eris threw off her sheets and jumped from the bed. She moved to fetch her clothes, but stopped as she glimpsed her reflection in the mirror. Her nose, which from what she could remember had been broken, was no longer damaged. It was, just as she was used too, petite with a slight upwards tilt at the tip and perfectly straight.

Nice.

Turning her back to inspect where the crossbow bolt had struck her, she saw no evidence to suggest she had ever been wounded at all. Running her fingers over her flesh, she felt no scar, not even a blemish.

Whomever these Sisters are, they are truly healers of the highest skill.

Dressing quickly, Eris noted that her clothes had been cleaned, pressed, and just as Máher had said, repaired. The fresh, and slightly warm, fabrics felt good against her skin. However, all notions of pleasantry were soon lost as she noticed that her daggers, and more importantly her boots, were not amongst the rest of her belongings.

Incensed, Eris stormed from the room, charged down the corridor and descended the stairs, screaming as she went.

'Máher! Máher! Where in the seven hells are my daggers and boots! I demand them back this instant!'

Máher did not respond.

Fury radiating from her scowling face, Eris looked around for any indication as to where the horned man could be. She saw nothing, but whispers and muffled voices emanating from the end of the corridor drew her attention. Without hesitation, Eris took off down the hallway.

Hurtling into the dining room, she found Máher sitting at a table, nonchalantly eating a forkful of bacon while he conversed quietly with a small group of women. There were five in all and they varied in age, from a hunch backed crone, wrinkled and grey, to a young girl barely into her teens.

They must be the Sisters. They don't look like siblings. Strange.

Máher faced Eris and as quietly as a mouse addressed her.

'Eris, welcome. Have a seat and eat your fill, there's plenty enough for all. Might I recommend the bacon, it is particularly good.'

She knew not how, by some magic Eris supposed, but her anger completely dissipated. Silently she sat in the only empty chair. Atop the table before her was a myriad of foods, each arranged appetisingly. An assortment of meats, both cold and warmed, vegetables, buttered and steaming, salads, crisp and fresh, breads, still piping from the oven. It was nothing short of a feast. For a moment Eris forgot her woes as saliva filled her mouth in anticipation and her stomach growled loudly, once more asserting its dominance. Picking up a fork, she started to nibble at some pork.

Gods, this is delicious. It would be so easy to gorge myself, but I shall refrain. A modicum of decorum should be maintained.

'Excellent, a bit of food will do you the world of good. Now. I do believe introductions are in order. These fabulous ladies are the Sisters.' Máher pointed to each in turn. 'Hygieia over there is the eldest followed by Iaso, Aceso, Aegle and finally Panacea. I have known them for many years and they are without question some of the best people I have ever met. They were kind enough to patch you up and grant us shelter while you rested. They also whipped up this splendid breakfast.'

As each was introduced to her, Eris bowed her head in respect and thanks. None of the Sisters spoke, but each returned Eris's deference with a smile.

'Now, the only person you have yet to meet is Beher. If you look over to that corner over there, you'll see him lounging about.'

Eris looked to where Máher was pointing. Audibly, she gasped in surprise. There was a dragon, albeit a small dragon, curled up in the corner. Crimson scales, speckled with ruby flakes, rose, and fell rhythmically as the creature breathed. The dragon lifted one of its leathery wings, revealing its head. Needle sharp teeth protruded haphazardly from a narrow snout. An eyelid rolled towards the back of the creature's skull and a singular yellow eye stared at Eris. With certainty Eris knew that the dragon was scrutinising her in the deepest way possible. The creature's nostrils flared as it snorted.

Eris felt a pressure build in her head. A tendril of thought, thin and winding, pushed against her consciousness. In panic she resisted its advances, but like a lance piercing a boar's side it thrust into her mind, sending shivers over her body as pain seared her temples. Eris breathed hard as the pain receded slowly. In its place a disembodied voice, far different to any she had ever heard before, filled her thoughts.

'*Hm, Máher seems quite taken with the elfling, Beher wonders why? Máher says more to the elfling than most other two-legs, what does Máher see in she-elf? Bleh. She-elf better not take Máher away from Beher or she-elf will be dinner for Beher.*'

Eris stared at the young dragon in challenge. It turned to face her directly, both of its yellow eyes staring back hungrily, purple tongue slathering the outside of his mouth with saliva, his meaning explicitly clear.

'*Whatever he may be to you, be certain that you have nothing to fear dragon. I am spoken for and have no designs on Máher, irrespective of what he has in mind for me.*'

'*Good. For the elfling's sake that is good.*'

Máher's eyes narrowed as he looked between Eris and Beher. For a moment they lingered on the dragon, only to return to Eris soon after.

'He spoke to you?'

In affirmation, Eris nodded.

'Well then. He's never spoken to anyone other than me before, aside from our father. I'm not sure if that's a good thing or bad. Regardless, I wonder, what is it that would have you leave so hastily, despite the risk?'

Eris took a deep breath and considered her options. She didn't trust Máher, not completely at any rate. Beher was an unknown, she had heard tales of dragonkin and their fickle ways. But this one seemed to be beholden to Máher and she doubted he would act on his own accord. She doubted Máher would do her any harm. Why would he rescue, and also heal her, just to do her harm? Unless, his motivations were far more nefariously twisted, like selling her to slavers or imprisoning her somewhere as his personal sex slave. Eris shuddered. Or he might just be a nice person wanting to help. Sighing, Eris told Máher everything.

Retelling how she murdered an innocent child affected Eris in ways she had never been affected before. Several emotions coursed through her chest at once, sorrow, guilt, anger, and confusion. It nearly broke her. However, the love that she felt for Mikael, coupled with the crystal-clear certainty that he was either directly in harm's way or already dead, shattered her. At her tale's end, her head was bowed as she wept unrestrained and unashamedly.

To enraptured by her grief, Eris didn't notice Máher stand, nor did she hear him cross the room. She only noticed his closeness to her as he tenderly placed a hand on her chin and gently guided her gaze to meet his own. Though he was not crying, his eyes shimmered with tears of his own. With a care and compassion, she had not yet witnessed from the man, Máher whispered to her.

'I know these are only words, and they mean little, but I am so very sorry. I have lost many loved ones, and came close to losing many more, in my time and I offer you my deepest sympathies and condolences. You must remain here until nightfall, but I do not. I will go to your dwelling and search for Mikael. All I need is some directions and I will leave immediately.'

Eris's soul surged with hope and instantly she dismissed all notions of mistrust towards Máher. Stammering through her tears, her message was garbled, but comprehensible.

'Th… th… thank you, we live in a loft. I… in the middle residential dis… dis… district, some three hundred feet due West from the Wh… White Stallion Tavern. L… l… look for the chimney covered in p… purple Verbena's, there's a hatch n… n… next to it.'

'Think nothing of it. Just stay here and try not to worry. I'll be as quick as I can.'

Máher rubbed Eris's shoulder consolingly and gave her a determined nod before he left, Beher following closely at his heels. The Sisters sat beside her as they ate their lunch, silently ignoring Eris and her troubles.

Chapter 17

Eris

Bothered by Máher's absence, Eris paced nervously around the living room. Three hours had passed and still he had not returned. Worry wore down her composure and inside her mind she spun tales of woe, each progressively more gruesome than the last. Although each was founded on nothing but her own insecurities, she started to see them as true, with a conviction bordering on fanaticism.

He's dead. They're both dead. I'll soon be dead. We'll both be dead. All dead. Gods no.

The front door opened and, distracted from her gradual descent into madness, she immediately ran into the entrance hall, the faintest glimmer of hope restored.

Before her stood Máher, gently closing the door behind him. He was alone. Eris clutched her breast as the full weight of her worry bore down upon her once again, crushing what little remained of her spirit.

She knew the answer before she asked the question, but still she asked it anyway, she had to hear him say it.

'Mikael?'

Máher turned to her, his expression pained.

'I'm so sorry. Mikael was not there. There were signs of a struggle, but no physical remains. Beher caught a trace of his scent leaving your loft. We followed it as far as we could, but he lost it in the market. Too many spices, the overpowering smell, his nose.'

Eris's face paled, but a mote of optimism remained.

He's not dead. Yet.

'Would he have went out on his own accord?'

Barely able to speak, Eris shook her head while mumbling her answer.

'No. But I know where he will be. We have to leave right now.'

'Wait, it's not yet dark. You'll be spotted.'

Something inside Eris snapped. She was sick of being told what to do, sick of being condescended, sick of everything. Furiously she shouted.

'I don't care! I would rather die knowing I did all I could to save him, than live with the knowledge that I chose to do nothing! I love him more than anything and cannot, nay will not, let him die! Help me or not, it's your choice, but I am leaving! Now, give me my fucking daggers and my fucking boots before I beat you to death with my bare, fucking hands!'

Eris stared at Máher as she waited for a response. Panting heavily, face flushed maroon, lips snarled angrily, she was ready for a fight. Surprisingly, he offered no resistance.

'Very well. We will leave immediately.'

Eris's anger instantly evaporated. She was not expecting Máher to concede so easily.

'Um, what?'

Ignoring Eris's surprise, Máher turned back towards the kitchen and shouted.

'Hygieia! Bring the boots!'

Máher twisted back to Eris, who still stood motionless with shock.

'Apologies, the Sisters have a fondness for magical trinkets and wanted to examine your boots. I allowed them to, as a kind of favour for healing you. Don't worry, while they did seem quite taken by that enchantment, they'll return them in perfect working order. As for your daggers, here they are.'

Máher reached into his furs, rummaged around for a bit, and pulled out Eris's two remaining daggers. Eris reached out and took them from Máher, re-sheathing them at her hips.

'Thanks.'

'I thought it best to hold onto them until we could become better acquainted, lest you try something rash. I would have hated to have to kill you.'

Kill me? As if buddy.

Before Eris could challenge Máher's preconception that he would be able to kill her, Hygieia waddled in from the kitchen, Eris's boots clutched firmly against her chest. She looked pleadingly at Máher, wordlessly begging him to be allowed to keep the magical footwear, if only for a while longer. Máher's face grew stern and he gestured towards Eris. Defeated, Hygieia visibly deflated as she handed the boots back to Eris, waddling away as soon as she did.

'All right then. Your belongings have been returned. Let's go. You take the lead and explain on the way.'

Eris exited the house, Máher close on her heels. She wasn't overly familiar with this part of the city, as the poor typically didn't have anything to steal, but she knew roughly where they were. Raising the hood of her cloak, she set off at a rapid pace. Máher kept up without issue, equally disappointing and impressing Eris.

To avert unwanted attention, the pair stayed close to each other and only spoke in whispers. Whenever another would pass within earshot, they would cease talking altogether.

'Okay. It's common for us, thieves that is, to go through the market, specifically, past the spice vendors, whenever we think that we are being pursued. It masks and confuses our scent, making it harder to be tracked. That's what happened to you and Beher when you tried to follow Mikael.'

Eris paused as a young couple crossed their path.

'Now. As far as I know, no one, apart from us, would be pursuing them. So, I doubt that they went to the market for that reason alone. However, it's a mandatory procedure whenever we travel to our headquarters, the Burrow.'

'I also know that it is me that they are after. I was the one that wronged them. Sure, they'll want to kill Mikael as well, but doing so will be pointless for them if they don't get me first. They'll want me to watch him die, as punishment. So, they'll use him as bait.'

'Now, it's true that we have plenty of safehouses throughout the city, but using Mikael as bait won't work if he's being held in a safehouse. I'd have no way of knowing which one he was in. It would also be riskier for them as it would be easier to rescue him or for him to escape. In short, they have to be in the Burrow, there's nowhere else he could be.'

From the corner of her eye, Eris could see Máher nodding, his face clearly displaying the complexity of his thought process as he analysed this information.

'Makes sense to me. Perhaps you should have been a detective instead of a th…'

Eris hissed at Máher, silencing him with a wave of her hand. A particularly large group of people were walking towards them. Too late to avoid them, Eris turned her face away from the crowd, hiding her face in her hood and hoping that she wouldn't be recognised.

Shit, shit, shit.

Two men, whom appeared more than a little shifty, stared at her. Eris felt their gaze burrowing into her as they inspected her intently, not at all subtly trying to peep under her hood.

Please gods, don't let them recognise me.

They must have seen something of interest, as spontaneously they started chattering to each other excitedly. With trepidation, Eris watched as the pair ran off, glancing behind their shoulders as they went.

That's not good.

'Máher. I think I've been recognised. Two men got a look under my hood and ran off once they did.'

'That's not ideal. Is if far to the Burrow?'

'No. Well, not exactly. We're practically there. Well, to one of the minor entrances anyway.'

'Good. Will there be any defences?'

'There should only be two guards outside the entrance. But on the inside, there will be traps and more guards, many more guards.'

'Stealth will be preferable then?'

'Indeed. Once inside, I'll take point, I know what most of the traps look like and can disarm them. Don't get in my way and only act if absolutely necessary.'

'This is your realm. I defer to your experience.'

Without warning Eris stopped, Máher bumped into her, but she ignored him and hissed out of the side of her mouth.

'We're here. That house is the entrance. Take cover and look for guards.'

The house before her appeared as an ordinary dwelling, indistinguishable from those around it. Its windows were open, dispelling any notions of hidden subterfuge, and it appeared well maintained, as if lived in. This was all nothing more than a façade. If you knew what to look for, and Eris did, it was easy to see several marks that identified the building as property of the Thieves Guild.

The first indication that the pair was in danger was the tell-tale hiss of an arrow in flight. The projectile whooshed past the duo and ricocheted off of the building behind them with a metallic plink. Pulling Máher along with her, Eris flattened herself against a nearby wall, manically looking for whomever had just shot at them.

'I don't see them. Do you?'

When Máher failed to respond, Eris turned to him. Amazed, she watched as his hair and eyes lit aflame.

'No, but Beher does. They're on the rooftops, one to the right and another to the left. Use your boots to take out one, Beher will take the other, I'll draw fire. Go!'

Eris had already started to move before Máher had finished talking, activating her boots as she did. A second arrow whizzed past her, barely missing her head. The enchantment now active, Eris climbed into the air as if she ran on an invisible stairway. She reached the roof in no time, but scarcely made it into cover behind a chimney before another arrow clattered against the nearby tiles.

So much for drawing fire.

Eris looked around frantically, still uncertain of exactly where her assailant was. Fortunately, the lack of cover made him easy to spot. Just as Eris was, he was hiding behind a chimney.

Got you.

Eris broke cover and ran towards him at full speed. The man saw Eris approach and hastily nocked another arrow.

He raised his bow at Eris. In desperation, she threw one of her daggers at the assassin. The blade spun gracefully through the air and miraculously the dagger struck the man in the throat, sinking deep. Before he collapsed, he released his bowstring, loosening the arrow he held. Eris saw the projectile fly towards her and dove to avoid it. Barely, Eris rolled under the arrow's flight path, leaving it to fly harmlessly over her head.

Gods, that was close.

Continuing to run over the rooftop, Eris reached the man's fresh corpse and retrieved her dagger, wiping off the blood that coated it onto the assassin's shirt.

I don't have enough of these to waste.

Staying behind the chimney as much as she could, Eris poked her head around its corner and looked for the other guard. Across the road she saw him, firing arrow after arrow towards the street, no doubt at Máher. Eris considered her options.

The gap between them was too far to jump and he was in reasonable cover, so a dagger toss would surely miss. The enchantment in her boots had faded, but it would be easy enough for her to reactivate it and then charge the man, just as she did the first.

A good a plan as any.

Eris had barely begun to chant the incantation when a glimmer of movement caught her eye.

Far above the thief, Beher was circling, his red scales twinkling in the afternoon sunlight. Although Eris had some reservations where the beast was concerned, she could not dispute the fact that watching him in flight was nothing short of awe inspiring. The elven words, uncompleted, died in her mouth as Beher tucked his wings into his side and dove towards the archer. Flaring them at the last moment to slow his momentum, he collided with the man, outstretched legs grasping the man, talons sinking deep.

From her vantage Eris heard the man's wailing scream. Almost immediately it was cut off as Beher tore out the guard's throat. Eris continued to watch, so disturbed she couldn't look away, as Beher tore strips of flesh from the man's lifeless body and consumed them hungrily. He must have sensed Eris watching him, for as he chewed on his meal, he looked directly at her. Eris felt a familiar pressure build up in her mind.

'She-elf must behave or this will be elfling. Food.'

Eris shuddered in disgust, but managed to shake that unpleasant thought from her mind before she was overcome with nausea.

Not going to happen.

Nimbly, she climbed down from the building she was on. Re-joining Máher, Eris noticed that he was clutching his thigh, face twisted into a stern grimace.

'What's wrong?'

'I was hit.'

'Will you be able to continue or will I have to go on alone?'

Between pained grunts Máher replied.

'I'll be fine, it's only a surface wound, nothing deep, just a scratch. Once I stop the bleeding, I'll be good to go. One moment please.'

Máher poked two of his fingers through a fresh hole in his furs. Both his hair and his eyes flashed briefly and his face clenched in agony. The air around them was filled with the repugnant smell of burning flesh.

He must have cauterised the wound.

'Gods, that's a sensation I'll never get used to. Argh, good to go.'

'Good. Let's get inside quickly, before that ruckus attracts any more unwelcome attention. Follow me.'

Eris took the lead, a limping Máher following closely behind. As she climbed the stairs her heart raced with trepidation, but her course was set and she could do nothing but continue. So, with a shaking hand, she opened the house's front door and entered the entrance to the Burrow.

Chapter 18

Neesa

With a purposeful stride, Neesa opened the doorway to the balcony and stepped outside. Crouching low, to avoid detection, she shuffled to the balcony's railing. Peeking through its cast-iron frame, she looked over the villa's grounds below.

Disgruntled guests, afraid that whomever had murdered the guards would do the same to them, streamed from the compound, seeking an escape in their waiting carriages. Guards, weapons drawn and alert, marched around the grounds, their heads pivoting constantly as they searched for their unwelcome guest. Only the guards stationed by the front door remained at their station, unmoving, but no less attentive.

Shit. I can't leave this way, too many guards. I could try to bluff my way out, but I doubt it'd be worth the risk. A distraction might help though, hm.

Without further hesitation, Neesa re-entered the Master's room, took the lantern from where she had left it and cast it against a wall. Shattering instantly, oil sprayed from its ruptured reservoir, coating the bed, the floor, and the dresser's doors. A second later, the lantern's flame ignited the oil and with a woosh her master's room began to burn. Acrid smoke started to fill the chamber and while it stung her lungs to stay, Neesa tarried but for a moment, both to enjoy the destruction she had wrought and to leave a parting gift, a globule of phlegm, for her master's corpse.

You deserved worse, may you find it in the hells, you bastard.

Leaving the room, Neesa glanced furtively around, checking to see if anyone had heard her slaughter the Master. There was no one. Thanking her continued good fortune, Neesa stepped quickly around a corner, interposing a wall between herself and the guards below. There, she waited.

As thin tendrils of smoke weaved their way lazily from under her master's door, Neesa considered her next move. Part of her thought it reckless, foolish even, to consider such a wild plan as viable. To simply walk from the scene of, not only a crime, but a crime that she had committed, in full sight of guests and guards alike. It was madness. Sheer madness. However, an ancient adage, a favourite saying of an old friend, wormed its way to the forefront of her mind offering her a modicum of solace.

Oft times an uninviting known is preferable to a seemingly welcoming unknown.

Sighing inwardly to herself, Neesa steeled herself. She could make this work, all she had to do was wait for the right time and hope that she could sell her lies well enough.

Her heart pounded in her chest as worry and the fear of detection gnawed at her insides. But, as fate seemingly smiled upon her, she remained hidden from those that sought her and soon enough it was time.

The slim wisps of smoke emanating from the Master's room had grown to thick wafting waves. Flames unbound licked into the hallway from beneath the door, as they sought to expand their domain. Clearly visible from the foot of the stairs, all it would take was a casual glance for her sabotage to be detected.

Perfect. Time to stoke the fires of chaos and escape in the bedlam. Hopefully.

Turning from her nook, Neesa descended the stairs in a haphazard run. Pushing as much fear and hysteria into her voice as she could, she shouted to the guards by the manor's entrance.

'*Help!* For gods sake, help! There be fire a burin' in the Master's chambers, I can see the smoke as clear as day in the hall. T'was an intruder that did it, saw him I did, as he ran off down the hall.'

Simultaneously, both the guards turned to face her. To sell her act, a river of crocodile tears streamed down her face and while they hindered her vision somewhat, the doubt in their eyes was clearly visible.

'What nonsense is this? Surely, you're mistaken love.'

'No, I never be. Look for yourself if you don't believe me.'

Neesa stretched her arm towards the top of the stairs. One of the men looked to where she pointed.

'*Oh, shit!* She might be on to something mate, there's a ton of smoke up there, just like she said.'

Now that Neesa's tale had a corroborating source, the second guard shifted his attention from Neesa to the manor's interior.

'Fuck me sideways, you're right. Get the lads and start with the water buckets as quick as you can. I'll check if there's anyone up there that needs a hand.'

Wordlessly, the first of the guards ran off into the stream of fleeing party guests, no doubt seeking his off-duty compatriots.

Well, when he gets to the barracks he's in for a surprise.

The second man pointed his finger squarely at Neesa's chest and barked out a curt order.

'And don't you be going anywhere sweetheart. We're going to have to ask you a few questions once this shitshow is in order.'

Remaining exactly where she was, Neesa watched as the guard pulled a fresh handkerchief from his pocket, used it to cover his mouth and ran into the villa. She waited for a moment, looking around to make sure if no one was watching her. Seeing that nobody was paying her any particular attention, she wiped the tears from her face, strode casually up behind one of the fleeing guests and addressed her.

'Terribly ghastly business this isn't it? Was having a cracking time when someone decides to go and ruin it. You don't know what the devil is going on by any chance?'

The guest, a well-to-do lady clad in silken vestments, which Neesa found garish, but were no doubt of the latest fashion, neither turned nor slowed. As she hustled along, she twisted her neck and spoke to Neesa from the side of her mouth.

'Yes, it is, isn't it? I haven't heard much, seen even less, but there's a rumour circulating amongst the ladies that there's been some fiend prowling about. Apparently, and I don't believe this for as second mind you, he even killed a guard. It was Lady Belmore's daughter that supposedly found the body. Poppycock. That slip of a girl is nothing more than an attention seeking hussy.'

Says you, ignorant old bag.

'By the gods, that's a worrying thought, isn't it? One would think it impossible for any old random to mosey on into such a secure estate as this. It rather does lead one to wonder as to the quality of the help, doesn't it?'

'Indeed.'

With that one word their conversation ended as the women entered her awaiting carriage. Neesa continued walking, trying to remain as inconspicuous as possible, beyond the line of coaches, hoping that no one would accost her. No one did.

Passing into the shadow of a nearby building, by appearances a groundskeeper's cottage, and broke into a sprint. She was no longer concerned with what lay ahead, but knew that those behind would catch her easily is she dared to tarry.

Neesa quickly came to a second building, far larger than the first and clearly a stable. Skidding to a stop, she peered through one of its windows. The building's interior was cloaked in a swathe of shadow, lit by only a single candle which shone dimly. Squinting as hard as she could she saw no one.

A light burning for no one? Doubtful. There must be someone inside. Somewhere.

It was risky, the odds of detection were high, but Neesa thought it to be worth it. Acquiring a horse would expedite her escape exponentially. Shrugging to no one but herself, Neesa opened a side door, as quietly as she could, and entered the stables.

Most of the horses were at rest in their stalls, brushed, fed, and relieved of their tack. However, there was one that appeared to be ready to ride. A snow-white stallion stood calmly in the centre of the building, saddled, and tied to a post.

Strange, but also fortuitous.

Moving to the beast, Neesa soothed it with gentle placations while brushing its neck with the palm of her hand. The horse reciprocated Neesa's affections, whinnying in appreciation as it nuzzled against Neesa's chest.

'There's a good boy. How about we go for a little ride?'

Untying the horse's reins from the pillar they were tied to; Neesa led the stallion to the building's main door. The door was already partially opened, but before she could open it completely a voice from behind stopped her.

'Just what do you think you're doing *girl*. That's the Master's horse. He'd gut you for touching it, let alone stealing it.'

Neesa spun around rapidly, to see an elderly orc step from the shadows. His tusks were long and twisted, his hair grey and stringy. He wore a pair of simple trousers and a scuffed leather apron covered his otherwise bare chest.

He must be the stablemaster. Shit.

Overcoming her initial shock, Neesa ground her teeth, narrowed her eyes into a scowl and poured as much menace into her words as she could.

'Somehow, I don't think he will. You see, I've met the Master and when we last parted, he was, how should I put this, fucked beyond all recognition.'

Neesa paused for dramatic effect, taking a single step towards the silent orc.

'Now, I would say I'm sorry for the intrusion, but I'm not. Just as I am not sorry for stealing this horse. I need it, so I am going to take it.'

She took another step.

'If you try and stop me, I will kill you and not lose a moment of sleep over it. But, and this is a big but, if you just walk away, letting me leave unmolested, then I will let you live.'

Neesa took a third step.

'You might believe yourself capable of stopping me by yourself. You're not. You might think a single cry of alarm will draw the guards to your aid. It won't.'

As Neesa took a fourth and final step, she witnessed the orc's face contort in fear as he finally recognised the rage that fuelled her.

'When the guards ask their questions, and make no mistake they will, lie. Tell them you fell asleep. Tell them you saw nothing. Maybe they'll believe you. At least against them you'll have a chance. Against me you won't.'

Resigned to the futility of further protest, the stablemaster sighed heavily and with slumped shoulders gave a single dejected shrug.

'Fine then, she-devil. Take what you have no claim to and leave. I shan't stop you. But mark my words hellsborn, on the day you're caught I'll be there and I shall revel in your passing.'

Neesa turned away from the immobile orc and pushed open the stable doors. They opened easily, as their well-oiled tracks offered no resistance, but before she crossed their threshold, she turned back to the stablemaster.

'If I were you, I wouldn't hold my breath.'

Springing deftly into the air, Neesa swung her leg over the back of the horse, mounting it. At first it was skittish, neighing madly and pawing at the ground, as it was unused to having anyone other than the Master upon it. But after a few gentle pats and some soothing words, it quickly calmed.

A flick of the reins and a sharp 'huh' was all it took for the stallion to spring into motion. In that moment it became a horse in the truest sense as it forgot the stifling bonds of captivity and remembered what it was to simply be. Similarly, for an instant at least, Neesa forgot her own incarceration and revelled in the air rushing harshly against her face and the wild liberty it represented as she galloped.

Beneath her, Neesa felt the stallion's muscles ripple and sensed its desire to run free. At her heart she wanted to let it, to allow it to surrender to its primal desires, but she couldn't, lest it be felled by exhaustion. Instead, she slowed the beast to a steady trot.

There is still one thing I must do before I leave.

Once she had exited the Master's estate, she steered her mount from the road and followed the exterior of the palisade. The ground was open, so the going was fast and easy.

Like thunder Neesa rolled into the slaves' portion of the estate. Without slowing, she grabbed a burning torch from its sconce. Under the flickering light of the flame her visage glowed as a hellish agent of vengeance. Spurring her stallion once she guided the beast to the barracks where the half-elf girl lay. She muttered a prayer to each of the gods that dealt with death, biding the girl's spirit to travel well, then threw the torch onto the buildings thatched roof.

The building caught fire quickly as it was dry from the recent lack of rain. For a while Neesa sat and watched it burn, captivated by the way the flames danced. In no time at all the roof collapsed, weakened by the raging inferno that consumed it. Unbidden the horse backed away from the heat, but Neesa's calming touch prevented it from bolting.

Idly, Neesa considered her actions. Consigning the body of the elf-girl to the flames seemed somehow inappropriate to her. She had heard it to be a common practice amongst some cultures, but every corpse she had thus far encounter had been buried.

What an odd thought, why should it matter what we do when with the body once the spirit is gone?

Far too long Neesa sat vigil, spellbound, as she paid her final respects. Only when the barracks was too far gone to be saved did she leave, guiding her horse out of the compound. Not from any sense of nostalgia, Neesa glanced back over her shoulder as she passed through the palisade gate. A deep sense of satisfaction surged in her chest as the night sky glowed from the flame consuming the Master's villa.

Chapter 19

Neesa

The morning air was still and a light mist hung over the wood. The trees creaked and moaned as the cresting sun cast its warmth over their branches. Chirps from birds and growls from miscellaneous ground dwelling beasts echoed throughout the forest as critters, both large and small, went about their business. A lone horse, once the property of the one called Master, pawed quietly at the soft earth as its new owner, Neesa, slumbered uneasily upon a bed of leaves.

The tell-tale snap of a dry twig breaking under the weight of a careless footfall was all it took for Neesa to awake. With a start, she sat up, breathing heavy, straining her ears, and squinting her eyes, scanning her surroundings intently. She neither heard nor saw a thing, but not for a second did she believe herself to be safe. While staying both as low and as quiet as she could, Neesa shuffled to a nearby tree and started to climb. Once she had reached a reasonable height, and believing herself to be well enough concealed, she stopped and waited.

Please gods, let it be nothing.

All the while staying as still as she could, Neesa scanned as much of the forest floor as she could. Her eyes darted from left to right, fixating on any movement, no matter how small, only to disregard it as an innocuous occurrence or an optical illusion. After a while Neesa felt hope begin to rise in her chest as she started to believe that what she had heard was nothing, that she was safe. Alas, that hope was proved to be false as the fern leaves below her parted to reveal a man traversing the underbrush. To Neesa he was a complete stranger, his face unrecognisable and his attire foreign.

An Imperial agent perhaps?

Almost immediately the man spotted the Master's horse. He rushed to the animal's side and while Neesa saw him wave his arms, bidding others to join him, she couldn't tell to whom, or how many there were, the man was communicating.

Motionless Neesa sat, hands fixed firmly over her mouth, afeared that even the smallest of movements, or an errant breath, would reveal her position.

Below her the first man was joined by three others. They offered no greetings and spoke in hushed tones, barely above a whisper, but if she focussed, Neesa could hear them well enough to discern what was being said.

'This is Telamon's steed all right, no doubt in my mind. Fits the description perfectly.'

Telamon. His name was Telamon.

'Good now we just have to find the blue-devil cunt that took it.'

'Yeah, and gut her.'

'Aint we gunna try and take her alive?'

'Nah. Fuck that. Reward's the same either way and hauling a corpse is easier than carrying a live one.'

'Suppose so.'

'Now, she shouldn't be too hard to find and she's probably close by. She would've taken the horse if she'd scarpered already.'

'Too right mate. Okay, fan out lads and keep your volume down and your eyes peeled, she could be anywhere.'

Neesa watched the four men spread out in separate directions. Thinking it best to act, she eased herself from the nook she had been resting in and climbed down the tree as quietly as she could. Going was slow, as the last thing she wanted was to be discovered while so exposed, but miraculously she reached the ground undetected.

Thank the gods for small mercies.

Crouching as low as she could, Neesa stalked through the underbrush, passing as a whisper, unheard and unseen. Falling in behind one of the men, she quickened her pace to close the gap between them. Once within reach she rose from the undergrowth as an avenging phoenix would from the ashes, clasping her hand over the man's mouth. He struggled, desperately trying to free himself, but it was for nothing. A single power twist was all it took for Neesa to snap the man's neck, wrenching his brain free from its stem. Slowly Neesa eased the corpse to the ground, all the while listening for the cries of alarm that would herald her discovery. She heard none.

Ducking low once more, Neesa moved in search of her next victim. Before long she found another man. Engrossed in his task he failed to hear Neesa as she snuck up behind him. Although she believed herself to be treading with the utmost care, she stepped on a dry branch.

Alerted to Neesa's presence, the man spun around. With the agility of a panther, he kicked out at her. Caught off guard, the man's foot slammed into Neesa's chest. Air rushed from her lungs and the force of the blow sent her tumbling across a floor of dead and dying leaves.

'On me lads! The bitch is over here!'

Quick to regain her footing, Neesa drew her sword and lunged at the man in one fluid motion. Startled by her speed the Imperial agent failed to parry her strike. The tip of Neesa's blade sunk into the man's chest, plunging deep. Blood spurted from his mouth as he exhaled in surprise. As he started to fall Neesa rapidly withdrew her sword from the man's torso and swung it backhanded across his throat. His eyes fluttered as a geyser of crimson erupted from his neck and he keeled over lifelessly into the leaves and dirt.

Alerted to her presence, the two remaining agents closed in on Neesa. The first charged at her, the edge of his longsword flailing towards her wildly as he swung with abandon. Neesa easily sidestepped the blow, but was caught off guard by the fourth man. Her shoulder exploded in a sudden blast of pain as a crossbow bolt thudded into her. The wound from the night before, which had barely begun to heal, reopened, soaking her kimono, and showering the forest floor with her blood.

A wounded cry, primal and terrifying, thundered from her mouth as the physical torment goaded the darkness within her broken soul. Neesa felt the rage in her chest rise, she offered it no resistance, instead she welcomed it, letting it consume her. All pain was washed away, replaced by fury.

Kill. Maim. Murder. Argh!

Snarling and wild-eyed, Neesa leapt away from the closest man and threw her sword at him. Dumbfounded by her illogical attack, the man stood frozen, unable to parry or dodge, as Neesa's sword skewered him. Impaled, and dying, the agent mustered the last of his strength to swing his longsword at Neesa once more. However, the blow was feeble and Neesa swatted it away as if it were nothing.

Utterly spent, the man fell to his knees. Pouncing upon him, Neesa grasped the hilt of her sword with one hand while choking the agent with her other.

Holding him in place, she stared into the man's fear filled eyes. She felt no sympathy, no empathy, nothing but hatred. Twisting her blade, Neesa wrenched it from the man's stomach. The agent's flesh was torn asunder, his entrails poured from the laceration and plopped sickeningly onto the ground. Captivated, Neesa watched as the light of life faded from the man's eyes.

More!

Still enraged, Neesa turned to the final soldier, her mouth curved upwards into a hellish grin. Walking slowly towards the man, she mocked his clumsy attempts to reload his crossbow with chuckles and sneers. Eventually the bolt was loaded. He raised the weapon to his shoulder and fired. Too hastily. Neesa didn't even react as the bolt flew past her harmlessly.

Instead of fleeing, which would have been prudent, the man lowered his crossbow and started to reload it. His hands shook, his face was warped by terror and the front of his trousers were soaked with piss. Despite these handicaps, he managed to rack his bow's string and place a bolt in its rail, but before he could shoulder his weapon, let alone fire it, Neesa was on top of him.

Neesa's hand shot out, encircling the man's throat. She squeezed tightly, her claws biting into the agent's flesh, droplets of blood welling from their tips. Weapons forgotten, the man gasped for breath, eyes pleading for mercy.

Kill!

Neesa raised her sword, pointing its tip towards the man's face. Sensing what was about to happen, he squirmed, desperately trying to break Neesa's hold. Calmly Neesa eased the point of her blade into the agent's eye. His twitching intensified, but still Neesa held firm. Meeting no resistance, the blade sunk deeper and deeper into the man's eye. A quick thrust drove the sword home, breaking the sphenoid bone behind his eyeball and piercing his brain. Immediately the man fell limp and Neesa withdrew her sword from the corpse, letting it tumble to the ground unhindered.

Victory claimed, the red haze blurring Neesa's vision dissipated as she calmed. As the rage faded the pain in her shoulder returned. Contemptuously, Neesa snapped the head from the bolt, wincing as a shot of concentrated agony stabbed into her arm, and ripped the shaft free from her wound. Kneeling, she cut a strip of cloth off of the nearest corpse's tunic and tied it tightly around her wounded shoulder, groaning in discomfort as she did so.

I definitely need to find a healer, or cleric, but for now this will have to suffice. Not ideal.

Echoes unnatural to the wilderness drifted into Neesa's ears. Perking her head in their direction, she listened for more. They were subtle, originating from quite the distance, but they were there. The thudding of hoofbeats and the shouts of men. In Neesa's mind there was no doubt, yet more had come, searching for her.

Shit. Time to go.

Desperation driving her, Neesa ran to where she had left the Telamon's horse. It was gone. Cursing, Neesa concentrated, gauging the direction where her pursuers came from the best she could. It was difficult, but thinking that she had discerned it well enough, she turned to the opposite direction and sprinted off as fast as she could.

Time lost all semblance of meaning as Neesa ran. It was definitely daytime, the sunlight peeking through the canopy above her alluded that, but as to the exact time, she had no notion. One tree looked much the same as the next, the uniformity its own form of sensory deprivation. Had she been running for hours or only minutes? In reality it mattered not. For Neesa there existed a simple truth, continue to run or die.

Bang!

Startled, Neesa ducked behind a nearby tree as an explosion echoed throughout the forest. Though it was loud, and appeared to be close, Neesa had no idea what could have caused it. She had never heard the likes of it before.

Bang!

Another loud explosion boomed through the trees. Was this one closer than the one before it? Neesa couldn't tell.

Bang!

This time it was definitely closer.

Bang, bang, bang!

More explosions.

What in the seven hells is happening?

Silence.

As unexpectantly as they had begun, the explosions ceased. Somehow, in the throes of this newfound peace, the woods seemed even quieter than what they had before. Neesa found it somewhat unnerving, unnatural even, but she pushed her worries from her mind and resumed running. Not for long. The forest soon thinned and opened to reveal a clearing before her. Cautious, Neesa slowed, hid herself on the underbrush and approached with care.

At the centre of the clearing two men sat, casually eating a fireside meal. She could smell the food from her hide and it smelt good. Her stomach rumbled, making its desires known, and her mouth watered.

Damn. I didn't realise just how hungry I was until now.

Neesa couldn't see much of the men themselves, but she knew that they weren't Imperial agents. Their grey hair and elderly frames contradicted such an assertion and their carriage, which sat nearby, was far too opulent for common footmen.

Hm, perhaps they can help. If they prove to be hostile, I'll just kill them.

Deciding to take a chance on these strangers, Neesa stepped from the underbrush and walked towards them.

Chapter 20

Baron Victor von Grumanhieser III

Scant few clouds blemished the cerulean sky as the sun crested its zenith. The grass that flowed across the hill dotted fields was far from lush, but was by no measure dry. Summer was still young and had yet to impose the full extent of its withering scorn onto the land. Save for the occasional bird of prey gliding in the sky, not a single animal could be seen, nary a deer, rabbit, or horse.

The landscape was pristine, save for a single road, even though in actuality it was barely more than a dirt track, that winded lazily from north to south. The trail was almost entirely empty. Only a single carriage juddered along the poorly kept track.

As carriages went, it was only moderately fancy. It was obviously not a common mail or passenger coach, the gold trim curving elegantly along its side dissuaded any such notions. But it was far from the grandest of coaches. The gold was only paint after all.

It was pulled by a pair of horses. Those who managed to get close enough would be able to tell that they were mares, but for those stuck at a distance they would simply describe them as black.

A lone man sat in the driver's seat. His grey hair betrayed his advanced age, but he did not hunch an inch, rather he sat ramrod straight. His head constantly swivelling from side to side, eyes alert for any danger.

Noticing no danger, but spying a promising spot to stop the carriage for lunch, the man examined the position of the sun. Gauging that the time was about right, the man guided the carriage off of the road and into a small clearing. A small copse of trees stood sentinel at its centre, providing welcome shade and the possibility of game.

As the carriage shuddered to a halt, a voice yelled from the inside of the cabin.

'Jeeves! Why in damnation are we stopping?'

The man had already stepped down from the carriage and moved to the cabin's door. Opening the carriage, he was met by the perturbed stare of a grizzled man covered in various alchemical substances.

'My Lord. We were passing a prime spot, so I decided it would be a capital idea to stop for a spot of lunch. If that suits my Lord of course, if not we can continue.'

The Baron's brow furrowed.

'Good gods Jeeves. It can't be time for a meal yet, I've barely finished my breakfast.'

'I'm sorry my Lord, but breakfast was several hours ago. It's currently past midday.'

'Really? It sure doesn't feel like it.'

The Baron pushed his head out of the carriage's doorway, Jeeves gracefully stepped out of the Baron's way. Looking towards the sky, he noted the position of the sun. He could see where it was, being the sun, it was hard to miss, but he had no idea of how its position related to what time of the day it was.

There's no way I'll admit to that smug bugger that I have no idea what I'm doing. Or what the time is.

Instead of revealing his ignorance, the Baron rubbed his chin and nodded in a knowing manner.

'I'd say your bang on Jeeves. Must have just got lost in my tinkerings, always surprised at how time flies when one's busy. Now, you get the food sorted and while I stretch out a bit.'

Jeeves bowed to the Baron.

'It will be done at once My Lord.'

Ha, fooled him.

Jeeves walked away from the Baron with a distinct purpose. Reaching the rear of the carriage, he opened one of the many compartments and methodically started withdrawing all of the necessities for a proper meal. First came a fold out table, then a red and white stripped table cloth, an assortment of cutlery followed and then, at last, the raw food stuffs.

The Baron stepped slowly from the carriage's cabin, stretching the kinks from his back and neck. Looking around the clearing, he was not at all surprised to see that Jeeves had indeed found the perfect spot to stop for a while.

Blasted man is either as lucky as a devil or just phenomenally skilled. Heck, the bugger's probably both.

However, as enticing as Jeeves's cooking was, the Baron was more interested in the possibilities that the nearby cluster of trees presented.

'Jeeves! I still need to field test Peacemaker and those trees over there might be hiding some critters. It'll be damn fine if I could rustle us up some fresh meat. Your salads are damn fine and all, but a man needs his protein. And for the love of the gods, do not get me started on your vegetables, they are positively awful.'

Not bothering to wait for a response, the Baron strode purposely towards the trees. As he went, he pulled Peacemaker from its makeshift holster and double checked that it was loaded. Six bullets sat in the gun, each in their own separate chamber, ready to be fired.

Capital.

Pulling the hammer back into the firing position, all the while keeping his finger outside of the trigger guard, the Baron squinted into the copse, eyes peeled for movement. He saw nothing, but a sudden thought popped into the Baron's head.

Hm, while I obviously need to test Peacemaker on live targets, examining the penetrative properties of the projectiles on inanimate objects may also be of scientific value. Plus, I could use the practice firing the bloody thing.

Spying a particularly thin sapling, the Baron raised his arm, pointed the gun at the sapling and gently squeezed the trigger. The hammer slammed into the firing pin, igniting the black powder.

Bang!

The ensuing explosion projected the lead bullet at a prodigious velocity. Missing his target by mere inches, the Baron readjusted his aim and fired again.

Bang!

This time the bullet struck just where he was aiming. Splinters flew from the young tree as sparks would from a grindstone. Severed in twain the sapling keeled over.

Not bad. Recoils manageable, larger grain counts could become a bit of bother to handle though, might need both hands to accurately fire it. Have to test it, but I doubt the accuracy of this weapon at longer ranges, perhaps a long-barrelled variant would be better suited for that?

Turning to a larger tree the Baron took aim and fired again.

Bang!

With a thud the bullet thumped into the tree. Pausing briefly, the Baron composed himself. Fanning the firing hammer while simultaneously holding the trigger down, the Baron fired three rapid shots at the oak.

Bang, bang, bang!

Only one of the three bullets hit the tree.

Well then. It's got a decent rate of fire if pressed, but the loss of accuracy might not be worth it. Plus, the increased fire rate might damage or wear out some of the gun's components. I'll need to test that some more. It'd probably be best if I avoid doing that, at least until I can improve the design or get better at shooting.

Walking up to his target, the Baron inspected the bullet impact sites on the tree.

It cut through the sapling just fine, but barely put a dent in this oak. Hm, light amour shouldn't prove much resistance, but denser materials might be a problem. I'll either have to increase the grains of powder in the bullet, use a different material for projectiles, use larger projectiles or some combination of those variables.

Opening Peacemaker's cylinder, the Baron emptied the spent brass into his pocket, being mindful to not drop any. Grabbing a handful of live rounds from a belt pouch the Baron carefully slid a single round into each of the six chambers, rotating the cylinder as he went.

Need to think of a faster way to reload the gun as well, sliding one bullet in at a time seems so damn inefficient. Maybe I could develop a clip or some such that allows me to load all six bullets at once? Bears further investigation and experimentation.

Field test completed, and lost in thought, the Baron wandered casually back to the carriage. Beside the picnic accoutrements a small fire was burning happily. Above the flames sat two plump rabbits and although they were not yet cooked, they already smelled delicious. Jeeves, who now wore a spotted apron over his suit, was in the middle of chopping a variety of plant-based foodstuffs, which the Baron thought looked suspiciously like vegetables.

'Nicely done Jeeves. It's coming along amazingly I see. Can't wait to have at it. Don't know how you do it my good man, I couldn't find a trace of wildlife at all.'

Blast. I forgot to try and hunt something. What would I do without that man?

'That's what I'm here for my Lord. It will be ready shortly my Lord, have a seat and make yourself comfortable.'

The Baron did as Jeeves suggested, sighing happily as he lowered himself into a foldout iron chair. He had barely begun to contemplate the engineering, and materials, required to build a bridge that spanned continents, when Jeeves presented his lunch to him.

A full cooked rabbit occupied the majority of his plate. Thin twisting tendrils of steam rose leisurely from the perfectly seasoned meat. It smelt even better than what it had before. Surrounding the rabbit was a variety of vibrant salads, green, orange, and red, dressed with a light coating of dressing. They were wonderful. The only fault that the Baron could find with the meal was the vegetables. Avoiding them to the best of his ability, while occasionally flicking them from his plate whenever Jeeves wasn't looking, he devoured the food with a gusto that betrayed just how hungry he actually was. Once he was finished, the remaining vegetables still untouched, the Baron wiped his chin with a napkin and expelled an epic belch.

'Oh dear, pardon my impropriety Jeeves, but that really did hit the spot. Didn't rightly know how hungry I was. Damned fortunate you found those rabbits by the by, just wouldn't have been as good without them. Meal would have been perfect, it's too bad you had to go and put fu…'

Though he knew it was rude to do so, Jeeves stopped the Baron mid-sentence.

'My Lord. It appears that we have a guest.'

'What now?'

The Baron noticed that Jeeves was staring over his shoulder intently. He turned his head to look at whatever it was that his manservant was fixated upon. There before him, barely beyond the treeline, was a lone figure staggering slowly towards them.

The Baron thought the figure most odd. Even at this distance he could easily see that it was a woman, but she was a woman the likes of which he had never seen before. Her complexion was the darkest of blue and her hair the deepest of purple. Two spiralling horns curved backwards from the side of her forehead and a tail slithered discreetly from her rear. She was clearly not human, though still humanoid in nature, yet as the Baron tried to place her lineage, he couldn't, he had no idea of what she was.

She's not one of the common races, that much is obvious. Not an iasgair, a builg or a dragonkin. Could be an elementarian, but I've never heard of one with her complexion. Confounding.

Whatever the woman was, as she got closer the Baron noticed that she was injured. Blood was dripping in a steady flow from her shoulder. Without thinking, the Baron leapt from his chair and moved to help the woman. However, he was stopped as Jeeves blocked his path with his arm. The Baron turned to his manservant, a quizzical look on his face.

'Apologies my Lord, but she's armed. It might be best if I go first, just in case things go awry.'

Although it pained the Baron to see an injured woman and do nothing about it, he nodded, gesturing for Jeeves to do as he wished.

'As pragmatically sensible as always Jeeves. Be my guest.'

Jeeves walked slowly towards the woman, his arms raised as non-threateningly as possible, palms facing towards her. The Baron felt his heartrate increase as trepidation stabbed at his chest. He looked on helplessly as the women reached for the blade behind her back. Jeeves stopped his approach and tried to talk her down, gesturing towards the Baron and their camp. The Baron couldn't hear what was said, but whatever it was clearly worked. Nodding towards Jeeves, she dropped her hand from her sword's hilt.

Breathing a sigh of relief, the Baron watched as the pair walked back to the clearing, the woman leaning on Jeeves, using him as a crutch. As they reached the Baron they did not stop and Jeeves only offered the simplest of introductions.

'My Lord, this is Neesa. Neesa, this is Baron Victor von Grumanhieser III, but everyone just calls him Baron, or my Lord if they're feeling formal.'

Uncertain of himself, the Baron waved nervously.

'Hello. Neesa.'

Neesa tipped her head and offered a single word as greeting.

'Baron.'

Oh my. As introductions go, that was not my finest.

Ignoring the Baron, Jeeves sat Neesa down by the fire, giving up his own chair. Then he knelt down so he could address the woman while looking her in the eyes.

'Unfortunately, there isn't much of our lunch left for you, but I'll tell you what. How about I mix the leftovers into a stew. Just need to add a few extra spices to the mix and I am certain it will turn out amazing. It won't take me more than five minutes. But first, let me tend to your wound. I have a needle and some thread in the carriage. I'll have you stitched up in no time, the Baron can attest to my skills. Just ask him.'

The Baron felt his face flush as Neesa gave him a sideways look, but she said nothing to him. Instead, she returned her attention back to Jeeves, dipping her head in thanks.

'Thank you.'

Chapter 21

Baron Victor von Grumanhieser III

The trio sat in silence around the campfire as Jeeves stirred his stew. True to his word, in less than five minutes it was ready. After pouring out a bowl, and handing it to Neesa, she attacked the meal with a vigour of one who had not eaten well for an age. She cared not for decorum, devouring the entire portion in a hurricane of mess and spittle. Once finished, she eagerly held out the bowl for a second serving. Jeeves abided. Wordlessly, the Baron watched on aghast, and more than a little impressed, by the veracity at which Neesa ate.

Good gods. That woman can eat.

From the distance, shattering the idle calm, the sounds of approaching hoofbeats drew the Baron's attention away from Neesa. Reacting faster than the others, Jeeves yelled to the woman.

'Neesa! Into the carriage and hide, quickly!'

Immediately, Neesa dropped the unfinished bowl of stew onto the ground, thick gruel spilling from its ceramic rim as it spun. As fast as a startled jackrabbit Neesa ran to the coach, climbed its stairs, and slammed the door shut behind her. Not a moment too soon.

Three riders charged into the clearing, swords drawn, angry sneers across their faces. Their mounts skidded to a halt scant few feet in front of Jeeves, each whinnying as they reared onto their hind legs. Jeeves stood impassively waiting for the riders to address him, his face stern and posture unyielding.

He didn't have to wait long. The central rider, apparently their leader, spoke first.

'Oi! Old man, we're lookin' for a blue devil-spawn. It was headin' in this direction and we need to know if you've seen it.'

As he responded, Jeeves's voice was low and calm, but having had known him for his entire life, the Baron could tell that his butler was tense.

'Good day gentlemen. It appears you have me at a disadvantage. Just what is a devil-spawn?'

A second rider, impatient at the delay or perhaps seeking to prove himself, interjected before his leader could respond.

'You know, it's a, what-ya-ma-call-it, an infernati, from the hells.'

Oh. She's an infernati. I should have known, it's practically obvious.

The lead rider said nothing, but glanced disapprovingly at his comrade, clearly mad at being cut off.

'Oh, I see an infernati. Well then, if I may be too bold, for what reason do you seek her?'

Inwardly, the Baron cursed. It was clear that they were seeking Neesa, but they had not mentioned their targets sex. All it would take would for the riders to uncover Jeeves's deception was the realisation of this fact. As sneakily as he could, the Baron eased Peacemaker from its holster.

'That's none of your business, Mr fancy-pants. Now answer our fuckin' question!'

'There's no need for vulgarities, my dear man. Let us remain civil. As to your initial inquires, I must regretfully inform you that neither myself, nor my master for that matter, have seen any devil-spawn, blue or otherwise, here, or anywhere else. I do wonder though, what is it that you will do to her once you find her?'

This time the Baron cussed audibly under his breath. For a moment he wondered what Jeeves was playing at, but then it dawned on him. The bloody fool was goading these men. He was actively trying to start a confrontation. However, it was not working. They were too dumb to realise. As quietly as he could, the Baron cocked his gun.

'For someone wo hasn't seen it, your actin' mighty concerned for its welfare. Why the hells should you care about what we do with our property?'

Jeeves's eyes narrowed.

'The measure of a man is not how he treats those he deems his equal. It is how he treats those less fortunate than himself. You and yours are scum of the highest order. Leave now.'

'You fuckin' wot mate?'

That's gone and done it.

The Baron reacted the fastest. Drawing Peacemaker, he pointed it at the chest of the rightmost rider. Holding his breath and bracing for the recoil, he fired.

Bang!

An explosion echoed throughout the clearing as a bullet flew incomprehensively fast towards its target. His aim true, the projectile slammed into the centre of the rider. His leather armour offered no protection, it didn't even slow the bullet down. Vanishing into the man's chest, only to burst from his back an instant later, blood, bone and organs gushed from the projectile's exit wound. Free from fanfare, the man simply slumped sideways off of his horse, already dead.

Jeeves was the next to act. Far spritelier than his age would suggest, he ran towards the central rider. As he moved, he slipped a metallic disc from up his sleeve into his hand and threw it at the leftmost rider. Humming as it flew, slicing the air in twain, it curved in a graceful arc. Jeeves's aim was exceptional and the blade sunk deeply into the rider's throat. The man's eyes went wide as arterial blood sprayed from the wound.

Desperately, the man clawed at the disc, urgently trying to remove it from his neck. He succeeded, which only served to hasten his demise. More blood spurted from the wound, pouring over his chest and down his gullet. Half drowned and half exsanguinated, the rider succumbed to his wound and keeled over limply in his saddle.

Barely having time to register the swift demise of his compatriots, all the final rider could cognise was the profound danger he was now in. Too afraid to fight, he broke. Spurring the flank of his horse, the rider spun his mount around. When the strangers were behind him, he dug his heels into his horse's side and started to gallop away.

Not today chum.

Re-arming Peacemaker, the Baron took a deep breath and held it. Steadying his heartbeat as much as he could, he gently squeezed the gun's trigger.

Bang!

A second resounding detonation reverberated throughout the clearing. One moment later the top of the rider's head exploded in a puff of red mist, bone and brains disintegrating as a bullet careened into them. Lifeless, the man's body toppled off of his horse and rolled over the grass.

'My Lord. I must say that was an absolutely cracking shot.'

'Yes. It was. Wasn't it?'

Too bad I was aiming for the centre of the bastard's back. I think Peacemaker might need some adjustments. Or some modifications for shooting at longer ranges. Perhaps both?

A shout from the carriage drew their attention.

'Quit your blathering! They were only scouts. More will be about soon enough, especially with all the racket you're making. We need to leave now!'

Both Jeeves and the Baron ran to the carriage as fast as they could. Jeeves climbed into the driver's seat, while the Baron joined Neesa in the cabin.

'All aboard, Jeeves. Now get us the hells out of here!'

'Hah'

Jeeves whipped the reins down the horses' backs. As if stung by a wasp, they whinnied and accelerated. Slowly the carriage rumbled from its standstill, momentum building as inertia was overcome.

Hitting a bump as they returned to the road, the carriage jumped. Both Neesa and the Baron gripped the wall of the cabin, cussing, as their arses flew several inches off of their seats. Sticking his head out of the window, the Baron yelled over the rushing wind.

'I know we're in a hurry Jeeves, but take a bit of care will you!'

'Sorry my Lord. I'll endeavour to be more careful henceforth!'

Sure, you will.

Pulling his head back into the cabin, the Baron regained his seat. As soon as he did, Neesa slid herself over to him, her face a hair's breadth from his. She hissed at him angrily.

'Where are we going?'

As he looked into Neesa's eyes, the Baron saw a well of pain and torment, but that was not what scared him. Beneath the hurt there was something else, a bottomless pit of endless rage and infinite fury. In that moment he knew, that to lie to this woman would be an error most grave and to make an enemy of her would be suicidal at best. Normally, he eschewed telling falsehoods, but in this instance telling the truth was his only recourse.

'North. We are bound for the Empire. You see, I'm going to visit a private collector of antiquities, concerning a scholarly matter. Never met the man myself, but he graciously invited me to his estate and I couldn't really turn it down. Um, why do you ask?'

The Baron saw the colour drain from Neesa's face as anger was replaced by concern and worry. Her purple locks flew behind her as she thrust her head out of the cabin's window. Just as the Baron had done just moments before, she shouted at the top of her lungs to Jeeves.

'Jeeves! Turn the carriage around! Take us south, towards Súthburh! Right now!'

The Baron felt the carriage slow as Jeeves prepared to turn it around. Neesa's head returned to the interior of the cabin and despite the fear of the woman he had felt before, the Baron lost control of his emotions. Spittle flew from his mouth as he raved.

'Who in the Seven Hells gave you permission to order my manservant around as if he was your own! Last time I checked he was my gods damned employee and this was my gods damned carriage and the destination of which was my bloody choice! Who the hells do you think you are, accepting my goodwill and welcome, only to throw it in my face and usurp me and my property for the satisfaction of your whims! Answer me this!'

If the Baron had thought Neesa angry before, that was nothing compared to how livid she was now. Her eyes burned with fire as she poked her sharply clawed finger into the Baron's chest. She responded not with a raised voice, but with one barely above a whisper. Rather than detract from her menace, it enhanced it. The Baron felt his vigour shrink under the intensity of Neesa's retort.

'Those that hound me herald from the Empire. If we cross the border into there we will be captured, tortured, and killed. The Empire will send more of its agents after me, but the further we are from their borders the lesser the risk will be. I could leave you, go my own way on foot, but I wouldn't get very far and with war on the horizon, your fate would still be death at Imperial hands. As far as I am concerned, I just saved your life. Perhaps that is what I owed you for your earlier assistance, but perhaps I just chose to do it because I don't believe you to be a complete asshole.'

Neesa paused. The Baron sat reeling, both at the manner he had just been spoken to, and as he tried to comprehend what he had just been told.

War. Can't be. The Empire wouldn't dare, would they? Blast you're a fool Victor, of course they would. What of me? Would they use a foreign noble, albeit a nobleman in name only, as leverage or as a sacrificial message to their enemies? Yes. They would. Bugger me.

'Now. I suggest that you prepare yourself, make ready that blast-tube-thingy you seem so fond of, there will be more riders to deal with soon enough. We shan't be able to outrun them.'

No sooner than Neesa had offered her warning, the Baron heard Jeeves shout out.

'My Lord! Look lively. There are riders approaching from our rear. They're coming up fast and they do not look friendly.'

Sticking his head out of the carriage's window, the Baron looked behind them. Just as Jeeves had said a group of riders, four in all, were storming up the road towards them.

Not good.

Before the Baron could retreat back inside, one of the riders raised a crossbow at him and fired. The bolt whizzed past the Baron's head, bare inches from his scalp. Aghast, he ducked back into the cabin as fast as he could and shouted to Jeeves.

'They most assuredly are not friendly. Jeeves! They are hostile! I repeat they are hostile! Kill them if able.'

Turning to Neesa, the Baron continued to talk, albeit at a much more pleasant volume.

'Now, that goes for us as well my dear. Let's show them a good ole what for.'

Sticking his arm, followed directly by his head, out of the window the Baron pointed Peacemaker at one of the riders. Another crossbow bolt zipped by his head, but this time he held fast, ignoring the danger to his person. He squeezed the trigger.

Bang!

One of the rider's heads jerked backwards violently as a geyser of blood spurted from his forehead. The rider fell rearwards off of his horse, disappearing into a cloud of dust.

Not the one I was aiming for, but a good result nonetheless. Should definitely tell Jeeves, and perhaps Neesa too, that it was deliberate.

One of the Imperials accelerated rapidly, overtaking the coach. Jeeves swerved, attempting to run the man from the road, but the rider was able to manoeuvre his horse out of the carriage's way. Drawing his crossbow, the rider took aim at one of the coach's horses. Before he could fire, Jeeves threw a silver disc from his jacket sleeve. The shuriken spun through the air, slicing through the rider's wrist. Screaming in pain, the man dropped his weapon and clutched his blood-soaked arm, desperately trying to stop the bleeding.

His original plan thwarted; the rider forced his horse into those pulling the Baron's carriage. Gradually, the coach started drifting towards the edge of the road.

Poking his head out of the cabin window, the Baron looked towards the front of the carriage.

Bugger. If that fellow isn't stopped soon, we'll be forced off of the road. At these speeds that would be disastrous. I can make the shot.

Looking down Peacemaker's sights, the Baron squeezed the trigger gently.

Bang!

The rider was unharmed, as was his horse. He had missed.

At least I didn't hit my own horse, that would have been so embarrassing.

When it left the road, the carriage shuddered violently as it soared across the uneven ground. Re-cocking his weapon the Baron slowed his breathing as much as he could. As he bumped up and down, he offered a silent prayer to the mysterious clockwork being that had shown an interest in him.

Please, whatever your name is, let this work.

He squeezed Peacemaker's trigger once more.

Bang!

This time he found his mark. The rider crumpled from his saddle. Now rider-less, the Imperial horse slowed to a canter and peeled away from the carriage.

Thank you.

Swerving wildly to avoid a tree stump, the coach skidded on the dry ground, drifting as it returned to the road.

The remaining two Imperial horsemen followed closely behind, but made no efforts to overtake the carriage, clearly unwilling to repeat their comrades' mistake. One fired their crossbow at the carriage. Ducking his head at the last second, the Baron barely avoided being skewered by the projectile. The bolt thudded into the coach's woodwork, quivering in place.

Bang!

Another cloud of smoke filled the air as the Baron fired a shot at the rider in retort. Seconds later the rider fell cartwheeling from his horse as the bullet shattered his sternum.

Ha. Take that you blighter.

Seeing his compatriot fall, the final rider fell back outside of the Baron's effective range, content for the time being to simply follow his quarry. Chagrined, the Baron fired his final two shots at the rider.

Bang, bang!

Cursing as each shot missed its target, the Baron slumped into his seat. Temporarily defeated, he tipped his spent casings into an empty pocket and slowly reloaded Peacemaker.

I can't allow him to keep following us, but how do I deal with the bastard if he won't come into range?

Before he could consider the problem too deeply, a question from Neesa drew him from his thoughts.

'Did you get them all?'

The Baron sighed.

'I'm afraid not. There's still one of the buggers left. I can't hit him though, he's out of my range you see.'

'Well then. Why don't you wait here and I'll sort it out, I shan't be long. By the way, it might be a good idea to ask Jeeves to stop the carriage.'

'What?'

With her final word, and after ignoring the Baron's query, Neesa opened the coach's door. Immediately, she swung herself underneath the carriage. Startled, the Baron rushed to the still open door, trying to see where Neesa had gone and if she was alright. The only thing he saw was a final swish of her tail as she disappeared from view.

Goods gods. Just what in the hells is she up to?

Taking this opportunity to take a pot shot at the Baron, the Imperial rider fired his crossbow. His aim was poor and the bolt shuddered into the interior of the swinging doorway, more than a foot from the Baron's head. Despite this, the Baron flinched.

Whatever you're planning on doing, I hope you do it soon.

A blur of blue and black, originating for the coach's undercarriage, caught his attention. Aghast, the Baron watched on powerlessly as Neesa slid along the dirt road, drawing the sword from her back as she went. If the rider saw her, he made no indication of doing so, for he didn't shift from his course.

Of all the crazy, hair brained schemes. Gods.

Hoofs flew over Neesa as she glided under the horse. All it took was two swipes of her blade and the beast's forelegs were severed from its body. Blood sprayed from its legs as the horse screamed out in a pained shriek. Eyes wide with terror, the horse attempted to arrest its momentum, but it no longer had any means to do so. Instead, the horse's chest slammed into the road, cartwheeling the creature back over front. Unable to hold on, the rider was thrown from the horse. In a glorious arc he flew through the air. His impromptu flight quickly ended as he crashed into the dirt with a sickening crunch.

'Jeeves! Stop the carriage immediately!'

The coach slowed and the Baron watched, stunned, as Neesa walked casually up to the fallen rider. The man was not moving, but he must have still been alive, for Neesa knelt by his side and ran the edge of her sword along the man's throat, finishing him off.

Cold, but perhaps necessary.

The carriage ground to a halt and the Baron waited patiently for Neesa to catch up. She didn't hurry.

'Well, that was exhilarating. Shame my kimono got a bit scuffed, but that's better than being dead I suppose. Shall we continue then?'

The Baron didn't respond as she climbed the carriage's stairs and retook her seat. He simply closed the door and called out to his butler.

'All aboard Jeeves.'

*　　*　　*

Several hours after their encounter, the heat of the day had just reached its peak and the Baron was feeling more than a little out of sorts. Sketches of mechanical devices, assorted metallic contraptions and crafting components of all ilk's lay scattered throughout the carriage, temporarily forgotten.

Neesa sat silently looking out of the window, staring at nothing in particular. Till that moment the Baron had tried to leave her be, refraining from prying into what he saw as her business, but his typically insatiable curiosity had finally got the better of him.

'Excuse my inquires, and feel free to not answer if you don't want to, but why were those men chasing you so doggedly? What did you do?'

Slowly, Neesa turned. Her eyes, emotionless, met his.

'I was a slave, had been for most of my life. I couldn't take it anymore. So, I escaped. I killed my former master. I killed a whole bunch of his men. He needed to die and they, well, they deserved it.'

Neesa paused, allowing the Baron to ask any questions that he may have had. He had none, so she continued.

'In the process of my escape I freed a large number of other women from a life of servitude, systemic abuse, and rape. Unsurprisingly, there were many within the Empire that took offense to my actions and decided to have me killed.'

Her eyes narrowed, presenting a silent challenge.

'Will this be a problem for you, Baron?'

The Baron returned Neesa's stare with a smile.

'Not in the slightest. In fact, I believe we'll get along swimmingly. I can't abide those that take advantage of women and as far as I'm concerned there are few things more abhorrent than rape. If I had known that such behaviours were commonplace within the Empire, I never would have considered going there. I'm glad you ridded the world of those that would conduct themselves in such a vile manner.'

Neesa's visage instantly softened and she returned the Baron's smile with her own.

'It means a lot to me to hear you say that. I thank the gods that I was fortunate enough to encounter you and Jeeves. Without the pair of you, I believe that I'd now be dead. Thank you.'

Chapter 22

Thoron

As he moved towards the portal, Thoron felt his chest tighten in trepidation. Such a mode of transportation was foreign to him and he knew not what to expect. Cautiously, he reached out with his hand, as if he were about to test the temperature of water. As soon as the tip of his finger contacted the surface of the gateway, he vanished from the cavern.

Thoron lost all sense of spatial continuity as he hurtled along a tunnel of spinning, flashing blue. His body was awash with the strangest of sensations, too odd to explain, no words he could think of sufficed. Regardless, he couldn't help but to smile as tiny pinpricks of feeling, glorious in their oddity, exploded across his skin.

Ach, 'is aint n'all bad.

Looking forward at his outstretched arm, Thoron blinked in confusion. Strangely, his limb had been extended beyond the horizon, he could no longer discern where it ended. Looking down, he gasped, his legs were similarly elongated. Wherever he was, it was as though he had been stretched to encompass all of existence.

He barely had time enough to process this absurdity when the arcane passageway he was travelling through disappeared. Instantaneously, he blinked back into reality. Overcome by a wave of nausea, he bent over, vomiting the sparse contents of his stomach onto the ground. Coughing one last globule of spittle out of his mouth, he cursed to himself.

Fuck me. I've changed ma mind. I bloody hate portals.

Looking around he couldn't see a thing. It was pitch black.

Where in buggery am I?

He could feel solid ground beneath his feet, so he knew he wasn't in the void. Tasting the air left a stale taste in his mouth, the biproduct of damp and mildew.

I must be underground.

At least there was air to breathe.

No' the afterlife then. The deid dae no' need tae breathe.

Sniffing, Thoron found no trace of brimstone and the air was cool, so no nearby fire.

No' the seven hells. Neither am I near a volcano nor so deep as tae reach the magma flows.

He couldn't feel any excessive magical forces permeating around him.

No' the celestial plane. 'At ainlie leaves the mortal worlds, o' which I cuid be oan any o' them. Bugger. Suppose it cuid be worse, I cuid be stuck wi' ma cousins an' their homemade ale.

Thoron shuddered at that thought.

Gingerly, Thoron extended his hand into the darkness. He was met by stone, cool to the touch and polished smooth.

No' a natural cave then.

Spinning around in place, he traced his hand along the wall, searching for some kind of opening or doorway. He found one. Gauging its width, Thoron held his arms in front of him, lest he walk unwittingly into a wall, and strode into the darkness.

As he passed through the opening he heard, as much as felt, a strange pulsating thrum in the air around him. Thoron froze in place, fearing the wrath of some dire device or mechanism. Nothing happened. Holding his breath, he waited for another twenty seconds. Still nothing happened. Seeing no other option, Thoron took another step.

The moment his foot touched the ground, a pair of braziers ignited, one to his left and one to his right. Lit by some unseen magics, their eldritch flames flickered, crackling as they burned. Glowing green, their fire revealed a long, narrow corridor of polished marble floor and smoothly carved granite walls. Every ten feet another pair of braziers stood jutting from the wall. As of yet they were unlit, but Thoron supposed that they were akin to the first pair, insofar that they would ignite when approached.

Glad for the light, if not a little spooked by the ominous nature of its source, Thoron continued along the corridor. Strange shadows danced across the walls as he moved, eerily enthralling, he did his best to ignore them.

A sharp pain stabbed at his side. Looking down, he found his armour caved in, sundered steel puncturing his flesh. Assessing the damage, he knew it could be fixed, but not here and not by him. So, even though it pained him to do so, he stripped off his plate and threw it to the ground, abandoning it. Thinking it strange to wear a helmet devoid of any armour, Thoron lifted his galea from his head and discarded that as well.

'At's a bloody shame. A gambeson is better than nothing, but if things go awry, I'd still lek tae be clad in steel.

As he continued, his earlier suspicions proved correct. When he arrived at the next pair of braziers, they burst into flame, just as the first pair had. Simultaneously, the light from previous pair of braziers disappeared, their flames extinguished.

For hours and hours Thoron walked along the corridor. Every now and again he would lose sight of its end as it was obscured by a bend. Each time this happened a spark of hope blossomed in his heart, that perhaps this monotonous drudgery was at an end, but each time he was disappointed as the hallway continued.

Alone with his thoughts, Thoron couldn't help but to ponder how the events of the day had affected him. His soul still ached from the loss of his kin, at the injustices that had torn it in twain. The core of his being still burnt with an anger that, for now, was dormant, but it still smouldered in his chest, threatening to explode at any transgression. Powerlessness was tempered with purpose, but he still felt somehow hollow, like he could never be truly complete until he had achieved some semblance of vengeance. This bothered him. What would he become once said vengeance was his? Would he shrink to nothing as a lack of purpose diminished him? Or would he be forced to find new crusades, to fight for the rest of his life, just to stave off cancerous stagnation? He knew not the answers to these questions.

Hope rose in Thoron's chest once more as the hallway ahead of him disappeared beyond his sight.

I swear tae the gods if 'is is jus' another bend, a'll fucking lose ma shite.

Thoron turned the corner. The hallway was at its end.

Aboot bloody time.

Before him stood a pair of heavy stone doors. Carved upon them was the mirrored image of a gargantuan man, standing some fifteen feet tall, the entire height of the door. He stood naked, tattoos of various designs covering his well-muscled frame from head to toe. In place of eyes sat two large emeralds that glimmered majestically in the eldritch light. Locked in eternal combat, the man wielded an ornate sword and shield as he fought off an assortment of foes, most of which were alien to Thoron.

Symbols framed the edge of the doorway. Examining them Thoron noticed that they were not all of the same language. He recognised some as elvish and others as gnomish. A few of these words he knew, but in their entirety, he could read neither. Others were completely foreign, to him utterly unrecognisable. Eventually he found some common and dwarfish, those he could read. Both said exactly the same thing.

"Here lies the mortal husk of Dalinar. Only son of The First. Protector of all. Infinite font. The fulcrum upon which fate weaves."

Wracking his brain, Thoron could think of no historical figures of note that were named Dalinar. In fact, he had never heard of the name at all.

Whomever 'is Dalinar wis, he must hev lived an age ago. He wis obviously someone o' great importance an' history's memory is vast, fur him tae be completely forgotten attests tae that.

Shrugging, Thoron pushed on the door. Without a sound, not even the squeak of a rusted hinge, it swung effortlessly inwards. Initially, he was greeted by only darkness, but as the door thudded gently against its stops, innumerable braziers erupted with a familiar green light.

Revealed before him was a vast courtyard replete with sculpted statues, intricate fountains, manicured gardens, and a carpet of well-trimmed grass. Each of the statues was so well carved that they appeared as real-life subjects petrified into stone. The fountains stood silent, having long since ran dry, but were free from any grime or taint. Although Thoron knew little of stone craft, he could tell that they were exceptionally well made. All of the plants were lush and verdant. Thoron had no idea how plants could survive without sunlight, and here they didn't just survive, they thrived. It was as though the entire courtyard had been frozen in time, at the moment of completion to preserve its perfection.

As he took in the splendour, Thoron walked along a stone path. Fine frescos and murals covered the walls. The same man from the doorway, Dalinar, Thoron supposed, featured heavily. Sometimes he was alone in the wilderness, other times he was at the head of an army on the march, but primarily he was depicted in the throes of battle.

An adventurer, a leader, and a warrior all. 'Is Dalinar must hev bin quite the man.

Looking up for the first time, Thoron noticed that the roof was resplendent with constellations of stars and other orbital bodies. Most were foreign to him, but he recognised Térrtha, its three moons and the other four planets of the mortal realm. To the depiction's accuracy, he had no notion, but in any case, it was a truly stunning sight.

As the path drew to an end, Thoron was greeted by a second door set in a curved wall. This one was far smaller than the first, but far more ornate. Gold inlays juxtaposed reliefs of ebony. Dalinar featured once more, this time as the god-like father figure standing protectively over a sea of others, smaller perhaps in stature, but as intricately carved as Dalinar himself. Elves, dwarves, gnomes, orcs and many more bowed in deference to Dalinar, happiness clear in their eyes just as much as in their smiles.

Thoron pushed on the door and, just as the first had, it opened easily. Unlike the rest of this underground space, there were no sconces lighting the room's interior. Instead, it was lit by a shaft of natural light, beaming from somewhere above. An innumerable mass of dust motes, flittered through the beam, casting a rotating kaleidoscope of shadows against the room's walls.

Stepping into the chamber, Thoron was immediately fixated by its centre. There, in the middle of the light, stood a stone plinth, atop of which lay a man. But it was not just any man. Immediately recognisable, it was the man from the carvings, it was Dalinar.

Daring not to touch anything, Thoron walked around the statues that ringed Dalinar's corpse, examining the body as he did so. Dalinar's remains were preserved to perfection, so much so that he appeared to be sleeping rather than dead. As in life, in death he remained a giant. Thoron could only guess, but he suspected that the man was no less than nine feet tall.

I've heard o' goliaths, a people as large as 'is, but 'is man, Dalinar, is clearly a human. He's easily the biggest man I've ever seen.

Laying atop a sheet of purple fabric, he wore nothing, save for a simple loincloth. His head had been shaved clean and his body bore the same tattoos as his artistic likenesses.

By his side sat a shield atop a sword, almost covering it completely. Booth seemed of simple make and each was covered in a patina of grime and rust, the fate of all uncared-for weapons. Though he knew them to be functionally sound, Thoron believed that neither appeared to be at all befitting of a man of such seemingly high status.

Perhaps they're magical, enchanted. That would make sense.

Typically, Thoron thought that graverobbing was an unhonourable venture and one to be punished at every opportunity. However, in the corners of his consciousness a nattering of voices, small and indistinct, started to convince him otherwise. Rationalisations normally beyond his cognition arose at the centre of his mind. He had lost his own weapons and would need new ones, he had to be able to defend himself if attacked. These ones wouldn't be missed, their owner was dead, he no longer had need of them. Who would know, he could proclaim them his and no one would be able to prove otherwise.

Thoron shook his head, trying to rid his mind of these notions, but it didn't help. The voices grew to a deafening chorus, pushing him, urging him to just pick up the sword and shield. Unable to take any more torment, he relented. With a profound urgency, Thoron scooped up the weapons, clutching them to his chest as one would the most precious of loved ones.

At first, nothing happened, save for the relief of a newly quietened mind, but after a few seconds the weapons started to change. Their sickly green hue faded, giving way to pristine steel. Luxurious carvings and the finest of details, that were previously obscured, revealed themselves. It was clear to Thoron, who had lived amongst smiths his entire life, that these were the works of a master craftsman.

By the gods. If Gobannos himself forged these, he wuid be proud.

As he stood admiring the exquisite workmanship of the sword and shield, Thoron heard a strange voice in his head.

'*Strewth, am I glad you picked us up. I didn't know if you were gunna at first, you're a right stubborn bastard aint ya? Me an' my pal here have been stuck in this tomb for absolutely yonks and I'm literally bored out of my mind. Say hi mate.'*

A second voice, remarkably dissimilar to the first, started talking to Thoron in his mind.

'Good day, old bean. It's an absolute privilege to make your acquaintance. Call me Harry.'

Completely stunned, and at a loss for words, Thoron stood there mute as the voices in his head continued.

'Any who, let's get down to brass tacks, shall we? Me an' my mate here, Harry, are the objects you are currently holding in your hot little hands. I'm, strewth, where in buggery are my manners? My name is Barry, but call me Bazza, and I am the sword. I know, I look amazing, but I'm not just about showing off, when it comes to functionality, I'm fucking top notch. Harry, that's the shield you've got, is an absolutely top bloke. He doesn't talk much, but is one hells of a listener. And now that you've picked us up, we're yours. Well, until you end up like ole Daly babe here and carc it. But don't worry about that though because me an' Harry will make sure that doesn't happen for a really long time. Now, any questions?'

More than a little taken aback Thoron stammered a response.

'Um, mair than a few I'd say. How in buggery is a sword talking tae me? Whit if I dae no' want you? Nae offense. How'd I get into 'is mess? And where the fuck is the bloody exit?'

'I take it then you've never heard of sentient objectification then. Well, let me explain. In essence a soul, willing or otherwise, is extracted from a sentient creature, such as a human, and is placed into an object during its creation process. Don't ask me exactly how this is accomplished, all I know is that the process employs a very specific magical ritual. Regardless, the soul loses all memories of their previous life and become one with the object they inhabit, living for as long as it does. Which is essentially forever as such objects are practically indestructible. That is what Bazza and myself are, sentient objects. As sentient objects we can communicate to anyone who is attuned to our magical essence. As soon as you picked us up, that was you. Oh, we can also talk to each other, consider us for all intents and purposes a pair.'

'Crikey, Harry, I haven't heard you speak that much since Daly asked what our favourite musical instruments were. Good on you for coming you of your shell mate. Ha, ha, shield pun, get it? No, oh well. Now, back to you Thoron mate, mind if I call you Thor, shorten everything I do, in regards to you not wanting us, well you don't get a choice. You see, we're a bit cursed, nothing to fret over it's only a little curse. It just means you can't get rid of us. If you try, we'll just 'pop' back to your side, teleportation style. Like I said mate, we're in this together till you die or we break and it's like Harry has already said, we're bloody indestructible.'

Thoron tried to keep pace with what Barry was saying, but it was hard. He could hear what the sword was saying, but it was like his brain simply refused to properly process the information it was given due to the absurdity of it all. He considered interjecting, attempting to slow Barry down, but he just kept on talking.

'That reminds me. Hey Harry! Remember that time when you stopped that fire giant's hammer from squishing Daly's head. There wasn't even a scratch on you, I was damn impressed.'

'That was most assuredly one of my finer moments.'

'Too right it was mate. Now, what in buggery were we talking about Thor? Mm, that's right messes. Well, buggered if I know how you ended up here, that's got nothing to do with me. But I'm bloody stoked you showed up because we can't get out of this place without ya. Fun fact, you can't leave without us either. Ha, ha, that Daly for all his seriousness was a bit of a joker, if you know what I mean. Using his resting place as a prison for me an' Harry, cheeky bastard. Oh well, we knew someone would be along eventually.'

Unable to take any more, Thoron cut Barry off, shouting at the top of his voice.

'Enough! Where's the bloody exit!'

'That? Oh, that's easy. Just take us to that wall over there, the one with the picture of Daly duelling an Elder Dragon, that was a bloody good fight by the way, and stick me into the slot just above his head. After that just give me a little twist to the right and she'll be apples as they say.'

Thoron stood motionless processing all that he had heard. It took him a while. All the while he felt Harry and Barry emanating an aura of expectation, like they were waiting on tenterhooks for him to act. After thinking his situation through, and seeing no other options open to him, Thoron walked to the painting Barry described. The slot was easy enough to find, so without any further hesitation he inserted the blade into the opening and gave it a twist.

Sounds of mechanical whirring and grinding filled the room as a bevy of unseen mechanisms sputtered to life. A sudden hissing noise emanated from a section of wall to Thoron's right. Turning towards the noise, he noticed that a section of the façade had sunk back further into the wall. More gears ground out a clanking tune and the façade rose upwards out of sight. Peering into the newly exposed space, Thoron saw nothing, save for the sheen of a polished obsidian wall. He waited for another minute. Still nothing.

'Well, I must admit that was a bit of a let-down. I mean I was expecting something a bit more really, like a spooky tunnel, some creepy stairs, something really atmospheric you know? I mean it was like...'

Barry stopped speaking mid-sentence as a portal exploded into being in front of the obsidian. Green energy spiralled in clockwise circles, projecting warmth and filling Thoron's ears with an arcane thrumming.

Shite. No' another portal.

'Crikey, that's more like it. I mean, it's not exactly spooky, but it's definitely a little on the snazzy side.'

Bracing himself for the now familiar experience of portal travel, Thoron approached this one with more than a little trepidation. He reached out to touch its surface, but before he could Barry yelled out to him.

'Wait! It completely slipped my mind before mate, but there's something still in here you might want to take with us. On Daly's plinth there's a carving of a daemon, stick your finger in its eye, should be the right one if my memory serves, and you'll find a button. Press it.'

Glad for an excuse to delay entering the portal, Thoron moved over to Dalinar's body and found the carving that Barry was talking about. Sticking his finger in the daemon's right eye, he found a button and pressed it. With an audible 'shuck' the daemon carving popped out from the plinth, revealing a cavity behind it.

Reaching into the space, Thoron felt around. Just within his grasp, his fingertips brushed against an object, made from some kind of soft material. Taking care not to push the object further away, he pinched a fold of fabric between his fingers and pulled. Whatever it was, it offered no resistance and was easily dragged from the cavity.

The object, now easily discernible as a small leather bag, plopped into his lap. Thoron picked it up and thought at first that it was empty, for it was practically weightless, but his curiosity was not yet sated. Opening the bag, he peered inside, hoping to find some treasure or trinket, but alas, all he found was an inky black void.

An oddity to be sure, but I don't see any value in it. Hm, I wonder.

Shrugging his shoulders, Thoron put his hand into the sack. Expecting it to barely fit, he was surprised when the bag fully accommodated his hand, all the way to the wrist, easily. He was even more surprised when his hand kept on going. By the time Thoron reached the bottom of the bag his entire forearm was inside of it.

A wee bag 'at's bigger oan the inside. Useful.

Grasping around blindly, he felt the metalic tinkle of coins. Seizing a few, he took them out of the bag, his palm shone with a small pile of gold.

Very useful.

Putting the gold back into the bag and tying it onto his belt, he returned to the portal. Cursing, he shut his eyes tightly, covering them with his hands for good measure, and walked slowly into the vortex. He felt his body tingle and his stomach lurch as the magic propelled him into the unknown. Almost instantaneously, he felt his body return to normal as he left the portal's wormhole. Nausea struck again and he heaved dry retching over the ground, his stomach already emptied.

I fucking hate portals.

Chapter 23

Thoron

For the second time that day, Thoron wiped the spittle from his lips. Standing up straight, he found himself in a small chamber. A single lantern hung from the ceiling, burning with green flame, highlighting a circle of arcane runes on the floor. He had no idea what they meant, or what they were for, but suspected that they had something to do with the portal he had just exited. So, careful to not touch them, Thoron stepped out of the circle. When nothing happened, he sighed in relief.

Thank the gods. I've had enough o' bloody portals tae last me a life time.

Directly in front of him a black lever occupied the centre of the wall. Seeing nothing else in the room he gave it a pull.

Grinding and groaning, a section of the wall beside him rose into the roof slowly. A gust of fresh air rushed into the room and Thoron felt a surge of joyous relief. Even though he was used to subterranean life, and the breeze was warm to the skin, of late he had spent too much time in the constricting confines of ancient tunnels, it felt nothing short of amazing.

Leaving the room, Thoron was met by the sights and sounds of the wilderness. Wide open fields of grass coated the ground, be-speckled with tufts of wildflowers bursting with colour. Thickets of trees, both large and small, dotted the landscape, their branches moving lazily in the breeze. Birds were chirping happily and the undergrowth rustled as the small creatures that called it their home went about their business.

Looking to the sky, he noticed the dimming light of early evening. Guessing that he had three, maybe four, hours until sundown, he knew that he had to get moving. If he was fortunate a town would be nearby, if not, then he would have to contend with both hunger and exposure, neither were appealing.

By his own admission, Thoron was not a skilled survivalist. Normally, this would not have been a problem. Whenever he ventured from Summa Antemurale, he was with the legion, where there were scouts who could fulfil that role. However, for obvious reasons, he currently had no legionaries to assist him. Besides himself, the only ones he could count were Harry and Barry.

Unfortunately, neither was much help. Harry rarely spoke and Barry, well, Barry was Barry.

'Oi Thor, chuck a right at the next tree, I'm dead certain that's where we'll find a town or some such. Hey Thor, lets hunt some critters. You could throw me and 'POW' they'd be cactus. Then you'd be able to get some grub in ya mug. You need to keep up your strength for the fighting, plus, and say this with all the care in the world, you're starting to look a little on the skinny side. Yo Thor, you should climb that big arse tree over there and have a gander about the place, I'd wager you'd be able to see for miles.'

Before long, it was safe to say that Barry's incessant 'advice' was wearing thin on Thoron's sanity. He was lost and he was tired. But still he continued on, at every moment resisting the urge to smash Barry against a tree. For as near as he could tell, he walked for almost two hours, before he stumbled upon a trail. Hope surged in his chest, for typically trails lead to somewhere and somewhere was where he intended to go, but the sun now tickled the horizon. It would be dark soon. He had to get a move on. So, ignoring Barry's adamant protestations that the correct way to go was to the right, he turned left onto the path and carried on.

Only a short time had passed, when ahead of him on the trail a twig snapped. Too tired to notice, Thoron continued walking, oblivious. As he passed a pair of yew trees, two furred creatures emerged from the shadows of their trunks. Sensing movement behind him, Thoron spun around. Before him stood two adult bugbears, thick of fur and long of limb, snarling pointed teeth threateningly in his direction. They held no weapons, but their claws, sharped to wicked points, were undoubtedly weapons enough.

Thoron backed away slowly, drawing his sword and readying his shield. Adrenaline pulsed through his veins, banishing his fatigue, and even though his heart raced, his breath slowed as instinct and training took over. He gauged his enemies. Fully grown bugbears were typically fast and strong, but these ones looked underfed and scrawny. Perhaps they would be weaker than normal? He could only hope.

More twigs snapped further along the trail. This time Thoron heard them, but he dared not take his eyes from the bugbears in front of him.

Thir's mair o' the buggers behind me. Am surrounded. 'Is cuid be a problem. Thir's ainlie one thing fur it.

He charged.

Screaming as he ran, Thoron drew back his sword, ready to strike. Startled by his ferocity, the bugbears cowered behind their upheld arms.

'Yes! Kill them all Thor. Woo.'

Thrusting his sword at the bugbear on his right, Thoron sent his blade deep into the beast's abdomen. It shrieked, high pitched and frantic, clutching its stomach as blood flowed freely from the wound. The bugbear backed away slowly, disorientated. Chest heaving, the creature collapsed to the ground, its lifeforce gradually ebbing away.

Frenzy overcoming fear, the other bugbear swiped its claws at Thoron's face. Thoron saw the blow coming as if it was happening in slow motion. He knew that he should try and block the blow, but he was frozen, a single thought occupying the entirety of his mind.

Oh, shite.

At the last second, his arm shot upwards, as if on its own accord, and intercepted the bugbear's fist. Thoron was momentarily stunned, that was not him.

'Thank me later chum.'

The bugbear's nails impacted the face of Thoron's shield with tremendous force. Sinking to one knee, Thoron groaned at the effort of staying on his feet. His arm numbed, but the magical steel of his shield would give no ground. Instead of puncturing it, the bugbear's claws snapped off of its fingers. Howling in disbelief and pain, the bugbear's eyes narrowed with a renewed, and increased, anger.

Bloody hells, 'at bugger can sure hit hard.

Thoron ducked low, rolling under an errant swing from the bugbear. Having moved towards his foe, he rose from the ground, swiping his sword at the creature's legs. With bestial agility, the bugbear leapt over the swishing blade easily.

Thoron didn't wait for the monster to regain its footing, rather he pressed the offensive. While the creature was still mid-air, he swung his blade once more. Unable to avoid the strike, steel carved into the beat's leg, severing it completely. The creature screamed in agony. Landing off balance, it fell awkwardly onto its back, arterial blood pulsating from its stump. Not waiting for it to bleed out, Thoron stabbed the helpless monster through its head, putting an end to its misery.

'Ha, take that you fucker! Who's next? Ha, ha.'

Turning around, Thoron was faced by another pair of enraged bugbears, both of which were charging towards him. In mere seconds a veritable flurry of blows were unleashed in his direction. His arm moved as a blur, assisted by Harry, as he tried to block as many as possible, but one got past his defences. Claws slashed through the sleeve of his gambeson as though it were paper, digging themselves deep into the flesh of his sword arm. Chunks of muscle sailed into the air as blood poured from cavernous lacerations. Pain, an unbearable torment exploded within him. Losing control, his hand spasmed and his sword fell to the ground.

A swipe from a bugbear's claw sailed over his head as he knelt on the ground, trying to retrieve his weapon. His fingers had barely brushed the blade's pommel when a mighty kick sent him sprawling. Rolling through the dirt, his chest heaved with pain, but compared to that which he felt in his arm it was nothing. Thoron's impromptu journey ended with him lying face flat in the dirt. Pushing himself off of the ground, he spat some soil out of his mouth and returned to the fray with gusto.

Knowing that he stood little chance without his sword, he sprinted towards it. Seeking to intercept him before he could reach it, the bugbears raced towards him. With a mighty leap the first of the beasts leapt towards him, scowling as it flew through the air. Barely reacting in time, Thoron skidded as low as he could under the creature. It sailed over his head harmlessly as he glided across the ground.

The second bugbear was only seconds behind the first. As Thoron slid it tried to pounce on top of him. Raising his shield above him, Thoron used the beast's own momentum against it, slapping it in the face and sending it flying harmlessly away.

Not waiting for his foes to recover, Thoron regained his footing and dashed over to his sword. Picking it up, he turned to see both of the bugbears hot on his heels. One flanking him to his right, the other to his left. He was being pincered.

Bugger.

As they simultaneously charged at him, Thoron shoved his shield into the face of the one on the left. With a resounding 'gong,' teeth sprayed from the creature's mouth as it spiralled away reeling. At the same time, Thoron thrust the tip of his blade at the other bugbear. Betrayed by its own momentum, the creature impaled itself upon Thoron's sword, he's blade sinking deep into the bugbear's chest, shattering its sternum, and penetrating its heart. With a twist, Thoron removed his sword from the creature's corpse, whereby it fell limply to the ground.

Rubbing the side of its face where it had been hit, the final bugbear was beginning to regain its composure. It eyed the battlefield nervously, assessing its odds of defeating Thoron by itself. Obviously concluding that it stood little chance of doing so, it turned and started running away.

Ach, am no' having 'at buddy.

Thoron, not wanting the creature to return later with others of its kind, drew back his hand and threw his sword with all his might. As it sailed through the air, Barry couldn't help but to express his glee.

'*Wee!*'

His aim was true. Barry impacted the bugbear in the centre of its back, severing its spinal column. Mid-stride, the creature's legs ceased functioning and it fell, tumbling uncontrollably into the dirt. As the creature lay on the ground helpless, no longer able to flee, Thoron walked calmly over to it. Careful of its still dangerous claws, he extracted his sword, then immediately pushed it gently into the base of the beast's skull. It died instantly.

Body flush with adrenaline, and mind consumed with survival, he had almost forgotten about his injured arm. Panting from exertion, he examined the wound. He grimaced. It was bad. He had seen plenty of injuries beforehand and knew that he required some serious medical attention, lest he lose the use of the limb itself or expire from the inevitable infection.

Shite.

Unbidden, a question entered his mind. What of his patron? Many times, he had heard of the miracles that the gods performed, why not his and why not for him? He had just pledged his life to her service after all.

Cannae hurt tae try.

Deciding to test his hypothesis, Thoron knelt in deference, bowing his head. Placing his hand over the wound, he prayed to Rivalitas. At first nothing happened, but he continued to pray, believing that his patron would hear his devotion and grant him her aid. After a few moments of continuous prayer, he felt a change.

A red light, warm and soothing, pulsated from his palm. The intense pain he felt was diminished to an easily manageable throb. The bleeding ceased and some of the damaged muscled reformed, knitting together before his very eyes. Boon granted, Rivalitas's light faded into nothingness. His arm was nowhere close to being fully healed, but it was functional, no longer threatened his life and would recover fully in time.

Thank Rivalitas an' her mercy. Praise be tae her.

Thoron stood and, even more exhausted than before, returned to the trail. The going was not pleasant, but he had little choice. The sun was now barely more than a sliver on the horizon.

'Hey, Harry. Whit wis it 'at happened afore? You ken, when ye telt me tae thank ye later. Thanks fur 'at by the way. Um, but care tae explain?

'*Well mister Thoron it's like this. We, that is Barry, you, and myself, are physically, psychically, and spiritually linked. Inseparably so in fact. This link means that we, just Barry and myself this time, perceive the world through your senses, be it sight, sound, or anything else. We can communicate with you, and you to us, telepathically, regardless of physical distance. It also means that we can, to a limited extent, influence your actions while we are in physical contact with you. That last one is what I did previously, I perceived through your senses that you were in imminent physical harm and took control, as it were, to circumvent said physical harm. I'm sorry if what I did was a surprise, but I'd wager that it was preferable to being dead.*'

'*Cor, crikey, look at him go. Good work on your explanation mate, really top notch. I'd clap if I could.*'

Before responding Thoron pondered what Harry had just told him and considered the possible ramifications.

'Reit, weel, again, thank ye fur 'at. It is mightily appreciated, but whit if I dae no' want ye tae take control? And can ye take control whenever ye want? Am I jus' a puppet fur yer amusement?'

'*Nah mate. We can only take control whenever the shit is really gunna hit the fan. Think of it like a reflex or something. Like how can I explain it better, hm, okay, it's like this. Your noggin gets information from your body that it has seen or heard some kind of danger. Then it sends that information back to your body to do something about it right? Well, what we do is we cut out the middle man, your brain. Your body sense some danger and we move to prevent it. Our way stops your brain from interfering with the proper reflexive way of dealing with shit by overthinking the whole situation. Now I know what you're about to say, Bazza, I can hear you say, how is that any different to normal? You're just taking the role of the brain; you're sentient too, what stops you from overthinking the situation and choking when it counts? Simply put, fucked if I know. It just fucking works.*'

'So, it's just a safety net and nothing mair?'

'*Yeah, that about sums it up. Hey. What's that? Ahead of us.*'

Thoron lifted his gaze from his feet and looked along the trail. Ahead of them, he sighted a cabin. It seemed as though, at last, fortune had smiled upon him. Reaching the building, too fatigued to care, he kicked open its locked front door, propped Harry and Barry against a wall and passed out on the floor.

Chapter 24

Eris

The interior of the house was dimly lit, only the barest hint of light peeked through the drawn curtains. Eris's eyes adjusted to the gloom quickly, her elvish heritage coming to the fore. Passing through the dwelling quickly, Eris hardly even looked around. She knew where she was and she knew where she was going.

To most it would appear as an ordinary house, the abode was replete with personal effects and the furniture was well kept. Only those with a keen eye would see past the façade. Unusually large piles of dust occupied the not-so-easy places to reach and barely visible tendrils of spiders' silk fluttered from the corners. Eris knew the building was a carefully constructed lie.

While she had never been in this house specifically, she had been in many others like it and knew exactly where to go. Making a bee-line towards the back of the house she bypassed the sitting room and the dining room. The kitchen was her destination and it was here where she stopped.

Lending credence to the subterfuge, the shelves were well stocked with provisions. Pots and pans hung from their hooks, clearly clean and ready for use. A small pile of kindling was arranged neatly beside the stove and a full array of knives were sitting safely in their block. This was a kitchen that could be put to purpose at a moment's notice. Eris ignored it all.

Moving to the pantry, Eris tried to open its doors. They wouldn't budge. Bracing herself the best she could, Eris put the entirety of her weight into the effort, groaning under the strain as she did so. They still wouldn't open. Sighing in exacerbation, she turned to Máher.

'If you would be so kind as to open these doors, please? They seem to be stuck.'

Wordlessly, Máher nodded and pulled on the doors handles. They opened without issue. Eris was momentarily stunned.

Gods, either he is really strong or I am really weak. I suppose it could be both. No. He must just be strong.

Ducking her head to hide her surprise from Máher, Eris walked into the pantry. Unlike the rest of the house, it was bare. Seemingly, the deception ended here.

Seeking the means of their ingress, Eris ran her hands over the pantry's back wall. Quickly, she found what she was looking for, a singular panel, raised higher than the rest. Pushing it with her palm, the panel gave a subtle click as it depressed into the wall. Hidden gears whirred as the back wall swung open, revealing a set of rough stone stairs that descended into darkness.

'Well, Máher. I hope that you can see in the dark because I'm all out of torches and we have no time to fetch any.'

Máher let out a low chuckle.

'I'll be fine.'

Confused, Eris turned to face him, a questioning look on her face.

Máher snapped his fingers and four balls of glowing light rose from his palm. Emanating a soft orange glow, their aura highlighted his smirking face as they bobbed around in the air above him.

'Lead on.'

Fool. How could I forget. He's a sorcerer.

Carefully, Eris descended the staircase, eyes peeled for any inconsistencies in the stonework or other tell-tale signs of traps. Ever anxious for the clicking of a trap sprung, sweat beaded upon her brow and her heart pounded in her chest.

Spiralling down, Eris followed the narrow curve of the stairwell, ever conscious of the fact that she could see its end at any moment. She went slowly, body crouched low to the ground, stalking her way onwards, her footfalls silent. The last thing that she wanted was to charge unprepared into a bevy of armed guards.

At several junctures Eris thought that her descent was at an end, as the stairs plateaued, but each time she was mistaken. The stairs continued.

Suddenly, Eris heard a pair of subtle sounds from behind her, a creak, and a click. Spinning around quickly, she saw one partition of the staircase depress under Máher's foot.

Oh shit.

Nothing happened. No missiles flew for their heads, no rolling stone came tumbling from behind to crush them, no fountain of scalding acid jetted from the floor to melt them. Nothing.

Perhaps the trap needs the victim to remove pressure from the plate to activate?

'Máher! Don't move.'

Hissed Eris.

Tersely, Máher whispered back to her as he stood frozen, clearly showing no intention of moving.

'Wouldn't dream of it.'

Still tense, Eris moved to inspect the trap.

Okay, the pressure plate is fully depressed. There's no obvious wire or any other discernible mechanisms, they must be under the plate itself. Curses. There's no way to access the trap without lifting the pressure plate, which is how it's activated. Damnations.

Unable to disarm the trap, Eris looked around the staircase for any obvious gaps in the masonry where projectiles from the trigger trap could originate from. She didn't see any.

Double damnations.

'Okay Máher. It's like this, you've stepped onto a pressure plate and I can't disarm it.'

There probably isn't any way to do so either, but you don't need to know that.

'I also have no idea what the plate will spring or from where. As far as I see it, we have two options. Either we stand here forever or run for it as fast as we can and hope that whatever you trigger doesn't hit us. As bad as those options are, I'm firmly leading towards the latter.'

Eris noticed Máher steel himself, his face twisting from its usual calm to a scowl of grim determination. Curtly, he gave a small nod to her.

'On the count of three we'll run. Ready yourself.'

Facing the darkness below, Eris rose halfway from her crouch, just as a sprinter would on the starting line of a race. Tensing her leg muscles, she prepared them for the initial push that would drive her momentum.

'One.'

Eris filled her lungs with one deep breath. Slowly, she exhaled through her mouth. Despite her circumstances, she felt a strange calm wash over her.

'Two.'

Tapping her heels together, she muttered the ancient elvish phrase her mother had taught her when she was a child. Her boots warmed as they tingled with magical energies. It was a pleasant feeling, one that buoyed her soul.

'Three.'

Pushing off from the floor as hard as she could, Eris launched herself forward. A blur of motion passed her by, so fast as to be barely perceptible, but it caused her no harm so, she ignored it.

Máher?

Knowing that running down the stairs would be slow, not to mention more difficult, she forwent them. Instead, she vaulted herself sideways and, trusting in her boot's enchantment, ran along the wall. Round and round she spiralled downwards, thankful that the stairwell was wider here.

A rumbling from behind her filled Eris's ears, but she dared not turn, for she knew that a lapse in concentration would kill her as certainly as any trap. Gradually, the sound grew in intensity. Whatever was behind her was closing the distance.

Later than she had expected too, she sighted the end of the staircase before her. There was a door. It was open. Unable to slow, Eris kicked herself off of the wall. With the barest of margins, she corkscrewed through the open door, scrapping her shoulder against the doorframe. Rolling as she landed to arrest her momentum, she drew her two daggers in anticipation of a hostile welcome.

There was none. Instead, there was only Máher, leaning nonchalantly against a wall, a pair of charred corpses smouldering by his feet. As Eris huffed from exertion, she couldn't help but to see the sly grin plastered on his face.

'Glad to see you've finally caught up. I was starting to think you'd gotten lost.'

Somehow Máher's comment irked her more than it should have, she scowled at him, but didn't respond.

Arsehole.

Behind her, a booming crash drew her attention away from Máher. A boulder, no doubt the product of the sprung trap, had collided with the doorframe, sending a shower of dust sprinkling over Eris's person. Inwardly Eris cursed, not for the sullying of her attire, but for the fact that their point of ingress was completely sealed, they would need to find another way out.

That might complicate things a little. At least there are other exits.

'Well, that was close.'

Eris groaned. She turned back to Máher, her glare intensified beyond all subtlety. Máher ignored her and continued as though nothing had happened.

'Now, I've looked about a bit and there are three ways to go. Suffice it to say, I have no idea which path we should take.'

Pushing past Máher, Eris studied each of the archways in turn. Scribbled on each of them were a series of seemingly random scratches. However, they were not random, they were in fact the written code employed by Súthburh thieves. Of course, Eris could read it.

'Okay then. The left path leads to the warren. That's the central hub of the barrow. It's where the sleeping quarters, barracks and armouries are. I'm familiar with it, there's several exits we could use that way, but we don't want to go there unless we really have to. At this hour it would definitely be full of thieves, more than we could possibly deal with. Mm, the centre path will take us to the mess hall and several storage areas. It'll be less guarded that way, but I can't see Mikael being held in the larder. Alright, now this is odd. The right path is labelled, but it doesn't make any sense. It doesn't give a description of what lies ahead, it just says "death".'

Máher snorted.

'Well, that doesn't sound ominous at all.'

'I have no idea what lies that way.'

'I'm guessing that it's something bad.'

'Well, the other two paths are out, so this one's it. Let's go.'

'Really? Towards "death." Willingly?'

Saying nothing, all the while keeping her eyes peeled for traps, or whatever "death" awaited them, Eris walked through the rightmost archway. If Máher had any further objections to Eris's decision, he did not voice them, instead he just followed her lead.

A shimmer in front of her caused Eris to stop suddenly. The glow of Máher's floating globules had reflected on some unknown object. Carefully, Eris moved towards the shimmering object. A thin line of fishing line spanned the entirety of the passage, a tripwire. With care, she sliced the line with a dagger. The two halves of line fell limply to the floor, the snare was disarmed.

That was a clumsy attempt.

Continuing along their path, Eris returned to her vigilant approach, scanning constantly for any signs of danger, certain that more traps lay ahead. Máher, on the other hand, was far more interested in the wall engravings.

'I knew that the city was built on dwarven ruins, but I have never seen them before now. They're quite a thing, aren't they? The quality of their stonework is nothing short of astonishing.'

Eris regarded the masonry around them and shrugged.

'I suppose some may take an interest in them, but to me they're just there, you know? I see them so often that they have become entirely familiar to me. Any mystique or rapturous intrigue they may have once held for me is now gone.'

'Ah, I see. It's a case of the old, familiarity breeds contempt. Shame.'

Ahead of them the hallway ended as a wall of earth and broken stone blocked their path. Beside her, Máher groaned in frustration.

'Damn. Looks like we'll have to backtrack and try another passage.'

'Hm, I don't think we will. Look over there.'

Tapping Máher's arm, Eris pointed to an unusual assortment of shattered stones on the ground. Their colour differed greatly from the dwarven masonry around them and they were clearly not a part of the collapse. Looking to the roof, Eris saw a hole.

Someone must have broken into the tunnel from up there.

'Hey, give me a boost. I think I'll fit.'

Máher grumbled in affirmation and kneeled. As Eris stepped into his hands, Máher pushed her towards the hole. Stretching out her arms, she reached it easily. Her hands clawed at the hard earth as she tried to find purchase. It was precarious, but with a bevy of grunts, groans, and sweat fuelled curses, she made it up. Panting, she rolled onto her back to rest her tired muscles.

After taking a few moments to catch her breath, Eris looked around. From what she could tell she was in a small tunnel. Unlike the dwarven ruins below, these walls were not carved, their formation was entirely natural. One direction ended almost immediately, but the other bent away out of her view.

Looks like there's a way to go after all.

Sticking her head back through the hole, Eris whispered to Máher.

'It looks like there's a tunnel up here. Give me your hands, I'll pull you up and we can see where it goes.'

'Um, not to directly call into question your sanity, but what, in your opinion, are the chances that this, tunnel, will lead us to Mikael?'

'Do you have a better idea?'

'No.'

'Well then, get over here.'

To say that Máher looked sceptical about Eris's plan would be grossly understating his entirely cynical expression. Sighing as he shook his head, Máher raised his hands towards Eris.

Laying on her stomach, Eris stretched out as far as she could. Her hands gripped his wrists, as his gripped hers. Taking a deep breath, she pulled as hard as she could. Her muscles burned at the strain, but it was working, she had lifted Máher off of the ground and was now pulling him towards the hole.

By the gods, it's working.

Eris's entire body was screaming at her to stop, but she did not. She could not. No matter what, she would not surrender the progress, nor forsake the momentum, she had already earned.

On the precipice of victory, Máher's hands poked their way through the hole. Once he had gripped the earth, Eris stood, taking this brief offering of respite to better her position in readiness to hoist Máher the remainder of the way. Free from her grasp, Máher's hold on the floor loosened and he started to slip. Quick as a hawk, Eris snatched at the man's furs and yanked him the rest of the way through the hole. Utterly spent, the pair fell into a heap, their breath short and chests heaving.

'Well damn me woman. That was an impressive display and entirely unexpected. Who'd have thought that a skinny lass such as yourself would have so much strength?'

'Thanks, I suppose, but next time how about you pull me up, okay?'

'Deal. Now let's see where your tunnel gets us.'

Begrudgingly, the pair eased themselves to their feet and started walking down the tunnel. They didn't have far to go. After the first bend, the narrow corridor opened up to reveal a grand cavern. Moisture hung heavy in the air and Eris found it difficult to breath, stifling a cough, she looked around.

Torches flickered throughout the cave, causing shadows to dance amongst the natural rock formations. Stalactites hung low from the ceiling, their sporadic drips echoing as an odd symphony throughout the chamber. Sheening stalagmites stretched waywardly towards their estranged cousins, yearning for reunification. A decrepit jetty stretched over a softly rippling pond.

I can smell the salt from here. It must join with the ocean.

Wordlessly, she tapped Máher on his shoulder and pointed at the water. She hardly heard him as he whispered back.

'I know. I've seen it too. I've already told Beher about it and he's going to try and find a way to swim in.'

Matching his whisper with her own, Eris murmured in response.

'Great. If this goes sideways his help will be useful.'

'Ha, ha. I think you mean when. Let's keep looking around.'

Working her way carefully through the stalagmites, Eris kept her eyes peeled for anyone or anything. A hiss from Máher made her stop. Looking towards where he was pointing, she felt her heart stop. It was Mikael. But it was not the handsome man she knew and loved, rather it was a pale imitation of that man, gaunt and decrepit. Tattered pants were all that he wore and his emancipated chest was riddled with scars and broken welts. Bound by chains, his arms stretched towards the roof as he dangled several inches from the ground.

Mikael. No. Gods no.

Lost in her grief, she almost missed the figure dancing around her lover, but a blur of garish pastels drew her attention. Vejovis. She had only met him a few times and was not overly familiar with the man, but there could be no mistaking him. Contrary to the stereotypical image of a thief, Vejovis wore a brightly patterned suit of coloured diamonds. Similarly brash, his hair was dyed green with streaks of purple.

Unexpectedly, Vejovis stopped dancing. His face twisted, as if in thought, and he tapped his finger melodically on his chin. Randomly, he spun in a circle, balancing on the tip of his toes. When he stopped, he was looking directly at Eris, grinning. Effeminate laughter cackled throughout the camber as he shrieked at her.

'There's no need to skulk in the shadows my lovelies, come on over and say hello. There is someone that is simply dying to greet you.'

Eris didn't want to break cover, but simultaneously she had to, Mikael needed her. Sharing a glance with Máher, who simply shook his head, she didn't feel any more reassured, in fact she felt even more conflicted.

Fuck it.

Raising her hands in surrender, Eris left the relative safety of her position and moved into the open. Sweat tickled her back as it slid down her spine and her heart pounded as she struggled for breath. Seeing her concern for Mikael, written on her face as clearly as the midday sun, Vejovis sniggered.

'What is it dearie that I tell all the youngling whelps that are brought into my fold? Oh, that's it. Don't get attached. You seem to forgotten that lesson my sweet and now I have to remind you why I teach it.'

As tears welled in her eyes, Eris screamed at Vejovis in desperation.

'Please, spare him! Take me in his stead. The error was mine, please don't punish him on my account!'

Ignoring her cries, Vejovis caressed the side of Mikael's face, far more tenderly than his nefarious demeanour dictated.

'Such a shame to waste such good stock, but needs must and all that. There, there Mikael. It will all be over soon.'

Eris watched on powerlessly as Vejovis bit down on the side of Mikael's neck. Mikael's eyes went wide as pain surged throughout his body. He tried to scream, to protest this transgression against his person, but the gag in his mouth stifled his cries. He struggled against his bounds and his attackers grasp, but both were too strong. He couldn't get away. He was helpless. Quickly, his frantic movements diminished in intensity to nothing more than sporadic twitches. Even these didn't last for long, as Mikael soon stopped moving entirely.

Vejovis lifted his head from Mikael's side and turned to face Eris and Máher. Eris gasped as she noticed the thin trails of blood trickling from either side of Vejovis's mouth. Recoiling in horror, she recognised him for what he truly was, a vampire, and for what he had just done to Mikael, he had drained him.

Desperately, she stared at Mikael's motionless form, searching for a sign of life, any sign, no matter how small. Her hands trembled and her stomach churned as she saw snakelike tendrils of blood twisting down Mikael's still chest.

He's not breathing.

Mikael's eyes were clouded a milky white, all colour and signs of life departed.

He's dead. Oh gods no. He's dead.

Chapter 25

Máher

Máher watched on helplessly as Eris visibly crumpled. The distraught woman fell to her knees, her face a twisted mask of anguish. She had lost her lover, more than that her soul mate, her life was now irrevocably altered. Máher knew her pain, he had experienced it more than once himself. He wanted nothing more than to comfort her, to hold her as she cried, to stand as a living testament that her pain would diminish in time, that her life still held meaning, but circumstances prevented him from doing so.

Vejovis wiped his chin with a silken handkerchief and covered his mouth as he let out a subtle burp.

'Oh, do pardon me. But then again, what is it people say? That's it. Better out than in, but I suppose it depends on what we're talking about. Ha, ha, ha. Now. Where was I? That's right I was going to kill you, that's what.'

Slowly, with an air of one who believes themselves superior to those around him in every conceivable way, Vejovis strutted casually towards Eris. Seeing Eris fail to react, her gaze locked unwaveringly onto the strung-up corpse of her deceased lover, Máher moved to her side.

'Eris! Snap out of it! I know too well how you feel, but this isn't the time or the place to lose your head.'

Nonchalantly, Vejovis drew a long sword from his hip. Holding it in a single hand, he twirled the weapon with a graceful ease that alluded to his supernatural strength. Still smirking, the vampire swung his blade at Máher. But much to Vejovis's chagrin, Máher deftly swatted the sword aside with his forearm. Not expecting Máher capable of fending off his strike, Vejovis overextended himself, stumbling on the uneven ground and coming close to losing his footing entirely. Instantly, his arrogant grin was replaced by a snarl.

'Ha. It seems that the horned mongrel has some skills. It matters not. You will fall to me!'

Máher's hair and eyes were engulfed by flame as he channelled his powers. Two axes, composed of pure fire, sprung to his hands with a blazing woosh. Not waiting for Vejovis to regain his composure, Máher attacked. His first swing barely hit the vampire, but the radiant heat his weapon emanated burnt the monster's skin, filling the air around them with the pungent aroma of singed flesh. Grimacing in pain, Vejovis deflected Máher's second strike, fiery sparks cascading from his blade as he did so.

'*Beher! Are you nearby? Your assistance would be appreciated.*'

'*Máher should not worry so much. Beher is very close and will be there to save Máher and the she-elf in no time.*'

'*Not to push you, but you damn well better hurry. I'm not sure this one is going to go…*'

Máher lost concentration as a crossbow bolt whizzed past his head, bare inches from his face. He turned towards its origin and glared fiercely at the man who had shot at him. Seeing Máher's ferocious stare, the man ducked behind cover, not only to hide from Máher's wrath, but to no doubt also reload his weapon.

Blindsided, a second bolt thudded into Máher's side. Air rushed from Máher's lungs as he huffed from the pain. Without a second thought, he tore the bolt from his torso and with wild eyes refocused his attentions upon Vejovis.

Before he could swing his axes, movement from the corner of his eye stilled his arm. With a slow and purposeful ascent, Eris rose from her knees, screaming a blood curdling banshee howl.

Drawing her daggers, she flew into a frenzy. Embodying the spirt of a hurricane, she pirouetted around Vejovis, hacking and slashing as she nimbly avoided the vampire's retorts. Her dance was a thing of elemental beauty and Máher couldn't help but to be enthralled. He was sure that she was yelling abuse at Vejovis, but he couldn't hear a word of it, so enraptured with her movements as he was.

Strangely, it was the subtlest of movements from the periphery of his vision that broke the spell. In a geyser of water, Beher shot from the subterranean lake. Droplets of ocean spray fell from his outstretched wings, just as rain would, as he soared throughout the cavern.

The man who had shot Máher must have sensed something because he turned just as Beher dived through the air towards him. The hapless man raised his arms in an attempt to fend off the young dragon, but it was no use. Panicked screams soon turned to whimpers, which were suddenly cut off completely as a sickening crunch heralded Beher claiming yet another victim.

'*Nicely done brother.*'

'*Bah. This is what Beher is for. Too bad this human tastes like sour goat, tough and sinewy. The things Beher does for Máher.*'

Not used to being resisted, let alone injured, Vejovis rubbed his scorched forearm off-handily, his eyes burning with hatred. Although his gaze never left Máher, he yelled an incessant stream of insults at Eris as he dodged around her blades.

'Just you wait, you insufferable bitch. Once I'm done with your half-breed pet, I'll be sure to give you everything you've got coming to you. Maybe I'll even fuck you before I drain you, show you how a real man does it. Ha, ha.'

Gripping his sword in both hands, Vejovis took a mighty swing at Máher. Seeing the blow coming from a mile away, Máher backed away, easily avoiding the strike. Thinking that Vejovis would follow with another attack, Máher readied himself, but Vejovis had other ideas. With a feline grace, he pivoted mid-swing, redirecting his aggression towards Eris. Mouth wide open, he lunged at Eris, trying to bite her. Máher felt his heart skip a beat as a tinge of concern spiked into his chest, but Eris swatted Vejovis's advance aside with a slap to his face.

Relieved that Eris was unharmed, Máher advanced towards Vejovis, slashing one of his axes under the vampire's guard. The fire-blade sliced along Vejovis's thigh, burning his pants, and scorching his flesh. The vampire screamed out in frustration and pain, a sound that buoyed Máher's spirit, but before he could press his attack, a movement from the corner of his eye caught his attention.

The man who had shot him previously had emerged from cover, exposing himself. Máher's body still throbbed with pain from being shot and the memory of that transgression triggered a surge of rage within him. Forgetting Vejovis for the moment, Máher threw one of his axes at the crossbowman. Sparks rained from the fire-blade as it spun sideways through the air, but much to Máher's disappointment, his aim was poor. Striking the wall behind the crossbowman, the blade embedded itself into the wood, singing its surroundings black.

Bugger.

Eying the fire-axe nervously as it dissolved into ash, its magic dissipated, the crossbowman struggled with his weapon as he tried desperately to reload it. Looking up at the battle before him, he saw his compatriot being torn apart by a dragon and his leader was, by all appearances, not faring very well either. Overcame with frustration, and dread, the man soon abandoned his task, dropping his weapon, braking from cover, and running from combat. Afeared, he didn't look back.

Máher saw this and was immediately concerned.

'*Beher! Stop playing with your food and stop the other one. We can't risk him finding help.*'

'*Do this Beher, do that Beher. Beher wishes Máher could hear what Máher says from Beher's point of view. Beher thinks Máher would think Máher to be a slave. But, okay, Beher will do this.*'

Beher swallowed the hunk of meat he was currently gnawing on and flapped his wings furiously. Taking to the air, he circled the cavern twice before racing after the fleeing crossbowman.

Bringing himself back to the immediate danger before him, Máher took stock of the situation. It was clear that Eris had taken Vejovis's latest taunts to heart as fresh tears welled in her eyes. Undeterred, she jabbed and slashed her daggers at Vejovis, but no doubt blinded by their stinging, her attacks lacked the effectiveness of her previous flurries. Vejovis was able to parry her strikes with ease, all the while laughing at her, goading her further.

'Ha, ha, what fun. You're pathetic dearie. To think I actually thought you capable, ha, ha.'

Sensing his inattention, Vejovis lunged towards Máher, thrusting his sword at Máher's chest. Had the blow landed, Máher would have been skewered, but at the last moment Máher raised a hand. His eyes blurred as a mystic wall of red flame enveloped him and Vejovis's blade skittered harmlessly off of its side. Enraged at being denied, Vejovis drew back his sword and with both hands swung it at the barrier as hard as he could. Scarlett energy engulfed the long sword as Vejovis tried to force his way through the shield, but it was no use, the magic would not yield to him.

Behind his shield, black spots filled Máher's vision and his head started to spin. Although his barrier was holding, he knew it was just a matter of time before it failed. He had felt the power behind Vejovis's last blow and that worried him.

'Beher. Sorry to be a bother, but we might need you back here to help us deal with the vampire. I'm not sure that this is going very well.'

Knowing that Beher had heard him, even though there was no response, Máher prepared to fall back. Mistakenly believing his shield would hold, he turned away from Vejovis. Too late he realised his error, for he felt his barrier's integrity wane, mere seconds before it vanished entirely.

Crap.

Capitalising on Máher's vulnerability, Vejovis swung at the now exposed Máher. The edge of his longsword slashed along Máher's back, carving muscle and sinew in two. Blood sprayed freely from the wound, soaking Máher's furs and staining the ground crimson.

Though he was in tremendous pain, Máher did not stop. He rolled away from the fray, staying as low as he could. Engaged by Eris, Vejovis was unable to follow.

Upon reaching a safe distance Máher turned to face Vejovis. Twirling his hands in mystic patterns, and focussing his will, he directed his energies into a ball of swirling flame. He caressed the conjured ball with his free hand as it floated above the palm of his other. The ball began to spin, slowly at first, but it's revolutions rapidly grew faster. Once the ball reached a critical velocity, Máher pushed it away from his person, launching it at Vejovis.

The sphere shot through the air, a trail of smoke and sparks streaming behind it. Curving as it flew, the ball ended its flight by careening into Vejovis's side with an explosion of fire. A horrendously pained scream erupted from the vampire as he burned.

All other thoughts left Vejovis's mind as he patted himself, furiously trying to quell the flames engulfing him. Eris took this moment of inattention to thrust her daggers into the vampire's torso. Each blade sunk deep into Vejovis's chest, buried to their hilts. In equal measures her face was wrought in anger and sorrow, but in that instant her eyes glimmered with a hint of triumph. Bringing her face as close as she could stomach to Vejovis's, she hissed into the vampire's ear.

'Well then, it appears it is you who is my bitch. Now die, you monstrous bastard!'

Vejovis just grinned, a sly and evil smirk, as though he was privy to some information Eris was not.

'Ha, ha. That's where you're wrong sweetie. Oh, how I will enjoy this.'

Ignoring the daggers in his chest and the flames that still smouldered along his side, Vejovis grabbed hold or Eris, locking her in place. Fearing what was about to happen, she struggled, trying to break the vampire's grasp. She couldn't.

Aghast, Máher stared on helplessly as Vejovis lent in towards Eris, placing his mouth over her neck.

Good gods, he's going to drain her as he did with Mikael.

He could have run over to intercede, he should have blasted Vejovis with magical fire, but in that moment, gripped by inaction as he was, he did nothing but watch. Thusly engrossed by this horrendous matinée, Máher failed to notice the subtle shift in air pressure above him as Beher flew overhead.

'Wake up Máher.'

Beher's prompting drove Máher from his stupor, but before he could act Beher dropped from the roof of the cavern and, like an errant thunderbolt, careered into Vejovis and Eris, sending them both tumbling. As Vejovis came to a stop Beher pounced on top of him. Pinning the hapless vampire to the ground with his claws, Beher tore into Vejovis's face with his maw. Chunks of undead meat were torn from the vampire's head in thick strips as he struggled underneath Beher's bulk, screaming madly as he sought an impossible escape. Deciding to end it, Beher stretched his jaw over the crown of Vejovis's skull and bit down. Bones shattered as the vampire's head collapsed under the pressure of Beher's bite.

At the moment of his death Vejovis's form exploded into a cloud of fine dust. Surprised, Beher coughed and spluttered as he tried to expel those particles he had inadvertently inhaled from his lungs. The cloud, all that remained of Vejovis, rose, and wafted gently from the cavern.

'Well done, Beher. Not a moment too soon either.'

'*Bah. Beher thinks it should be the she-elf that does the thanking. Foolish elfling was the one who was almost bleed dry. Maybe Beher should get the she-elf to buy some piglets for Beher's supper?*'

'*Ha, ha. Feel free to ask her. I'm sure she'd be more than happy to oblige you.*'

Searing pain bit through Máher's joviality and he grimaced. Reaching behind him, he traced the length and width of his wound. It was bad, but by no means the worst he had ever suffered. No arteries were severed and as far as he could tell no tendons were torn.

There's no time to cauterise it now. Blast. No matter. I shan't bleed out.

Examination over, Máher withdrew his hand. It was now coated in a thick glaze of crimson, but he cared not. In truth he barely noticed for he was far more concerned with Eris's plight.

Running to her side, Máher rolled her prone body over. On the side of her neck a pair of red dots, fang-marks, oozed blood. The memory of Mikael's death still etched graphically in his mind, Máher felt his heartbeat increase in tempo as worry wore at his soul.

Placing his hand upon her sternum, searching for signs of life, Máher calmed as beneath his touch Eris's chest rose and fell slowly.

Good she's still breathing.

Similarly, he placed a pair of fingers onto the side of her throat. Immediately, he found a pulse. It was weak, but better than nothing.

She's still alive, thank the gods, but not by much. I need to get her out of here.

'*Beher! Did you manage to stop that crossbowman I asked you to chase down?*'

'*Beher did not. Máher called Beher back before he could catch the human. It surprised Beher that the man was so fast.*'

'*Mm, not ideal. No doubt he'll be back with friends anytime now. Bugger. There's no way we can leave the way we came in. We'd be too slow. They'd catch us. Okay then, how long did it take you to swim through the water passage? Do you think me and Eris could make it?*'

'*Beher doesn't know. It wasn't too long, but Beher can hold his breath for a long time and is good at swimming. Beher thinks that Máher and she-elf would probably drown if they tried.*'

'*Shit. What if you pulled us out? Would that be something you could do?*'

Beher stared at Máher and cocked his head, as if in thought. Blinking a few times, the dragon snorted and shook his entire body.

'*Beher thinks Máher soft in the head. Of course, Beher could do this. That being said, Beher would prefer not to. Bah. Fine. Beher will do this for Máher.*'

'*Excellent. Let's get out of here.*'

Scooping Eris from the ground, Máher carried her limp body to the water and jumped in. Shivering involuntarily as a wall of cold hit him instantly, his discomfort surged to new heights as the seawater soaked through his clothes. Salt seeped into his wound, stinging with a fury that threatened to propel him from consciousness. It took all of his effort to avoid blacking out from the agony. Beher dove into the water next to him and surfaced by his side, waiting for instructions, his reptilian eyes a clear depiction of concern.

'*Worry not brother, I'll be fine.*'

Shifting Eris, Máher wrapped his legs around her waist and cradled the back of her head with his hand. Taking a few moments to breath deep and oxygenate his bloodstream, Máher floated gently as he treaded water. Once prepared, both mentally and physically, he nodded to his companion and grasped the dragon's hind leg.

'*Okay, I'm going to channel some magic directly into you to expedite our escape. Once my incantation is complete, you'll only have one minute of enhancement. So, please, as soon as you feel the effects of my spell, swim as fast as you can.*'

Taking a deep breath, Máher channelled his powers into Beher, willing his younger brother to hasten. The dragon started to shimmer with an orange-red glow and as his power left him, Máher felt himself tire, but he continued anyway.

Not three feet from his head, a geyser of water erupted upwards as an errant arrow shot from the cavern floor missed its mark. It was soon followed by another splash, this time closer, but Máher paid it no heed.

As the final vestiges of Máher's power were absorbed by Beher, thus completing Máher's spell, Beher dove under the water, dragging both Máher and Eris with him.

Water surged past Máher as the trio rushed through the ocean tunnel. He gripped Eris as hard as he dared, both fearful of harming her and of letting her go. Holding onto Beher was equally difficult, albeit for different reasons, as on more than one occasion during their journey he felt his grip on his brother slip. Fortunately, he managed to hold on.

They zipped past subterranean walls of craggy rock, bereft of any life, but Máher saw nothing as he closed his eyes fast against the torrent of oncoming water. Consigned to a darkness of his own making, he had no idea for how long they travelled, but he knew it wasn't long, for Beher maintained his magically enhanced pace.

As Máher's lungs burned, desperate for a breath of fresh air, Beher breached the surface of the ocean. Driven by desperation, Máher gasped, drawing in as much oxygen as he could. Still wrapped in his legs, Eris had regained consciousness and was similarly spluttering beside him.

Chapter 26

Máher

As he held her, lolling in the surf, Máher checked on Eris. Save for the wounds on her neck, which still wept blood, she was physically fine, but he could easily see that she was psychologically tormented. From watching her love be murdered before her very eyes, to her narrow escape from death by exsanguination, her eyes were hollow, haunted by both pain and fear.

'If you would be so kind Beher, please take us to shore. Thank you.'

As Beher fulfilled his request, Máher leaned in towards Eris, placing his forehead on hers, and whispered gently to her.

'I know you don't feel it now, but it's going to get easier. The pain will fade and the beauty of the world *will* return to spark joy in your heart once more. It is going to be hard, I know this, but should you want me to, I *will* be here for you, I *will* help you.'

Fresh tears welled in her eyes as Eris whispered back.

'Thank you.'

Staring into her soul, Máher felt her sincerity and a stirring of long-unfamiliar emotions sparked at the core of his chest. Without a second thought, he supressed them.

It's neither the time, nor the place, for that.

'Think nothing of it.'

Much to Máher's relief, this moment of intimacy was interrupted by an interjection from Beher.

'Beher wishes Máher to know that the water is quite shallow now. Would Máher please be so kind as to let go of poor Beher? Beher is quite sure that Máher and the she-elf can walk from here.'

After releasing his hold on Beher, Máher unwrapped himself from around Eris. Stretching his legs out below him he immediately found sand. Standing slowly, he helped Eris to her feet, but still weak she stumbled. Instinctively, Máher grabbed her waist, stabilising her before she could fall. Abashed, Eris turned her head away, hiding her face behind her hair.

'Sorry. I'm a bit out of sorts.'

'It's okay. You have nothing to apologise for. I'll help you.'

Stooping, Máher scooped Eris up, cradling her in his arms.

'I'll carry you.'

Eris said nothing but buried her head into Máher's chest as he walked from the surf. Beher was already some twenty feet ahead of them, shaking himself dry, just as a dog would. It was a comical display, with his dragon hide being naturally hydrophobic, but the novelty of the spectacle was lost on Máher who's attention was thoroughly elsewhere.

No. She's just lost the love of her life. I cannot think of her as anything more than a friend. For Now? Damn.

Abandoning his thoughts, and once more supressing his emotions, Máher evaluated their current situation. He knew that, soaked as he was, the cold he now felt would bite even more fiercely in cooling afternoon air. He, just as much as Eris, had to get dry, they needed shelter. He scanned the beach looking for just that and, despite the odds, fortune smiled upon him. There, not too far in the distance, was a cave. By all appearances it was small, but for their needs it would more than suffice.

'*Beher. Along the shore, to the east, there is a cave. We will take shelter there for the night. Could you please make yourself useful and fetch some firewood please?*'

Beher stopped his shaking, turned his neck slowly and starred at Máher. Without responding the dragon huffed and squinted his eyes in his direction, clearly displeased by Máher's request. Five seconds passed before Beher stormed off down the beach, away from the cave.

'*Thank you.*'

As Máher entered the cave, hunching to avoid its low opening, a twinge in his back agitated the already painful wound in his back. Grimacing, he propped Eris gently against the cave's wall, trying to make her as comfortable as he could. Slowly he lifted his furs, peeling them gingerly from his torso, growling as the pain intensified. Throwing them into the corner he faced Eris and whispered.

'I need to cauterise this wound, but I cannot see it. Would you please help me? All I need is for you to guide my had, my magic will do the rest.'

Biting her lip, she nodded.

'Of course, I can.'

'Excellent.'

Channelling magical energies into his hand, the tips of his fingers started to glow red-hot and emanate a scolding heat.

'Grab my hand, but be careful not to not touch my fingers as they will be very hot. Then just move my hand so my fingers burn shut the laceration.'

Taking his hand in hers, she did as Máher asked. Her touch was tender, and in that Máher took comfort, but as soon as his superheated fingers contacted in gash in his back, his body stiffened from the pain. Supressing the desire to scream, Máher remained silent as his flesh burned. A horrid stench filled the cave, which almost made Eris vomit, but stoically they both continued with their morbid task. After a couple of minutes, Eris released Máher's hand.

'It is done.'

'Thank you. Do you have any wounds that need tending?'

Eris grasped the side of her neck and flushed.

'No, I'll be fine. Thanks for asking though, I really do appreciate it.'

Eschewing words, Máher simply nodded in understanding. Believing the conversation over, he started to turn away, wanting to let Eris rest, but her gaze, which was locked firmly upon his chest, held him in place.

'What is it?'

Her cheeks darkened to a deeper shade of red and in embarrassment she bit her lip.

'Oh. Um, you have so many scars, I was just a bit taken aback. And then there's the, um. The you know. The scales. I was not expecting scales.'

Máher laughed.

'Ha. As to the scars, I've led a difficult life, harder than most in fact. And, well, not wearing armour has its drawbacks. But I manage. The scales. Now, they're a biproduct of my parentage. My father is a dragon, an ancient red dragon to be specific. I get the scales from him.'

Pausing, Máher pointed to the horns on his head.

'I also get these from him. And, before you ask, yes, Beher is his. He's my younger brother, well, technically half-brother. That's the reason he's travelling with me.'

Eris's eyes went wide with surprise.

'Wow. I was not expecting that. When I first saw your horns, I just thought you were descended from infernati. I never even dreamed you were a dragonkin.'

Máher shrugged.

'Don't worry about it, most people think I'm part infernati when they see me, I've never seen the need to correct them. Now. Get some sleep, if you can. It's been a long day and I'm sure you could use the rest. I'll take watch.'

Not bothering with his discarded garments, Máher slumped to the ground and leant against the wall of the cave. Although it was uncomfortable, Máher was so tired that as soon as he was seated, he sighed audibly in relief. For a time, he fought his drooping eyes, but weary as he was, he soon succumbed to slumber.

An amount of time later, he knew not how much, Máher awoke. Bleary eyed, he looked around the cave. Eris was dozing where he had left her, snoring daintily as she did so. Beher was curled up by the entrance, similarly asleep. A large pile of misshaped wood lay strewn in the centre of the chamber.

Damn, so much for keeping watch. At least Beher fetched enough wood for a decent fire.

Stretching his stiffened frame as he stood, Máher shuffled over to the driftwood and arranged it as best as he could. Channelling his powers, Máher conjured a flame into his hand. Kneeling, he held his hand underneath the wood and waited for it to catch alight. It took some doing, as it was damp in the extreme, but eventually he was satisfied that the burgeoning fire would hold. Quelling the flame in his hand, he moved back to his spot against the cave wall and sat, content to watch the dancing of the fire's flames.

However, no matter how he wanted to, Máher could not sit peacefully. An itch, never welcomed, but all too familiar, scraped at the back of his mind. He knew what it heralded, Dolos, but he was too tired to fight.

Fine. Just give me a moment.

Satisfied, the presence withdrew and the urge to change eased, but Máher knew that should he renege on his promise, then the itch would return tenfold the stronger. Sighing, he crossed over to Eris and gently shook her awake.

'Eris. I'm sorry to wake you, but we need to talk.'

Eris woke with a start and immediately she was overcome with concern. Panicked, she bolted upright, looking for whatever peril had caused her to awaken. However, she soon calmed when she realised that it was only Máher and that there was no danger present.

'Máher? What's going on?'

'I apologise for the rude awakening, but we need to talk. I've been thinking and we can't stay here, nor can we return to Súthburh. We need to leave. Although I've never been there, I know of a small town to the north. I suggest that we go there, for now anyway. We can think about what comes after that later. That is, unless you can think of a better plan?'

For a moment, Eris sat immobile, deep in thought, a profound look of concertation on her face. When she answered it was an air of profound dejection.

'Súthburh is all I've ever known. I've never even been to another town before. I'm not sure how I feel about leaving it, about leaving everything I've ever known behind. But you're right, we can't stay. I'm certain Vejovis's men will be after us and I don't think that anywhere in the Southlands will be truly safe, but I'll follow your lead, if you say this town is our best choice then that's where we'll go.'

'Okay then, that's settled. But before we can depart, we'll need some supplies, and maybe some horses. There's also one other…'

Máher trailed off, uncertain of how he should broach the topic of Dolos with Eris. After a second's thought, he decided that the most direct path would be the simplest.

'Sorry. As I was saying, there's one other thing you need to be made aware of. Please, don't be alarmed.'

Twisting his ring, Máher's form shimmered as it shifted to his alter ego, Dolos. Once the transformation was complete Eris gave a startled cry, her hand shooting to the hilt of her dagger, ready to throw it if the need arose. Seeing Eris's anxiety, and wishing to asway her of any violent actions, Dolos swept his arm flamboyantly in a formal bow.

'How do you do my dear. I am Dolos and I assure you, I mean you no harm. Unlike that social buffoon Máher, I have a certain way with people, not to mention words. Now, I can see you are surprised, but never fear my sweet. I am as much an ally to you as Máher. Consider me to be, for all intents and purposes, one side of a coin, Máher being the other. We are different, vastly so in my opinion, but we are also the same. We share the same memories and, for the most part, have similar goals. I will care for you as he would, just don't get any ideas about bedding this hot piece of ass. As alluring as you are, I am well aware of your recent loss and would never besmirch Mikael's memory in such a scandalous manner. Oh gods, where are my manners, please accept my sincerest condolences.'

Dolos bowed again as Eris's mouth gaped, her mind whirring as she tried to comprehend exactly what it was that had just happened and who it was that now stood before her. Dolos barely noticed her bemusement as he worked a spec of dirt out from under one of his fingernails. Breaking through her discombobulation, Eris stammered to Dolos.

'Oh, my. Well. This is a lot. So, you're the same person? How? Just how?'

Instantly, the imaginary piece of grime was forgotten and Dolos spun to face Eris, his face a mask of excitement.

'*Well*, it's like this. See this ring here, it's not really to my taste, but it wasn't me who chose to wear it. Máher, the lout, picked it up on one of his adventures and instead of identifying it, you know to make sure it was safe and not cursed or haunted or otherwise problematic, he just slipped it onto his finger, as easy as anything. Guess what? It turned out the bloody thing was cursed. Brilliant. Now, it's not a super bad curse, like oh no I'm going to die if I don't collect one thousand souls for a daemon lord in the space of three years bad. It's more like an oh no I can't get this ring off of my finger and it clashes horrendously with my outfit kind of bad. That being said, *I* can't complain, without it I wouldn't even exist. You see the ring also had the nasty effect of splitting Máher's personality into two divergent people, Máher is one and I am the other. Each of us can use it to shift into the other, which, if I'm entirely honest, can at times be useful, but it can also be damned insufferable when Máher chooses not to let me out.'

Dolos paused for the briefest of moments before shouting at the top of his lungs.

'You hear that Máher! Damned insufferable!'

After taking a deep breath, he continued at an ordinary volume.

'There's probably more to it, but I couldn't tell you what. To be honest magical gubbins are more of a *Máher* thing. I hate to admit it but I'm a bit clueless where enchanted artifacts are involved.'

If Dolos would have been paying attention to Eris at all he would have noticed that nothing he had said had remedied her original bewilderment. If anything, her confusion had only grown more intense. But, lost in the flow of his own monologue, he didn't. He just kept on talking.

'Oh well, don't worry your pretty little head about it pumpkin. Now. Where was I? Mm, that's right, supplies. Okay then, you wait here dearie, have a nap or, good gods woman, you're soaked! Máher's bloody useless. He could have dried you out in an instant, but didn't. I swear there's something wrong with that man. Anyway, warm yourself by the fire, you'll catch a cold otherwise. I'll leave Beher behind to keep you company, in your enfeebled state I don't want to leave you alone, I shan't have you dying on my account. Plus, a dragon, no matter how small he is, is about as inconspicuous as a naked magistrate walking down the promenade.'

At being referred to as small, Beher growled deep within his throat and bared his teeth in the most menacing way he could. Dolos being Dolos, failed to notice.

'Yes. That settles it. Stay here Beher. I'll be back right quick Eris, expect me on the morrow's morn. Ta, ta folks.'

With that Dolos bowed for a third time before exiting the cave. Leaving an utterly befuddled Eris, and a less than pleased Beher, behind him.

Chapter 27

Dolos

The walk back to Súthburh was not particularly long, but for Dolos it was a welcome change to, what he considered to be, the utterly droll void-space of nothingness, that he occupied whenever Máher was in control. The sky was clear and, even though it was nearing the horizon, the sun still exuded a pleasant warmth that reaffirmed Dolos's desire to live.

Shame it will be dark soon, I would have liked to frolic in a field of daisies as I caught some rays while cavorting with someone's willing daughter. No matter. I'm sure some other devilish diversions will present themselves. One can only hope I suppose.'

A slow trickle of farmers shuffled through Súthburh's eastern gates, their workday complete. Dolos didn't waste his time joining the que, but rather nudged and shouldered his way through the crowd. A stream of empty placations, 'Excuse me, thank you, don't mind me, on important business, make way and cheers,' followed every physical interaction. Perhaps they worked, for each farmer Dolos bumped simply returned his rudeness with a vicious stare. Not a one challenged him openly. But then again, maybe they were just too exhausted to bother, or too wary of the stranger's confidence.

At the end of the line a pair of bored looking watchmen flanked the gates. Each making a show of waving through the citizens, as if their guidance was the very reason why the procession remained civil. Most were allowed through without interruption, as they were known to the watchmen, but as soon as he reached their post Dolos was immediately stopped for questioning.

'Hello, hello, hello. What do we have here now?'

'Well Charles, I'd say it appears to be a stranger attempting to gain entry to our fine city at a hitherto irregular hour.'

'I think you're right George, I think you're right indeed.'

It was an odd exchange to be sure, and more than a little comical, but Dolos opted to remain silent, forgoing his usual wit, as he had no wish to incur any more inconveniences to himself.

Bloody morons, just let me through.

'So, good sir, what is your reasoning for entering Súthburh today?'

Dolos grinned as wide as he could, hiding his increasingly violent thoughts, and bowed.

Hopefully an abundance of civility will ease my passage into the city. Not to mention the greasing of palms.

'Good day sirs. I am but a humble traveller who has, through no fault of my own, found himself in the unexpected need of supplies. Bandits you see.'

At the mention of bandits, the guards gave a knowing nod, their expressions grim. In recent years the Southlands rulers had taken drastic steps to eradicate banditry in their lands, to great effect, but every now and again fresh tales of some outlaw's nefarious deeds reached Súthburh's walls.

'So, naturally, I made for Súthburh. This was not my original intention, hence the late hour of my arrival, but necessity dictated that I did so.'

Dolos held out his hand, a pair of gold coins hidden behind his fingers. Without missing a beat, George took his hand and shook it firmly.

'My condolences friend. Be sure to make a report with the Senchal, I'm sure he'd want to hear your tale firsthand. He makes a habit of hunting down bandits whenever he can and who knows, it could be that your property is recovered. In any case, the city welcomes your patronage.'

Breaking his hold upon Dolos, the guard waved him through the gates. The gold was gone. In thanks, Dolos bowed to the pair once more.

'Thank you kindly, good sirs.'

Well. That went better than I expected. I mean it's not like I look like the most nefarious villain ever, but I certainly look a little shifty. I sure as hells wouldn't have let me in, but then I suppose I know what I've been up to, not to mention what I plan on doing. Then there's the fact that they didn't even try to extort more coin from me. Bah, amateurs.

Following the main boulevard, Dolos looked casually at the buildings he passed. Despite their ancient age, their windows and wooden trims were clean and well maintained. Their stonework however was nothing short of immaculate. While it was not as though he expected dilapidation, Dolos found it somewhat surprising that there was no evidence of degradation at all. Not even an errant scratch or chip.

Dwarves. Gods did they know their stuff.

Quickly, Dolos lost interest in masonry and his thoughts drifted.

Hm, what to do first? I could track down a lustful tavern wench for a bit of rumpy pumpy. Or perhaps 'persuade' a shopkeeper to give me all their valuables and gold. Oh, I know. How about I murder someone, that's always fun. But who? A miscreant or a whore? Well, whichever I find first I suppose. Mm, so many good options.

Mid-thought a searing pain erupted in his mind. Instantly, he stopped walking and clutched the side of his head in vain effort to lessen the torment.

'NO!'

That single word reverberated around Dolos's skull, drowning out the city around him and diminishing all his other senses. Blinded to everything, save for that word, he stammered a response into the darkness, with every word hoping that he would be delivered from his suffering.

'Ah, cripes. Hey Lord Kyrios, how's it going big man? Um, so no fun, that's cool, that's cool. What would you have of me?'

'KNOWLEDGE. DALINAR. SUPPLIES. ERIS.'

With every word Dolos winced as the voice of Kyrios boomed in his head. Passersby looked at him strangely, thinking him more than a little disturbed, unaware of the internal conflict that tore at his insides.

'I will do as you ask, at the earliest convenience of course, how could I say no? But and I mean no disrespect when I ask this, as you're the one true God and all, why don't you just snap your fingers and 'bam' everything sorted?'

Dolos braced himself as he waited for Kyrios's reply, anticipating the agony of God's words. Nothing. Two minutes passed, still nothing. Relaxing slightly, Dolos sighed in relief, thinking himself free from further torture. Glaring at everyone who dared look at him, Dolos began to skip along the cobbles, humming an offbeat tune as he went.

'THAT WOULD BE BORING.'

Caught completely by surprise, Dolos nearly jumped out of his skin.

'Goodness gracious your lordliness, you scared me half to death. Message received your eminence. I'll get right onto it.'

Reeling from Kyrios's latest tirade, Dolos increased his pace and headed directly towards the Peoples Depository of Knowledge. Head bowed, he ignored everyone and everything he passed.

I don't know why he had to choose me. He could have picked anyone, but no it had to be me.

To those that lived in the city the Peoples Depository of Knowledge was an impressive building, but to foreigners it was truly awe inspiring. Like the other buildings around it, numerous spires jutted from its roof, each twisting towards the sky like gargantuan facsimiles of a narwal's horn. Elegant banisters and balconies framed the plethora of windows on the upper floors. At a distance they were stunning, yet so intricate in their design that they were, it was impossible for passersby on the ground to discern the true extent of their detail. In short, this was far more than an ordinary library, it was an architectural masterpiece.

While this was the first time Dolos had ever visited the Depository, his access to Máher's memories afforded him with a certain level of familiarity with the building. For Dolos it was a peculiar sensation. Though it was foreign, it was also strangely familiar. As though from a dream he recognised many of its features and instinctively knew exactly where to go. As he walked along the marbled entrance hall, he found an unaccustomed, yet comforting, warmth swell within his breast. As near as he could express it, he felt as though he was coming home after a long stretch abroad.

Máher, what a strange fish you are.

Before him, at the end of the hall, stood a singular desk. It was simple in its design, but unequivocally massive. Behind it sat a lone clerk, an ageing woman who was well past her prime and clearly bored. Very bored.

As he reached the woman, she was so engrossed in whatever it was that she was doing, which as far as Dolos could tell was the drawing of infinite doddles on an errant scroll, that she completely ignored Dolos. He doubted that she even knew that he was there. To gain her attention, Dolos coughed. She continued to ignore him. Impatient, and still more than a little disappointed at Kyrios ruining his fun, he tapped the tabletop in front of the clerk furiously.

'Good day madame. I have come to this esteemed establishment in the pursuit of knowledge and was wondering if it would be possible for me to browse the tomes held within.'

Without looking from her incessant drawing, the clerk responded in an unenthusiastic monotone.

'The main atrium is open to the public at all times, so feel free to peruse it at your leisure. If you're after something specific, and don't know the author, I'd recommend asking one of the librarians. They'll be able to find what you're after much faster than you will. Scrolls and tomes in the atrium can be borrowed for a short period of time, no longer than a week, if a small down payment is provided to serve as collateral.'

Pausing briefly, the clerk stared off into the distance as she twirled a strand of hair in her fingers. Looking up at Dolos for the first time, the clerk continued her unenthusiastic welcome.

'If you can't find what you're after in the atrium then the Depository also provides access to our restricted section for a small fee. Entry to the restricted section is provided under the proviso that you will be always accompanied by a Depository employee. No texts are to be removed from the restricted section under any circumstances. Failure to comply will result in your arrest and a lifetime ban from the Depository. If you have any questions feel free to ask the nearest Depository employee.'

Speech over, the clerk turned away from Dolos and resumed her sketching. Somewhat chagrined by this less than warm welcome, Dolos raised his arms in admonishment and stuck out his tongue at the clerk. She did not see it. Mumbling unpleasantries under his breath, Dolos left the receptionist and entered the main atrium.

Bloody bint. Useless at her job and as sour as a dried up cootch.

It was massive, nay it was beyond massive. Craning his neck Dolos gazed towards the ceiling as he attempted to count the floors. However, he gave up at twenty when his head started to swim with vertigo. Around him there were no walls in the traditional sense, rather there were bookcases. Giant bookcases organised in rows which portioned each section from the other. Each of which was packed full of books, scrolls and loose parchments.

Oh my, I certainly do not have time to wade through all this. That would take an eternity. It's time to find some help.

Sighing as he grew ever more impatient, Dolos looked around the chamber for assistance. The first, and only, person he saw was an elderly human. Although he was completely bald, his epically proportioned beard made up for that fact. Pure silver, it stretched to the man's stomach, where it was tucked neatly into his belt. The small cart that he pushed squeaked as he shuffled behind it, putting away books as he went. Shrugging, Dolos decided to introduce himself to the man.

'Good day sir, my name is Dolos. It's a pleasure to meet you. Am I correct in the assumption that you are a librarian?'

The squeaking stopped as the man halted his cart. With a broad and warm smile, he returned Dolos's greeting.

'Greetings my good man. Why yes. Yes, I am. Archibald at your service. Is there something that I can do for you?'

'Capital. Indeed, there is. I was wondering if you could help me find any information you could on an historical figure I've been researching. I'm not sure if you would have heard of him, Dalinar is his name.'

The librarian's face morphed to form a quizzical expression. Repeating the name to himself under his breath, the man rolled the name around his mouth as if it were a wine that he was tasting for the first time.

'Dalinar. Dalinar. I must say there's something familiar about the name, but for the life of me I can't quite place it. Hm, most infuriating, normally my memory is quite infallible. Maybe some extra information regarding this individual might spark something in the old brain pan. When was this, Dalinar didn't you say, alive?'

'I'm afraid that I have absolutely no idea.'

'Mm, less than ideal, but not the end of the world. Okay. So, do you happen to know where this fellow resided? Or do you know if he was present in any particularly important historical events?'

'Unfortunately, that would be a no and another no.'

'Cripes. You're not making this easy, are you? Okay then, no location, no known historical links, no notion of time of prevalence, what's left then? Mm, we could tackle this from another direction I suppose. Do you know of this chap's parents or if he sired any prominent children? Perhaps there were some siblings?'

'No, no and no. All that I've found in my research thus far is this fellow's name, Dalinar, and some evidence to suggest that he was, and still could be for all I know, a very important person. The whole point of me coming here was to find out more.'

'Hm, well, I know I've heard that name somewhere before and it's not like it's a common name, so I reckon your man is in this place somewhere. Tell you what, you wait here and I'll go and consult with my fellows, maybe one of them has heard of this fellow and can remember where from. Sit tight and I'll be right back.'

Dolos watched, frustrated, as the elderly librarian shuffled off, leaving him alone. Having no choice but to wait for the man to return Dolos slumped to the floor and waited for his return, eschewing the mountains of knowledge around him for his thoughts.

Blast this. I could be off having some fun, but no, I must wait here for the slowest man alive to make the rounds. I haven't had a decent shag in forever. Maybe I could find a comely lass for a game of hide the sausage in the stacks. Mm, not likely though. All these librarians seem old, yuck, and not to mention male, even worse. There aren't any patrons about either. Bugger. Maybe I could light a fire and watch the whole place burn. Hm, I haven't got any matches though. Damn. I've never thought I'd be jealous of Máher for anything. Insufferable bastard.

Used to being alone with his thoughts, Dolos failed to notice the librarian amble back to him. Ever polite, the elderly man waited for Dolos to notice him. After waiting for what he deemed to be a polite amount of time, the man coughed. Startled from his musings, Dolos glared upwards, ready to reprimand whomever it was that had disturbed him. Seeing that it was the old librarian, all plans of scolding fled from his mind and enthusiastically he leapt to his feet.

'Well? What have you found? Don't leave me in suspense.'

'We found mention of your man. To be honest I'm not surprised that I couldn't remember where I had heard that name before. It has been more than twenty years since I read the book that contained his name and in all our archives it's the only one that does. What's most fascinating is that particular tome originates from almost three thousand years ago, long before man occupied these parts of the world, long before we had even thought about building walled cities.'

On the verge of losing his temper, Dolos hissed furiously at the librarian.

'Yes, yes, that's wonderfully fascinating, but what does it say of the man himself? What of Dalinar?'

Ignoring, or ignorant of, Dolos's hostility, the librarian sighed and shook his head.

'Precious little I'm afraid. Just a small poem that, in my opinion, is more artistic then informative. Here I'll read it to you.'

> *A hearthless stranger walked were all feared tread*
> *Wrought fellowship and bound the broken*
> *He faced the immortal foe and left them sundered*
> *But fear ye should, for in time they will be awoken*
> *All hail Dalinar! Saviour of the living, Lord of Men*

'We made a copy for you, as the original is far too valuable to lease. As you can see, it's not much. I'm dreadfully sorry that we couldn't be of more use.'

As the librarian finished the poem, Dolos simply stared at the man in shock. Re-mouthing the words he had just heard he shook his head and snatched the parchment from the librarian. Reading the verse for himself, and finding nothing new, he hissed angrily.

'Is that it? This is the only mention of Dalinar? In all the scrolls, tomes and held within this archive, *this*, is all you have? Worthless!'

Furious at this disappointment, Dolos scrunched up the parchment and threw it to the floor. Ignoring the librarian's indignation, he turned and stormed from the Depository.

Fuck this place, if I never see it again, I'd be eternally grateful. I'll fetch those damned supplies so we can leave this cesspool of humanity post-haste, fun be damned. Ha, I never thought I'd think it preferable to let Máher take the reins. Oh void, at least you never disappoint me.

Lost in thought, Dolos failed to notice the hooded figure leave the shadows behind him and begin to trail his movements.

Chapter 28

Baron Victor von Grumanhieser III

As the carriage trundled along, rattling with every pothole, the Baron smiled, Neesa's gratitude warming his heart.

'Think nothing of it. A gentleman such as myself couldn't bear standing idly by when a lady was in the need of aid. That just wouldn't do. Ha, not to mention there's the fact that Jeeves would up and leave me the instant I contemplated doing so. Now, don't tell the bugger I said it, but I'd be utterly lost without him. I honestly doubt I'd survive the parting.'

'Be that as it may, I feel as though I should repay you. I don't have much, but I can give you this.'

Neesa leaned forward, unslinging the Master's rapier from her back. As she held it before her, she hesitated. In her eyes, the Baron saw an ocean of conflict and on her face, he witnessed clearly the memories of deep traumas etched profound. Yet, from somewhere, the baron knew not from where, other, more pleasant, thoughts fought their way to the forefront of Neesa's attention and she smiled. Supressing her grin, as though she found it improper, Neesa handed the sheathed blade to the Baron.

'Here. Rapiers don't suit my fighting style and this looks like a decent piece, so take this with my thanks.'

The Baron gingerly took the blade, rotating it slowly as he examined it thoroughly.

'Well, I'll be. This is indeed an exquisite piece. I'm flattered that you'd think to gift it to me, but I'm not sure I'd be the best fit for it. In my youth I was a poor swordsman and, though I hate to admit it, I've only gotten worse with age. I fear I'd be more likely to stab myself with it, rather than my enemy, if I ever tried using this in actual combat.'

Neesa shrugged, her grin returning with gusto.

'That's okay. Take it anyway. I could always give you a few pointers. You know, just so you don't stab yourself with it.'

He knew what Neesa had said wasn't entirely said in jest, but the Baron couldn't help but to chuckle at her words. Laughter echoed from the carriage's walls as his belly shook with mirth.

'Ha, ha, ha. No one would want that, least of all me. Very well then, I'll take it off your hands, but I'll hold you to your offer. I expect some lessons in the near, nay very near, future. Thank you.'

Taking another look at the rapier, the Baron smiled as he fastened it to his belt.

It's been a long time since anyone has given me a gift this fine. That's one of the downsides of being an adult I suppose, people expect you to just buy whatever you want whenever you want it. Hm, there's also the fact I don't have many friends. That might have something to do with it. Maybe I should get Jeeves to take me out of the estate more often?

Lost in his thoughts, the Baron was oblivious to the awkward silence that had overcome the cabin. As far as he was concerned, their conversation was over and he was more than happy to return to his inner musings. Neesa was not so content. A polite cough from her direction told the Baron that she was not done conversing. Ever the epitome of good manners, the Baron refocussed his attention on Neesa and waited politely for her to say her piece.

'If you don't mind me asking Baron, I've told you why I'm in my current predicament, but what about you? What was it that was driving you north?'

For a moment the Baron considered how he would respond.

Should I tell her the truth? I hate to lie and I can't really see the harm in it, so I may as well. But perhaps some omissions might be wise.

'Quite simply my dear, I am seeking knowledge. You see, I came across an icon that I had never seen before and just had to find out more about it. One of my contacts said that he recognised the icon, so I was travelling to meet him. We could have just conversed through letters, but sometimes one prefers to do business in person I suppose.'

Finding and unimportant scrap of parchment, the Baron quickly sketched the symbol that was secretly tattooed on his chest and handed it to Neesa.

'This is it here. You wouldn't happen to recognise it would you?'

Neesa scanned the page quickly, a perplexed look clear upon her face.

'No. It's just a pair of cogs. It could literally mean anything.'

'Truth be told, I would have been flabbergasted if you had recognised it. And yes, I know it appears unimportant, but I have reason to believe that it's divine in origin. I haven't the foggiest as to which one of them it belongs to. Everyone I spoke to about it was as stumped as I was, but it must mean something to someone. I haven't pondered all the ramifications yet, but I suspect that it could very well be the mark of a new divine.'

Neesa shrugged.

'So?'

'You see, there hasn't been a new divine in centuries. So, this in and of itself would be a remarkable occurrence, but there's more to it. Every time, throughout the entirety of our known history, the rise of a new divine has coincided with a profound change in the mortal realm. Sometimes good, sometimes bad, but always profound. Therefore, *if*, and I cannot understate the if, this symbol is the hallmark of a new divine, we could all be in for a bumpy ride, so to speak. I believe that it would be prudent of us to be prepared for this ride as best we can. And that requires knowledge.'

The Baron felt the carriage slow and come to a stop. Perturbed, he looked out his window, trying to ascertain what was going on. Seeing nothing that offered an explanation, he turned back to Neesa.

'Have you any idea as to what in blazes is going on?'

She didn't have to answer, her quizzical expression was evidence enough that she did not, but regardless, she shook her head and shrugged her shoulders. Frustrated, the Baron stuck his head out his window and shouted to Jeeves.

'Gosh darn it all Jeeves. Why have we stopped this time? And, please, don't tell me it's time to make camp already, we've only just recently finished lunch.'

'No, my Lord. Um, this is not what you would call a scheduled stop. You see, my Lord, the road ahead is blocked. We cannot pass.'

Sighing deeply, the Baron hung his head, massaging his brow with his knuckles.

'Well Jeeves, this is less than ideal. Are you certain there is no way past? Can we turn around? What of this blockage, can it be moved perhaps?'

'I'm sorry my Lord. We have so little room that turning around is quite impossible. And as to the blockage, well, it would be best if you saw that for yourself.'

'If you say so Jeeves. Shall we my dear?'

Opening the carriage door, the Baron gestured for Neesa to exit the coach. Wordlessly she stepped down from her seat, onto the road below, her tail swinging lazily behind her. Following immediately behind her, the Baron skipped down the steps, curiosity replacing frustration.

I wonder what it is. A landslide? A treefall? Hm, if it were something so mundane Jeeves would have just said. It must be something different.

Easing his way past the stationary Jeeves and Neesa, the Baron's vision was filled with what it was that blocked the road. Utterly taken aback, he stopped, gasping at the spectacle.

'Well. I'll be. You certainly don't see one of them every day, or ever, as it were. I only know what it is because I've read about them. What in the seven hells is one doing taking a nap on a main road of all places?'

Before the trio, occupying the entirety of the road, lay an adult forest giant, curled up and snoring loudly. The creature wore no clothes, but blessedly its more intimate anatomies were shrouded by wavy drapes of lichen. Its white beard was scraggly to the point of frizz and its grey hide was dappled with a smattering of green and brown splotches. Though he only caught a whiff of it, a musky aura emanated from the beast, reminding the Baron of damp earth and decomposing leaves.

I would never have guessed it to be a forest giant. Colour me surprised.

Casually noting the raised embankments to either side of the road, the Baron swore under his breath.

Of course, Jeeves was right. The bloody giant's blocking the only way out. Bugger.

Without another thought, or consultation with his fellows, the Baron yelled towards the creature, seeking to wake it.

'Ah friend, if you don't mind terribly, we were wondering if you would be so kind as to move? It'll only be for a moment, just so we can pass! We hate to be such a bother, but we have little choice in the matter!'

Apart from the steady rise and fall of its chest as it breathed, the giant remained motionless.

'I'm not sure it heard you, my Lord.'

'I do believe you're right Jeeves. It appears something more extreme might be in order.'

With a confidence of a man who believed himself incapable of doing any wrong, the Baron strode purposefully towards the sleeping giant.

'My Lord? Are you sure that's prudent?'

Reaching the beast, the Baron gave the creature's foot a firm kick. *Thud.* The giant didn't react. Sighing in frustration, the Baron kicked the giant again, this time much harder. As before the creature did not wake, yet this time the Baron's body contorted in agony as a searing pain shot upwards from his toe. Jumping on his uninjured foot to avoid contact with his damaged digit, the Baron unleashed a chain of unfiltered vulgarities.

'Fuck, fuck, fuck! Bloody, fucking ball sacks of maggoty fuckery!'

The sweet melodic tinkling of feminine laughter broke through his pain fuelled haze. Turning around, he saw Neesa bent over, clutching her sides as she was overcome by the amusement she found in his discomfort. Jeeves, in his typical fashion, was disapprovingly shaking his head.

At least he could manage some restraint.

'Gods be damned woman, it's not funny. That bloody well hurt.'

'Yes, yes, it is. Ha, ha, ha. It's absolutely hilarious.'

'Alright you bugger, have a taste of this!'

Growling, the Baron drew the rapier from his hip and thrust its tip into the giant's foot.

Immediately, the snoring stopped and the giant's eyes shot open. Originating from somewhere deep within the creature's chest, a pained roar exploded from its mouth. Soundwaves reverberated off of the nearby dirt mounds, rattling the Baron's bones. Groggily, the giant rose from the ground, wobbling as it found its footing. Looking around for the source of its pain, the creature's head swivelled from side to side, an angry grimace affixed firmly on its face. Finding the Baron, it squinted in his direction.

'Ow dat hurt. Wot you do dat for?'

Okay, that might not have been the best of ideas. I'd better be tactful if I want to talk my way out of this mess. He's a lot bigger than me and could literally squash me like a bug.

Chapter 29

Baron Victor von Grumanhieser III

A thin sheen of sweat grew upon the Baron's brow. In his chest he felt his heartbeat surge and, in his ears, he heard its steady thumping clear. Praying silently to the gods, he licked his lips and took a deep breath.

'I'm terribly sorry for that, but we had to wake you. You see, we need you to move so we can pass. I tried yelling, really loudly I might add, but you wouldn't wake. I tried kicking you, apologies for that too, but that also didn't work. I didn't want to stab you, really, I didn't, but it was the only option I had left, again sorry. But, let's be honest, I only stabbed you in the foot and not that badly either.'

The giant scratched its head, his brows furrowed in a puzzled expression. He wasn't great with words at the best of times and this was by far from the best of times. He had only just awoken, forcibly torn from a peaceful dream, and his brain was foggy, his cognition impaired. In short, he had no idea what the Baron was saying. Granted, he knew that they were words, even he used words on occasion, but he didn't know which words. To him it was just noise that held no meaning. The only thing that was clear in his mind was the knowledge that this little man had hurt him. He did not like being hurt.

'Small thing meanie. Me no like meanies. Argh!'

Panic griped the Baron as the giant closed the gap between them in a single step. The beast drew an arm back and swung it towards the Baron. Telegraphed grossly, the Baron saw the attack coming a mile off, yet, paralysed by fear as he was, it was only by the barest of margins that he escaped. Fuelled by desperation, the Baron leapt out of the giant's path, thudding into the ground with an audible oof.

Carried buy its momentum, the giant momentarily lost track of his immediate prey, but immediately found others to vent its anger upon, Jeeves and Neesa. As the pair stood idle, awestruck by the beast's sudden ferocity, the creature bellowed at the duo. Lowering it head, just as a bull would, it charged recklessly towards them.

Jeeves, despite his advanced age, reacted faster than Neesa and yelled out towards her.

'We can't win this! Run!'

Without looking back to see if she followed his command, Jeeves sprinted off towards the oncoming giant, counter-intuitively forsaking his own advice.

Flat-footed, Neesa was caught between two unsavoury options, to surrender to cowardice and flee or to assist a pair of relative strangers in a helpless endeavour. To her there was no choice at all. Drawing her sword, with an exhilarated grin, she embraced the thrill of impending combat and dashed after Jeeves.

Rolling onto his back, the Baron drew Peacemaker, placing the rampaging giant firmly in his sights. Gently he squeezed its trigger, hoping beyond all rational hope that his shot would stop their quarry, or at the very least give the creature pause.

Bang!

The gun kicked violently as it boomed, launching its payload toward its target.

Moving too fast to be seen, the bullet zipped through the air, crossing the divide between the Baron and the giant in an instant. As the lead smacked into the back of the creature's head a small puff of green blood bloomed from its scalp. Instantly, the beast stopped its charge and grasped at its wounded head, howling as its own blood seeped from between its fingers.

Veering to stay beyond the giant's reach, Jeeves threw two silver discs towards the beast. Each hit their mark, but skittered ineffectually off of the monster's hide. Reaching the Baron, he held out his hand to help his master to his feet.

'Another cracking shot my Lord. You are definitely getting the hang of that thing, but we have to get out of here. We can't fight that monster.'

Gripping Jeeves's hand firmly in his own, the Baron grimaced as he pulled himself to his feet.

'Agreed. However, it seems our new friend is intent on doing just that.'

With a sublime grace Neesa danced between the giant's feet, slashing her sword at the creature's legs whenever an opportune moment presented itself. Her blade barely scratched the giant's thick skin, but after repeated blows both its legs were coated green as blood from a patchwork of wounds seeped freely.

Time and time again the giant swatted at Neesa, but with every attack she darted away, pirouetting inches from death each time. Her kimono's sleeves fluttered about her as she twirled, her face beaming with enrapturement as she duelled.

'By the gods, she's magnificent. I've never seen anyone move like that before. Have you?'

'Yes, my Lord. Many years ago, there was an Imperial warrior I witnessed fight in the arena. The similarities between the two are uncanny and while Neesa's got a long way to match the skills of that particular swordsman, I think that in time, if she survives, she could surpass him.'

Tired of the biting fly at his feet that it couldn't quite swat, the giant changed tack. Kneeling with a single knee on the ground, the giant swept his arm in a low, sweeping blow. Having nowhere else to go, Neesa summersaulted over the careening forearm. Expecting this, the giant snatched Neesa from the air. Now caught in its grasp, the beast raised Neesa's struggling form to its eye, laughing manically at her feeble attempts at escape.

'Har, har, me got you now. Squish, squish time!'

Bile rose in the Baron's throat as he heard Neesa scream. Bloodcurdlingly frantic, it was one born from the pain and desperation of one who knew that they were about to die. Reacting instinctively, he sheathed his useless rapier and drew Peacemaker. Too desperate to take careful aim, he forewent caution, instead intending to fan the weapon's hammer as fast as he could, releasing the entirety of his payload in one savage salvo. Squeezing the trigger, he anticipated the explosion, but when its hammer fell there was nothing but a soul wrenching '*click.*'

Oh no.

Urgently, the Baron pulled back the gun's hammer and squeezed the trigger again.

'*Click.*'

Dammit, why won't you work.

Acting as the avatar of insanity, the Baron squeezed Peacemaker's trigger for a third time.

'*Click.*'

Gods. I know there's unfired rounds in the cylinder. Blast. The firing pin must be knackered. The gun's useless.

Mortified by his own impotency, the Baron turned to an equally horrified Jeeves and stammered wordlessly. All the while Neesa's shrieks intensified.

Lost in his hopelessness and unable to see a solution to Neesa's plight, the Baron stood immobile, frozen in place. Fortunately, the mistress of fate had deemed Neesa worth saving and as such provided her salvation. Eyes locked unwaveringly on her struggle, the Baron barely heard the thrum of bowstrings, but he clearly saw the carnage that they heralded. A trio of bolts impacted the beast with tremendous force, their bodkin tips easily penetrating the giant's flesh.

Startled, the creature wailed in pain and dropped Neesa. As it flailed about recklessly, she seized her chance and dashed to a safe distance. Three more blots slammed into the giant's flank. Knowing it was beaten, and fearing yet more pain, the giant howled in frustration before fleeing up an embankment disappearing into the woods beyond.

Seeing that Neesa was now safe, the Baron spun around, wishing to thank their timely saviours. In the middle of the road sat four riders, each draped in dappled cloaks, their faces hidden behind hoods pulled low. Three of them cradled crossbows in their arms, while the fourth, who was closer to the Baron than the rest, simply held his reins loosely near his lap.

No insignia, but they look to be scouts or some such. There might be a larger force following behind them. Curious.

'My appreciations friend for your timely intervention. If not for you and your companions I do believe our friend, not to mention both my manservant and myself, would be dead.'

The lead horseman just waved the Baron's words aside.

'Is that your carriage?'

His voice was deep and laced with a commanding tone. This was a man, the Baron could tell, that brooked no weakness and demanded the uttermost respect. However, at the man's query, the Baron wondered as to the sense of that question.

Do you see anyone else about? Who's else would it be? Bloody dullard.

Yet despite his thoughts, the Baron responded with a more civil answer.

'Yes, it is. Why?'

'Remove it from the road immediately.'

'We would love to, but we cannot turn around, too narrow you see. We have no choice but to continue onwards. Once we're through this cutting we'll be sure to drive as far to one side as we can, so you, and your fellows, can pass by safely. If we hadn't been delayed, I would have happily ceded the whole thing to you, but it would be best if we made it to town by nightfall.'

The rider raised his hand, flicking two fingers into the sky. One of his fellows spurred the flank of his steed, spinning it around to face the east. After whipping his mount with his reins, and bellowing a mighty 'huh,' he galloped away. His two remaining subordinates similarly mushed their steeds, accelerating swiftly past the Baron westward.

Now alone, the lead rider rode close to the Baron and nodded in affirmation.

'That will suffice. Just don't tarry.'

Conversation over, he urged his horse after the pair of riders heading west.

Well, he was certainly a cheery chap. Not to mention an exquisite conversationalist.

'Alright folks, I'd hate to get on that fellow's bad side, so let's get out of here. Oh, Neesa my dear, that was a bloody close shave, are you okay?'

Neesa didn't immediately respond, but after the pair had climbed into the carriages cabin and made themselves comfortable, she replied meekly to the Baron's question.

'I'm fine.'

As the carriage began its journey once more it resumed its incessant rattling. Ignoring his discomfort, the Baron inspected Neesa's face, searching for the truth behind her words. Somehow, she looked far wearier than he remembered her to be. Instinctually he knew that she was lying, erecting a veneer of bravery over a wealth of insecurity, but out of respect chose to not push the issue.

'That's good. However, feel free to let me know if that ever changes. I may not have the greatest of emotional intelligences, but I will listen to anything you have to say and do my darndest to solve any problem.'

'Noted.'

An awkward tension filled the cabin and the Baron found it impossible to look Neesa in the eye. Whenever he would meet her gaze, she would turn away, immediately fixating upon something outside her window.

And my parents still wonder why I never married. If they could see me now perhaps, they'd understand.

Knowing full well what the Baron had promised the cavalryman, once they were clear of the embankments Jeeves steered the carriage to the leftmost edge of the road. As soon as he had done this a thunderous cacophony of hoofbeats pounding against the earth overwhelmed the carriage. Peering out the window, the Baron saw an endless blur of colour as brightly dressed men atop similarly coloured mounts cantered past.

'Looks like Estmirian cavalry to me and a lot of them to boot. Tensions must be really heating up between the Southlands and the Empire for Estmire to get involved militarily.'

Neesa sneered.

'Good. The more that stand against the Empire, the better. All Imperials need to be slaughtered, every last one of them.'

'Hm.'

Poor girl. I wonder, what did they do to you to warrant such hatred?

Soon losing interest in the passing horsemen, the Baron drew Peacemaker and started to examine the piece. He broke it down quickly, removing the barrel and the cylinder. After inspecting them both carefully, he found nothing wrong with either component. Satisfied, he extracted the hammer mechanism and examined it.

Ah, just as I thought, the firing pin has snapped. An easy fix, I just have to slide in a replacement, lucky I thought to bring spares. Hm, maybe I should consider using a harder alloy for this component in future, lest it break again. Then again, if I harden the steel, then that should suffice. Oh well, that's something to explore in the future, for now it just needs to function. I'd hate to run into trouble without it.

Just as he was putting the final screw back into Peacemaker's frame, Jeeves banged on the carriage's roof and shouted through its window.

'My Lord! We've arrived at a town shall we stop for the night?'

Startled from his tinkering, the Baron dropped his screwdriver. Abashed, he looked coyly to Neesa, just to see if she had seen his clumsiness. She hid an amused grin behind her hand, but remained silent. Ignoring the growing heat in his cheeks, the Baron refocussed his attention out of his window. He was amazed to see that the sun had long since descended beyond the horizon and been replaced by an ocean of stars.

'Already? Gosh. It always surprises me how fast time flies by, especially when one is having fun. Ha, ha, hm. Anyway. Yes Jeeves, absolutely yes. Park when you see a decent spot and we'll see if we can't find an inn or some such.'

'As you wish my Lord.'

Once stopped, the Baron climbed down the carriage's stairs, Neesa following closely behind. Jeeves stepped down from his driver's chair to join them. Before they had walked three steps down the earthen road, the Baron grasped Jeeves by the shoulder and pulled him close.

'What a damnable day Jeeves. The answers I seek are out of my reach, we were almost killed by a bunch of Imperial soldiers and to top it all off, an angry forest giant nearly squashed us to jelly. But, as bad as all that may be, not all is lost, for I smell ale on the wind. There must be a tavern nearby.'

The Baron's proclamation was proved true as the trio rounded the next corner. A pair of drunken farmers, already deep into their cups, stumbled from a porch, clearly oblivious to the oncoming strangers. One of the men tripped on the feet of the other, carelessly losing hold of his tankard. The vessel flew from the farmer's grasp and ended its short flight by thudding heavily into the dirt by Jeeves's feet. A geyser of alcohol spurt through the air towards Jeeves, but the butler deftly steeped to one side, avoiding the entirety of the spray.

'I must say that was awfully close.'

'That it was Jeeves, ha, ha. Let's get inside, I'm properly parched.'

Chapter 30

Neesa

As Neesa entered the tavern sounds of boisterous merriment filled her ears and the pungent smell of spilt ale assaulted her nose. Serving wenches flittered between the full tables, trying to keep up with the insatiable demand for alcohol. Men wolf-whistled at the girls, especially the prettier ones, and in response they laughed, taking the men's advances as nothing more than harmless fun, just as they were intended to be.

However, one of the patrons took it a little too far. Neesa saw the man grab one of the younger women firmly on her behind. The woman didn't laugh, nor did she smile. She simply froze. Anger surged within her chest, her heart racing as it fuelled her rage. She wanted to act, to stop this vile ingression, but she could not. She was just as frozen as the girl, captured by one of her worst memories she was catapulted into her past.

*   *   *

'Hurry up girl! Fetch more wine, the good stuff! Those nobles at table four won't take to us kindly if their goblets go dry. By the gods do we need their patronage.'

Shook from her daydream, Neesa stammered in response to the publican.

'Oh course. Um, I'm so sorry Ed... Edgar, I'll g... get str... straight onto it.'

As fast as she could, Neesa rushed to the store room, almost falling down the stairs in the process. Shaking with nerves, she reached for the bottle of wine. It slipped from her flustered fingers. Seeing the bottle fall in slow motion before her, Neesa reached out to catch it. But, instead of catching the bottle, it bounced off of her closing hand and shattered against the wall. Shards of glass clinked to the floor as the purple wine splattered over everything in the room, save for Neesa. Somehow, she manged to avoid the spray.

Oh no, oh no. Edgar will lash me for this, I'm sure of it. Darn it. Oh well, I'll tell Edgar about this later, much later. I have to deal with those nobles first. If I do well, he might even forgive me.

Fortunately, for Neesa there was another bottle of the same vintage. But only one more. Taking extra care to not drop this one as well, Neesa picked up the bottle gingerly, making sure to hold it firmly in both hands. She climbed out of the cellar slowly, her tongue poked shyly from the corner of her mouth as she concentrated on not falling.

I'm not going to drop this one as well.

The nobles at table four were deep in their cups by the time Neesa got to their table. She offered the wine to one of the men, hoping that he would take the bottle so she could leave, but he wouldn't have it. Instead, he thrust his goblet into her face.

'Hic, don't be shy love, fill 'er up. Hic, all the way to the brim if you would please.'

Neesa curtsied and did as the man asked, all the while taking great care to not spill a single drop. In turn, each of the nobles offered their glasses to Neesa. Around the table she went, filling all of the men's goblets.

'As I was saying, before I was interrupted by Frankie over there, the Emperor needs to spend more coin on infrastructure. The first rule of economics is to save when it's good and to spend when it's bad, and I don't need to tell any of you which we are currently enjoying, do I?'

'You're not wrong Eugène, but the Emperor has his heart set on saving as much as he can. Rumour is that he's building a war chest to fund another expansion.'

Neesa was halfway through filling one of the noble's glasses when the man grabbed at her behind. She could feel the man's hand caress her skin through her dress, the fabric doing nothing to shield her. Blushing, but saying nothing, she kept filling his glass.

Oh gods. What do I do?

Casually, the man squeezed her gently. Gasping in surprise, it took all the control she had to prevent herself from spilling the wine. Her entire body was trembling and her heart raced. She was afeard, desperately so, but she didn't know what to do, she was frozen in place. Noticing her discomfort the man simply chuckled.

'Ha, ha. There's no need to be scared girl, I won't hurt you. Who knows, you might enjoy it. Ha, ha.'

The man's wineglass was long since full, but Neesa lingered. Standing petrified, incapable of movement, she felt his gaze linger on her body. She felt her blush deepen as it spread throughout the rest of her body, as his stare burned her, devouring her physique with a carnal hunger. Her heart pounded in her ears and her breath came fast and shallow. Amused by her suffering, the man slapped her arse softly, all the while laughing heartily.

'Ha, ha. Run along then girl. Leave the bottle.'

Freed from her bindings, Neesa ran away as fast as she could, a foul melody of sniggers chasing her from behind. Finding refuge in the washroom, she leant against the wall and tried to steady her shaking frame. Her head swam with dizziness as she wiped away each of her errant tears, but it was futile, they just wouldn't stop. Sniffling, Neesa sank to the floor, forgoing all attempts at composure. Surrendering to her sorrow, she drew her legs to her chest and as she cuddled herself, she wept.

Neesa didn't know for how long she sat there crying, in her grief the passage of time was an irrelevancy beyond all consideration. She knew that Edgar would be mad at her for shirking her duties, not to mention the broken bottle of wine, but that no longer mattered to her. Overcome by sorrow, nothing mattered to her at all.

Why did he have to do that?

The washroom door clattered open, causing Neesa to jump in surprise.

'What cha doin' down there girl, cryin' an' such? We've got folks tha' need servin'.'

It was only Ellie, Edgar's wife. Relieved that it wasn't Edgar himself, Neesa leapt from the floor and hugged the welcoming matron. Through her tears, and sobs, she told Ellie what had just happened.

'There, there child, it's goin' to be fine. I know they shouldn't do it, an' I suspect tha' many of them know they shouldn't do it, but for whatever reason there will always be some menfolk that treat us womenfolk as nothin' more than objects to use for their pleasure. I hate to say it, but there's nothin' that either you nor me can do to change that.'

Neesa felt better for Ellie's touch, she took comfort in it, but her words only solidified her melancholy.

'Now, you wipe your face an' dry your eyes. Edgar has asked me to send you his way, up in the main suite. You'd best hurry off; we both know what he gets like when he's angry.'

She didn't want to leave Ellie's arms, but Neesa knew that the longer she tarried the worse it would be for her. According to Edgar, tardiness was a mortal sin, second only to disobedience. Breaking her hold of Ellie's midriff, she grabbed a dishcloth and cleaned her face. Once she was satisfied with her efforts she ran to the door, but before leaving the room, she looked back at Ellie.

'Thank you.'

Ellie simply smiled, shooing the young infernati away.

As Neesa ran through the tavern, she ducked and dodged around the dancing patrons. The bard was strumming a simple guitar while belting out a catchy tune. Neesa was no aficionado of music, but it sounded good to her. It made her smile, despite her mood. At any other time, she would have enjoyed dancing to its beat, and perhaps would have even sung along with the minstrel, but not tonight. Edgar was waiting.

Gods be damned. The one night we get a decent bard, is the night I can't enjoy it.

Jogging up the stairs two at a time, Neesa couldn't help but hum along with the music. Spirits lifted, she skipped along the hallway, right up to the main suite's door. It was closed. Abashedly, Neesa knocked on the door. From the other side Edgar's familiar voice answered.

'Enter.'

Doing just as she was bidden, Neesa entered the room, ensuring that she closed the door behind her. Standing in the centre of the room was Edgar, just as she had expected, but he was not alone. By his side stood the man who had groped her. She froze as her blood ran cold.

Oh no. This can't be good.

Seeing her hesitance, Edgar grabbed Neesa's arm and led her into the centre of the room. All the while she felt the other man's eyes follow her. It made her skin crawl, but there was nothing she could do. Edgar remained silent, and Neesa knew better than to ask questions, instead it was the other man that broke the silence.

'Now girl, take off your dress.'

Neesa spun towards Edgar, her face twisted in disgust, and looked into his eyes, searching to see if she should follow the directions of this man. He gave her the slightest of nods. Stammering, Neesa pleaded with Edgar.

'Pl... please sir, I don... don't want to.'

The bedroom echoed with a resound crack as the man backhanded Neesa across the side of her face. Her head was wrenched sideways and despite herself, she cried out in pain. Unable to look at the man, she kept her gaze averted as she rubbed her numbed cheek. Her tongue tasted a metallic twang as her cut lip bled into her mouth. Despite the taste she swallowed it, thinking it unwise to spit it out.

'That was not a request. Now strip.'

Oh gods, oh gods, oh gods.

Seeing no other option, Neesa abashedly pushed her dress's straps from her shoulders. Momentarily getting caught on her bosom, she wiggled it down and once past her breasts the dress slipped easily from her slender frame. The cool air chilled her naked flesh and, despite the heat that burned her flushed cheeks, she felt goosepimples spring up all over her body

'My word. She is quite the specimen, isn't she? What of her age, do you know it by any chance?'

Edgar shook his head.

'Alas, my lord, I do not. I know she was taken when she was still young, but her birth year has never been known. However, if I were to hazard a guess, I would say around fifteen or sixteen. Her first cycle was almost four years ago now, so that would make sense.'

Neesa dared not raise her head, but she heard the man walk around her and could feel his eyes devouring her nakedness. His footsteps stopped.

He's standing right behind me.

She didn't move, she was far too scared to. She could feel the man's breath on the back of her neck, hot and heavy it burned her skin. She felt the slightest of touches against the outside of her thigh as the man stroked her leg. Shivers ran down her spine as his hands moved to cup her buttocks and rub the base of her tail. Barely managing to remain standing, she quivered as silent tears streamed from her eyes.

'She's a virgin then?'

'As far as I know my lord.'

Neesa gasped as the man ran his hand down the front of her belly, right to the pit of her stomach. Almost tenderly, he parted the lips of her womanhood. Neesa felt a single finger push gently against the mouth of her vagina. Discomfort wracked her body and she bit her lip in distress, but still she remained motionless.

'Mm, excellent. Her hymen is intact and she is clearly ripe for the plucking. I will have her. Wait outside, we can arrange payment once the deed is done.'

Bowing to the man, Edgar left the room without another word. As the door clicked shut behind him, the man started unbuckling his belt. Instinctually, Neesa knew what was about to happen. Her chest tightened as a surge of fear constricted her chest.

He's going to rape me. Oh gods no. Please no.

'Get on the bed girl. Lay on your back and spread your legs.'

Neesa was torn. She wanted to refuse the man, but at the same time didn't want him to beat her. After the briefest of considerations, Neesa concluded that a beating would be the preferable option. As such, she offered another protestation of resistance.

'Please sir, no. I don't want to do this.'

The man crossed the distance between them in an instant and wrapped his hands around Neesa's neck. Struggling for breath as his fingers dug into her throat, she flailed desperately at the man's hands, trying to loosen his grip. In response he tightened his grasp. Neesa's vision swam with dots as her body screamed out for oxygen. Reluctantly, she accepted her defeat and abandoned all notions of resistance.

He's too strong for me, there's nothing I can do.

Though he still held her tightly, his grip loosened. Blessed relief surged through Neesa as her lungs filled with air, but the man gave her no time for respite. Forcefully, he twisted her head, compelling her to look into his eyes. Within them she saw a hatred that was soon echoed by his venom laced words.

'Listen closely you little daemon bitch. I am going to fuck you. That cannot be avoided. The only choice you have is to do as I say or to continue defying me. Doing as I say is the easier option. Refuse me again and I'll fetch the rest of my fellows. They'll hold you down while I screw you, then when I'm done, they'll each have a turn as well. We'll all fuck you. Repeatedly. And just between you and me, Eugène has a particular penchant for sodomy. It will not be pretty. Do you understand me?'

Unable to speak, Neesa nodded as much as she could, her glimmering eyes wide with fear.

'Good.'

The man released her neck and looked expectantly at Neesa. Sighing, she resigned herself to her fate and lay on the bed. She turned her head to one side, averting her gaze. She didn't want to look at the man, nay, she couldn't bear to look at him. Tentatively, she opened her legs.

Gods. Let it be over quickly.

With an impassioned ferocity, the man gripped Neesa's legs and pulled her towards him. Taken off guard, Neesa yelped as she slid across the sheets. Anticipating what was about to happen, she closed her eyes as tightly as she could.

Neesa felt him for an instant, rubbing his erect member against her labia, before he thrust himself inside her. Pain, sharp and fierce, stabbed at the pit of her stomach. She wanted to remain silent, to stay strong, but it was too much for her, she screamed in agony as yet more of her tears flowed. She felt herself rip at his vigorous advances, each of his thrusts tearing more of her most intimate parts. A wet warmth dripped from her and ran down the cleft of her buttocks. She was bleeding, but lost in the constant pain and shame she barely noticed.

Mercifully, the man's lunging stopped as he groaned in release. Neesa felt the man leave her insides and, knowing it was now over, rolled onto her side, curling into a ball. As her blood mixed with the man's spilt seed, Neesa sobbed uncontrollably atop the bed, overcome by the anguish that infested her being.

Lost in her grief, she barely heard the man dress, nor did she hear him open the door or call to Edgar. She did however hear the man's final words to her master and his response.

'Should she fall pregnant make sure it's taken care of. I will not be the father to a bastard hellsborn mongrel. Do you understand me?'

'Of course, Lord Balor. We wouldn't want such a, scandal, either.'

Neesa's sobbing intensified as these words compounded her grief. For they removed the only potential silver lining of this torrid affair, a child.

*   *   *

A bump from a nearby patron tore Neesa away from the past. Shaking the final vestiges of her memories from her mind, she wiped away an unwanted tear and refocussed on the man. His hand had not left the girl's rear and she still had not moved. Reminiscent anguish gave way to anger. Incensed, Neesa shouldered her way through the crowd towards the man.

I'll fucking kill him, the bastard.

Fists clenched, ready to strike, Neesa neared the pair, but movement from the girl gave her pause. Bending her waist, the girl lowered herself towards the man and kissed him passionately on the mouth. Neesa froze. Though she couldn't hear what the girl said, she could easily read her lips, what they spelled out was unmistakable. *I love you.*

Conflicting emotions surged within Neesa. She loathed it whenever men encroached upon the personal space of women uninvited, but in this instance the man's advances were not only tolerated, they were welcomed.

By the gods. I almost struck a man for showing affection towards his sweetheart. Is there something wrong with me?

Flustered, and more than a little annoyed with herself, Neesa turned from the couple and pushed her way outside. Devoid of any care, angry growls and admonishments followed her as she bumped into the other patrons. As she stormed from the tavern, she heard Jeeves's surprised exclamation as he wondered to where she was headed, but she ignored him.

Heart a flutter, Neesa turned down random roads and paths, first left, then right and finally left again. Heaving with emotion, she stopped, leaning her head against a house's wall. Furious with those that had wronged her in the past, and with her own flaws, she punched the wall as hard as she could.

It hurt, by the gods did it hurt, but strangely the pain gave her some small measure of comfort. It was familiar to her, like a mother is to her child, and somehow, she felt more at ease within its embrace. She knew this made no sense, but that was how she felt. Welcoming the pain, Neesa punched the wall again. The skin over her knuckles split, oozing blood that coated her hand and smeared along the house's side. Grimacing wildly, she hit the wall again.

'Hello, Neesa.'

Startled, Neesa stopped mid-swing and turned towards the voice. Before her stood a human woman. Covered by a simple grey cloak, a raven hued fringe poked shyly from beneath her broad brimmed hat. Neesa tried desperately to see the woman's face, but all of her defining features were masked by shadow.

A myriad of questions circled her mind, most prominently how did a stranger know her name, but before she could ask any of them, the woman continued speaking.

'We were deeply impressed by the manner in which you dealt with that insufferable Imperial pig, you knew him as the Master, when you took your freedom. Suffice it to say, we were very pleased to see him go. In fact, we were so impressed that we have decided to extend an offer of invitation to you. We would like you to join our order.'

All of the questions she had planned on asking were immediately forgotten. Instead, Neesa simply stammered.

'What?'

'We believe that you would be, with a little time and refinement of course, an invaluable asset to us. Just as we believe that we could be of great service to you. As such we want you to become one of us.'

'What? Why would I do that? I don't know who you are, or what you do, or what your plans for me are. Why would I join you?'

'They are all fair questions and your concerns are not without merit. But, have no fear. We are nothing more than a small, albeit powerful, group of people that seek to rid our world of its more unsavoury elements. We strongly believe that you would be of tremendous help in this objective. As a gesture of good faith, we have a morsel of information for you that you might find interesting. I assume you are familiar with the name Lord Balor?'

The memory of her first encounter with a rapist still fresh in her mind, Neesa paled as her stomach turned.

'Yes.'

'We thought as much. The man you know as Lord Balor is currently residing in Estmire, specifically in Evonium. We have no idea for how long he will remain so, but if you find yourself there in the near future, it might be to your advantage if you sought him out and 'dealt' with him as you did the Master.'

'Why are you telling me this? What do you want from me?'

'We currently don't require anything from you Neesa, but if that ever changes, we will contact you directly. For now, just stay close to the Baron. We are uncertain of his intentions and that makes us uneasy.'

The woman paused, waiting for Neesa to ask more questions. Flabbergasted, and unable to compile a single coherent thought, Neesa said nothing.

'Very well. Welcome to the Collective, Neesa.'

The skittering of an errant stone over a cobbled walkway drew Neesa's attention away from the stranger. A trio of youths rushed by, hiding their faces from Neesa's view as they did so.

No doubt they're outside without their parents' permission and were worried that I'd rat them out. Well, lucky for you, kiddos, I have no idea who they, or for that matter any of you, are.

Once they had passed Neesa returned her attention to the stranger. She was gone.

Chapter 31

Thoron

As he floated in nothingness, pulsating lights flashed blue and distant stars rushed across the ink black sky, impatient to reach their destination. Beautiful in their simplicity and naturally awe-inspiring, they found ingress into the depths of Thoron's soul. He couldn't help but to smile.

All around him colours, an assortment of infinite variety, exploded into the pallid void. Twisting and blurring together, they brought a kaleidoscopic insanity to the previously mundane. The colours merged to form a muddy brown, only to explode into joyous vibrancy once more. The cycle repeated itself over and over again, seemingly eternal. Finding it similarly beautiful to the star-scape he had previously witnessed, but for intrinsically different reasons, Thoron watched on enthralled.

Without warning the sequence stopped, frozen in place the overly saturated colours gradually bore their way into his weary eyes. Brighter and brighter, they shone, till all semblance of colour was gone and he found himself drifting in an endless expanse of white. Lost in nothingness, without a single point of reference, Thoron felt uncertain as anxiety clawed at his heart. Was this a dream or a nightmare?

Three dots, distant and tiny, appeared in front of him. Squinting till his eyes burned with tears, Thoron tried as hard as he could to discern what they were. The outlines of their silhouettes blurred, but they remained as indiscernible as ever, barely visible blemishes on an otherwise pristine landscape.

Sound. Up until this moment Thoron had been unaware that wherever he was now, was a vacuum devoid of any sound. It was only until his ears rang with the all too familiar echo of war horns did this fact become unbearably obvious. The transition from silence to all-encompassing noise jarred his senses. Thoron grasped the side of his head with his hands, trying to keep the overwhelming sound at bay. It was futile.

Grimacing, he turned his head towards the source of the noise. Hovering in the air beside him was a sword and a shield. Their forms were instantly recognisable as Harry and Barry, but they differed markedly from the weapons he knew.

Arms and legs protruded, for lack of a better term, from their bodies. They both swayed rhythmically from side to side as their legs propelled them around Thoron, just as dancers would. In their hands they each held a horn, pressed firmly against their torsos. Although neither had any lips to speak of, it was clear to Thoron that their horns were the source of the din. In their other hand they each held a top hat, like the kind that some nobles took to wearing in the larger cities, above their heads. With each step they would bring it down, only to thrust it above them upon the next.

Thoron was thoroughly perplexed. Even though he knew it was impossible for inanimate objects to display any form of emotion, he would have sworn, if asked, that the both of them looked happy.

As Harry and Barry continued to frolic merrily around him, movement from the corner of his eye drew Thoron's attention away. The three black dots had grown larger, and as he stared at them it was clear that they were rapidly growing larger still. Blurred outlines became clearer and Thoron felt the clawed hand of dread seize his chest. He had seen these figures before, one orc and two goblins.

He tried to turn away, but was unable, his head would not move. He flailed his arms and legs, desperately trying to gain some momentum, attempting to get away, but he was stuck, unable to move. Eyes wide and mouth agape, Thoron watched as the trio got closer still, eyes kindled with black flame and mouths sneering in vindictive smirks. Still, Harry and Barry danced on.

For no discernible reason the goblins stopped, keeping their distance. The orc continued to approach. It grew larger as it advanced, to sizes far greater than any real orc could. Soon it was as big as a horse, and then as large as a house. Eventually, it became so large that it encapsulated the entirety of Thoron's vision. His heart beat with a tremendous pounding, sweat poured from his pours, drenching his entire body. As fear relented to terror, he attempted to avert his gaze from the creature, but no matter how hard he tried he could see nothing other than the beast's face. Harry and Barry were gone.

Starring into the creature's eyes, Thoron saw nothing but a profound emptiness, devoid of any emotion or empathy. He thought that if this beast had a soul to be found, it would certainly be as black as tar, a perfect facsimile of the shadow that burned in the eyes of its minions.

Opening its mouth, the orc gave a maniacal cackle, born not from mirth, but rather rage and anger. Warm spittle flew from its maw and covered Thoron. It stank of rotting and rancid flesh. Nauseated, Thoron felt his own bile rise in his throat and, unable to control himself, a wave of vomit gushed from his mouth. Pain tickled at his throat as he retched the last vestiges of his stomach's contents from his body, his eyes clouded by tears, stinging. Finding Thoron's display of weakness amusing. the orc laughed for a second time, deep and cheerful, clearly revelling in Thoron's misery.

The laughter stopped, yet its echoes continued reverberating within Thoron's head. The orc's mouth opened, rotting teeth lined a cavern of mottled purple and a tongue, covered in vast pustules, flittered in his direction. Like an anaconda encircling its prey, it wrapped itself around Thoron's stationary form. Dragged into the abyss, the orc's face vanished as Thoron's sight was completely obscured by wall of wine shaded muscle. Tighter and tighter, the orc's tongue squeezed around his body. Slowly the pain built from a tolerable irritant to an overwhelming and all-encompassing crescendo. Thoron felt as though his body would burst at any moment. He tried to move, but he couldn't. He tried to scream, but he couldn't. He couldn't do a thing.

A blinding flash of red flame shattered through the purple wall and the pain instantly receded. A searing light washed over his body, but he was not blinded by it, nor did it cause him any pain, rather it gave him comfort. Thoron felt a sense of completeness, one that his soul had always lacked, and he felt glad. He smiled a knowing smile borne of welcome and acceptance. Before him, floating as her wings flapped gently, Rivalitas returned his smile with that of her own.

Thoron blinked and as quickly as it had arrived, the light vanished. He was no longer floating in a shapeless void, but rather lying on the wooden floor of the hut he had discovered the night before. He blinked again and the hut remained. It appeared to him that his dream, for that is what it must have been, was over.

Gods. 'At wis the strangest dream I've ever had, an' tae be honest I'm glad it's over.

Groaning as he stood, Thoron massaged his stiff muscles. Absentmindedly, he inspected his wounded arm, wary of infection. He need not have worried, for it was completely healed.

Cor, it appears 'at bein' a man o' faith has its uses. 'At shuid have taken another week at least tae come right.

Shrugging, Thoron shifted his attention from himself to his surroundings.

The cabin he occupied was old and in a poor state of repair. Crooked floorboards twisted haphazardly from the building's foundation, ever seeking an escape from their bondage. A plethora of holes pierced the cabin's wall, which granted entry to an equal number of sunbeams. An ocean of tiny dust motes floated carelessly through the rays, light refracting alluringly off of their surfaces. For the most part the roof was intact, save for a collapsed portion at the room's rear. Throughout, rubble debris lay scattered across the floor.

Overall, the building was small, but by no means tiny. A family of three would have found it cosy, four would have found it stifling. Aside from the entrance, there was only one other door. Surrendering to his curiosity, Thoron crossed the room, all the while careful to not trod on an upturned nail, and gingerly opened the doorway, uncertain of what he would find. A high-pitched squeak aggravated his barely awake ears as the door's hinges protested his advances.

Stepping through the threshold, his eyes were drawn by a singular pillar of light. Caught in its glow, pale reflections of the softest white emanated from the mildew encrusted remnants of a bed. As his eyes slowly adjusted, Thoron moved with trepidation towards the light, his attention fixated firmly upon the centre of the halo. Two skeletons, one much larger than the other, lay atop the bed, their frames entangled in a loving embrace.

It was apparent that they had been human, or at the very least humanoid, and that the smaller of the two was the remains of a child. Perhaps, Thoron thought, they were parent and child or siblings who differed vastly in age. Whatever in actuality the case was, he knew not.

Poor buggers.

Morbid curiosity overcoming any notions of propriety, he inspected the corpses further. He could not tell how long they had been here like this, nor could he fathom the nature of their demise. He was unable to determine either of the skeletons sex's, unsurprisingly, as he had no notion of how that would even be done. As far as he could see, which was also the extent to what he could gather, what lay before him was a collection of bones from what was once two people.

The barest of glints, a twinkle of silver, caught Thoron's eye. A thin metallic chain peeked shyly from the closed fists of the smaller body. He knew that he should have left it alone, that there was no real need to pry, but a part of him wanted to, so that's what he did. While trying to be as gentle as possible, Thoron pried the finger bones away from the object they held. Long since devoid of any tissue or ligaments to bind them, the bones fell into a rough heap upon the bed. Thoron cursed under his breath, mouthing an apology to the child.

'Sorry.'

However, atop the pile of bone was the trinket he sought. Picking it up, as reverently as was possible, he dusted some grime from its surface and inspected the piece. It was a locket, either silver or silver coated, simple and unadorned. It was fastened to a thin chain of steel, strangely free from rust.

Opening the locket, Thoron was met by the smiling faces of two young girls, human girls. Each wore their hair up high, tied in neat buns, and their eyes shone with a mirth mirrored by toothy grins. It was clear to Thoron that the smaller of the corpses was one of the girls in the painting, as to which one, it was impossible to discern.

'At means the larger corpse must hev been their mother. Or perhaps their father. Tis a shame either way.

Shaking his head at the waste of it all, Thoron closed the locket and placed it back onto the bones of the child. Muttering a prayer to Hecate, he wished the departed souls well upon their journey to the afterlife.

A shiver ran itself up Thoron's spine as the temperature in the room shifted. Although it was mid-summer, and not at all cold, a strange chill permeated throughout the bedchamber. As he breathed out his breath hung heavy in the air and he couldn't help but to rub his hands together in a vain attempt to warm them.

An ethereal globe of light blinked into being, directly over the two corpses. It swirled chaotically through the air before splitting into two identical spheres. Each of the orbs looped upwards before silently slamming into the floor directly in front of Thoron. From the impact sites two wraithlike figures apparated, one of whom Thoron immediately recognised as one of the girls depicted in the locket. The other spectre he had never seen before, but knew instinctually to be the mother of the child.

They each smiled warmly towards him, the mother holding the hand of her child firmly within her own. Their hair and clothes rippled as if they were caught in an unseen wind, but to Thoron they didn't seem to mind. The elder bowed her head towards him, clearly expressing her thanks. Enthusiastically, the younger spirit waved her free hand towards Thoron. Then, with no more fanfare, the two spirits vanished with a puff and were gone.

Weel bugger me, ye dae no' see 'at every day.

Curiosity more than sated, Thoron gathered his arms and left the building. Not knowing in which direction he should travel, Thoron simply shrugged, turned away from what was familiar and strode into the unknown. Almost immediately after taking his first step, Barry's voice echoed in his head.

'Good morning, mate! Have a lovely snooze, did ya? Nice. So, what's the plan then? We goin' to find something to stab? Or maybe slash? What about bash?'

Thoron sighed.

'No' if I can avoid it. Am gunna find a toon an' get me some food. Then, once I've figured oot exactly where I am, I hev tae get myself back home.'

'Well mate that sounds like a bloody fantastic plan, save for the distinct lack of violence that is. Oh well, I'm sure something will turn up. Anyway, let's get a bloody move on shall we!'

It was still early and the air had a touch of chill to it, but as the skies were clear of clouds, Thoron knew it would soon warm. As he walked, Thoron swivelled his head constantly, keeping an eye out for any sign of civilisation or danger. He saw neither. After cresting a small hill, his stomach rumbled, clearly proclaiming its anger.

Ach, whining willny dae ye any good, thir's nary a thing tae eat and ye weel ken it, so shut it!

The day wore on and the sun reached its zenith. Still nothing. True to his premonitions, the day had grown warm, uncomfortably so. Sweat soaked both his shirt and trousers, making his every move an infuriatingly irritating exercise. Thoron was most assuredly not at all happy. Grumbling as he trudged along, he kicked a particularly large stone in his path, wishing to vent his frustrations. It was a poor kick and the stone barely moved, but worse than that, it had hurt his toe.

'Fecking wanker, shite balls an' pus filled arse cracks!'

'Hey mate, I can tell you're not doin' so great, so, um, I've got some news that'll cheer you up right quick. I just spotted some smoke trails over that hill to your left an' I reckon there must be a town or village nearby. It's a dead cert that they'll have some grub for you to mung out on.'

Thoron turned towards the direction Barry had mentioned, squinting. He saw no smoke.

'Ach, ur ye sure? I cannae see a thing.'

'Dead certain mate. When has old Bazza ever led you astray?'

Thinking of all the times Barry had done just that, Thoron chose not to respond to Barry's assertion. Instead, he just altered his heading and walked towards the hill. As he crested it, he was met by an assortment of buildings and several distant people bustling about their business. It was a town.

'See mate, told ya.'

The town, more like a village, was relatively small. Sure, it had several dozen houses, a blacksmith, a general store, an apothecary, an impressive town hall and from what he could see at least one temple, but it only had one tavern. It was literally a one tavern town. Fortunately for Thoron, a single tavern was all he needed. Ignoring everything else that was on offer, he made a beeline for it.

Chapter 32

Thoron

Entering the tavern, a quaint establishment ubiquitous the world over, Thoron strode straight to the man behind the counter, a portly human with no more than three hairs spread over his head. The man stopped wiping the glass he was cleaning and boomed happily towards Thoron.

'Good evening, friend! What can old Nicholas do for you?'

'Greetings. I wis wondering if ye had some food tae eat, somewhere tae bathe an' a room tae rent fur the night?'

'Hm, I most assuredly have those. Do you want anything in particular for your meal or are there any dietary requirements I need to be aware of? I only ask because some folks, like those finicky elves for instance, won't eat meat. Ha, silly buggers if you ask me!'

'Ach nae. Whatever ye hev cooking will dae me jus' fine thank ye.'

'Excellent! What about your drink? We have wines, beers, ales, ciders, spirits, and some non-alcoholic choices, like milk or water, ha, not that I think you'll be wanting any of those, ha, ha!'

'I reckon I cuid dae wi' a mulled wine, if ye hev any 'at is.'

'Ha, of course we do! Okay then, a drink, a meal, a bath, and a room, um, that'll be seven silvers please.'

Thoron reached into his money pouch and pulled out a single gold coin. He tossed it to the barman.

'Keep the change.'

Mid-air, Nicholas caught the coin and, without even looking at it, slipped it into his pocket.

'Thank you very much, master dwarf! Here's a key for your room, up the stairs and last on the left. Now, would you prefer to eat or bathe first?'

Thoron didn't have to sniff his armpit to know that he stunk.

'I think it wuid be best if I bathed afore I ate.'

'Very well, there's a basin in your room, feel free to head on up and I'll have one of the girls bring you some heated water. Once you're cleaned up, just find a table, anywhere you please, and I'll get you your food.'

Thoron nodded to the barman in thanks and left for his room. It was a simple space, constructed of stained pine and furnished with woven wool rugs, but it would service Thoron's needs. The bed was fit for a couple, though he was alone, and the wash basin, being designed for humans, was larger than he was accustomed to. All in all, Thoron thought, it was worth the silver.

Not bad, not bad at all.

He had just taken off his gambeson when there was a polite knock on the door. Opening it, he was greeted by a young maid holding a heavy jug of steaming water and a towel that was impossibly fluffy. Curtsying as she left the items, the girl scurried away wordlessly, leaving Thoron to his business.

Thoron striped hastily, and washed with just as much alacrity. The hot water felt amazing on his skin, and he was long overdue a cleaning, but he longed to quench his thirst and fill his belly.

Ach that'll do, thir's nae need fur perfection.

Coming back downstairs, after he had dried and dressed himself, Thoron found himself a table. As usual, he chose to sit with his back to the wall, so he could see all the goings on in the tavern, and waited for his meal. He didn't have to wait long. A young serving girl, by appearance a sibling of the girl he encountered earlier, scurried out with his order, placed it carefully in front of him and curtsied before dashing off.

The food was simple, but it was well-seasoned and barely touched the sides of his throat as he scoffed it down. The wine was surprisingly good and Thoron found himself downing the tankard far faster than he had originally intended to. Letting out a mighty belch, he signalled for another, which was hastily provided.

By the gods did 'at hit the spot.

Thoron gripped the second mug tightly and in a deliberate attempt to make it last longer than he first, he only took sporadic sips of the mulled wine held within. Even though he was tired from the day's trek, he deigned it too early to retire for the evening, so he sat in the still empty tavern, enjoying his drink and the quiet in equal measures.

Soon enough however, the tavern started to fill with those who had just finished their day's work and the previous silence was quickly overridden by banter. Thoron inspected everyone who entered, not for any reason other than simple curiosity, but none held any particular interest for him, save for an odd trio. One of which was an elderly man, dressed as a butler or manservant, the second of which was a middle-aged man, who had aged less than gracefully, and the third of which was a young infernati woman, who departed almost immediately after entering.

Strange tae see wan o' them 'is far south, or at all fur 'at matter.

'Strewth, it's an infernati! I've always liked infernati. There's just something so appealing about them, maybe it's the tail or perhaps the horns, but amongst all the races they are my favourite. Daly travelled with one for a time and she was top notch in all the right ways. A perfect ten, if you catch my drift.'

Ignoring Barry's interjection, Thoron stared at the remaining duo as subtly as possible, assessing them. They were strange insofar as they were most assuredly not locals, but as travellers were commonplace that was not overtly suspicious. The younger of the two was obviously well off, dressing as a nobleman would, but as far as Thoron could tell, there was nothing noticeably sinister about them, so he returned to his drink.

A short while later, Thoron noticed a young halfling woman walk casually onto the stage. She was tall for a halfling and curvaceous in the most appealing of ways. Frizzy chocolate brown hair sprouted wildly from her head, all attempts to tame it clearly having failed. Her clothes were plain and simple, but nestled almost reverently in her hands she held a battered violin and a bow. Only the most particular would have not considered her to be gorgeous.

The rest of the tavern ignored the halfling; they continued to talk amongst their tables and quaffed their ale greedily. Thoron, on the other hand, was enthralled.

As she took her position, she brought the violin to her shoulder. She scanned the crowd and for the briefest of moments her eyes met with Thoron's. In that instant, she smiled modestly and gave a respectful nod to Thoron. He felt his chest tighten as his heart began to race. Thoron was momentarily flummoxed. He had seen many beautiful women before, and even bedded more than a few of them, but Thoron felt that there was something special about this woman. It wasn't as though she was the most attractive woman he had ever seen, objectively she wasn't, yet there was something about her, something he couldn't quite explain, that led him to feel as though this halfling was precious beyond measure.

Gods. Whit a woman.

The Halfling brought the bow up to the violin and stroked it gingerly along the instrument's strings. A single solemn note reverberated throughout the tavern. All conversation ceased immediately and collectively the tavern turned to face the halfling minstrel. For a perceived eternity, the note continued to build in volume, until it utterly filled the minds of the audience. For them nothing but this note existed.

Thoron watched entranced as the halfling closed her eyes and let the music consume her entirely. Her hands moved slowly at first, a series of low notes painting a scene of bitter sweet melancholy. Thoron not only heard the music, but felt it gently caress his soul. He was struck by the beauty of it, but it also saddened him. It reminded him of all of those he had already lost and alluded to a future where he would lose more.

Gradually, both the pitch and the tempo increased and the beautiful despondency was replaced with impassioned understanding. Thoron felt that he understood the inevitability of loss and the need for it as the harbinger of renewal. He felt as though he could let go of all his grief and not forget those he had lost, but rather remember them at their finest.

Hands a blur, the halfling increased the pitch and tempo once more. In his mind's eye Thoron saw himself in a meadow bathed in warm sunlight surrounded by a sea of blooming wildflowers. They swayed, dancing in in time to the music, boundless optimism unleashed. Around him stood all of those he had ever loved, each smiling joyfully towards him. Thoron felt their pride in him and knew that his current path was where he needed to be and no matter the outcome all would be well.

The music ceased abruptly and as it did so Thoron felt a keen loss as the magical grip upon his heart was released. All illusions were shattered and his attention returned to the now still and noiseless tavern. The halfling opened her eyes and bowed to each of the tables in turn, her gaze lingering briefly when it met Thoron's. Somewhat shocked by this unconventional performance, the tavern patrons were slow to show their appreciation. Thoron was the first to applaud, but gradually everyone else followed suit. It was by no means a resounding roar, but it was indeed hearty.

Several more songs followed suit, each as affecting as the first. At the saddest moments, grown men couldn't help but weep softly into their cups. At the most jovial, the entire room shook from the combined laughter and huzzas of the crowd. Throughout it all, Thoron sat spellbound, as caught up in the emotional turbulence as everyone else, but never once did his gaze leave the halfling.

At the end of her final ballad, and as the praise for her performance washed over her, she met Thoron's stare. Unabashedly, he held her gaze and was rewarded with a sultry grin and a wink.

Cripes, gods strike me down if 'at wasn't the clearest invitation I've ever received.

Ceding the stage to, who Thoron assumed was her father, the halfling headed towards the bar. Many of the patrons congratulated her as they passed, offering her handshakes and tips. One of the more inebriated patrons was bold enough to slap her gently on the behind, but she just laughed it off with a smile and wiggled her finger at him.

Driven by something more than pure lust, Thoron left his table to join the halfling at the bar. Initially, she was surrounded by numerous admirers, each pressing for her affections, but much to Thoron's amusement, she rejected each in turn. She was never rude in doing so, yet as each one failed in their advances they stormed angrily from the tavern. Buoyed by their failure, Thoron walked up behind her and talked softly in her ear.

'Lass, 'at wis the best performance I hev ever seen, you've sure as buggery got a talent fur it.'

The halfling turned towards him and Thoron felt his heart skip a beat. Up close, her beauty was amplified to near goddess levels of perfection. Despite his stubborn nature, he had to admit that his earlier assessment of her was incorrect, she was easily the most attractive woman he had ever met. She looked him up and down, evaluating him, for what he did not know. Then, unexpectedly, she smiled at him.

'Thank you so much. I noticed you by the way, when I was onstage, I don't think anyone has ever stared at me that hard, or for that long, before.'

'Weel, clearly they dae no' appreciate yer beauty as much as me.'

'Ha, ha, you're not subtle are you. Good. I like that. I'm Jovita by the way.'

She held out her hand towards Thoron. Without hesitation he grabbed it, but instead of shaking it he drew it to his mouth and kissed it.

'Thoron, at yer service.'

'Oh my, it's excellent to meet you Thoron. Tell me are you staying here tonight?'

'I am.'

Jovita leaned in close to Thoron and whispered in his ear. He barely heard it over the crowded tavern, but hear it he did.

'Perfect. How about you take me upstairs for a bit of fun then?'

Heart pounding, Thoron nodded in acceptance to Jovita's proposal and took her hand once more. He led her through the crowd and up the stairs. The door to his room had barely clicked shut when Jovita untied the straps of her dress and wiggled it down over her bosom and waist. Thoron felt his pulse accelerate, and his loins strain, as he drank in her naked form.

By the gods she is perfect.

Without direction, he crossed the room and locked his lips with hers. As he kissed her mouth, Thoron lay Jovita gently onto the bed. Moans of pleasure left the halflings mouth as he massaged her breasts. Moving downwards slowly, Thoron kissed Jovita's neck tenderly, his hand tentatively exploring the mouth of her vagina. Arching her back, Jovita's sighs intensified.

Further down he moved, kissing as he went, stopping as he reached Jovita's bosom to suckle her nipples. First the left and then the right. He felt the welcoming warmth of Jovita's vagina engulf him as he eased his fingers inside of her. As they slid in, Thoron felt Jovita quiver. Leisurely at first, he eased his digits in and out of her, the halfling moaning with every thrust. His tempo built, faster and faster, until Jovita's entire body shuddered and she sighed in pleasured satisfaction as she came.

Jovita smiled up at Thoron, brow coated in sweat, chest heaving from exertion. She started to say something, but Thoron placed a finger over her lips and shook his head. He was not done.

Untying the drawstring around his pants, Thoron let them fall. Fully erect his penis throbbed and pulsated. Jovita moved onto her knees, gripping his phallus with one hand while the other fondled his balls. Up and down his shaft her hand blurred. Thoron groaning at the profound pleasure of the experience.

Before it got too far, Thoron stopped Jovita. Gently he guided her onto her back and eased her legs apart. Moving down on top of her he started to massage the head of his penis against her vulva. He stared into her eyes, seeking permission, his intention clear. Jovita bit her lip playfully and nodded in response.

In one powerful thrust, Thoron jammed the entirety of his member inside Jovita. The halfling's eyes shot wide and she let out a tiny scream, overcome by the glorious sensation of it. To Thoron it was heaven, Jovita's vagina was so wet and warm, he couldn't help but to groan in ecstasy.

Pumping in and out, his balls slapping repeatedly against Jovita's arse, Thoron thrust himself harder and harder into Jovita. Already tight, Jovita clenched as she achieved orgasm, compressing the walls of her vagina around Thoron's cock. Combined with Jovita's impassioned moans, it was too much for Thoron. Unable to hold it any longer, he gave one final thrust and expended his seed, groaning as his semen spurted from the tip of his penis deep inside Jovita.

Utterly spent, he rolled off of the halfling and lay next to her. Caressing her side, he looked into her eyes and smiled. Between his laboured breaths he whispered to her.

''At wis amazing lass.'

Jovita smiled in return as she stroked the side of his face.

'You weren't half-bad yourself.'

Thoron pulled Jovita's head towards him and kissed her more tenderly than he had before. Although the deed was done, he felt no desire to leave, nor did Jovita. So, instead they lay together, barely more than strangers, but locked in each other's embrace, sharing kisses, and exploring the depths of each other's souls.

Chapter 33

Eris

Many attest to the calming nature of the ocean. The rhythmic sloshing of waves as they impact the shore, the tender caress of a calm sea breeze. All of it combined, equated to an experience both soothing and comforting. However, Eris felt nothing of the sort. In actuality, she felt nothing at all. Not happy, nor sad. Not angry, nor jovial. For the first time, in the longest time, Eris's seemingly bottomless reservoir of love and mirth was dry. It's source, Mikael, was gone and in its place was nothing but nothingness and it left her feeling nothing but numb.

As she lay in the cave, a rock dug uncomfortably into her side, but the discomfort didn't even register in her mind. The fire that Máher had lit had diminished to tiny embers that did nothing to warm her. She stubbornly refused to remove her sodden clothes, not due to any bashfulness on her part, she simply couldn't bring herself to move.

Over and over, she replayed Mikael's final moments in her mind. Though she knew it foolish, a tiny part of her refused to accept the reality of his passing. She had witnessed him die, his lifeforce be drained, she knew him to be dead, but the irrational part of her brain questioned the certainty of this fact.

He can't be gone, he's just hurt. Yes, just injured. He isn't dead, he'll be fine eventually, all he needs is to heal, I just know it. It's going to be okay.

No Eris, no it isn't. You're in denial.

Her frail psyche shattered as that realisation sunk in. It was not going to be okay. It was never going to be okay again. Her love, the only love she had ever known, was gone, eternally and irrevocably gone. Nothing could be done to change that. His love irreplaceable, perfection nigh unattainable, would never be found again.

The worst part of it all was that it was her fault. If she hadn't botched that simple robbery Vejovis wouldn't have taken Mikael in retribution and he'd still be alive. If she hadn't killed that child, none if this would have happened.

Gods, I killed a child. A child for fuck's sake. I'm a monster.

Though she sat immobile, too tired to even cry, her conscience screamed furiously at her. Words laced with vitriol and hate bombarded her from within. Internally quivering, she did nothing to repel them, how could she, when her attacker was her own self.

Hours passed and the sun dropped below the horizon. Slowly the night wore on, but Eris could find no relief in slumber, her racing mind drove away all possibilities of that. The ocean waves did nothing to calm her, in fact, lost in her self-loathing stupor, she didn't even hear them.

Time moved on, implacably as ever, and the soft moon-glow of the evening relented to the harsh brightness of a cloudless day. Subconsciously, Eris noticed the change, it would have been impossible for her not to, but in her current state it meant little, such trivialities as the passage of time could not have been further from the forefront of her mind. Similarly, she barely noticed Máher's return.

She first realised his arrival when he grabbed her shoulder and in his signature whisper, consoled her with gentle words.

'I know your pain and I also know that it will fade. You will never get over Mikael's loss completely, but I promise you, it will get easier.'

Her pain still raw, Eris was thrust from her depressive state, and oblivious to Máher's good intentions, she snapped at him angrily.

'What do you know of my pain? Hm? How can you understand what am I'm going through, well? My life is ruined, the love of my life is dead, and it's all my fault! How dare you claim to know what I'm feeling!'

Máher's form shimmered as Eris's eyes filled with fresh tears. Ashamed, she wiped them away with the back of her hand. Stifling a sniffle, she bowed her head, abashed by her outburst.

'I'm sorry. That was uncalled for. Since the moment we've met you've only ever meant well and here I go spitting in your face.'

Máher waved her apology away, his face stern, but his eyes shining with kindness.

'Bah, think nothing of it. Me and pain are well acquainted. I know well its effects.'

Eris felt her chest tingle with emotion as Máher's understanding warmed her heart. Though she was in no mood for it, she mustered a brave smile.

'It's kind of you to be so understanding, but that's still no excuse. I'm so sorry.'

Máher shrugged his shoulders.

'That's okay.'

'Um, I know that this is a personal question, but if you don't mind me asking, who was it that you lost? You say you know my pain, so you must have lost someone, you know, your version of Mikael.'

Eris noticed his eyes un-focus as a faraway look overwhelmed his face. His furs rustled loudly in the close confines of the cavern as he paced restlessly around its interior. He wrung his hands together, the strain of their forceful contact clearly evident. He took a deep breath and exhaled slowly.

'No, I don't mind. I know the origin of your grief, so it's only fair you know mine. Over the years, I have witnessed many of those close to me fall to old age, disease, or circumstance, but there was one that affected me far more than the others. Her name was Hannah.'

Máher paused, inhaling slowly as he gathered his thoughts. Eris remained silent, waiting for him to continue.

'I first met Hannah during a particularly bad time in my life. I was alone and truly believed that I would always be. I had no friends, no family and not an ounce of love in my life. This was before I knew my father, or that Beher even existed, you see. Anyway, back then, I only knew despair and, on several occasions, I considered ending my life. I only ever came close to doing so once, but the dark thoughts were ever-present.'

'Anyway, it happened on an ordinary autumn day, nothing at all special about it. I was sitting on a park bench, lost in some particularly dark thoughts, when out of nowhere a small human woman sat next to me and just started talking. Not about anything special, it was just small talk, but that was enough, it made me feel something good for the first time in the longest time. We talked for hours and it was simply amazing, but eventually she had to go. I'm sure I tried to hide it, but she must have seen the pain on my face because before she left, she told me her name and where she lived, so we could meet up again.'

'I visited her the next day, a bit keen perhaps, but I just couldn't wait to see her. She didn't mind though, in fact she seemed pleased by my eagerness to be with her. From then we spent the next three weeks together. It was the best time of my life. She saw past my gnarly visage and into my soul. She saw who I really was and she still loved me. It goes without saying that I loved her in return. She was everything to me.'

'Then, like everything good I had ever known before, it ended. I don't know why, but one day she just stopped seeing me. She wouldn't even open her door for me. It was like she no longer knew I existed. That killed me.'

Oh, Máher. I'm so sorry.

'I couldn't take it. I relapsed into my depression so deeply that I gave up on life completely. I rode to the local cliffs and without a second thought I jumped from them. I wanted to die and I intended to do just that.'

'It was the Sisters who found my ruined body on the seaside rocks. I was alive, but only just. They nursed me back to health and helped me learn how to deal with my own twisted thoughts. I owe them everything.'

'Anyway, when I was back on my feet I went to try and talk to Hannah one last time. You know, to say goodbye, and all that. But she was gone. I found out from her neighbour that she had fallen ill, around the same time she stopped seeing me, and had passed away not long after I jumped off of that cliff.'

'When I learned what had happened, I was mortified. I thought that I could have been there for her, no I should have been there for her, at the end. That I could have helped her, somehow, but I let my own insecurities get in the way of her welfare. I didn't know if I could have saved her, I still don't, or even have helped her, but what if I could have? What if the reason she died was because I wasn't there to help her, to save her? I know now that I shouldn't have dwelled on what ifs, but at the time I couldn't help it, they were literally all I could think about.'

'It took me a long time to come to terms with the manner of her death, but come to terms with it I did. It still hurts when I think about her, but I no longer ponder the reasons for her passing. I've come to accept that good people are not immune to bad things, that's just life, bad things happen all the time and sometimes no ones to blame, it just is.'

Aghast, Eris sat frozen, unable to move or speak.

My gods. What he went through. The pain he must have felt. What he still feels. He can understand me.

Máher crossed the cave, stopping when he was practically on top of her, and held out his hand. Unsure of his intentions, but unarmoured by his heartfelt tale, she took it. A small squeak escaped her mouth as he pulled her from the ground. Before she could protest, he placed his hands on her cheeks. Her face flushed with a comforting warmth that spread throughout her entire body, drying her clothes, and kindling a spark of hope in her heart. Although it was unasked for, once it was received, Eris couldn't help but to be deeply thankful for it.

'Eris, I know Mikael's gone, and I know it hurts to have lost him, but try to focus on the good times you had with each other. I do that with Hannah and that's what makes her death bearable. Let Mikael live on in your memories in the best possible light and use that to better yourself. You can do this, and for as long as you want me to, I'll be here for you.'

'No matter how you feel about it, Mikael's death is not your fault, that is Vejovis's alone. He killed Mikael and he will answer for it. Maybe not today, or even tomorrow, but in time I will see to it.'

Eris wanted to doubt him, she wanted to slap him and his hollow words aside, but she couldn't. There was something about them, something about him, that consoled her troubled soul and planted the seeds of hope in her heart. For better or worse, she believed him and in that she found comfort.

'Thank you.'

'It's okay. Now, we've got a long ride ahead of us, so let's get out of here.'

Buzzing filled her head as a force pressed upon her consciousness, a flicker of recognition in Máher's eyes told her that he was experiencing the same sensation.

'Beher hates to interrupt the conversations of others, but in this instance Beher feels that Beher has to. A group of people are outside and Beher's not sure that they're friendly, they smell, odd. Hopefully they won't be a problem as Beher would love to leave this boring sea-cave behind, but Beher knows the kinds of people Máher usually attracts.'

'Shit.'

Máher withdrew his hands from Eris's face and strode purposefully towards the cave entrance. At its threshold he turned back towards her, his face stern.

'There are extra daggers for you in that pack. For some reason you keep throwing yours away. Hurry, you may need them.'

Without another word, he exited the cave. Hastily, Eris scrambled towards the pack and tore it open. Digging past various sundries and foodstuffs, she found the daggers that Máher had mentioned. As quickly as she could, Eris slid them into the empty sheaths around her person and rushed after Máher.

As she exited the cave, Eris had to shield her eyes from the sun, for while it was still low in the sky, its harsh rays assaulted her dilated pupils. She blinked furiously, willing her eyes to adjust, all the while searching for those Beher had mentioned. It took her a moment, but eventually she found them. To the east three robbed figures stood evenly spaced along the beachfront, another two were similarly arranged to the west.

Gods, if they mean us harm, we're screwed. There's no way past them. Fuck.

Like a caged animal, Máher paced the sand between the two groups anxiously. His face was flustered, his mouth curled snarling and his eyes glowered angrily. At his feet, Beher looked just as spiteful as he darted back and forth growling deeply at either group in turn.

Uncharacteristically, Máher shouted at the figures.

'You will not take her! You will not take me! You will not take us!'

Máher's hair flared as he sent a bolt of fire towards one of the figures. Contemptuously, his intended target simply flicked his wrist, deflecting the missile with no apparent effort. Harmlessly, it sailed into the ocean, exploding into a geyser of steam as it landed in the water.

Enraged, Beher leapt towards the figures, his teeth bared and ready to bite. As he neared the men, he leapt into the air, lunging towards them. However, before he could reach them, one of the figures raised his hand. Instantly, Beher lost all forward momentum and froze, hanging helplessly in the air. Seeing his brother rendered helpless, Máher bellowed a call driven by a primal furry and charged towards the one holding his companion captive, an axe of summoned fire held tightly by his side.

Another figure spoke a single intangible word and a wall of pure force blasted from his mouth. Máher couldn't stop, nor could he avoid the blast. He had nowhere to go. It hit him head on. Máher's flesh rippled as the thundering gale slammed into him. Unable to stand against the onslaught, and no longer in control of his movements, he flew backwards, tumbling through the air.

Sand sprayed violently into the air as Máher thudded onto the ground. His face twisted, contorted by pain, as the contents of his lungs were expelled violently from his body. His conjured weapon, vanished as he lost concentration on the enchantment holding its form in place.

Worried for his welfare, Eris took a step towards her companion, seeking to render aid to her prone companion. But that single step was all she could manage before Máher raised an arm towards her and yelled in her direction.

'No! Stay away!'

Biting her lip, Eris stopped, and though she didn't want to, she backed away. As a myriad of emotions roiled in her chest, fear, doubt, worry, anxiety and more, she watched on helplessly.

One of the hooded figures took a step towards Máher and spoke with a strangely high-pitched squeak.

'You mistake our intentions sorcerer.'

A second figure, this time from the other side of the beach, growled in a deep baritone.

'Yes, very mistaken.'

A third figure, who stood beside the first, snapped sassily at Máher.

'We are not here to take you, as you put it. Nor are we here to take your companions, they are irrelevant.'

When the fourth figure spoke Eris could barely hear what was said, as he whispered in a scarcely perceptible hush.

'No, we are here to warn you.'

To Eris's ear the fifth figure resembled an automaton as he droned with an emotionless matter of fact monotone.

'Cease your questions and desist your research. The one you seek is not for you. To find him will release a great peril upon this world. One it may not survive. You have been warned.'

As the final word from the hooded man was spoken, each of the figures spontaneously burst into a murder of crows. The birds scattered randomly into the sky, flying in every direction.

Free from his hold, Beher plopped ungracefully onto the sand. In an attempt to balm his battered pride, he roared into the sky, believing in his mind that he was chasing the figures away.

'That's right run from the mighty Beher you fiends! One minute more and Beher would have freed himself from your devilry and feasted on your bones.'

Danger seemingly gone; Eris ran to Máher's side.

'Are you okay?'

Wincing as he stood, Máher nodded towards her.

'I'm fine. Thanks.'

'That's good. Now, who the fuck were they and what the fuck is going on?'

Eris saw the answer on his face before he spoke the words, and it was obvious that he was worried. Really worried.

'I have no idea.'

Chapter 34

Máher

Máher saw the mistrust on Eris's face, it was unmistakable.

She doesn't believe me. But to be fair, I wouldn't believe me either.

Matching the uncertainty of her expression, Eris's voice radiated an aura of doubt.

'You must have some idea of what those hooded, things, wanted. What have you done to draw their ire?'

Unable to hold her gaze, Máher bowed his head and stared at his feet.

'What should I tell her, Beher?'

Beher trotted up to Máher and nuzzled his snout against Máher's midriff. The entirety of Máher's vision filled with the ruby red scales of his sibling and he felt somewhat comforted. As the familiar pressure of Beher's presence pushed at his skull, the dragon's sunset-coloured eyes blinked at him expectantly.

'Beher says you should tell the she-elf the truth. Maybe not everything, but at least something. That way the she-elf will stop pestering Máher.'

'And put her in more danger? I will do no such thing.'

'Beher thinks that the she-elf is already in danger. Being near Máher has that effect.'

'Granted, but I won't make it worse for her.'

Knowing full well that what he was about to attempt was at best a hard sell, Máher lifted his head and looked directly into Eris's eyes, mustering as much warmth and sincerity as he could.

'Eris, please believe me when I say this. I have no idea who, or what, those things are and I have no idea what they want.'

For a second Eris remained utterly still. Máher tried to read her face, but could ascertain nothing. Without warning her mouth twisted into a scowl and she aggressively pointed her finger at his chest. Practically spitting at him, she yelled.

'Bullshit! Do not lie to me!'

'See, Beher was right. Máher should have told the truth.'

'Look, I'm really sorry. I really am. I just don't want to see you put in harm's way and I feel that getting you further involved will do just that.'

Eris practically exploded.

'Didn't want me to get involved! Then why the fuck did you save me! Why didn't you let me die! I'm already involved and it's all because of you! Now that I am involved it should be up to me whether or not I stay involved or leave! I'm a grown woman who can make her own decisions. My life is my own to spend as I want, so don't you fucking dare use my wellbeing as an excuse to lie to me!'

In a physical display of his exacerbation, Máher threw his arms into the air.

'Look, things have changed. That was before those hooded freaks showed up. Everything I've promised you, I meant, I will help you in every way I can. I will not break my word to you. But I worry that if you become entangled with my quest, then they'll use their power against you too. From what they've already demonstrated I'd say that they're very powerful. I don't want to see you in harm's way on my account.'

Eris folded her arms across her chest, sass practically radiating off of her.

'Oh, would you rather I just leave you then? At least then I wouldn't be in any danger!'

'No, I don't want that. I don't want that at all. I just don't want to see you hurt, least of all because of me. I wouldn't be able to live with that.'

Unfolding her arms, Eris's body shifted as her demeanour softened.

'Well, that's kind of nice, but you shouldn't have lied to me. Now, back to your quest you mentioned. The truth. Now.'

Máher took a deep breath and exhaled slowly. He didn't want to tell Eris the truth, but the look on her face told him that she wouldn't let this go. He was going to have to tell her something, maybe not everything, but certainly something.

'Okay, I'll tell you what I can, but I'll do so as we ride. We need to get some distance from Súthburh and we're wasting daylight. I'll see to the horses; you get our things from the cave. Please.'

Unhitching the two grey mares from their posts, Máher gently ran his fingers through their manes. At first, they shivered at his touch, unaccustomed to the intimacy, but quickly they warmed to it, eventually neighing in appreciation.

'*Beher wonders, will Máher tell the she-elf everything?*'

'*No. That would be unwise.*'

298

Eris exited the cave and handed Máher one of their packs. Simultaneously, he gave her the reins of her horse. Abashed, he was unable to meet her gaze, so he mumbled his thanks to her midriff. Quickly throwing his pack over his shoulder, he mounted his steed and coaxed it forward, Eris following closely behind.

Cantering north, they quickly left the beach behind. The sound of the waves faded slowly until they were imperceptible over the rustling of trees and the chirping of birds. Forgoing the road for the sake of expediency, they rode in silence over mound and hillock, tiny vessels forging their own path atop an ocean of wild grass and flowers.

Inevitably, Eris became sick of following Máher's lead. Spurring her horse, she came up beside him. As she kept pace with him, Máher could feel her stare. She said nothing, but he could feel the expectation in her gaze and he knew exactly what she wanted. Without looking at her he raised his voice over the steady tempo of their mounts hoofbeats.

'I know that you've met Dolos and that he's tied to me magically.' To emphasize his point, Máher held up his ring. 'Well, soon after we were bonded, for lack of a better term, we were contacted by one of the gods. He tasked the both of us with uncovering all that we can about a particular someone. We were told nothing but this person's name, Dalinar.'

Pausing to take a sip of water, Máher gathered his thoughts before continuing.

'When Dolos went into the city he didn't just fetch supplies, he also went to the Depository. He tried to find some information on this Dalinar, as we have been tasked, but found nothing save for an ancient poem that, as far as we could tell, meant nothing substantive. I can only assume that these hooded figures we encountered on the beach want us to stop our research.'

Máher paused for a second time, taking another sip of water, but Eris interjected before he could continue.

'Why in the seven hells would those creeps be interfering with the business of a god? It makes no sense.'

For the first time in their conversation, Máher turned and faced Eris.

'Agreed. In all honesty not much about this whole situation makes a lot of sense. I know how it looks and I don't like it either, but one rarely refuses a god.

Unless they have a death wish, that is. No matter who, or what, those things were, I have to continue along this path. For better or for worse.'

'This feels off Máher. I think that there's more to it all than what you're telling me, whether you're aware of it or not.'

'I'm telling you all I know, but yes, I also believe there is more to this. What that is, I cannot say.'

Eris sighed.

'I'll continue to journey with you for now, but don't ever lie to me again.'

'That'll be a hard promise to keep, but I'll try.'

Máher saw Eris's face flush with anger, but she calmed as soon as she saw Máher's grin. Although it was a poor one, it was a joke. Unable to help herself, Eris smiled.

'That'll have to do.'

For hours the duo rode onwards in silence, only stopping to answer calls of nature and to have a lite snack once the sun reached its peak. Máher found comfort in the wilderness. He was used to being alone, save for the company Beher provided, and deeply appreciated the tranquillity. All in all, he was enjoying the ride. Eris was not. She sat poorly in her saddle and complained incessantly to its lack of comfort. Also, whenever some leaves rustled, or a twig snapped, her head would whip manically towards the noise, worried that it was the precursor to a predator's attack. Normally, Máher would have poked fun at her, but knowing that things were already strained between them, he refrained from any friendly jibes.

She's a city girl through and through. No matter. She will adapt soon enough.

After cresting a hill, most alike to each of the countless others they had already crested that day, Eris called out to him.

'Hey, look over there.'

Máher looked to where she was pointing and was surprised to see a middle-aged gnome, who was wearing a simple fur coat and tall bear-skinned hat, pacing around a toppled cart crossly. While he wasn't waving his arms around wildly, he would vigorously gesture between his wagon and a nearby horse. Impassively, the horse just stood there, chewing on grass as it watched its owner rant.

'*Beher, we've encountered a traveller. It might be best if you keep yourself hidden, we both know how most folks react when coming face to face with a dragon. Even a small one like you.*'

'*Beher's stalking deer, so Beher will do as Máher wishes. By the way Beher's not small, he's young, like to see you call him small when Beher's all grown up, ha.*'

'Do you want to see what's up with him?'

Eris shrugged.

'Sure.'

As the pair got closer to the gnome, they were able to make out the specifics of his grumblings.

'No, no, no, zees veell not do. Khow veell ve gyet to town now Fedosia? Cart not yet syeason old and alryeady brokyen. Oh, ze gods.'

The nearby horse, who Máher could only assume was Fedosia, whinnied as it shook its head. Not wanting to sneak up on the fellow, and cause undue alarm, Máher raised a hand in greeting and yelled to the gnome.

'Hail, friend.'

Turning around to face Máher the gnome's frustration disappeared instantly as a toothy grin spread across his face.

'Ah, travellers. Oppologees for these poor appyearances, eet breengs me much shame. But, vhere are my manners. I'm Bogdan, purveyor of mageecal treenkets and syellyer of many feene zeengs. Zees is Fedosia, gryeatest of fryends.'

Gently easing his mount forward, Máher bowed his head in respect.

'Greetings Bogdan, I'm Máher and this is Eris. It's strange to see a cart, let alone a laden one, so far from a road, what possessed you to journey this way?'

'Vell, mostly fooleeshness on my part. Lookeeng for ze mytheecal shortcut. Ve vanted to get to market earleer zan usual. Beeg meestake.'

'We've noticed that you're in a bit of a bind. Could we be of assistance perhaps?'

Bogdan's smile grew even wider and even more toothy. Máher didn't know how it was possible, but Bogdan managed it.

'Da, vat vould bye perfyect. As you can see, I khavye fixed vheel, but not have strength to leeft cart. Veef your help ve veell khavye no problyem. Eris, yes? Vhen ve leeft you put vheel on spoke please.'

Each of them got in position, Máher and Bogdan by the fallen quarter of the cart and Eris by the horizontal wagon wheel.

'Okay fryends, ve leeft on zree. Onye, two, zree, leeft!'

Máher placed his hands on the lopsided cart. Bracing himself he prepared to push with everything he had, and on the count of three he did just that. As he groaned deeply, a reflexive outburst to the expected physical intensity of the task, he was surprised when the cart rose effortlessly. Upon reaching its zenith he held it there, barely feeling any strain.

Well, that was far easier than I expected.

Eris, however was struggling with her task.

'Um, Bogdan, a little help please?'

Eris had only managed to lift the cart's wheel a small amount. Her face was twisted into a red tinged grimace and beads of sweat were dripping off of her forehead in a torrent.

'Now would be great!'

'Da, da, da.'

Bogdan released his grip on the cart and left Máher to hold it by himself. Perplexingly, Máher noticed no change in the wagon's weight.

Cheeky bugger, he wasn't lifting anything at all.

Scurrying over to Eris, Bogdan joined his hands with hers on the wheel. As Bogdan grunted a string of words Máher couldn't understand, but guessed were curses, the wheel slowly lifted. Once it was completely vertical Eris and Bogdan nudged it towards the cart. With a loud thunk it slid onto the wagon's axle and the job was done.

'My gods! Zat was pyerfect Máher, you wery stong my friend, I did nusseeng. Eris, not so much, but ve get zhere een ze end. Een thanks look at my vares, beeg deescount just for fryends.'

Bogdan walked to the side of the now righted cart and banged on its side. The air filled with the sound of cracking wood as one of its panels split into two. For a second, Máher thought that Bogdan had accidentally broke his own wagon, but this was not the case. Slowly, the sundered board folded outwards to reveal a myriad of shelves and hooks, each replete with a collection of curios.

'Velcome to Bogdan's travelleeng vonders!'

Potion bottles of various shapes and sizes glinted as their varying contents reflected the sun's rays. Piles of scrolls sat in lopsided pyramids alongside numerous leather-bound tomes. Weapons and articles of armour, all elaborate in detail and wonderous in design, hung from their hooks resplendently. It was a wonderous collection and Máher had no idea where to begin for he was enamoured with it all.

From out of nowhere, Eris's arm shot over his shoulder as she exclaimed loudly. 'What's that?' Máher followed the point of her finger to see what had her so interested. It was a dagger, but by no means any usual dagger. The face of its black blade was replete with fine patterns, the intricacy of which astounded Máher, and its straight edge was as fine as a razor. The guard of the piece was subtlety curved into the shape of a sweeping s. Inlaid gold contrasted against the obsidian handle and inset gems, large enough to impress, yet small enough to avoid vulgarity, sparkled wonderfully in the sunlight. While he was not normally interested in physical armaments, Máher had to admit that this particular weapon was indeed exquisite.

'Ah, ha, ze lady has good eye. Zat ees blink dagger, eet khas twin, but I only khave ze one. Ven eet ees zrown,' Bogdan snapped his fingers, 'it blinks to ze target. Zen ven you vant eet back', he snapped his fingers for as second time, 'eet blinks back to your khand to be thrown again. Wery useful, unleemeeted throws. Vould ze lady leeke purchase?'

'It looks amazing and daggers are definitely my thing, but I have no coin. Sorry Bogdan, I'd certainly buy it otherwise.'

Hearing the disappointed inflection in her voice Máher interjected.

'How much does it cost?'

'Mm, khonestly I do not know. Let's say for fryend, vun khundred gold.'

'Are you sure? That seems really cheap.'

'Bah, eet no problem, I got eet from deceased estate, wery good deal and you fryend, so et all good.'

'Okay then, one hundred gold it is.'

After fishing around his pockets, Máher held out three different sized coin pouches to Bogdan. Greedily, the gnome snatched each of the bags and began to count out the gold, his eyes shining with glee.

Eris grabbed Máher's arm and spun him around to face her. He could see that the emotion on her face was mirrored by the pleading in her voice.

'Please Máher no, this is too much. I don't want you to spend all your gold on me, I don't deserve it.'

'Consider it an apology gift for my earlier behaviour.'

'You don't need to do that.'

'But I feel like I should.'

Eris bowed her head to hide the flush of her cheeks, but she wasn't quite fast enough. Máher saw her emotional reaction clearly. From beneath her hood Máher heard her whisper, 'thank you.' He was about to respond, to tell her that it was nothing, to say that it was fine, but he was interrupted by Bogdan.

'Gold accounted for. Khere you go.'

Bogdan removed the blink dagger from its hook and threw it to Eris. Catching it deftly, she spun the blade in her hand, appreciating its perfect balance and excellent craftsmanship. Máher saw her gratitude clearly and felt a warmth bloom in his chest. He couldn't help but smile for, though it was a trivial thing, his gift had made her happy and that in turn pleased him.

Careful Máher.

'Vell Bogdan zanks you for ze khelp and ze buseeness. Farevell fryends, onvards Fedosia!'

Gobsmacked, Máher watched on as Bogdan's cart went from a standstill to a full gallop in a matter of seconds. Before he could wave, or even shout, a farewell, the merchant was beyond sight. A rapidly dissipating cloud of dust and the dagger Eris now held, were the only evidence of their peculiar encounter.

Hold on, did he tie Fedosia onto the wagon? He must have, but I can't remember seeing him do it. Come to think of it, I never saw him climb up to the driver's seat either. Strange.

'Were you able to understand him at all?'

Pushing his perplexation aside, Máher turned to Eris.

'Yes, of course. Why?'

'I was just wondering because I had no idea what he was saying the entire time. The only thing I understood was blink dagger, that seemed a bit self-explanatory. Anyway, thanks again for the gift, it really means a lot to me. Shall we continue on?'

Suppressing his disbelief, Máher just nodded.

'Um, yes, let's get going.'

As they continued their journey, the awkward tension that had dominated that morning's travel was gone. It wasn't as if they talked much, fast overland voyages on horseback don't lend themselves towards deep conversations, but Máher no longer felt obliged to remain silent or avert his gaze whenever Eris looked his way.

The afternoon wore on and was nearing its end when the pair encountered a main road. Having a basic understanding of the region, Máher bid them to follow the road westward. Knowing nothing of the area, Eris accepted his suggestion without complaint. Thus, westwards was the way that they rode.

Some hours later, the light had faded and dusk had taken hold. The night sky was clear of cloud and exceptionally beautiful, but Máher paid it no heed as he was focussed on guiding his mount through the darkness.

Lost in his own mental exertion, he had forgotten that Eris was even there. So, it came as a surprise to him when she accelerated beside him and shouted in his direction.

'Hey Máher! Riding at this pace in the dark doesn't seem like the best idea, shouldn't we slow down or make camp?'

Startled from his concentration, Máher became acutely aware of just how fast they were going. Easing back on his reins, he slowed his horse down.

'Sorry. You're right of course, I just didn't realise how fast we were actually traveling. Normally I'd stop, but I know that there's a town close by, so we may as well push on. You would like to sleep in a bed tonight, right?'

'Ha, ha. I sure would dragon man. Let's keep going, but not too fast, okay?'

Chapter 35

Selene Amakiir, King John of Estmire

As Selene fell, her perception of time shifted and moments passed seemingly as eternities. Intensely aware of everything around her, she flittered her attention from one stimulus to the next. The air flowing over her near-naked flesh, cooling her to the point of discomfort. The clouds above, slow moving, and irreverent to all beneath them. The cliff-face, which provided purchase for a myriad of small plants and tiny creatures.

Her eyes blurred as they burned from free-flowing tears. She blinked, trying to force them away, for a time she succeeded, only for more to fill their place. In her ears, each beat of her heart sounded as loud and as distinct as a war horn's call. Surely, she thought, at any moment her ear drums would burst.

Long wisps of golden hair surrounded her face as it streamed upwards, stretching towards the heavens. Errant strands tickled her cheeks, but she didn't care enough to brush them away.

Her stomach growled, protesting its emptiness. She couldn't remember the last time she had eaten, yet, even if she could have, she would have chosen to starve. The thought of putting food in her mouth made her nauseous.

Despite everything she witnessed, and everything she felt, it was all secondary to the emptiness she felt in her heart. Ronar was gone. Her best friend for the longest time, her confidant and protector, was gone. There was no way to bring him back and no way her life would ever be the same again. As far as Selene was concerned the best thing for her to do would be to die. For then, her soul would be reunited with Ronar's in the beyond.

Unexpectantly, her mind cleared of all thoughts save one, overwhelming pain. All the air in her lungs voided her chest in a whoosh as her back slammed into the river's rippling surface. Columns of opaque glass shot up around her, blocking out the entirety of the sky. Failing against the gravitational pull of the planet, the towers buckled and keeled over. As they collapsed on top of Selene, she was swallowed utterly by the cold water and everything went black.

*   *   *

Shaking from a combination of exertion and fear, King John stormed to the doorway. Thrusting it open, he searched the corridor for a servant, guard or, to be frank, anyone at all. Fortuitously, there was a lone chamber maid going about her business.

'Girl! Come here, I have a task for you.'

Hastily, the chamber maid scrambled over to the King, always ensuring that her eyes never met his. Unused to being found in such company, the girl stammered shyly.

'Yes, my Liege?'

'Fetch Ronald immediately, and with haste. I have an urgent need of him.'

With her head bowed the chamber maid curtsied. 'At once my Liege.' The girl scurried off quickly, her dress swishing violently around her feet.

Turning back to his wife The King's spirt was buoyed by the sight of her cuddling their sleeping daughter. He couldn't help but to smile.

'Fear not my love, it is all going to be okay, both you and Esmerelda will be safe. I will see to it.'

The Queen returned her husband's smile with one of her own.

'I know.'

So enraptured by the Queen's radiance, The King would have traded everything to remain in that moment, free from all burdens and stately responsibilities, for but a second longer. However, it was not to be. A heavy rapping on the door shattered the intimacy of the moment and propelled The King back into reality. Knowing it to be Ronald he opened the door, exited the chamber, and closed the door behind him.

'Ronald! You made good time, excellent. Listen close and don't interrupt. There has just been an attempt on my life, not to mention the lives of my family.'

Ronald's face visibly paled. His mouth gaped and his eyes danced with questions, but at the command of his liege, he remained silent, waiting for the king to continue.

'Before you ask, no, I do not know who was behind it or for what purpose. You know that I'm no stranger to this nasty business, but this feels different. I'll fill you in on all the details later, but suffice it to say, I think that something quite bizarre is going on.'

The King paused for a reflective moment. His posture shifted as he wrung his hands together in an unordinary show of doubt riddled emotion. Ronald, not used to seeing his liege display any weakness, was stunned by the King's radical transformation. However, after recovering from his pervious shock, he did nothing to betray his surprise. As stoically as he could he maintained his composure.

'Though it pains me greatly, I've decided that it would be best for the Queen and my daughter…'

Despite the well-established, yet entirely unwritten, rule that one should not interrupt the King, Ronald couldn't contain himself.

'A daughter! This is excellent news my Liege, congratulations!'

The King didn't say a word, he didn't have too. Daggers shot from his eyes as he scowled aggressively towards his subordinate. Detecting the animosity directed at him instantly, and not wanting to make the situation worse, Ronald bent his head in submission.

'Apologies for the interruption, my Liege.'

'Thank you, Ronald. So, as I was about to say, I've decided to send the Queen and my daughter off continent, specifically to Anátristé. Those Iasgair are a good bunch and I'm certain will keep my family safe. The head of our embassy there is also a decent chap, Lord Byron if I remember correctly, and I'm sure that he'll be more than up to the task. Anyway, I need you to make the appropriate arrangements, they need to set sail at the earliest convenience.'

'Of course, my Liege, it will be done at once.'

Ronald bowed and was about to leave, but a look from the King gave him pause. Patiently, he waited for his Liege to say whatever it was that he needed to say.

'Ronald, this has me spooked. I know it's contrary to protocol, but I'm going to take a few of the royal guard and escort them to Súthburh. If something were to happen to them and I wasn't there, but could have been, I'd die Ronald. I'd simply die.'

*　　*　　*

Selene opened her eyes and struggled to see. The world around her was nothing more than a murky gloom, where every feature was indistinguishable from any other. Her eyes burned and itched. She moved to scratch them, but was perturbed by her sluggish movements. Yes, her arms were indeed moving, but it was as if they were moving through syrup. Reaching her eyes, she rubbed them, but no amount of scratching could ease her discomfort.

Feeling the need, she opened her mouth, seeking the relief that only a chest full of fresh air would provide. Nothing. There was no air around her to breath. Panic surged within her breast, her heart racing as and her heart raced as she flailed in the molasses like dark, trying desperately to fill her lungs, but failing.

Relax.

That single word permeated throughout the entirety of her mind, echoing from every hidden corner. Knowing not where the word had come from, but not knowing what else to do, Selene closed her eyes and tried to do as bidden. To relax.

Her panic eased and her pulse slowed as she came to the realisation that wherever she was, breath was not a necessity.

How strange.

Now calm, she reopened her eyes. The darkness was not as it was before. A light, formless and distant, pulsated with a constant rhythm. Seeing this beacon, Selene's hope was rekindled and she smiled, for she knew that despite all appearances, everything was going to be fine.

Rise!

No longer confined to just her mind, this bellowing cry shook the entirety of her being. Her body vibrated with purpose as Selene felt a giddy mirth build within the pit of her stomach. She wanted to scream, nay she needed to scream. To let everything go, to rock the heavens with her pain, sorrow, and anger. To change what needed to be changed.

Unable to supress her desire for release, she arched her back and unleashed a horrifying shriek. Her scream was utterly soundless, instead, rays of the purest light burst from her mouth, and every other orifice besides. As the darkness around her was banished, she returned to the mortal realm, ushered by an ocean of white.

Not fully cognisant, but not unconscious either, Selene rose out of the river's embrace. Her skin glowed as sunlit crystal and her eyes blazed as bonfires. Hovering three feet above the water her hair defied gravity as it wafted in every direction and the rags that she wore flittered in a non-existent breeze.

Gazing towards the horizon, Selene saw and understood all mortal life. This comprehension pained her, for it alluded to the futility of it all. However, she was also encouraged by its inherent beauty, derived not only from its fleeting nature, but its intrinsic hopefulness. Succumbing to the perils of curiosity, she turned her stare towards the heavens and the houses of the gods. But before she could gleam a thing, her skin faded and her eyes dulled. Motionless, yet still alive, Selene fell back into the water.

*   *   *

As the King walked along the courtyard's cobbled surface his armour rattled and clanked. With every step a heavy clunk echoed throughout the otherwise silent square. Truly resplendent, his gold and silver plate gleamed and twinkled in the low torchlight of the dimly burning scones around him. His cape, more of a status symbol than a functional garment, fluttered around him as the silk caught the slightest of breezes that passed him by otherwise unnoticed. He cut a truly inspiring figure and, despite the anxiety that roiled throughout his insides, he played the part well, exuding nothing but confidence.

He was the last to arrive. The unassuming carriage that held his wife and child was flanked by four of the royal guard, each of whom was on horseback, and driven by another three. To deflect unwanted attention, they were each dressed not in their usual uniform but as simple travellers. Only those with a keen eye would be able to mark their swords as castle forged steel and see through their deception.

'Good evening gentlemen. Is everything ready?'

In unison, each of the guards bowed towards the King, but it was only the driver that responded.

'Yes, my Liege, we only await your command to leave.'

'Excellent. Let me mount and we can be away.'

A lone horse, far larger than the rest, stood rider-less near the exit to the courtyard. Its snow-white mane contrasting vividly against its chestnut coat. As The King approached the horse it pawed nervously at the cobblestones, whinnying apprehensively.

'Be still Skinfaxi, it's only me.'

The horse calmed immediately at the King's soft murmurs. Muscle, both thick and powerful, shuddered under his hand as the King stroked Skinfaxi's neck, the horse clearly appreciating the attention. In an impatient attempt to hurry The King along, Skinfaxi pushed gently against The King's chest, bidding him to mount her and for them to ride.

The King chuckled and patted her muzzle. 'Soon Skinfaxi. Soon.' Skinfaxi neighed as she shook her head, as if disgusted, but made no further attempts to coerce The King into action.

Knowing that subterfuge was the goal, and that his current attire ran contrary to that, The King removed his cape of office. After folding if deferentially he placed it in a saddlebag. From the same bag he removed a heavy flax cloak and donned it. Once it was fastened almost all traces of his armour were obscured.

Far from perfect, but it will have to suffice.

As prepared as he was going to get, The King mounted Skinfaxi and signalled the guards. Loud enough to be heard, but quiet enough to not carry beyond the courtyard the King whispered to his men.

'Sergeant, if we should be waylaid within the city stop for no one and nothing. You must make it past the outer walls. The rest of you follow my lead. If we're separated regroup at the rendezvous. May the gods be with us.'

With a wave of his finger, the King spurred the flank of his horse and the procession began its journey.

*   *   *

Hardly consciousness, Selene floated downstream, entrapped by the flow of the river. Her eyes fluttered sporadically as she tried in vain to open them fully. Catching nothing more than glimpses of indistinct shapes, and the occasional hint of a sunbeam, she was perturbed. She felt as though there was something that she was missing. Something that she was forgetting.

She remembered how gruesomely Ronar had died, for how could she possibly forget something so affecting? She remembered her fall and subsequent dunking. She remembered her journey into the darkness and all that had transpired there, but somehow, she knew that there was something more. It nagged at the corner of her mind, as an itch that demanded to be scratched, but no matter how she tried she couldn't bring her lost memories into focus. Frustrated at her impotency, Selene gave in and surrendered to forgetfulness.

Gently, the flow of the river nudged her against the bank. Devoid of any energy she groaned, but made no move to stand. For a second time she was pushed against the bank. Selene felt her annoyance rise, but still did nothing. At the third shove her apathy was broken. Releasing her frustration in a low sigh she clawed at the soft earth weakly. Slowly, she started to drag herself out of the river.

Rise!

It was far from easy going, as the grass tufts she used as handholds constantly broke, hindering her progress. Both her shift and her body were quickly coated with mud. The extra weight bogged her down, threatening to drag her back into the river, but she persevered. Driven by that one word that still rang in her mind, *rise*, Selene pushed herself.

She wanted to stop with every fibre of her being. She wanted nothing more than to curl up into a ball and sleep, but she didn't concede to these feelings. She knew that if she stopped, she would be ceding her life to the river below. For Eris this was unacceptable, she couldn't die yet, there were still things that she needed to accomplish.

I will not surrender.

Cresting the top of the rise, Selene's triumph was rewarded with the briefest of reprieves. As she teetered upon the edge of her earthen summit Selene wheezed heavily, desperately trying to reoxygenate her system. Carelessly, she leant just a little too far forward and lost her balance.

Unceremoniously, Selene tumbled down the other side of the embankment. As she rolled wildly, stones and twigs alike ripped her clothes and tore at her flesh. Pain became everything to her; it was all that she felt and all that she knew. Her descent ended abruptly with yet more pain as she thudded into a patch hard-packed dirt. Though her journey was over, the pain persisted and it was all she could do to not pass out from it.

Lying on that hard-packed earth, Selene was torn, bloody and barely hanging on to life. Trying to stand, she pushed her arms against the ground. She made some headway, but they quickly buckled and she collapsed into the dirt once more.

Utterly spent, shivering from the cold and shock, she placed her palm upon her breast and offered a silent prayer to Freyr. It must have been heard. Her hand started to glow as it radiated an ethereal blue light. Gradually, Selene felt her energy return, her cuts heal and her bruises fade. Although her injuries lingered, Selene couldn't help but to moan in satisfaction as her previous agony decreased to nothing more than a dull ache.

Reinvigorated, but by no means of perfect health, Selene eased herself to her feet and assessed her surroundings. Now in control of her senses, it was abundantly clear that she was on a road, and a main one at that. The sun was making its way towards the horizon, so she marked that direction as West. There were far fewer trees around her than what she would expect to see if she was still in the Oldeen Forest.

I'm somewhere south of the Forest on a major road that goes from East to West. Shit, this must be the highway between Estmire and The Southlands. How by all that is holy did I end up here? It's going to take weeks to get back home on foot. Fuck.

Subtle vibrations in the road, closely followed by the unmistakable sound of hooves, quickly drove all of her ruminations from her mind. Taking the chance that these unknown riders would be friendly, Selene walked to the centre of the road and raised her hand.

Gods, I do hope they stop.

*   *   *

Skinfaxi's hooves pounded against the road as she galloped freely. Happy to be set running amongst the wilderness, but chagrined at being held back by her slower and altogether inferior kin, she devoured the miles with a ravenous delight. The King found no such joy in the journey. For him it was nothing more than a bitter tonic borne from necessity. As much as he knew that he had to do it, he assuredly didn't want to.

The King saw the woman standing in the middle of the road long before he reached her. Wary of ambush and trickery, even this far from Evonium, he slowed the convoy. Easing Skinfaxi forward, while maintaining a firm grip on his sword, The King inspected the stranger closely.

The woman was strikingly beautiful, though not in the most traditional sense, and clearly a full-blooded elf. Sharp, pointed ears poked proudly from beneath her golden hair. Her high cheekbones and otherwise hawkish features served to accentuate her doe-like eyes. Bright blue, and exceedingly round, The King couldn't help but to be drawn in by them. Contradicting her slender figure, they betrayed a deep reservoir of strength that the King couldn't help but to respect.

'Please, stop! I mean you no harm.'

As melodic as the most sublime windchime, the woman's voice reached The King's ears as the most welcome summer breeze. He examined each of her words for even a hint of deceit, finding not a trace and believing her to be entirely sincere, the King approached the woman.

'Good lady, what has befallen you to see you so stranded,' The King gestured to her garments while averting his gaze from her shapely breasts and all too clearly visible nipples, 'and so poorly equipped for travel?'

'That's a tale that I'm more than willing to share, but it would be unwise to tarry. As we speak those that are responsible for my poorly equipped stranding are no doubt moving against me. I sense that you and yours are also in a hurry so, may I join you? Or will you leave me to my fate?'

It was obvious to the King just how nervous she was. The elf hopped anxiously from foot to foot, all the while swivelling her head from bush to shrub.

She's afraid. It's as though she believes something will pounce upon her at any moment.

In the midst of his thoughts, The King turned his head and looked at the carriage behind him.

Honour dictates that I help her and I don't believe her to be an enemy, but I'm not sure that I'd be comfortable with her being so close to my family. Then there's my daughter. I cannot let this elf see her eyes. Damn it.

Sighing under his breath, to keep his frustration hidden from the stranger, The King turned back to the elf.

'It would be repugnant of me to refuse you aid. Alas, we have no room to spare in our carriage. Perhaps, if it isn't too forward, you would find riding with me acceptable?'

'It appears that I have little choice. But first, let us not remain strangers. I am Selene Amakiir of the Taoiseach Spire. And you?'

The King paused, thinking on how he should respond. With the truth, or a lie?

There's nothing for it. I have no doubt she'll see through any falsehoods I spin. Subterfuge be damned, the truth it will have to be.

'I am King John of Estmire. It is a pleasure to make your acquaintance.'

Selene swept her arms behind her with an elegant flourish as she curtsied.

'It would appear that the honour is mine, your Majesty.'

The King waved her formality away with a swipe of his hand.

'Bah, there's no need for that. You're hardly one of my subjects, you don't have to be so proper. Now, what is your preference? Front or back?'

'Mm. I've always found the front to be far more stimulating than the back, so the front it shall be.'

'Excellent.'

The King bent down and offered his hand to Selene, but before she could take it, a realisation dawned upon him, and he withdrew it. Unfastening his cloak, he pulled it from his shoulders and held it towards Selene.

'Here put this on first. I know you didn't choose your current attire and I would never question your honour, but I'm not sure my wife would approve of us being in such intimate proximity, with you so scantily clad and being as beautiful as you are.'

Adding almost as an afterthought The King continued, far less certainly.

'Plus, I daresay you're cold.'

If Selene was offended, she didn't show it. Instead, she just gave The King a slight nod as she took the cloak and wrapped it around her.

'Thank you, your Majesty.'

Thusly covered, Selene mounted Skinfaxi. The King wrapped an arm around her waist, thinking it as nothing more than providing her support, and he felt her body tense at his touch. He wondered if he had somehow crossed a line, but soon abandoned all fears of impropriety as Selene soon relaxed and laid back against him, snuggling herself up against his chest.

Good gods, I'll be in a pickle if the Queen decides to glance out her window. It'll be the couch for a week. Perhaps a month.

Gently spurring Skinfaxi's flank, The King eased the convey back into motion. Once a steady rhythm had been established, he leant forward and spoke into Selene's ear.

'So, who is it that's after you and for what reason?'

There was no response.

'Selene?'

When Selen still did not respond, the King bent forward to check on her welfare. The elf's eyes were shut tight, but her chest rose and fell gently as she breathed softly.

Just asleep. Must have been truly exhausted to have passed out so quickly. Poor girl.

*   *   *

Muffled and garbled, Selene heard her name wander lazily into her mind. *Selene... Selene.* Soft at first, barely audible, it grew in both volume and intensity. *Selene!* She struggled against it, wanting to ignore it's call and remain in the darkness, for she felt safe there. However, the voice would not be denied. It grew to a thunderous crescendo and Selene was utterly overwhelmed by its force as it shattered her slumbering consciousness. ***Selene!***

With a gasp, Selene opened her eyes. Disorientated, she jerked her head around, trying to figure out where she was and what was going on.

'Easy there Selene. Calm down. It's alright, you're okay.'

Upon hearing The King's voice, Selene's faculties returned to normality and all the memories of the past twenty-four hours rushed back to her. Her grief over Ronar's demise hit her hard, and fresh tears welled anew, but she forced herself to maintain a measure of composure, refusing to break down entirely. It helped that she found comfort in being so close to the King, but despite this a small worm of worry tickled the pit of her stomach.

'What's happening? Why did you wake me?'

'Wake you? I have no idea what you're referring to. I did no such thing, nor make any attempt to do so.'

The worm, that was only moments before slithering benignly across Selene's abdomen, now bared its fangs and bit into her stomach deeply. Instantly, she felt her intestines knot. It took all of her will, but somehow, she managed to supress the overwhelming urge to vomit. Recovering her composure enough to speak she stammered weakly to The King, her words laced with worry and concern.

'No. I heard someone. They were calling out my name. Repeatedly, I might add. That wasn't you?'

'No. You were sleeping peacefully and then you just suddenly awoke. I said not a word.'

All colour drained from Selene's face and she felt her head swim with dizziness.

Oh gods, please no. It's him, isn't it? No. It can't be. It's too soon. He couldn't have found me so quickly. Just a bad dream, nothing more. Breath Selene, breath. It's fine, it's all fine.

A familiar buzzing filled Selene's ears and she winced, not from the discomfort of the sensation, but because she knew what was about to follow it.

'*I see you, Selene. Why did you run from me? That was most unwise Selene. You know you can't hide from me Selene. I see you.*'

The voice vanished from her mind, as did the buzzing from her ears, but the awful truth stabbed violently at her heart. Her torturer, her captor, and her nemesis, had found her. Antrayus was here. As this horrid fact became fully realised the howl from a single wolf pierced the air. From every direction, a myriad of other howls answered its call.

Selene twisted her back and turned to face the King. Her voice quivered in abject terror as she hissed at him.

'He's here! The one who pursues me. Hear me now King John and hear me well, we cannot overcome him. We must flee and hope to find aid, for that is our only chance.'

Seeing her expression and noting the tone of her voice, The King didn't bother with questions. His soft features shifted and his face locked into a determined grimace.

'There's a town nearby. It's small, but it will have to suffice. Hold on.'

The King whipped Skinfaxi's reins and shouted a single, 'hah.' Defying belief, the large warhorse accelerated to even greater feats of speed. Stifling a yelp as she was pushed against the King's chest, Selene grabbed the arm that was still affixed firmly around her waist and held on for dear life.

Oh gods.

*   *   *

Skinfaxi's hooves sang as she thundered down the town's cobbled road. Houses and other small storefronts blurred beside them as the King and Selene whizzed past. Noting Selene's iron grip upon his arm, The King squeezed her hand reassuringly. Selene did not loosen her hold.

Skinfaxi shot into a wide and open space as the narrow corridor of buildings opened up into a large square. Knowing little of this town, but correctly surmising the importance of it, The King steered Skinfaxi towards the largest building of the courtyard. As he closed with the structure, the words *Town Hall,* written along its face in faded blue paint, became legible.

This will have to do. I doubt there'd be better in the whole town.

Besides the Town Hall's doors stood two towns-guard. Pulling alongside the drowsy guardsmen, both Selene and the King dismounted Skinfaxi. Provoking not a single response from the guards, the King shouted towards the elder of the two.

'Guardsman! Rouse your fellows to take up their arms. Your town is in peril and we have need of them.'

Having spent his entire life fulfilling the needs of the nobility and social elite, the elderly man knew what was required of him. He wasted no time in questioning this stranger, he simply saluted the King, pivoted from his post, and rushed inside.

Exiting her carriage, The Queen looked around, perturbed by the obviously stressed demeanour of her husband.

'What's wrong my love?'

Though he wished to shield her from the dire nature of the situation, the King never lied to his wife. So, with a heavy heart and a terse word he told her the truth.

'I have good reason to believe that an attack on this town is imminent.' The King sighed heavily. 'I'm honestly not sure if we'll survive the night. Please, take Esmerelda into the Town Hall. You'll both be safer there and I shan't suffer from worry.'

The Queen smiled warmly towards him.

'Never fear my love. I am certain that everything will be fine.'

As stunning as always, The Queen's smile was all The King needed. He felt his spirits lift as hope warmed his heart and buoyed his soul. Though the situation didn't warrant it, the King returned his wife's smile with his own. Pulling her close, he kissed her forehead, then her lips.

Gods do I love this woman.

A serendipitous gurgle drew his attention downwards. Esmerelda was wriggling around furiously in her mother's arms, begging for attention. Upon seeing his daughter, the King's smile grew even wider. He tickled her chin and Esmerelda's gurgling intensified as her eyes shone with joy and her mouth beamed with toothless delight.

'I haven't forgotten about you little one.'

Bending down, The King planted a kiss on his daughter's cheek. Contented, she stopped squirming immediately.

'Now, inside with the pair of you.' Pointing at the remaining towns-guard, The King continued. 'You take care of them understood? If any harm should befall them, then far worse will befall you.'

The guard, not long past his coming-of-age day, visibly paled. Trembling terribly, he presented a shaky salute and stammered his understanding.

'Ye... yessir. Um, this way my L... Lady. If you'd follow m... me, I'll get you sorted out.'

Not wanting to prolong an already difficult goodbye, The King turned away from his rapidly departing wife, his fears and misgivings overridden by purpose and duty.

Gods give me the strength to see them to safety.

Before him, his royal guard were standing at attention, waiting to receive their orders. Their faces were grim, but they stood tall and proud. The King knew them all personally and he had no doubt that each of them would die for him if that's what was necessary. He knew they didn't need a fancy speech or pep talk, they were professionals, all they needed was direction.

'Men! Form a defensive line in front of the Town Hall, defend it at all costs at let none enter! No matter what we face this night, we will hold firm!'

In unison, the King's guards bent their knees to the ground, bowing deferentially to their liege. The slightest of nods from the King was all they needed to rise and disperse around the hall.

From the corner of his vision, the King saw a flutter of green fabric. He didn't bother to turn around, he knew exactly who it was.

'Selene, it would be best if you went inside with my family.'

'Nonsense. I'm no frail maiden, I can fight. I'll be of more use out here with you and your men.'

Not used to being disobeyed, but sensing the steely determination behind Selene's words, The King simply shrugged.

'As you wish.'

Conversation over, the King turned to face the courtyard. Though he knew not what destiny had in store for him, he was as ready as he was going to get. Taking a deep breath, he waited for his fate to reveal itself.

Chapter 36

Neesa

Neesa was perturbed by the stranger's spontaneous disappearance, even more so by her words. She had never heard of this Collective and had no notion of what being a part of such a secret organisation would even mean. She couldn't help but to wonder.

Why me, what is it that they could possibly want? What is their purpose? Are their intentions good or ill? And what of Lord Balor? I haven't thought about that bastard for years and now he has crossed my mind twice in a day. Shit. I would love to rip the cunt's throat out though. Maybe that's a good enough reason to travel to Evonium. Damn it, Neesa. That's how this collective will get you, they want you to kill him. Fuck. Problem is I want to kill him.

Still feeling queasy from her memory of Balor, and frustrated by her weakness, Neesa punched the wall again. Contrary to what many would believe, it did help.

Gods be damned. I'll go to Evonium and see what happens. Got nothing else planned anyway. I wonder if the Baron will join me? He's not that bad, for nobility anyway.

A lone howl pierced the night sky. All idle ruminations were thrust from Neesa's mind as she felt a shiver creep up her spine. Her body tingled unpleasantly and she shuddered involuntarily. Hailing predominantly from the north, more howls echoed the first.

Hm, too many for a single pack. Something strange is going on.

A shrill scream reverberated along the alleyway's walls, followed by a desperate plea. 'Help me! Please!' A second more frantic shriek, that of a child's, chilled Neesa's blood. Not thinking of her own safety for a second, Neesa broke into a sprint towards the cries. Rounding a bend, she was met by a horrific spectacle.

One of the youths she had seen before, a thin girl who couldn't have been any older than ten, was running towards her. Tears were flowing from her eyes and snot was trickling from her nose. Her mouth was wide and twisted, the innocence of childhood perverted by the terror that overwhelmed her

Upon seeing Neesa, the girl sensed salvation and pushed herself to run all the harder. A glimmer of hope flashed over her face, the seeds of a small smile peaking the corner of her lips. Too soon.

The girl's arms wind-milled as she was propelled violently into the ground. A tiny yelp escaped her lips just before her face smacked into the ground. Hard. The cobbles tore at her cheeks, leaving her bloody and whimpering.

Behind the child a wolf, much larger than normal and by far more vicious, stalked casually towards its prey. Its muscles rippled beneath its mottled jet-black and grey fur. Its coat shone as still-fresh ichor reflected the moonlight. But Neesa saw none of this. All of her attention was fixated firmly upon the twin flames, black and flickering, that danced in lew of the beast's eyes.

Not yet dead, and stubbornly clinging to hope, the child clawed weakly at the cobbles as she tried desperately to pull herself away from the monster behind her. Neesa should have tried to save her, by the gods she could have, but she was frozen. Held in place by those enthralling flames, she did nothing.

Easily, the wolf reached the child and placed one of its paws upon her back. The child's scrambling intensified as she doubled her efforts at escape. A low growl rumbled from the wolf's throat as it dug its paw into the girl's back. The girl froze, but raised her head slowly towards Neesa. Trembling violently, she looked up at Neesa, stuttering imploringly.

'Pl... please. H... help. M... me.'

Still captivated, Neesa did nothing.

Gods. I cannot move. I need too, I must, but I cannot. Gods.

Slowly, the wolf arched its back, raising its snout to the sky, and howled. By virtue of its proximity, more than anything else, Neesa felt the creature's call in her bones. Wincing in pain, she clasped her hands over her ears, trying to keep the sound at bay. Alas, it seemed to do little, for she still felt as though her eardrums were about to burst.

At the wolf's feet the girl was screaming. Neesa couldn't hear it, but the child's face was twisted into that tell-tale horror born mask. The girl had given up trying to escape, she knew it was useless. All she could do was scream.

Abruptly, the howl ended and as quick a lightning the wolf bit down on the girl's neck. Viciously, it whipped its head from side to side, tossing the girl around like a child's rag doll. Neesa felt bile rise in her throat as the girl's neck snapped, her scream ending in a pitiful gurgle. No longer of any interest to the wolf, it threw the girl's limp form against the alley wall.

Free from the wolf's enrapturement, Neesa looked into the girl's sightless eyes and something inside her broke.

I'm sorry. I'm so sorry.

The wolf was snarling angrily at Neesa, its next target clear, but she paid it no heed. Bowing her head, she muttered a prayer to the gods, pleading with them to care for the girl's soul. Only once she had said what she needed to say did she succumb. Embracing the rage that burned within her soul, Neesa stared directly into the fires that smouldered on the wolf's face and unleashed her anger in a single fury fuelled shout.

Sliding her sword from its back sheath, Neesa charged headlong towards the wolf. The beast didn't move, but its legs twitched in anticipation. Nearing her quarry, Neesa swung her blade wildly. Propelled by the purest anger there was no technique or subtlety to her form, she meant only to hit, and hit hard at that.

Either by instinct or conscious thought, the wolf ducked under Neesa's attack and darted nimbly past her guard. Skipping agilely beside her flank, the wolf struck at Neesa's calf. Pain, as though it was derived from literal fire, shot into her as the creature's fangs sunk into her flesh. Most would have fell, or perhaps even been staggered, but Neesa embraced the pain. She welcomed it. It fuelled her.

Movement from the end of the alley draw her attention away from the first wolf. A second wolf launched itself into the air, its mouth wide as it flew towards Neesa's face. In one fluid movement, Neesa spun out of the beast's path, while reversing the grip of her sword. Passing but a hair's breadth from her face, Neesa thrust her blade's pommel towards this new attacker. With a satisfying crunch, the wolf's jaw shattered into splinters as the hefty hilt collided with its chin.

Unable to arrest its momentum, the wounded wolf skidded uncontrollably along the cobbles. After thudding heavily into a wall, it picked itself up from the ground slowly, whimpering pathetically. Padding gingerly back towards Neesa its fire-eyes burned far less robustly than before.

Succumbing to the errors of a rookie warrior, Neesa let her mind focus too keenly on the enemy before her. Momentarily forgetting about the first wolf, she left herself unguarded and open. Seizing the opportunity, the first wolf barrelled into Neesa, knocking her from her feet. All the air she held fled her lungs was expelled as her chest pounded into the stone floor. Neesa swore, even though her ribs were not broken, they sure as the seven hells hurt.

They're probably just bruised.

Before Neesa could stand, the wounded wolf leapt on top of her. Unable to bite with its broken jaw, it clawed at her torso. Talons, as sharp as razors, raked over her unprotected skin, tearing her kimono, and the shirt beneath it, just as easily as she would tear a baguette at dinner time. Her abdomen stung as blood seeped freely from her wounds. They pained her, and she knew that they would hurt all the more in time, but in that moment, they were just what she needed.

Filled to the brim, the monster inside her unleashed itself upon the world. Without thinking, Neesa snarled, throwing the wolf off of her with a casual ease as she leapt to her feet. Its compatriot charged at her, but Neesa pirouetted away from its open maw. In a flash, her sword slashed along the wolf's side, carving deep. Blood splattered against the stonework and the beast fell prone. Though severely wounded, it was not yet dead. Desperately it tried to stand, but its legs buckled at every attempt.

No longer an immediate threat, Neesa turned her attention to her other quarry. It stood at the alley's opening staring, if it were possible to stare with fire for eyes, directly at her. Its jaw hung loosely open, gloopy saliva oozing slowly from its lolling tongue. Caught in a moment of indecision it flicked its head away from Neesa as it contemplated the eternal conundrum, fight vs flight. Fight prevailed.

The wolf pushed off of its hind legs in an explosive burst, accelerating from a standstill to peak velocity far faster than what should have been possible. Neesa stood her ground. Judging the wolf's speed, she waited. As it neared Neesa, the wolf leapt into the air, aiming for her throat.

Seemingly at the last moment, Neesa jumped towards the alley wall. Kicking off of its grippy surface, she summersaulted over the flying wolf. As it soared beneath her, confounded by her spontaneous disappearance, Neesa whipped her sword-arm downwards. Her blade sung as it hissed through the air and she barely felt a jolt as her sword carved through the wolf's neck.

The wolf's head cartwheeled clear from its body, spraying gristly ichor as it flew. Momentum carried the corpse forward, but inertia forced it to slow. Inevitably, it came to a stop, oil-like blood pumping from its neck.

Landing with her knees bent, Neesa scowled towards the other wolf, her heart still pounding with rage. It was still frantically trying to stand. No longer interested in combat, escape and survival were its only intentions. But broken as thoroughly as it was, it was incapable of fulfilling this desire.

Seeing her foe helpless, Neesa walked casually towards the creature. After flicking the remnants of wolf-blood from her blade, she re-sheathed her sword. Anger still surging within her, she gripped the wolf around its neck. Ignoring the rancid stench and foul texture, Neesa squeezed. The wolf's scrambling intensified, but it couldn't break free from Neesa's hold. As the beast's lungs run low on oxygen its movements slowed.

Neesa's rage roiled as it protested against such a slow and peaceful death. Shouting angrily, Neesa torqued her hands as hard as she could. Offering not even the slightest resistance, the wolf's neck omitted a mighty crack as it snapped in two. Instantly, all vestiges of life fled from the wolf and the creature collapsed, deceased.

Appeased by the twisted karmic retribution she had bestowed upon the wolf; Neesa felt her anger subside and her heart rate slow. With the morbid curiosity of someone who just has to know, she walked with pained steps towards the body of the girl. Neesa was certain that the child was dead, and unsurprisingly when she reached the girl, not a trace of breath or pulse were to be found.

In lieu of rage, sadness threatened to consume her as tears blossomed in the corners of her eyes. Wiping the beginnings of sorrow away with the sleeve of her gown, Neesa stood and looked along the alleyway. The girl's two friends, that she had initially seen her with, lay broken and bloody near the end of the alley. Neesa felt no compulsion to check on them, their spilled intestines and crushed craniums dissuaded any such desire. But, just as she did with the girl, she bowed her head and prayed for the gods to care for their souls.

I'm sorry I couldn't save you, any of you. I'm so sorry.

The adrenaline was starting to fade and Neesa felt the pain from her wounds increase markedly. Through gritted teeth, she peeled back the blood-soaked cloth that covered the scratch marks on her stomach. Blood, of the deepest crimson, oozed slowly from the claw made furrows.

They're not too deep, but will still need stiches. Either that or a decent healing spell. Maybe an apothecary's potion could do the trick?

Illogically, Neesa's femininity took the reins from reason and her thoughts shifted from her own well-being to that of fashion.

Damn, I really like this kimono. Maybe I can get it fixed?

Whether through her subconscious recognising the absurdity of such concerns or the involuntary shaking of her head, Neesa abandoned that train of thought and examined her calf.

Hm, worse than the scratches and more likely to get infected.

Testing her wound, Neesa put the entirety of her weight onto her injured leg. It hurt more than she would have liked, but it was far from unbearable.

Might cause issues in a fight, will have to be extra careful with it.

More howls echoed around her. Instinctually Neesa knew that these howls were identical to that of the twisted child-slayers she had just dispatched. She also knew that they originated within the town's borders.

Shit.

Loathe to disturb the poor child's remains in such a disrespectful manner, but having more need than a soulless corpse, Neesa tore off a strip of cloth from the girl's tunic. Wrapping it around her calf, she bound her wound tightly, grimacing as she did so. It would need to be attended to more attentively in the near future, but for now this rudimentary wrapping would have to suffice. Not having the materials, nor the time, to see to her torso, Neesa ignored it.

Retracing her steps at a steady jog, Neesa left the alley, turning right and then right once more. Warry of more hostile creatures, she slowed before reaching the main road. Crouching low, she shuffled along slowly, hugging close to the wall beside her. Straining her eyes and ears for any indication of danger, her heart thumping noisily in her head.

Reaching the main road, Neesa stopped, taking shelter in a particularly deep shadow, and looked around. Small packs of wolves, complimented by the occasional bear, jogged silently down the road. Every so often one or two would break off from the main force and head off down a side road or alley. Fortunately for Neesa, they ignored the lane she was sheltering in.

Fuck me. They're fanning out over the town in an organised manner.

Initially, this observation perplexed Neesa. Why, she thought, would wild animals act in such a way? The answer hit her like a runaway carriage.

Oh gods. They're not wild animals. It's an invasion and they mean to take the town. They're going to encircle the town and then kill everyone.

As she watched on helplessly, Neesa felt anxiety stab at her chest. She knew that the longer she was outside the more likely it was that she would be found. She also knew that the longer she squatted there inactive, the harder it would be for her to escape. A break in the invaders procession was all she needed.

C'mon, C'mon.

Smiling upon her, fate provided.

As quietly as she could, Neesa emerged from the shadow and ran towards the tavern. No wild cries of alarm sounded nor bites from an unseen foe impacted. She made it to the tavern doors unseen and hurried inside, closing them silently behind her.

The tavern was as rowdy as it was when she left it. It appeared as though the outside troubles had not yet marred its jovial interior. Pushing past a pair of drunken farmers as they danced, Neesa joined the Baron and Jeeves at their table.

As Neesa sat down, the Baron beamed towards her, freshly filled tankard of ale clutched protectively under his beaming face. He bobbed and swayed in his seat, having clearly already downed a few similarly filled tankards. Though inebriated, his faculties were not entirely hindered. All vestiges of joviality dissipated as he noticed the bloodstains that Neesa bore.

'By the gods Neesa! What in the seven hells has happened to you? We need to find an apothecary or a doctor or something. We'll get you fixed up right quick we will. Jeeves!'

Neesa held her finger to her lips to quiet the Baron's bombastic protestations. 'Shh!' Gesturing the pair to come over closer, Neesa whispered to the pair as loudly as she dared.

'Please be quiet. I'm fine, please don't worry about me. A panic will only make things worse.'

Neesa sighed heavily, she didn't know how to phrase what she had to say tactfully, so she decided to just tell it plainly.

'The town's under attack. Wolves and other wild creatures are running wild in the streets killing everyone they come across. I encountered two and,' Neesa gestured to her stomach, 'you can clearly see how that went.'

The Baron sobered up immediately.

'What would possess them to do such a thing? It's damned unnatural, that's what.'

'Unnatural is putting it mildly. These wolves are different, they're not normal. They don't have eyes and they're not eating their victims. They're killing for killing's sake and nothing more.'

Jeeves's eyes went wide. The Butler leaned in even closer towards Neesa and hissed at her forcefully.

'What exactly do you mean when you say that they don't have eyes?'

'Just that. They don't have eyes. It's not like there's nothing there, they have these small fires, I suppose, but they're black and I'm not sure if they produce any heat. It's really strange and kind of creepy.'

Jeeves's face turned as white as a freshly laundered bedsheet and small beads of sweat formed atop his brow. Neesa saw his concern plainly and noted her pulse accelerate in response.

'I know of what you're describing and if it is as you say, we are in the direst of perils. As is the whole of Ulandir and, dare I say it, all of Térrtha.'

Sighing heavily, Jeeves turned away from Neesa and stared directly at the Baron.

'I'm sorry my Lord. I implore you to continue your quest, as I have no doubt that it is important, but I can no longer travel by your side. There is someone that I have to see at the earliest convenience and I must go there alone. I will see you and Ms Neesa out of the town and to safety, but after that I will no longer be able to serve you.'

Usually eloquent to a fault, the Baron could only stammer his protestations.

'Je... Jeeves, no.'

'I'm sorry my Lord. It must be so.'

Chapter 37

Baron Victor von Grumanhieser III

'*I'm sorry My Lord. It must be so.*'

Jeeves's words echoed painfully in the Baron's head. The man who had cared for him for his entire life. The man who had been more to him than even his parents, was leaving. No explanation, no justifications, nothing but a 'trust me, it's serious.' A lesser man would have become enraged, would have lashed out in anger, would have said, and done, things to be later regretted. Not the Baron. All he felt was pain. All he felt was abandonment.

The Baron stared into his friend's eyes searching for any hint of reason, hoping to find even a trace of explanation. He found none. Voice shaking terribly, he resorted to the direct path.

'Why? Tell me that at least.'

Sensing the Baron's pain, Jeeves placed his hand upon his master's shoulder. He met the Baron's eyes with his own and smiled, trying to impart as much compassion as he could.

'Believe me my Lord, when I say that I'm sorry. This whole business hurts me just as much as it hurts you, perhaps more. I have long viewed you as the child that I never had, but I cannot tell you any more than I already have. It's not my place and I don't wish to burden you further.'

'But I want to know. I need to know.'

Before Jeeves had a chance to respond, Neesa hissed angrily from her chair.

'Enough! We don't have time for this. We need to get out of here.'

Jeeves just shook his head and turned away. From the corner of his mouth the Baron heard him whisper, 'I'm sorry.' Knowing that any further protestations would be futile, the Baron returned to his ale. It didn't taste anywhere near as sweet as it did before.

Bathing in the awkward silence enveloping him, the Baron reeled. Deep down he knew that Jeeves was his own man and could pursue life in any manner he sought too, the Baron would never prevent him from pursuing his destiny. But, the lack of trust in him that Jeeves was demonstrating hurt. It hurt him deeply.

How could he leave me? Why now? What has gotten the old goat so riled up? Why won't he explain anything?

The relative clam was shattered as the tavern door exploded inwards. More than just being knocked cleanly off of its hinges, shards of broken window and pine splinters littered the floor as detritus was all that remained. Disturbed from his inner thoughts, the Baron looked up from his mug of ale. Standing at the entrance to the tavern was a wall of dishevelled black fur, occupying the space that the door had mere moments before.

Well, you certainly don't see that every day.

Gawking stupidly, disbelief froze the tavern patrons in place. All merriment ceased and a strained silence enveloped the tavern. A glass tinkled against another and a woman gave a nervous cough. Somewhere near the back of the tavern an elderly man deep in his cups, utterly oblivious to reality, exclaimed loudly. 'Who turned the music off. Hic. Like tha' tune I did. Hic. Put it back on. Hic.' If the situation wasn't so serious his outburst would have been comical.

Poking its head around the tavern, fiery pupils undulating rapidly, the bear roared. Released from its shackles, pandemonium erupted vengefully. Patrons leapt from their chairs screaming. Ensnared by panic they ran mindlessly from the monster at the door, trampling those poor sods who were knocked to the floor in the stampede.

Damned by proximity and ill luck, one of the tavern wenches shrieked as the bear raked its claws along her torso. She collapsed twitching as her entrails spilled from her stomach. Whimpering softly, the young woman tried to hold her intestines in check, but the slippery organs slithered uncontrollably through her hands, slopping grotesquely onto the floor.

Lunging inside, the bear snatched a patron's head in its jaws. In some ways he was far more fortunate than the wench, for at least he died quickly. A mere moment of abject terror was all the man felt before his skull crumpled into nothing. Blood, viscera, and brain matter drooled from the bear's maw as the man's lifeless corpse thudded to the floor.

Caught utterly by surprise and stunned by the horrendous scene before him, the Baron could do nothing but look on ineffectually.

By the gods.

Sitting speechless beside him, both Neesa and Jeeves were equally astounded and no less indecisive.

Simultaneously, the two windows beside the remnants of the main door shattered inwards. A pair of wolves, one for each of the windows, flew inside through the broken portals, vehemently snarling at those around them. Blood oozed from the glass shards that had punctured their matted hides, but neither paid their afflictions any attention.

Foolishly, an elderly patron turned his back to one of the newly arrived threats as he tried to flee. Without hesitation, the wolf leapt on top of the hobbling geriatric's back, pinning him to the floor. Impassively, the wolf ignored the man's cries for mercy and bit into his back. The man's face twisted horribly as he scraped desperately at the floorboards, trying to escape. His exercise in futility soon ended as he succumbed to shock and ceased struggling.

Caught in the gaze of the second wolf, a middle-aged woman quivered in place. Too afraid to move, yet fully aware of her fate, her body reacted in the only way it could. Geysers of urine gushed from her urethra as her bladder emptied involuntarily. Acidic piss soaked the front of her dress and filled her shoes as it poured down her legs.

The wolf lunged towards its target. The woman screamed as she was knocked off of her feet. Burrowing into the woman's chest the wolf ripped apart her ribcage, sinking its snout inside her chest. Still conscious, the woman writhed as blood filled her mouth, stifling an as of yet stillborn scream. With one final spasm the woman went still and her open eyes glazed over.

Raising its head from the woman's chest, her heart firmly pincered between its teeth, the wolf glared menacingly at the Baron. Feeling his blood run cold and his heartrate pound his ribcage as it surged, the Baron licked his lips. Easing Peacemaker from its holster as gently as he could, to avoid the wolf's ire, he cocked the gun's hammer and assessed his adversaries.

Which one first? The bear? That's obviously the biggest threat. Or the wolves? They're faster and will kill me just as quick as the bear if they get close. Shit. At least all the patrons have fled, I would have hated to have hit one by mistake.

Flicking its head towards the roof, the wolf threw the heart into the air. With a casual snap of its jaws the wolf snatched the organ from the air and swallowed it whole. Crouching low on its haunches, it growled menacingly as it stalked slowly towards the Baron and his companions. On the opposite side of the tavern the other wolf followed suit. Still standing stationary in the doorframe, the bear flittered its attention between the trio, as if deciding who it should attack first.

Casually, Neesa rose from the table, her chair scrapping noisily upon the floorboards as she pushed it backwards. With her eyes fixed firmly on the wolf closest to her, she spat a single curt sentence from the corner of her mouth.

'Deal with that fucking bear.'

Still stunned, the Baron watched on meekly as Neesa's arm blurred. Sword now in hand, she vaulted over the table, skimming gracefully across its surface. Having no intention of passively waiting for its prey, the wolf pounced towards Neesa. Unbelievably, she caught the creature.

Clutching the beast around the throat, Neesa thrust her blade into the wolf's chest, driving it backwards. Her sword sunk deep into the creature, but the wound inflicted was by no means mortal. With a desperate ferocity, the wolf raked its claws against Neesa's arms and chest. Incensed, Neesa ignored the blows, even as her blood began to mix with that of the wolf's.

In the tavern's doorway, the bear was no longer procrastinating. Its gaze was fixed firmly upon the Baron. Apparently, it had chosen its next target and that target was him. Gulping heavily, the Baron stood and, bracing himself as best as he could, levelled Peacemaker at the bear.

Perhaps the creature sensed the threat that the Baron posed and felt threatened, perhaps it just wanted to assert its dominance, maybe it was simply being spontaneous. Whatever the reason, the bear bellowed another mighty roar spraying gore and spittle throughout the room. Desires satiated, the monster padded heavily towards the Baron, knocking aside both chairs and tables as if they were the epitome of irrelevance.

Aiming down Peacemaker's barrel, the Baron took a deep breath, then holding it, he squeezed the trigger gently. Reaching their tipping point the internal mechanisms of Peacemaker whirred. The hammer fell, striking pin slammed into primer and spark ignited powder.

Bang!

The resounding boom echoed throughout the close confines of the tavern. The Baron's ears rang uncomfortably as Peacemaker's recoil pushed the Baron's arm roughly upwards, but his shot had been on target.

A small wobble as it carved its way along its flight path did nothing to diminish the effectiveness of the shot. Slamming into the bear's chest with a heavy 'thwack,' the projectile ricocheted off of a rib and burst out of the monster's side. Fragments of bone and meat sprayed from the bullet's exit wound, closely following the squashed lead slug. A pained whine emanated from the bear's throat as blood gushed from both injuries, but still it ran towards the Baron. Intent on the murder of man, nothing short of death could dissuade it.

Witnessing his rapidly approaching demise, the Baron took a desperate step backwards. The chair behind him toppled over and clattered noisily against the floorboards. To the Baron the sound barely registered as the entirety of his focus was on the mass of enraged muscle charging towards him.

Desperately, he moved to cock Peacemaker's hammer, to take another shot. But, at his core, he knew that there was not enough time. The bear would reach him before that would ever happen.

If I live through this, I'm going to have to find a way of shooting without having to cock the hammer after every shot. It's too damn slow in a pinch.

Ever his unasked-for saviour, Jeeves sprang into action. Vaulting from his chair, he leapt onto the table. A pair of silver discs, originating from gods knows where, slipped down his sleeves and into his palms. With not a trace of fanfare, the elderly butler flicked his wrists and sent the missiles spinning towards the oncoming bear.

Each throw in its own way was masterful. The first disc flew straight and true, imbedding itself deeply into the beast's forehead. The second disc curved at an extreme angle, flying wide of its target, but sweeping back towards the bear's flank. Either through good fortune, expertise, or divine intervention, the second disc flew into the bear's weeping exit wound and buried itself deep in the monster's flesh.

Internally broken, the bear's legs ceased functioning. Crashing onto the floor with a ground-shaking thud, it slid limply across the floorboards, tongue lolling uselessly to one side. Carried far by its momentum, the corpse only stopped once it had bumped lightly against the Baron's table.

Still fearful of the monster, the Baron peeked over the table's edge apprehensively.

'Is it dead?'

'Unmistakably, my Lord.'

The Baron sighed, relieved by this news.

'Excellent. Capital throws Jeeves, I would have been for the daisies otherwise.'

An enraged cry drew the Baron's attention away from the carcase beside him.

'Stop fucking talking! This is not the time!'

Capitalising on Neesa's momentary inattention, the wolf she was tussling with clamped its jaws around Neesa's wrist. Neesa yelled angrily as the creature's teeth bit down upon her, puncturing her flesh and numbing her hand. Reflexively, she let go of her sword.

The wolf spasmed, pushing the blade out of its chest. As the blade fell towards the floor Neesa released her grasp of the wolf's throat and snatched the sword's handle from the air. Whilst ducking under an errant lunge from the wolf, Neesa pointed her sword-tip upwards and rolled forwards.

With the combination of her momentum and that of the wolf, Neesa's sword carved a deep gash along the length of the creature's belly. In a waterfall of gore, putrid organs reeking of death and decay cascaded onto the floor. By either sheer will, or the foul magics that drove it, the wolf was not slain. Snarling as it landed awkwardly, it hobbled behind Neesa clumsily.

Temporarily forgotten, the second wolf barrelled unchecked into the Baron. The room spun around him and he lost all vestiges of spatial sense. Tumbling across the floor, he lost his grip on Peacemaker. Clattering uselessly beside him, the gun slid to a halt barely a hairs breath out of reach.

The wolf leapt on top of him, pinning him firmly to the ground. Reacting just in time, the Baron shielded his face with an arm. Held momentarily at bay, the wolf gnashed its plaque riddled fangs towards his exposed throat. Drool and bile sprayed the Baron's face as he struggled to prevent the monster from eating his face off.

Desperately, the Baron reached out towards his weapon as far as he could, willing his fingers to stretch just a little bit further. All the while the wolf's jaws snapped ever closer to his face.

Gods be damned. I will not let this be my end. I'll give you a good old what for, you bloody, mangy mutt.

Feeling his strength wane, the Baron gave one final push towards Peacemaker. Hope surged in his chest as he felt the tips of his fingers brush against the cold steel of the gun's frame. Praying silently to the gods, the Baron attempted to shimmy Peacemaker towards him. It worked.

Finding a larger purchase on Peacemaker than he had previously, the Baron scooted his weapon even closer towards him. His palm rubbed tantalisingly against the tell-tale leather of Peacemaker's grip and he knew that it was now in reach.

Greedily, the Baron snatched Peacemaker up off of the floor. Cocking its hammer against his thigh as he brought it towards the wolf, the Baron wasted not a moment to consider optimal firing vectors or the anatomy of wolves. Instead, he simply pressed Peacemaker's barrel against the wolf's side and fired.

Bang!

Peacemaker barked an angry retort as it propelled its lead projectile deep inside the wolf's torso. The smoky scent of charred fur filled the Baron's nostrils and he felt the pressure exerted by the wolf against him slacken as the monster reeled from being shot. Though it was a welcome reprieve, the Baron knew that any celebrations would be premature. The wolf was still alive and it was still a threat.

Frantically, the Baron tried to re-arm Peacemaker, cocking it as he had done so before, but frustratingly he could not. His hand, and by extension Peacemaker, was pinned beneath the floundering form of the wolf. Blood seeped from the hole in the wolf's torso, soaking the Baron's hand. He found no comfort in the macabre warmth it offered.

Gods that's disgusting.

Spurred onwards by the prospect of its imminent demise, the wolf redoubled its efforts. Though its legs could no longer support its own weight, it was no less ferocious. Cringing as the beast's teeth came mere inches from his face, the Baron did what he always did when he didn't know what else to do. He called for Jeeves.

'Jeeves!'

Never one to disappoint his master, Jeeves quickly came to the Baron's aid. Pulling the wolf's muzzle backwards, he slashed the edge of a silver disc across the beast's throat.

Where in the seven hells does he get all those discs from? I swear the bugger has an infinite supply of them.

Arterial blood pulsed rhythmically from the wolf's wound, spraying both the Baron and the wall behind him with hot crimson gore. Unavoidably, he breathed in some of the wolf's blood. Coughing and spluttering as he tried to clear his lungs, the Baron felt a great weight lift off of his torso as Jeeves pushed the wolf away. Thudding onto the ground, the creature spasmed wildly as it haemorrhaged the remainders of its lifeblood.

Free from the burden that was holding him down, the Baron staggered to his feet, assisted by Jeeves. With no delay, the butler produced a simple white cloth and held it out to him.

'Are you alright my Lord?'

The Baron took the cloth, having not the faintest clue where Jeeves had pulled it from, and wiped his face clean.

'Yes, thank you kindly Jeeves. Another timely rescue. Whatever will I do without you?'

Jeeves flushed red and turned away in response to the thinly veiled jibe implanted within the Baron's words. However, always the consummate gentleman, he quickly recovered his composure. Choosing to deflect, rather than engage, the Baron's assertations he redirected his master's attention elsewhere.

'I'm sure you'll be fine my Lord. Speaking of which, I do believe miss Neesa is mopping up the last of those foul critters as we speak. And, considering the difficulty of which, she's not even that worse for wear. Impressive.'

Wiping the last vestiges of blood from his brow, the Baron looked to where Jeeves was gesturing. Neesa casually sidestepped a wolf as it lunged carelessly at her thigh. Torquing her torso with tremendous force and precision, her blade hummed as it blurred through the air. The wolf's head rolled free from its toppling body and a spray of wolf-blood shot as high as the ceiling, painting an upturned table with a speckled red star-scape.

At the end of her stroke, she held her pose, as if waiting for the next foe to attack before responding. None came. They were all dead. Coming to this conclusion, Neesa wiped her sword clean on an abandoned dishcloth and re-sheathed it.

Seeing that neither Jeeves nor the Baron required any assistance, Neesa gave them both a curt nod of respect. She then walked over to the woman whose heart had just moments before been devoured. While the Baron could clearly see her lips moving, he could not hear what she was saying.

What the devil is she up to?

Her mouth stopped moving and much to his surprise, Neesa tore off a strip of the woman's dress. Quickly, she stood and wrapped the cloth tightly around the forearm of her sword-arm, all the while grimacing in pain.

That must be unpleasant. Poor dear.

Noting that both Jeeves and the Baron were staring at her, she scrunched up her face in a quizzical expression.

'What? It's not like she was needing it.'

Simultaneously, the pair shook their heads and quickly looked away while muttering a variety of apologies and platitudes. The problem was however, for the Baron at least, that the room was far from a pretty sight. Never one to foster much of a morbid curiosity, the remnants of their encounter made him feel more than a little queasy.

Oh no, don't look there, intestines should not be on the outside of one's body. Oh dear. Look somewhere else, oh bugger, that's worse. Oh my. Is that brain? Not good.

'Hey Baron, are you okay?'

'Um, yes, indeed. I'm glad to report that I am unharmed. Though, if I'm entirely honest, I'm finding it hard to not vomit. It appears that recent events,' the Baron gestured to the plethora of blood and gore decorating the inside of the tavern, 'have tested my constitution to its limit. Oh gods.'

A sudden surge of nausea overwhelmed the Baron. Clutching his stomach, he bent double and heaved. A torrent of bile tainted ale spewed from his mouth. As it gushed uncontrollably over the tavern floorboards the Baron shuddered internally as the putrid liquid splashed onto his feet and legs.

This is a long call from my finest hour. A long call indeed. Disgusting.

Standing behind him, well clear of the splash zone, Neesa rubbed the Baron's back.

'There, there Baron. I know some folks think it's better out rather than in, but they're wrong of course. It's always better left inside, especially for me, but for now let's go with that. Let it all out.'

Retching the final remnants of his stomach's contents onto the floor, the Baron straightened. Jeeves already had another clean cloth at the ready and without any hesitation the Baron took it.

Goodness gracious, another one? Maybe he has an infinite supply of cloths as well as silver discs?

After wiping his bleary eyes and foam crusted mouth, he looked between Neesa and Jeeves.

'So then. What's next?'

Chapter 38

Thoron

Thoron ran his hand through Jovita's hair as he gazed into her lust filled eyes. Those silken curls, as smooth as liquid butter, slipped easily between his fingers. Jovita smiled and Thoron's heart skipped a beat as the halfling's digits tickle his bare buttocks. In that moment, he couldn't help but to contemplate his good fortune and prayed that it would last.

Lowering his hand to the side of Jovita's face, Thoron grasped her cheek and tenderly drew the halfling towards himself. Not to be left wanting, her lips pushed out to meet his and the pair embraced, tongues darting, playfully intertwined.

Deep in the throes of passion, the pair writhed uncontrollably over the bed. Wanting more, and subconsciously knowing that Jovita wanted more too, Thoron passed his hand along Jovita's stomach. She offered him no resistance and parted her legs.

Slowly at first, Thoron rubbed the tips of his fingers over Jovita's clitoris. Jovita's body tensed and spasmed at the pleasure of it. With a primeval urgency she groaned huskily into Thoron's ear as she nibbled on his lobe.

'More!'

Without hesitation, Thoron slipped two of his digits inside her. Moaning deeply, Jovita bit down on his shoulder and clawed his back wildly. Rapidly, he thrust his fingers in and out of her, sliding easily back and forth as Jovita's pussy ran heavy with warm juices. As she panted heavily in his ear, Thoron felt Jovita's vagina clench down upon his fingers and her body stiffen. Shuddering violently, the halflings head snapped backwards as she screamed in uncontrollable ecstasy.

'Yes!'

Though she had already orgasmed, Thoron kept on fingering Jovita. Gradually, he slowed his rapid pace, thrusting his fingers inside her one last time, as deep as he could. At this final thrust Jovita trembled, whimpering softly.

Thoron withdrew his fingers, now coated with Jovita's juices and his own seed, from inside her, and noting a hungry glint in her eyes, held them up to her mouth. Greedily, she suckled Thoron's sopping digits, her slurping tongue cleaning them thoroughly. Once Jovita was done, she swallowed heartily, smacking her lips in satisfaction.

'Mm, delicious.'

Turned on by her debaucheries, Thoron felt his loins stir. With his throat coated in gravel he forced his words from his throat.

'Ye ready fur rood two?'

Jovita licked her lips, collecting one last drop of cum that had spilt there. After rolling the semen around her throat for a moment, she swallowed for a second time and nodded her head eagerly.

'Yes. By the gods, yes.'

Jovita's eyes dipped towards his groin and her lips twisted into a coy smirk.

'By the looks of it you're about ready too. Get on your back, it's my turn to be on top.'

Thoron obeyed. Jovita pounced on top of him, her mouth quickly encompassing his semi-erect penis. Hot saliva drenched his member as Jovita's head bobbed up and down, her velvet lips sliding along the side of his shaft. Thoron groaned in pleasure. Hot blood rushed into his cock and it stiffened fully.

Objective accomplished, Jovita stood, seductively turned to face Thoron, and slowly lowered herself downwards. Squatting above him, she rubbed Thoron's erect member against the outside of her vagina. A mixture of her own love juices and his semen oozed from her womanhood, dribbling all over Thoron's cock. Jovita stopped moving and slowly started easing herself down onto him. Thoron felt a warmth engulf the tip of his penis and he groaned in ecstasy.

Before he had fully entered her, a barely audible crash echoed from downstairs. Instantly, Jovita stopped, head spinning towards the door. Her face, just moments before a masque of pleasure personified, was twisted by a primal concern. Motionless, she waited.

'Dae no' worry aboot it lass, it's probably nothing mair than a drunkard falling over himself. Nothing tae fret over, am sure.'

As soon as he had finished speaking, a fierce roar bellowed from below, shaking the very walls. Immediately, Jovita let go of Thoron's still-throbbing member and leapt from the bed. Scooping her dishevelled dress off of the ground, she started working it over her heaving frame.

'Ah, come oan lassie, cannae we jus' ignore it? Surely someone else can deal wi' it?'

The briefest of glances was all that she gave him, but it was enough for Thoron to see the concern and regret in her eyes.

'Sorry lover-boy, I'd love to have you fuck my brains out for a second time, but my father is down there. Whatever's happening, he's in the middle of it and he might need my help. I can't just leave him.'

Giving her dress one final rub, smoothing out its wrinkles the best she could, Jovita opened the door. At first, Thoron thought to protest some more, to try and get her back in bed, but any such notions died stillborn upon his lips as Jovita scurried outside without another word. The door clicked shut behind her rapidly departing form, leaving Thoron alone.

'Shite!'

Rolling grumpily off of the bed, Thoron gathered his garments and dressed quickly. He heard more sounds from below, he couldn't make out exactly what they were, but they didn't sound pleasant.

Best get a move oan.

With the deftness of a man who had been forced to dress hurriedly on many a previous occasion, Thoron hitched his trousers and slid on his top. His fingers blurred as they rebuttoned his shirt and fastened his britches. After slipping his boots onto his feet and easily as a whore slides between the sheets, Thoron donned his gambeson and tightened his belt firmly around his waist. Dressed in record time, he fetched his sword and shield from the corner. As soon as he touched Barry's hilt, the voice of the enigmatic weapon echoed throughout his mind.

'Hey mate, what's the go? We haven't been put down for long, something's up, isn't it?'

In no mood to dawdle, Thoron moved across the room, replying to Barry as he went.

'It sure is. I cannot say whit, but I hev a feeling we'll be in fur a scrap. Something is going oan downstairs and I dae no' lek the sounds o' it.'

Even though he always sounded chipper, there was an evident upward spike in Barry's tone.

'Bonza! I do love me a barney.'

'Hm. In ma experience at' depends oan the barney.'

Opening the door by the slimmest of margins, Thoron peered carefully into the corridor, wary of danger. The corridor to the right was empty, and to the left he saw nothing. Pushing the doorway open to its full extent, Thoron stepped into the hallway, his shield held protectively in front of him and his sword pointed warily outwards.

'*Crikey, mate. I should have told you this before now, must've slipped my mind, but you don't need to talk out loud when you speak to me an' Harry. We can hear you just fine when you talk in your head. Just think it and we'll hear it, telepathic like.*'

Turning right, towards the downwards stairwell, Thoron tentatively eased himself forwards, eyes and ears keenly focused.

Bang!

Despite his training, Thoron flinched as a peculiar explosion reverberated off of the hallway walls. It was a sound completely alien to him. He was familiar with underground gas explosions, and they were the nearest facsimile to this new sound he could think of, but in actuality this was nothing like those at all.

Bugger me, whit in the seven hells is going oan doon thir?

Overcoming his momentary confusion, Thoron's reflexes took control of his actions. Crouching low behind his shield, he ducked into an open doorway. Feeling his heart beat faster in his chest and cold beads of sweat from on his brow, Thoron took a deep breath in an attempt to ease his intensifying nerves.

'*I didn't let on to Daly about that particular pearl of wisdom for absolutely yonks. Poor bugger got himself into a fair few pickles because of it. And it was bloody hilarious, but eventually I had to tell him.*'

After waiting to see what the unknown noise would portend, and seeing no discernible effects, Thoron left the door frame. Creeping slowly down the hallway Thoron strained his ears, ignoring Barry's incessant chatter in his head, hoping to gleam whatever information he could about the ruckus below.

Bang!

A second booming explosion sent a shockwave of sound echoing off of the walls. Now knowing that the sound harboured no immediate threat, Thoron ignored it. With his expression locked in a stoic grimace, he didn't even break his stride.

'We were in a tent with a bunch of tribal big-wigs and Daly lost his temper at me, can't say I really blame him for it though. Anyway, he yelled out some right colourful language and the tribal fellas thought Daly was yelling at them. To cut a long story short, Daly was almost killed and we had to scarper out of there right quick.'

Thoron's head snapped towards the top of the stairs as movement drew his attention. The muscles in his forearm twitched as he prepared to skewer whoever, or whatever, was approaching him. In the moment between preparedness and action, Thoron assessed the potential threat and in that split-second determined it to be harmless. It was nothing more than an old man, unarmed and shuffling uneasily. Thoron relaxed, but didn't lower his guard.

As the man meandered past, barely noticing Thoron and unaware of how close he had just come to death, Thoron heard him mumble incoherent ramblings.

'Blasted nonsense, they don't belong here strange critters. It's those foreigners I say, stirring up trouble as always. Natures wrath, that's what it is, shouldn't have disturbed him I say, chopped it down they did. Bah fudge sticks.'

Keeping his gaze fixated on the stairwell, Thoron ignored the muttering geriatric. Keenly aware of everything around him, he heard from somewhere behind him the tell-tale creak of a poor oiled door hinge. First as it opened, and then again when it closed. The mumbling stopped.

Whit a bizarre man. Can 'is night get any stranger?

'Too right mate, that bloke sure was an odd duck, wasn't he? Not the strangest thing I've ever seen, but certainly up there. That's for sure.'

While his heart pounded in his ears, Thoron tiptoed slowly down the stairs, wary of a squeaky floorboard and a keen eared foe. Despite his caution, one of the stairs emitted a high-pitched squeak as soon as his foot touched it. Instantly, he froze. Tightening his grip on his sword's hilt and straining his senses to their limit, he sought the seemingly inevitable cry of alarm. There was none.

Sighing audibly in relief, Thoron, even more tenderly than before, continued to ease himself down the stairs. One step, two and then three. There were no more squeaks.

Voices, muffled by distance and obstruction, wafted sporadically into Thoron's ears. He couldn't make out all that was said and the words he could hear made no sense, but he knew that they would cover any noise that he would make during his descent. He quickened his pace.

'There... some folks... better out... always better... inside... for me... let it all out.'

The voices stopped and Thoron immediately froze, afeared of discovery. They were soon replaced by the signature melody of a torrent of liquid splashing onto the floor. A cacophony of wracking coughs and spluttering retches followed immediately after. Thoron continued downwards.

Sounds lek someone's losing their stomach contents all over the ground. They cannae hold their drink most likely.

'Maybe there's blood about and they can't stand it? Before I met Daly, I knew a sheila like that. One speck of blood was all it took for her to lose her guts. Projectile vomit at that. It was fucking spectacular. Shame she was absolute dogshit in a fight though, as useless as tits on a bull that one.'

Stepping off of the final step, Thoron assessed the room before him, ready to react to any and all threats.

It was a disaster zone. Corpses, mutilated and twisted, lay torn and scattered throughout the tavern. Men, women, the old and the young, none had been spared whatever nightmarish slaughter had transpired here. Blood coated the walls and ceiling alike. Entrails lay snaked across the floor and what was unquestionably brain-matter was splattered against an upturned table. Dotted amid the corpses of the innocent, bodies of forest beasts lay equally maimed.

By the gods.

'Strewth, it looks like someone had some fun. Shame it wasn't me.'

Much to Thoron's surprise, no one called out in alarm, nor attacked him, nor even acknowledged his presence at all. The only living things to occupy the room were the three strangers he had witnessed enter the tavern earlier that evening, the blue infernati, the well-dressed noble and the elderly man. Standing in a close-knit circle, with their backs to Thoron, none of the trio had as of yet seen him.

Hugging the wall, Thoron moved around the edge of the room, not for a second taking his eyes off of the strangers. The elderly man handed the noble a handkerchief, who then wiped his mouth with it.

He must be the wan we heard vomiting.

'Bah, looks like a soft-cock to me mate. Those other two on the other hand, they could be trouble. Still, I'm dead cert we could take them though.'

The middle-aged man cleared his throat before looking between the infernati and the elderly man.

'So then. What's next?'

Utilising the bar to cover his left flank, Thoron answered the question that was most assuredly not directed towards him.

'At's a good question laddie, but I've an even better wan. Whit the fuck's goin' oan here?'

'Aw shit mate, why the hells did you do that for? We could have bopped them before they even knew we were here. Now we'll have to talk to them, groan.'

Simultaneously, the trio of strangers each turned to face him, their surprise clearly apparent. In a blur of movement, the infernati's hand shot to the hilt of her sword, while the elderly human drew a silver disc from his jacket sleeve. Though they did not attack him in that moment, Thoron knew that their inaction could cease in an instant. The infernati's eyes narrowed.

She's gauging whether I'm a threat or not.

A low growl escaped from the corner of the infernati's mouth, but her hand left her blade and she relaxed her stance. The old man's silver disc disappeared up his sleeve as quickly as it had appeared and he too relaxed.

'Looks like they don't consider you a threat. That's a bloody insult in my books mate. Let's stab the pricks.'

Tipping his brow to the strangers, Thoron reciprocated their peaceful gesture by sheathing his sword and lowering his shield.

'Well master dwarf, time is not currently our ally so, I'll give you the short version. No pun intended. At this moment the town is being assaulted by a large number of wild creatures.' She waved her hand, gesturing to the animal corpses strewn around the room. 'Much like these ones, which are determined to slay everyone, including ourselves, that currently resides in said town. My companions and I were about to leave when we were attacked.'

The infernati shifted her gaze, again towards the slain beasts, but also to the slaughtered townspeople. For the former, Thoron saw that a deep hatred burned in her eyes, for the latter all he witnessed was sorrow tinged with regret.

'As far as I see it our only course of action is to flee. We are far too outnumbered to stand and fight, if we stay, we die. That being said, even escape will be difficult. I have no doubt that we will stand a better chance united, so how about it dwarf, will you join us?'

'*Don't do it mate, we don't need these milksops, we'll be fine on our own.*'

'*I do say. You are mistaken my good man, alone we perish. It would be best to accompany these folks if you ask me.*'

'*Sigh. Fine. Do what the bloody shield says.*'

''At sounds lek a good plan tae me, but let us no' dae so as strangers. Ma name is Thoron, clansman o' the Nam Beann.'

'I wish I could say well met Thoron, but under these circumstances, it would be a lie.'

With an outstretched arm, the infernati dipped her head in acknowledgment towards Thoron.

'In any case, I'm Neesa, the fellow with the crusty mouth is the Baron and the dapper gent is Jeeves.'

Thoron took Neesa's hand and with a firm grip shook it heartily.

'Greetings all. Now, let's get the fuck out of here.'

Chapter 39

Máher

Máher preferred the night over the day. He found solace in the solitude and privacy it provided. There were no awkward stares, nor any uncomfortable questions, it was just simpler. Even now, despite the presence of Eris, he felt as though he was free, as though nobody and no one could touch him. That calmed him.

Cool air rushed over his face as he rode and, not for the first time, he gave thanks for the heavy furs he wore. Though he did not despise it, the cold was not his friend. At his core he was a literal being of fire, the progeny of fire made flesh. Whenever he roamed in cooler climes, he always ended up feeling lethargic and uneasy.

At least I'm not in the far south. If I were, I'd be little more than comatose.

Carried by the same air that chilled him, Máher heard a chorus of howling wolves. Used to the wilderness, he would never have normally paid any real attention to them, but in this instance, they aroused his slumbering apprehension.

How strange. By the sounds of it there's too many for a single pack and they seem to be coming from Thered's Field. This cannot be good.

Thinking it prudent, Máher extended a tendril of his consciousness to his draconic friend. Though he did not know how far away Beher was, it mattered not, regardless of distance they could always find each other. Sensing the distinct pulse that Beher's soul emitted into the world, Máher probed the essence of his sibling with his own and projected his thoughts into the dragon's mind.

'Beher! Are you awake?'

At first there was no response, so Máher gave Beher a wordless prod. Beher's soul stirred in response to the assault, but gave no higher display of recognition. More forcefully than before, Máher repeated his original question.

'Beher! Are you awake?'

This time there was a response.

'Mm... what?'

'I said, are you awake?'

'Beher hates to say it, but Beher is now. Why does Máher interrupt poor Beher's dreams of endless lambs and piglets. What does Máher want?

'Something's wrong. Just a moment ago I heard more wolf howls than I've ever heard at once before. By the sounds of it, they came from Thered's Field. I would appreciate it to no end if you would rouse yourself and investigate. I would hate to run headfirst into danger without any forewarning.'

'Pfft, why Máher worries about such things Beher knows not, Máher always ends up in danger anyway, regardless of Beher. But Beher is a good brother and will do as Máher asks. But, Máher should know, Beher is quite far from human town. Beher thinks Máher will get there first.'

Pushed from Beher's mind like a stubborn turd expelled from a constipated man's bowels, Máher's consciousness was thrust back into his own body. Shaking his head at the indignity of it, Máher swore under his breath.

'Shit.'

Having not noticed just how close Eris was riding to him, he was taken aback when she called out. Evidently, she had heard him cursing.

'What is it?'

'There might be trouble in the town. I just asked Beher to check it out, but he's a long way out. For now, we'll be without him.'

Máher signalled to Eris, pointing to the side of the road. She nodded in response. Pulling back on his reins to slow his steed, he guided his horse off of the road.

'I'm sorry, I know that you were fearful of our previously rapid pace, but I feel as though we now need to match it, if not surpass it. I'll do what I can to ease our journey. Try to stay close behind me.'

Reaching inside of himself, Máher drew upon the font of energy that nestled within his chest. His visage flared for a moment as he pulled a small ball of eldritch energy into his palm. Banishing the night, a bright light blossomed around the pair. Directing the ball with his will alone, he prompted it to float over the head of his mount. Affixing it to the forehead of his horse, he willed the ball to change, slowly morphing it into a cone. Now, in lew of an omnidirectional aura of sunlight, a focussed beam projected forwards, revealing the road before them.

'Máher, even if there is trouble ahead, why don't we just avoid it and go elsewhere? We should let someone else deal with it. Why do we have to get involved?'

Staring out at the clearly illuminated road before him, Máher saw nothing. Granted he could physically see what was there, but his mind was unable to process the details. It was too busy contemplating Eris's question.

Why do I want to get involved? Why do I always get myself involved in the issues of others? Why can I never just walk away?

Whatever the answers to these questions were, Máher had not the time, nor inclination, to discover them at present. So, he chose to do what he often did. He deflected.

'To be honest, that would be the smart thing to do.' Máher sighed deeply and turned towards Eris, looking directly into her eyes with a sly grin. 'But, what can I say? I've a curious soul. I shan't force you to follow me and I'd understand if you chose to go your own way.'

As she sat, still in her saddle, Máher could see the cogs in Eris's brain turn as she considered her options. Obviously coming to the end of her deliberations, she shook her head.

'No. Currently you're the only person in this world who doesn't wish me dead or isn't a complete stranger, other than Beher of course. I'll stay with you. For now, at least. But, and this is a big but, if you get me killed, I'll haunt you for the rest of time.'

Máher couldn't help his smile from widening.

'Somehow your decision comforts me greatly. Thank you.'

Without another word to Eris, Máher spurred the flank of his horse with an uncharacteristically loud shout, 'hah!' Neighing skittishly, the creature pushed off of its hind legs and accelerated from a standstill to a full gallop. He took a cursory glance over his shoulder to ensure that Eris was keeping pace with him. She was.

Together, they bounded along the road. Máher's eyes never strayed from the illuminated cone before him, ever on the lookout for potholes and other such hazards. He knew that a single error could cost him his life. As focussed as he was, he left no room for thoughts or worries. He never once looked back to check on Eris's welfare. For him there was only steely concentration, devotion to the task at hand.

They soon reached the outer limits of Thered's field. Wilderness gave way to lonely houses and pasture. Sporadic wolf howls, louder now as a result of proximity, still marred the usually quiet night, but they were now joined in concert by a myriad of fear fuelled screams.

Máher was no stranger to the atrocities of this world. He knew that a violent death was just as common as a peaceful one, but it still hurt to hear the cries he was hearing now. Being there in person and witnessing their manifested pain was fundamentally different to knowing it in the abstract. This was worse. Far worse.

By the gods, these poor souls.

Ahead of him, a particularly old woman stepped onto the road and into the light. She was waving her arms wildly as she hobbled ungracefully into Máher's path. For the most part she appeared ordinary, simple peasant garb covering a wiry frame which had only ever known hard work. It was her expression that alluded to the sinister events of this evening. Her flustered face was devoid of any mirth and her eyes bore the mark of one who had recently witnessed horrors.

Pulling back on his reins, Máher slowed his steed. At a gentle canter, he guided his horse to where the woman stood and stopped beside her. Though worry wormed deep within his chest, he had no intention of causing the woman any further grief, so he lied, reassuring her the best that he could.

'Easy there, it's going to be okay. We shan't let any harm befall you. You're safe now. Madam, I know it must be hard, but please tell me, what is occurring here?'

Flustered and out of breath, the woman panted in response.

'Oh, good sir, horrible it is. Never seen anything like it I have. Monsters they are. Invaded the town they did. Slaughter most foul it is.'

Máher could see the pain etched clearly on her face, just as he could hear it in her voice. He couldn't fathom the exact nature of her grief and he knew that he couldn't undo the damage already done. He also knew that there were no words he could provide would balm her violated soul, however, he felt that he had to offer her something. If only to lift her spirits for a time.

'I'm sorry for everything you've had to contend with this night. I truly am. I will do my best to provide a remedy.'

With a heavy heart Máher, prompted his horse away from the old woman. Once he was at a safe distance, he spurred his mount's flank. He accelerated swiftly, but was able to make out one final shout from the rapidly disappearing woman.

'Wait good sir! If hellsbent on death ye be, seek the King in the main square. Mounting a defence when I saw him last, he was.'

The King? What king?

Buildings blurred past him as his horse thundered along the town's road. The screams around him intensified, threatening to tear his soul asunder, but he pushed them from the forefront of his mind.

Focus Máher, you can't let yourself become overly emotional.

Illuminated before him, Máher saw a horrendous sight emerge from the gloom. Held tightly within the clutches of terror, a young mother was running away from a pair of wolves, her baby held snugly against her chest. He saw their evil intent in their movements and he knew that if he did nothing to intervene the pair would surely be slain.

Offering a prayer to the gods, Máher whipped his steed to even greater feats of speed. He rode as though he was pursued by minions of the hells, but as he did so, he gauged the distance between himself and the mother. Already burning with power, Máher released his reins and drew the fire he held in his palm into a long spear. Holding himself steady, with nothing more than his legs, he drew the weapon back. Growling with exertion, he threw the spear towards the closest wolf.

Sparks and embers cascaded from the glowing beacon of death as it flew through the air. As the magical spike soared, Máher hoped and prayed that it would land on target. His aim was true. The tip of the fiery spear sunk deeply into his target's forehead, the fur around the molten weapon smouldering as the wolf's earthly remains unceremoniously slid to a tumbling halt.

Pleased with his own success, Máher felt a surge of satisfaction within him. However, his positivity was tempered by the knowledge that the one he was aiming to save was still in imminent danger. Mind racing with possible strategies, he settled on his next course of action.

When the right moment struck, Máher threw caution to the wind and leapt from his horse's saddle. No one would ever describe him as an agile man, but in that moment, he soared as gracefully as the most skilled of acrobats. Landing perfectly, he inserted himself between the young mother and her pursuer. Rolling out of the fall as he touched the ground, his momentum was diminished, but not entirely arrested. Wanting to put more distance between the inevitable conflict and the woman, Máher accelerated and sprinted towards the wolf.

As he got closer to the beast, he could see that it was no ordinary wolf. It was larger than usual, that much as obvious, but that was not of any specific significance. In actuality, what was truly peculiar were the creature's eyes. For in fact there were no eyes. In their place black flames flickered excitedly.

Taken aback by this oddity, the eldritch energy he was holding in his mind slipped away from him. Defenceless and flat-footed, Máher failed to react in time as the beast lunged madly towards him. Crashing into his chest, it knocked Máher off of his feet. Thumping into the road, his head spun in dizzy circles and his vision deteriorated out of focus. Not waiting for its prey to recover, the wolf pounced onto Máher's chest, pinning him down.

Still disorientated, Máher flailed madly in an attempt to fend of the wolf. Ignoring Máher's futile protest, the wolf wrapped his jaws around Máher's throat and began to squeeze. Máher felt a sharp stabbing pain as razor sharp fangs eased themselves into his skin. In a panic, Máher grabbed the creature's maw and tried to pry it off of him. The pressure on his neck eased, but in his heart, he knew his efforts would ultimately prove futile.

I will not allow you to take me. Not like this.

Born from desperation, rather than any mindful intent, Máher reached out to the font of magic pulsing within him. Energy surged through his chest, down his arms and into his hands. Manifesting as it always did, as fire, wild and uncontrollable flames surged from his hands in a geyser of molten fury.

In a scant moment, the fur around the monster's muzzle was atomised, prompting a foul stench to waft nauseatingly up Máher's nostrils. Its flesh charred, dropping shrivelled and blackened from its bones.

Consumed by pain, the creature released its grip on Máher's neck. Blissful relief washed over him as the wolf shrieked intensely while it backed away, trying to escape the flaming torrents engulfing it. Máher let it go, but did nothing to quell his firestorm. Staggering as it gradually lost control over its functions, the beast surrendered its hold on life and collapsed into a smouldering heap. Only when the corpse stopped twitching, did Máher douse his flames.

Hearing the tell-tale sounds of a horse's hoofbeats clip-clop behind him, Máher turned around, wary of danger. It was only Eris.

'Did the woman make it to safety?'

'Yes. There was another wolf, but I dealt with it.'

'Good. That's good.'

Even though he knew that his horse would be long gone by now, he looked along the road for it anyway. It was nowhere to be seen.

'Hm, I seem to have lost my horse. May I ride with you?'

Eris shrugged. 'Sure. Just don't get handsy.'

Eris offered her hand towards him and Máher took it gratefully. Groaning with effort, he pulled himself up, mounted Eris's horse and sat behind her. The saddle was not designed to be ridden double and instantly Máher questioned his decision to abandon his own mount.

As uncomfortable as this will be, I won't have to put up with it for long.

Trying as best as he could to not get 'handsy,' Máher clinched his legs tightly around the back of the horse as Eris prompted it forwards. The beast accelerated quickly, despite the increased load, and Máher did his best not to fall. Beside them, the buildings of the town blurred, but Máher paid them no heed. He was to focussed on their destination and the invariable combat that awaited them there.

Without warning, the blurring tunnel of buildings vanished as the horizon opened up around them. Thundering into a large, open square, all thoughts of the future, and the growing discomfort in his rear end, evaporated as the scene around him took precedence over everything else.

Having succumbed completely to the clutches of chaos, the courtyard around them was nothing less than an exemplar of pandemonium. Corpses lay bloody and torn across the cobbles, while shadow marked creatures mercilessly tore down those seeking to avoid a similar end. For most, their efforts were pointless as, despite them, they fell victim to their pursuers.

Small enclaves of resistance stood as pockets of order amongst the entropy. For a while they repulsed the shadow wolves and bears, but inevitably they succumbed to the insurmountable odds arrayed against them.

Individuals, and small family groups alike, all seeking refuge the onslaught, trickled into the square as they sought their salvation. Perhaps they hoped to find allies there to aid them, or perhaps they were simply driven by circumstance. In either instance, it was only a few that found redemption, the remainder found nothing but misery as they witnessed the death of their closest loved ones before meeting a violent end themselves.

The greatest misfortune was felt by those who were not killed outright. Incapable of movement, they lay groaning in perpetual agony. Coated by an ensemble of piss, shit and vomit they slowly faded away as their blood pooled around them.

Unsurprisingly, the screams were far louder here than what they were on the outskirts of the village. Just as he did before, Máher tried to push them from the forefront of his mind, lest they affect his cognition. But it was growing harder to do so.

Of all the horrors I have witnessed in this world, this is by far the worst. Oh, gods why?

At the far end of the courtyard Máher noticed a loose line of guardsmen and soldiers standing in front of a large building. They skirmished with the creatures assaulting them, but never broke formation, even when it appeared to be prudent to do so.

That must the King's forces that the old woman spoke of earlier.

Máher tapped Eris on her shoulder and pointed towards them.

'I see them.'

Unbidden, Eris steered her steed towards the King and his men. Máher squeezed his legs even tighter around the horse, lest the centrifugal force of the turn throw him off.

Máher felt the tendrils of another's consciousness reach out towards him. Recognising them instantly as those of Beher, he dropped his mental guard and let the thoughts of his friend mingle with his own.

'*Beher wishes to inform Máher that Beher has arrived at the town. Beher's circling above it now.*'

'*Nice of you to join us. It would be for the best if you stayed up there for now. It's an absolute mess down here, but I'll be sure to call if I need you.*'

'*Beher will do as Máher wishes. As always.*'

Tapping Eris's shoulder once more, Máher leant closer towards her and spoke into her ear.

'Beher's above us, should we need him, but for the meantime I'd prefer him to stay aloft. As an ace in the hole, as it were. Now, shall we join the fray?'

'I thought that was the plan. Um, wasn't it?'

Despite the circumstances, or perhaps because of them, Máher couldn't help but to laugh. Contrary to his usually stoic resolve, his demeanour broke down before the sneak-attack from his own unconscious self. Which, for some inexplicable reason, found hilarity in a situation truly underserving of any humorous response.

With his belly quaking in nervous mirth he whispered in response, as much to himself as he did to Eris.

'It sure was.'

Chapter 40

Baron Victor von Grumanhieser III

Taking cover beside the shattered doorframe, the Baron eased his head slightly beyond its edge. Careful to not reveal himself, he squinted his eyes into the gloomy night, trying to see if any of their quarry posed an imminent threat. He saw nothing.

'Well, as far as I can tell, the coast is clear. Which way are we headed?'

Neesa moved silently to the opposite side of the door and whispered out of the corner of her mouth.

'When I saw them before they were coming from the north. So, I suggest we head south.' Neesa paused as she looked out of the window, left and then right. 'It would also be prudent for us to stick to side roads and alleys, we're less likely to be spotted that way.'

'Very well, that sounds reasonable to me. Alright then, let's get out of here.'

The Baron was about to move when a low whistle from Neesa stopped him. Raising his eyebrows in a quizzical expression, he mouthed silently, 'what?' Neesa just pointed. Emerging from a side-street were a pair of wolves accompanied by a black bear. If he would have left the building when he thought to do so, he would have been detected.

Good gods, that was close. Tis a fortunate thing that Neesa has such good eyes.

Nervously, the Baron waited for the creatures to pass. Though it was cool, beads of sweat gathered on his brow and, though it wasn't something he'd usually do, his lips moved in a silent prayer to Eleos. Either they were blessed by Eleos, or lady fate smiled upon them, for the animals passed them by and they remained hidden. The Baron breathed out a sigh of relief.

'Nicely spotted. That would have been messy otherwise.'

Neesa just shrugged as she looked out the window once more.

'Okay, it's clear. Follow me.'

Neesa left the tavern and turned left, avoiding the open ground of the road as much as possible by hugging the wall of the building tightly. Hot on her heels, perhaps even too closely, the Baron followed, wishing to remain close to someone he viewed as 'proficient at close quarters combat.' Jeeves and Thoron followed, at an entirely respectable distance, behind him.

The rapidly cooling evening air chilled the Baron's skin as it bit into him. After the welcoming warmth of the tavern's interior, it as an uncomfortable change. He had always preferred warmer climates and as a rule never ventured far from his hearth during the evening. His mood was additionally soured by the myriad of screams and pain fuelled howls that echoed from all around him. They drilled into his very soul and were even less welcome than the cold.

Having lived a life of relative luxury, the Baron was a stranger to pain and misery. Sure, he was aware that the world was at times a nasty and merciless place. He was under no illusions to how hard it was for those less fortunate than himself, but this was somehow worse than what he had ever imagined, than what he could possibly imagine.

These were the screams of the hopeless. Those that cried out had each relinquished every possibility for salvation. Their resignation to their grisly fates tainted the air with a palpable sorrow. It was in every respect a symphony of true torment for upon hearing it the Baron felt his soul decay within him. What made it worse was the knowledge that he could offer no remedy. For either himself nor the forsaken.

Pushing both his inadequacies and the cacophony of madness that plagued him to one side, the Baron focused on following Neesa, trusting her to lead him to safety.

There's nothing I can do. Just keep on moving Baron. Just keep moving.

Through the narrow laneways and alleys of Thered's Field, a deceptively complex labyrinth of fences and building walls, they ran. Oft times fast, other times slow. First this way, then that. They stopped at every intersection to make sure the way was clear. When it was, they never tarried, immediately resuming their mad dash to safety. When it wasn't, they let the roving bands of creatures' pass, all the while praying that they wouldn't catch their scent. It was a tense journey and for the Baron it was the worst experience of his life.

The constant fear, worried his mind and wore at his soul. He knew that at any moment they could be discovered. That any moment any manner of beasts could descend upon them, catching them unawares, and tear them asunder before they could react.

I imagine this is what a fox feels like when on the run from the hound. By the gods, if I ever get out of this mess, I'll never go on another hunt again. Social standing be damned.

Neesa stopped by the corner of a building and the Baron held his breath, thinking that danger lay ahead. Neesa waved, gesturing for them to press themselves against the wall. The Baron complied and wordlessly waited for her to give the all-clear, as stress induced sweat ran uncomfortably from his armpits.

Neesa peered around the corner, looking to see what lay ahead. As the moments passed, they passed as eternities and the Baron felt his stomach knot as anxiety clawed at his insides. After what seemed to be an age, Neesa turned back to the trio and with addressed them with a hesitant whisper.

'Listen, as crass as this may be, I have to ask.'

As quietly as he could, while still remaining audible, the Baron whispered back.

'What is it?'

'I've seen what's ahead and we have a choice. There's a crossroad, one way leads back into the streets, and perhaps eventual safety.' Neesa paused, as if thinking how to phrase what she had to say. 'The other way, well I couldn't see who it was, but there seemed to be a group of people fighting, resisting. They didn't look like farmers, much too organised. We could help them.' She paused again, took a single deep breath and the exhaled slowly. 'So, that's the choice, try and help or leave the people here to their fates.'

The moral implications of Neesa's question were immediately apparent to the Baron. He saw the prudence in advocating for a hasty withdrawal from the town, but in his heart, it seemed to be a poor decision. He was not a particularly brave man, or at least didn't believe himself to be, but he thought the idea of abandoning those he could help, and potentially save, repugnant. For him there was no choice.

'I understand the need to ask for our opinions, but for me at least the choice is clear. We help those we can. We fight.'

It was nothing more than a glimmer, but the Baron would have sworn that he saw a hint of satisfaction, and maybe even a modicum of respect, creep into

Neesa's dour expression. Rather than say anything overtly emotional, Neesa just dipped her head in a simple act of appreciation.

'Good. What do you say, Thoron?'

'A fight? Ha, 'at sounds lek a good time tae me. Let's dae it. Let's help them oot. An' mibbe we can put a stop tae whatever the fuck is causing 'is madness tae boot.'

Just as she did with the Baron, Neesa dipped her head towards Thoron.

'Excellent. Jeeves?'

'I go where the Baron goes.'

Neesa bowed for a third time.

'It's decided then, we go to their aid and we go together.' Neesa inhaled deeply, steeling herself. 'Stay together and watch each other's backs, danger could come at us from any direction.'

Steel hissed softly as both Neesa and Thoron drew their blades. The Baron pulled Peacemaker from its holster and carefully cocked its hammer. And Jeeves, well Jeeves was as always just Jeeves. Somehow, and from somewhere, he held in his hands a pair of serrated silver discs. In concert, and without further ado, the quartet rounded the corner.

Before them was a large cobbled square, simultaneously the literal and metaphoric heart of the village. Strewn across its stones were a number of deceased. Women, children, and men. Soldiers and farmers alike. All of those who tried to flee, but failed, joined by those who chose to fight and lost. It was an horrendous vista of blood, guts, and bodily excretions. Of a chaotic, hate fuelled slaughter. It was a disturbing and an unnatural sight to be sure, but it was also one that the Baron was becoming all too accustomed with. It was this familiarity which troubled him the most.

The dead were juxtaposed starkly beside those that still clung to life. Desperately they tried to stave off the same fate as those who had already fallen. For the most part it was a futile endeavour. Untrained civilians, no matter their gumption nor armaments, make for easy prey when pitted against that which nature designed to be killers.

Feeling for their plight, and riling at the injustice of it all, the Baron raised Peacemaker. While still walking forward he, exhaled slowly and held his breath, steadying himself the best he could.

Bang!

Imperceptibly fast, a bullet shot from Peacemaker's barrel, a puff of grey smoke trailing far behind. With a deeply felt satisfaction, the Baron grinned as the shot hit its mark. Entering by the base of its skull, the bullet bore its way through the head of an unsuspecting wolf. A shower of burnt grey-matter spurting from the beast's eye socket served as a celebratory fanfare as the creature unceremoniously collapsed.

Ha, now that was a shot.

Now noticed by the flame-eyed wildlife, a bevy of wolves departed from harrying their previous victims and charged towards the Baron and his compatriots. The first to react, Jeeves threw a single silver disc at one of the wolves. With precision bordering on godlike, it arced through the air and sliced across the throat of the lead wolf. The creature kept running as blood poured from its throat, as of yet unaware that it was already dead. Eventually, the wolf yielded to the inevitable and collapsed. Twitching as it continued to bleed, it slowly returned to death.

Not to be outdone, both Neesa and Thoron ran ahead of the others, meeting the wolves charge with one of their own.

Thoron slapped the snout of a wolf to one side with his shield. Following up, he swept his sword upwards, carving his blade through the creature's exposed neck. Steel sliced through sinew and the wolf's head parted from its toppling body.

An idol of rage made manifest; Neesa plucked a leaping wolf out of the air as it leapt towards her. Holding it at bay by its throat, she drove the beast onto its hind legs, whilst screaming into the flickering flames on its face. As she sang her hellsborn solo, she stabbed her sword into the wolf's side. Again and again, she thrust her blade into the soft underbelly of her foe. It was only when the creature went limp, did Neesa release her hold upon the wolf, casually letting it fall, her face lined with a contemptuous, wrathful smirk.

The Baron re-cocked Peacemaker's hammer and levelled it at the final wolf. Caught in the heat of the moment, he forwent his usual care and hastily squeezed his gun's trigger.

Bang!

Peacemaker kicked, as it always did, and a bullet shot from its barrel at tremendous speeds. It flew straight, as the laws of physics demanded it to, but victimised by the Baron's impatience, the bullet failed to achieve what he had hoped it to do. He had hoped for a killing blow, but instead he only managed a crippling one.

Dash it all!

The bullet slammed into the creature's shoulder. Mid-stride, the wolf's snout drooped, scraping its way across the cobblestones as the creature's crippled leg collapsed. Though it could no longer control its movements, momentum carried it tumbling forward. As it came to a rest Thoron stepped forward, and with a single precise thrust, stabbed his blade through the wolf's heart.

Ahead of them, Neesa pointed to a particularly large group of creatures that were harrying a small cluster of survivors and shouted.

'This way!'

Brooking no argument, they followed.

Out of the corner of his eye the Baron saw a rider, nay a single horse ridden by two, gallop into the square from the south and veer sharply to the east. They too, it seemed, were headed for the survivors.

How odd. I would have thought that most folks would flee from danger, not hasten towards it. Then again, that's exactly what I'm doing. Blimey, we all must be mad.

Bolts of fire shot from the hands of the rear rider, immolating all those that they struck. Thankfully, the Baron noted, they only seemed to target the bewitched woodland creatures he also fought against.

An enemy of my enemy and all that, but a pyromancer? This is easily the most peculiar day of my life.

Taking care to not endanger any of his allies, or any of the survivors for that matter, the Baron chose an isolated black bear, took aim with Peacemaker, and squeezed the trigger.

Bang!

A heavy retort was followed by the weighty impact of flying lead slamming into muscle and bone. It was a hit, but not a fatal one. The bear still stood.

Readjusting his aim after the shot's recoil had thrown it off, the Baron squeezed Peacemaker's trigger for a second time.

Bang!

This shot was as accurate as the first, but differed in its results. Almost immediately after the bullet smashed into the bear, the creature let out a low mournful groan and collapsed.

Huzzah! It seems to me that I'm getting the hang of this 'gun stuff.'

Thoron and Neesa quickly reached the creature's assaulting the survivors and engaged with them in melee. Soon after that, the riders joined them, dismounting in a flurry of motion. The lead rider, a woman, rolled from her saddle, dancing lightly over the cobbles as she moved, dagger blades glimmering in her hands. Her passenger, a man, landed with a heavy skid, both his hair and eyes aflame, whilst bursts of fire sprouted from his hands. With the aid of these newcomers, they made short work of the remaining wildlife.

Panting heavily, Neesa withdrew her blade from the flank of a freshly killed wolf. Wary of danger, the Baron spun around, looking across the square for any sign of more foes, Peacemaker at the ready. He saw nothing. For now, they were safe. He took no comfort in this realisation.

Overwhelmed by those that assailed them, the small group of survivors had dwindled. Even with the aid of the Baron, his friends, and the mysterious riders, only two remained. A human man and an elven woman. The man, noted the Baron, stood tall and broad, jet-black hair contrasting markedly against his pale skin. The woman was distinctly different, aside from being an elf, she was tall, albeit in a slender fashion, and her brow was framed by halo of golden locks.

He sure is a powerful looking chap, I'd hate to cross him. But oh my, what a vision of beauty that elf is.

'Thank you all for the assistance, if only you had arrived sooner. More may have yet lived.'

The man sighed a heavy sigh and bowed his head in an act of remembrance and respect for those that lay around him.

Overcame by his usual curiosity, the Baron looked to the fallen. Immediately he was taken aback by their apparel, specifically the insignia embroidered upon their chests.

Oh gods, I recognise that mark. Estmirian Crowns Guard. What in blazes are they doing here? Oh, I see… that means… Oh my…

'I wish we had the time for proper introductions, but for now this will have to suffice. I am King John of Estmire and each of you are most welcome. Now, I fear that this was just a prelude to the trials that shall quickly follow.'

As I live and breathe, the King of Estmire. Gods.

The man paused and looked around the periphery of the square. Whatever it was that the King saw, or perhaps sensed, the Baron could not discern, but the worry that lined the Monarch's face was clearly evident. Afflicted by the contagion that is fear, the Baron felt a knot in his stomach tighten.

Oh gods, what now I wonder? How in blazes could this night get any worse?

'Gods, where are my manners this is…'

Before the King could say another word, or complete his introductory gesture towards her, the elven woman beside the King exclaimed loudly.

'By the gods.'

The tone in the elf's voice cut through the survivors' jubilation and collectively they turned to face her. Obviously twisted by dread, the elf's eyes were open to their full extent and her visage was utterly bereft of colour. The corner of her mouth spasmed uncontrollably as a stress-born tick manifested itself.

Oblivious to those around her, the elf sank to the ground while staring out across the square. Speaking to no one but herself, she stammered a barely audible whisper.

'He's here.'

Chapter 41

Neesa

A palpable chill washed over the courtyard and, despite her natural affinity for the cold, Neesa shuddered in discomfort. The world seemed to somehow shrink as she noticed for the first time that the unbearable sounds of death echoing around her were no longer present. The night had grown completely silent. She knew not if this boded for good or ill, but deep down she suspected that it was not the former.

Eying the prostrate elf with a sideways glance, Neesa felt the sense of uneasiness in her chest rise as the elf's fear bit into her soul. With more than a hint of trepidation, she tracked the elf's gaze and turned to face what she was staring at.

From the far end of the square, Neesa watched with a rabid curiosity as a low fog rolled in from the north. At her core she knew that such a phenomenon was unnatural, that it could only be the harbinger of more ill fortune, but all the same she stood as a motionless witness to the unfolding horrors before her.

An eldritch energy, the likes of which Neesa had never seen before, crackled from within the fog. A figure glided above the crackling mist, floating above the unnatural lightning beneath him. Strands of his tattered robe meandered lazily in the air around him. From this distance Neesa was unable to make out all of the figure's defining features, but she could clearly see, from the tears in his robe, pallid and sickly skin clinging tautly over his emancipated frame. Sharp, pointed ears swept backwards fitting snugly against his bald head.

He's clearly an elf, but of which subspecies I cannot say. Whichever it is, he does not look friendly.

Beside the elf strode another figure. Unlike the first, this man was tall and of a powerful build. Clad from the neck down in thick, black armour, he waded through the mist, completely unphased by the arcing maelstrom of power dancing by his feet.

The sounds of armour scraping over hard-pressed earth broke the unnatural silence. Not three feet away from the floating elf's feet a wounded guardsman was trying desperately to drag himself out of harm's way. Without slowing, or even looking in his direction, the elf held out his hand towards the guardsman. A purple glow flared in his palm and several tiny drops of white light beaded along the guard's back.

A guttural scream born from the combination of abject terror and the worst pain imaginable, echoed from the guard's mouth as he spasmed uncontrollably. The drops of light coalesced into one large ball and rose slowly into the air, a single miniscule tendril of light keeping it affixed to the guardsman. Driven by the will of the floating elf, it tugged repeatedly against its tether, seeking to free itself from its bondage. Each time it did so, the guard's screams reached new heights of intensity.

Fixated upon the macabre scene before her, Neesa only heard the King growl in anger at the injustice of a man's lifeforce being toyed with so casually. But in her heart, she knew that his face must have mirrored the rage that was building within her.

I'll kill him.

Neesa saw the moment the guard gave up. Surrendering his hold on life, he collapsed limply onto the ground beneath him, trading desperate shrieks for pitiful whimpers. Bored with his plaything, the floating man tugged the ball of white light free from its tether with a single strong pull. Soul brutally stolen away, the ill-fated man fell still and silent as he succumbed to a fate worse than death.

Gripping the hilt of her sword and grinding her teeth in frustration, the seeds of fury deep within her sprouted to fruition. Throwing caution to the wind, Neesa took a step towards the advancing duo and drew her blade. Snarling, and visibly enraged, she took a second step.

Enough! I will end you!

Before she could take a third step, a hand grabbed her shoulder. Neesa whipped around towards this unwelcome interference, madly hissing spittle at whomever it was that dared to touch her. Her ire was quickly quelled as she was met by Jeeves's caring gaze. The red mist clouding her vision was somewhat parted and coherent thoughts crept slowly into her mind, but still an ember of her anger smouldered within her.

Jeeves must have seen it in her eyes. He squeezed her arm gently and shook his head.

'I know, but not yet my dear. We'll do it together.'

The final vestiges of her rage dissipated, replaced by embarrassment.

Gods be damned! Why do I always let my emotions control me so easily?

Neesa nodded towards Jeeves and the elderly butler returned her appreciative smile with one of his own.

'Thank you, Jeeves…'

The words that Neesa was about to utter died in her throat as distraction murdered all possibility of continued conversation. From behind her the elf gasped a pained exclamation.

'No. Oh Ronar, no.'

Neesa noticed the wracking sorrow written clearly across the elf's face, noticed the tears mar her unwavering stare, noticed the faint glimmer of recognition in her eyes. Knowing not what had affected the elf so profoundly, Neesa turned to look where the elf looked. There, still walking implacably towards them, was the tall armoured man.

Just as the wild things that assaulted the town, twin obsidian flames flickered madly upon his face. Similarly, his exposed flesh bore the wounds of one who had met a violent end. Most notably in this instance, a gaping hole, flanked by slivers of flapping skin where his larynx was once housed.

That must be Ronar. I wonder who he was to her?

The elf shouted the man's name.

'Ronar!'

In that single word, a wealth of emotions and desires were conveyed. Keenly, Neesa felt the elf's grief and began to understand her loss. Neesa understood that the elf loved, truly loved, the man that was once Ronar and that she was pleading for him to return to her. But she also detected the dejected realisation that such love was irreplaceably gone. Neesa was so moved, a tingling shiver spread its way uncontrollably across her body and tears welled in her eyes.

Every trace of humanity gone, Ronar ignored the elf's cry. There was no reaction at all, save for another aggressive step forward.

A pain, the likes of which she had never experienced before, stabbed into Neesa's skull. She winced as words, impossibly loud, boomed in her head. They were all she could hear and, no matter how she tried, she was unable to see past their unbearable universality. In that moment, only these words existed.

'*You lost him, Selene. You forfeited your claim upon him. He's mine. For now. For always.*'

The elf, who Neesa now knew to be Selene, had her hands pressed to her ears. In either a futile attempt to lessen the pain or block out the floating elf's words, Neesa knew not. Selene cried out once more, loud enough to breach the agony induced cacophony raging in Neesa's head.

'Lies! I will reclaim him!'

It lacked none of the emotion, nor desperation, of her previous plea, but Neesa could tell that Selene was failing. She could hear it in the cadence of the elf's voice. All bravado was gone, replaced by an insubstantial veneer, which thinly obscured Selene's own subconscious doubt.

'*Why did you flee Selene? You knew that I would come for you. You knew that I would find you. You knew what that would mean.*'

Neesa felt the pressure against the inside of her skull mount. Black spots marred her vision as her blood flow slowed and unconsciousness threatened. From the corner of her fading vision, she saw Selene's eyes roll into back of her head as she keeled over. As if possessed by a hell born spirit, her prone body spasmed uncontrollably while blood seeped from every orifice.

Feeling a wet warmth upon her cheek, Neesa wiped the side of her face. Looking to her palm she was greeted by a crimson streak of her own blood. Looking towards Selene once more, Neesa was met by a confronting realisation, if she did nothing that would soon be her.

No. I refuse to be helpless. I will not succumb.

'*Because of you more will now die. Because of you more will join me. Because of you I will become even more powerful. Ha, ha, ha.*'

Neesa looked to her centre. To that place in her chest where the darkness lived. Choosing to face what she normally kept buried, she brought all of her worst memories to the forefront of her mind. All of her loss, all of her heartache, all of her trauma. All of the injustices she had been forced to endure. She remembered it all. She became enraged.

Blinking rapidly, fuelled by her fury, Neesa pushed aside the agony. Compared to the hurt she had been forced to endure, that she had carried for the entirety of her life, this was nothing, a mere trifle. Though the words of the floating elf still seared the inside of her mind, she held them in contempt. She held him in contempt. Infuriated beyond all reason, she screamed a scream of hells born fury.

'*Your new friends cannot save you Selene. They will join me just as Ronar did. Why did you flee Selene? Why do you resist?*'

Through the scarlet lens that tinted her vision, Neesa barely noticed the purple light that flashed around the floating elf. It illuminated the square in a surreal violet hue, but all she saw was red.

Around her, seemingly sentient tendrils of energy, that emanated from the heels of the floating elf, snaked their way around the courtyard. As an obvious target for her ire, Neesa lashed out at one as it passed her by, but her blow could find no purchase and the immaterial entity continued unscathed.

Noticing, but far from understanding, Neesa observed the eldritch tentacle wrap itself around the torso of a nearby corpse. Momentarily, rationality peeked its way through the haze of madness that consumed her and she looked more discerningly around the courtyard. For whatever reason, it seemed that these tendrils sought out the dead and whether it be humanoid or forest creature, they found what they sought.

'*Now you all die!*'

A wave of physic energy exploded from the chest of the floating elf. The shockwave, a lavender tinted wall of force, sped unbelievably fast across the square. Neesa braced, and with a snarl, readied herself to meet this new challenge. Air rushed across her chest as the wave broke upon her. It pushed into her, threatening to knock her over, but she resisted and remained standing. Not so for those around her.

Throughout the square, those eldritch tentacles Neesa had marked before sunk their tips into the lifeless bodies they surrounded. In unison the tendrils pulsed once, a singular flash of violet. For a second there was nothing, but then each of the tendrils vanished in a shower of dust. The corpses they had just seconds ago held, twitched manically and then stood, black flames burning where their eyes once were.

A rational person would have in that moment felt afraid, even if only just a little. Neesa, once again lost to the throes of rage, felt nothing of the sort. In fact, she was pleased. A fight, irrespective of the foe, was exactly what she needed. Grinning manically, she willed it to begin.

Come on! Fight me! I'll kill you all!

She barely noticed those around her pick themselves up off of the ground. She barely noticed the King rush to Selene's side. She barely heard the King shout to everyone.

'I'll look after her while I coax her from this stupor, but until then I'm afraid you're all on your own. I'll try to be quick.'

Neesa was solely focussed upon the impending combat and the inevitable death of those that opposed her.

Chapter 42

The Heroes of Thered's Field

Having spent the entirety of her life living from moment to moment, Eris wasted no time on idle thought or irrelevant ruminations. She reacted as she always did when faced with open hostility, with haste and with purpose. Giving no mind to the others around her, she broke free from the stupor of inaction and charged towards the nearest risen Crown's Guard.

While she ran, she slid her blink dagger from its sheath and flicked it towards her quarry. With a twist and a twirl, the blade vanished as it popped out of existence. Mere moments later the dagger reappeared, a scant few inches from the guardsman's chest. Before any notion of blocking, or even dodging, the projectile could enter his mind, it drove its way through his chainmail shirt, penetrating deep into his heart.

The lightless flames of the Crown's Guard blinked out. Devoid of life once more the corpse toppled backwards. As it fell Eris snapped her fingers and her dagger reappeared in her hand, ready to be thrown once more.

Already beyond the scope of her attention, the guardsman thudded heavily into the dirt. Eris paid it no heed; she was already on the hunt for another adversary to vanquish.

*   *   *

Not wishing to be at the forefront of the ensuing melee, the Baron eased himself backwards. He nearly fell as his foot bumped into the town hall's stairs, but fortunately he caught his balance just in time.

Careful old man, it wouldn't do to take yourself out the fight. You'd never hear the end of it from Jeeves.

With a haste tempered by caution, the Baron pulled himself up the stairs. Though he had not intended it to be so, his decision to fall back afforded him an improved view of the skirmish. Making the best of this advantage, he surveyed the battlefield.

It was pure chaos made manifest. People moved in seemingly random patterns as they jostled for advantageous positions and avoided the attacks of their adversaries. The situation was rendered even more complex as risen woodland creatures danced around the living, all the while nipping at their proverbial, and literal, heels.

Good gods, if this is any measure of one, I'd hate to be in a real battle. I daresay I'd barely know which way was up.

For the briefest of moments, the Baron's eyes locked onto Jeeves's darting form just as he ducked under a wild swing from one of the risen Crown's Guard. In retort, the elderly butler slashed one of his silver discs along the risen's throat, severing it cleanly. Immediately, the risen guard fell, no longer a threat to the living.

That a boy Jeeves.

Inspired by Jeeves's success, and thinking it well past time that he made his mark on the fracas, the Baron drew Peacemaker from its holster. Levelling it towards those in front of him, he cocked its hammer and waited for a clear opening to take his shot.

It didn't take long for a brown bear to present itself as the most obvious target. As it lumbered towards Neesa, oblivious to everything else, those around it parted long enough for the Baron to seize the moment. Looking down the barrel of his gun, the Baron took a deep breath, held it in his lungs and slowly squeezed Peacemaker's trigger.

Bang!

Peacemaker kicked in his hand as the explosion rang in his ears. His held breath rushed from his chest and he looked towards the brown bear, hoping that his shot had incapacitated, or at the very least hurt, the risen monstrosity. Alas, he saw nothing of the sort. As a matter of fact, the bear appeared to be entirely unscathed. He had missed.

Confound it all.

* * *

All around Thoron purple energy flowed into the dead. His mind instantly flashed back to the deep road and the slaughter of his legion. Just as his comrades had then, the fallen by his feet now shrugged off death and returned to a pale reflection of the life they once enjoyed.

'*Well fuck me sideways with a spiky, soap covered fruit, that shit sure aint natural. There's only one thing for it mate. Kill the fuckers!*'

Momentarily stunned, he stood frozen, not through fear, but in thought. The neurons in his brain fired in rapid succession as he regarded his current predicament and the appropriate course of action he should take.

At his core he knew that a sorcerer, in this instance the floating elf, had to be behind the attack on Thered's Field, just as the orcish sorcerer was behind the destruction of his legion. He knew that simply slaying the magically risen would be futile as the sorcerer would simply raise them again. And though he knew little of the laws of magic, he could see no logical way for a risen magical entity to persist after its sorcerous progenitor was rendered deceased.

If we don't kill 'at sorcerer then we're all deid.

Lost in his own thoughts and memories, the first Thoron saw of the risen Crown's Guard rushing towards him was a blur of motion in the corner of his eye. Reacting instinctually, he turned to face the oncoming threat, still not fully able to process exactly what was going on. He was met by steel humming viciously towards his face. It was all he could do to curse inwardly.

Oh shite.

Unbidden, his arm seemed to move on its own accord. It darted to intercept the sword swinging towards his head. Making it just in time, the blade clanged harmlessly off of his raised shield.

'*Best be on your toes chum. I won't be able to save you every time.*'

'*Holy shitballs mate! Snap out of it and get your head in the game!*'

Inwardly thanking the gods for his good fortune, Thoron brought himself back into the moment. His far-away look was replaced by a scowl of steely determination. His panicked heartbeat slowed as he abandoned surprise for acceptance. Ready to do what he had always done, what he did best, what he lived for, he waited for his adversary to make the next move. He didn't have to wait for long.

Casually, he slapped aside the Crown's Guard's second swing with the face of his short sword. Stepping inside the risen man's stroke, he thrust the rim of his shield as hard as he could into the leg of his quarry. The man's bone snapped with a satisfyingly sickening crunch and he fell soundlessly to his knee as his leg gave out beneath him. Not waiting for the man to recover, Thoron twisted his arm and swung his sword with all his might.

Barely meeting any resistance, his blade carved through the neck of the guard, severing the man's head from his body.

'Damn did that feel good! Now, who's next?'

*   *   *

Neesa felt the rage explode within her. Her pulse surged as her heart worked overtime to pump the oxygenated blood her body so desperately craved through her veins and arteries. All of the aches and pains she had acquired over the course of the evening dissipated into nothingness. Invigorated by the thrill of battle, she felt alive, nay she felt fantastic.

A risen guardsman stood before her, but he was nothing to her. With a purposeful glee, Neesa strode towards the magically animated creature. Vainly, he thrust his sword at Neesa's chest. Without pause, she side-stepped his lunge, shunting his arm away with her own forearm. Without letting the guard recover, Neesa thrust her other arm towards the man's neck. Unable to react in time, the guardsman could do nothing in response.

Neesa's fingers wrapped around the man's throat, her talons sinking deep into his still-warm flesh as she squeezed. Unnaturally black tinged blood trickled over Neesa's fingers as the man flailed desperately against her. Neesa ignored the guard's feeble blows and squeezed even harder. Neesa felt a simultaneous tingle of satisfaction and a stab of regret as the risen man's neck snapped. Seeing no point in continuing to flog the proverbial dead horse, she dropped the once more lifeless body.

Neesa's thoughts instantly turned to finding the next kill, but before she could begin her search an angry roar from behind her drew her attention. Slowly, she turned to face the source of the bellow. It was a brown bear. An angry brown bear.

Ignoring everything else around it, the bear was lumbering in her direction, black flame-eyes clearly fixated upon her. Immune to fear, Neesa cowered not before her latest challenge. In fact, she embraced it. With a wicked grin curling her lips upwards and an inspired twinkle in her eyes, she growled a low, animalistic growl, drew her sword from its sheath and charged towards her foe.

*   *   *

Following the Baron's lead, Máher ignored the melee around him and fell back towards the town hall, climbing the stairs at its entrance. Reaching out to the familiar well of power within him, he felt the magic warm his skin. Both his hair and his eyes burst into flame as he drew the magical energy into the palm of his hand. Twirling the eldritch power between his fingers he waited.

I don't want to metaphorically blow my load too soon, best to save it for the right target. It would be foolish to waste it on the chaff.

Unexpectantly, Máher felt a force push upon his temples and his mind begin to itch. It was similar to the feeling he experienced when he communicated with Beher, but more painful. Much more painful. The pressure increased and a trifling annoyance transformed into a sharp stabbing pain. Máher tried to fight it, to push the interloper from his mind, but his adversary was just too strong. Wincing, his head rang with words laced with contempt.

'*Ha, ha, ha. Your attempts at resistance are futile. Surrender to me. Succumb to death and be reborn anew.*'

The floating figure pointed his hand towards the King and his allies. Taking this as his que for action, the armoured man increased his pace, breaking into a casual jog. Máher's senses narrowed as they focussed entirely upon this man. The sounds of the battle before him faded into the distance, replaced by the clanking of the man's armour. His vision receded and all he saw was the man, his flickering eyes and torn asunder throat. Instinctually, Máher knew that this man was the greatest threat upon the battlefield, save for the elven sorcerer himself.

Half-way along his journey, the man bent down, scraping his hand through the cobbles and into the dirt below. Wherever his fingers passed, ripples reverberated across the ground.

Máher pointed towards the armoured man and shot a small bead of energy at his chest. It was more of an experiment than a real attack, but he hoped it would do some damage all the same.

Without breaking his stride, the man withdrew his fingers from the ground's surface, the stone-crusted hilt of a great sword held firmly within his hand. As though it was weightless, the man spun the obsidian blade and with ease, deflected Máher's shot. Máher's heart sunk as he realised just how difficult this threat was going to be to overcome.

Máher's attention snapped away from the armour-clad man as purple light flared from across the square. Cursing inwardly as several small balls of purple energy shot into the air, Máher lamented at just how easily his attention had been distracted from the wider array of events around him.

Dammit. I could have countered that spell, or at the very least shielded my compatriots from harm.

Seemingly controlled by a sentient mind, their trajectory changed as they reached their zenith. Arching downwards they streaked towards the town hall. Máher tracked their path with his eyes and saw their intended target. Knowing that he had too little time to offer any arcane protection he did what he could. Shouting at the top of his lungs, and pointing towards the oncoming missiles, he attempted to warn his fellows of the oncoming danger.

'Look out!'

Too late, Jeeves saw the approaching peril. The old man tried to jump out of the way, but the missiles would not be denied. In quick succession, each of the orbs slammed into the butler. Though each was not particularly powerful on their own, their culminative effect blew Jeeves off of his feet. No longer in control of his movements, he slid wildly across the stone. When he came to a stop he lay still, several tendrils of smoke rising lazily from his charred suit.

'*Shit. Beher, that sorcerer is going to be a problem. Would you mind lending us a hand perhaps?*'

'Beher could, but Beher thinks staying alive is better than not. Maybe if it gets really bad Beher could help. Maybe.'

'Thanks for nothing.'

Máher focused on the energy still roiling in his hands. Utilising nothing more than his will, he compelled the magic to form three small balls of fire. The balls rose from his palm, flying in-between his fingers at an ever-increasing pace. Holding a mental image of the enemy sorcerer in the forefront of his mind, Máher threw the balls into the air.

Small trails of red light trailed behind the projectiles as they zoomed across the square, making a beeline for the enemy sorcerer. Máher saw the tell-tale sheen of a magical screen as the elf raised a shield in defence, but it did nothing to stop Máher's spell. Each of the fiery balls smashed into the sorcerer's chest. However, unlike Jeeves, he did not fall.

An overwhelming pain, identical to the one that had afflicted him mere minutes before, surged through his mind. Groaning in agony, he clutched his head as his consciousness rang with the enraged protestations of the floating sorcerer.

'Argh! Such impertinence! I will end you all!'

*   *   *

Eris's head pounded uncomfortably as it rang with the echoing monologue of the distant floating man. Ignoring it the best she could, she sprinted behind a Crown's Guard currently engaged with the dwarf. He neither saw nor heard her approach.

With a brutal efficiency, Eris wrapped her arm around the guard's head. He struggled in a futile attempt to escape, but she held him fast. Knowing the limits of her own strength, and that she would not be able to hold the guard for long, she plunged her dagger into the hapless man's chest. The guard grunted in retort, but continued to wriggle violently as he tried to free himself. Eris was not going to have that. Withdrawing her blade, she thrust it into the guard for a second time, then a third and finally a fourth. Eris felt the man slacken. Withdrawing her dagger for the final time, she let the guard's body collapse limply onto the ground.

'I wuid hev bin fine lassie, but I appreciate it none the less.'

As Eris felt that a verbal reply was unnecessary, she simply gave the dwarf a humble nod of acceptance. The dwarf grunted and shuffled off begrudgingly towards one of the risen black bears, his shield held protectively in front of him.

Eris was about to follow suit, deciding that fighting together would be more efficient than fighting alone, but was stopped by a blur of motion in her periphery. Acting by pure instinct, Eris ducked. Above her, she heard the hum of a blade slash the air and knew that she had just barely avoided decapitation. Not letting herself freeze in the moment, she tumbled deliberately to the ground, rolling clear of the anticipated follow-up swing.

Eris rose from her roll, the blink dagger already in her hand ready to be thrown, and spun around. With the briefest of glances, she sighted her target, another one of the risen Crown's Guard, and let her weapon fly.

Eris's arm shot out in front of her and the blink dagger vanished in a twirl of movement. Almost instantly, it reappeared, embedded in the abdomen of the Crown's Guard. Ignoring the blow, the guard readied his sword for another attack while advancing implacably towards Eris.

Lamenting the far from lethal wound she had inflicted upon her foe, Eris cursed and summoned the dagger back to her hand. Crouching, to lower her centre of gravity, she steeled herself for the oncoming duel.

*   *   *

The Baron's heart leapt into his throat as he saw Jeeves get blasted by the sorcerer's magical missiles. Seeing his oldest friend lay immobile on the ground, tore at the Baron's insides. Should he help him or should he continue the fight? Inaction gripped the Baron as he stood indecisively, weighing the options in his head.

Before he could commit to any course of action, Jeeves tentatively eased himself to his feet. Relief flooded through the Baron's chest. As he stood, the butler stumbled, restoking the fire of concern at the Baron's centre, but Jeeves quickly righted himself and returned to the fight with gusto.

That's the spirit old boy. Now back to the task at hand.

The Baron breathed deeply through his nose, filling his lungs to capacity. Exhaling slowly through his mouth he calmed himself. Levelling his gun towards the risen brown bear once more, the Baron squeezed Peacemaker's trigger.

Bang!

Now used to the percussive force and booming sound of his weapon, neither registered as the Baron focused intently upon his target. With a grim satisfaction he smiled as he saw his bullet strike home, tearing a sizeable chunk of flesh from the bear's shoulder.

Shame it's not a fatal wound, but at least it's a hit.

*   *   *

From somewhere behind her, Neesa heard the familiar sound of the Baron's gun as he fired a shot. The bullet whizzed over her head with a sharp crack. Instinctually, she flinched as felt the projectile's shockwave washed over her.

Damn you to the hells Baron, take a care would you.

Despite her discomfort, Neesa grinned in wicked satisfaction as the bear's shoulder exploded in a cloud of blood and viscera.

That's more like it.

Seemingly unphased by the wound, the beast reared up onto its hind legs. Arching its muzzle towards the sky, it bellowed a deep and mournful cry.

Neesa felt the soundwaves reverberate over the entirety of her body. Gritting her teeth, she ignored the troubling sensation and adjusted her grip on her sword. Ceding the initiative to the creature, she bent her knees, willing all of her strength into her legs. She knew that the bear would charge her, it was an inevitability. She would be ready for it.

Come and get it you bastard.

Perhaps seeking to intimidate her, the bear fixed its shadowy stare unerringly upon Neesa. A twinge of suspicion gnawed at the corner of her mind as she sensed the hint of an alien intelligence hiding amongst the flames. Holding the creature's gaze, she searched deeper, seeking an explanation for this peculiar feeling, but alas, whatever she had detected was gone.

The creature was the first to break the stare, shaking its head as if clearing its mind of an unpalatable thought. Crashing back to all fours with a heavy thud it raked its claws experimentally across the cobbles. Seemingly satisfied with whatever it was that it sought to ascertain, the bear grunted once and then lunged towards Neesa.

Though she was expecting it, Neesa was caught off guard by just how fast the creature was. Not normally one to cede ground to a foe, in this instance she had to. Backpedalling to give herself space to correctly time her swing, she waited as long as she dared to before leaping out of the bear's path.

As it passed her, she could smell the fresh scent of woodland dirt and decomposing foliage intertwined with its fur, juxtaposed starkly beside its rotten breath. It was a small thing to notice, and considering everything that was occurring around her, an almost irrelevant one, but for Neesa it was all that occupied her mind. In that moment there was nothing else.

It's strange. I'm somewhat drawn to, and yet simultaneously reviled by this creature's odour.

Drawn from her ruminations by the tickle of fur upon her cheek, Neesa reached into the well of rage that permanently simmered at her core. Using it to bolster her strength, she shouted in anger and swung her blade across the bear's flank. From the feel of it, Neesa could tell that her blow didn't bite as deeply as she would have hoped, but knew that her quarry would still be sporting an impressive gash.

Quicker than she would have believed possible, the bear circled back towards her. Utterly caught off guard, Neesa cried out in surprise as the bear slashed at her torso. At first, she felt nothing, believing that the creature had misjudged its attack. But then she felt it. The pain. The agony.

She wanted to scream, she needed to scream, but her mouth could no longer make any sound. It was as if her body was no longer her own. She willed her legs to move, she willed herself to raise her blade in defence, but it was to no avail. Her body ignored each of her orders.

Helplessly, Neesa collapsed to her knees. For a moment she balanced upon her sword, desperately trying to remain vertical, but it was no use. Slipping from her grasp, her sword clattered uselessly on the cobblestone beside her. Unsupported, she keeled over beside it.

As Neesa lay on the ground, she knew that she was dying. She could feel her own blood pooling around her, more than her body could stand to lose. Her vision started to lose its focus, blurring, and narrowing. She knew that she was about to pass out and that there was nothing she could do about it.

So, this is how I die. I'm on my way mother.

Chapter 43

The Heroes of Thered's Field

Rolling out of the path of a charging black bear, Thoron thudded heavily into the ground. Briefly, he considered launching an attack at the bear's side, but quickly discarded the notion as inviable. His footing was wrong, to attack now would only serve to off-balance him and leave him vulnerable to counterattack. Instead, he opted for a more defensive posture by correcting his footing and raising his shield.

The black bear roared at Thoron and pummelled his shield with one of its paws. Thoron grunted under the force of the blow and was forced back a step, but held firm in his defence. Twice more the bear slapped his shield, trying as hard as I could to breach Thoron's bulwark.

Holy shite, 'is bugger hits hard.

'Not to worry old bean. I've had far worse than this. I shall not let us down.'

For whatever the reason, the bear abandoned its assault upon Thoron. With a mild confusion, he peeked over the rim of shield. His perplexion intensified as he watched the bear lumber away towards one of its kin, who was currently attacking the elderly butler.

I cannae say I dae no' appreciate the reprieve, but 'at wis mair than a tad strange. How wuid it jus' leave combat lek 'at?

'Too right mate, something fishy is going on here. Ah, strewth. That. Is. Not. Good.'

Worried by the obvious concern in Barry's voice, Thoron looked over the battlefield, trying to find the source of his concern.

'Whit is it?'

'It's that blue sheila, Neesa, wasn't it? She's in a bad way mate, best get over there and lend her a hand. Quickly mate, that way!'

Even though Barry didn't specify exactly which way, that way was, and, as he was a sword, was unable to physically point the way, Thoron knew instinctually which way the sword was referring to. Turing his head Thoron saw the blue Infernati, Neesa, lying motionless on the ground as a brown bear circled her helpless form.

Pointing his sword towards where Neesa lay, Thoron shouted out to Jeeves.

'Oi! Jeeves!'

The butler looked to where Thoron was pointing and nodded back to him in understanding.

A blur in his peripheral vision drew his attention back to his immediate surroundings. Instinctively raising his shield arm to defend his previously exposed torso, Thoron grunted as another blow rattled his bones.

'Hey, firemancer! Get these fuckers aff o' ma back will yer!'

*   *   *

At least he didn't call me a pointy headed bastard. That's happened before.

Máher groaned at being told what to do by the dwarf, but he saw the wisdom in his request. Without further ado, Máher drew upon the energy within him and coaxed some of it into his palms. He held the twirling flames in his hands and formed a picture of his intent for the fire in his mind, but paused before letting the energy go.

Hm, I'm going to need a bit more than usual, I think.

Máher's hair grew even brighter. Normally a bright orange, his hair flared to the purest of whites, as he channelled even more energy. He knew that channelling so much power so quickly was dangerous, but he decided that taking the risk was a necessity. Time was not a resource they had an abundance of. Besides, he knew his limits.

Máher released the energy he held. Three rays of scorching fire burst into the air. Arching towards their destination, the two black bears, they crackled as they flew, dropping a cascade of tiny glowing embers beneath them.

With a deep satisfaction, Máher grinned as the two risen bears were engulfed in flames. However, jubilation was quickly replaced by unease as he felt his legs tremble. Black spots clouded the periphery of his vision and he grew nauseous. Swallowing the little saliva in his mouth to supress his urge to vomit, he wobbled precariously in place, barely managing to remain standing.

Oh gods, I did that a bit too quickly.

*   *   *

The putrid stench of burning flesh and fur filled Thoron's nostrils. It was undoubtedly unpleasant, yet entirely welcome. Raising a skyward pointed thumb above his head, he yelled back towards the town hall.

'Nice wan, ye pointy headed marvel!'

Free from immediate danger, Thoron sprinted towards Neesa's unmoving body, hoping desperately that she could still be saved.

Hang in thir, lassie. Am oan ma way.

All the while, he stole quick glances around the courtyard. More risen, who's number included a large number of undead villagers, were beginning to enter the square from its periphery. Thoron's mind once more turned back to the recent calamity in the under roads, he knew that they would soon be overwhelmed. He knew what he had to do.

Mustering his voice, he turned back to his allies and yelled to whomever would listen as loud as he could.

'Kill 'at fucking sorcerer! He dies or we dae!'

Knowing not if he was heard, or if any would heed his warning, Thoron raced towards the downed infernati and the brown bear that circled her. Sensing that it would be close, he shouted at the beast, attempting to draw it away from Neesa. As its attention was firmly locked onto its hapless prey before it, the creature paid Thoron no heed.

Thoron redoubled his efforts. His legs burned, his heart pounded in his ears and his lungs ached under the strain he put them in. Yet, still harder he pushed.

Ach, a'll no' let it get ye lassie, jus' a wee bit further tae go.

For Thoron, time seemed to slow as the bear raised one of its claws into the air, poised to finish Neesa off. He saw the paw fall, ever so slowly descending towards the blue infernati. Judging himself close enough, Thoron pushed off of the ground as hard as he could and leapt into the air. Just as the bear's claw was about to tear into Neesa, Thoron landed on top of the infernati, his shield interposed between himself and the monster.

Razor sharp claws skittered harmlessly against the face of his shield, but yet enough force remained in the blow to force a pained grimace from Thoron's face.

Bidding a silent prayer of thanks to Rivalitas, he peeked out from behind the rim of his shield. The bear had already raised its claw once more to strike. Offering a second silent plea to his patron, Thoron felt Barry's hilt grow warm as his blade shimmered with a faint iridescent glow.

'Steady on mate, that shit tickles. Not gunna lie though, I kinda like it.'

For a second time, Thoron saw the bear's paw descend, but in that instant, he was devoid of any emotion other than an inexplicable calm. Acting instinctively, and from a deep serenity, he slapped away the monster's claw with his shield. Without allowing the bear to recover, Thoron followed immediately after with a downwards slash with his sword.

The bear's forehead offered no resistance as Thoron's steel carved it in twain. Though it had been entirely bisected by the cut, the monster's face remained in place. Instantly, the black flames in the creature's eye sockets blinked from existence and the once-more lifeless corpse slumped gracelessly to the ground.

Sensing a presence behind him, Thoron turned expecting another foe, but it was only Jeeves. Between gasping breaths, he pointed towards the elven necromancer across the square.

'I can deal wi' 'at bastard. 'Gasp.' Keep the lass safe old man. 'Gasp.' I hev a job tae dae. 'Gasp.'

His expression grim, the elderly butler bowed his head towards Thoron in respect.

'Understood. Gods speed.'

*   *   *

Máher blinked the distortion from his vision and shook the weariness from his mind. Looking across the courtyard, he surveyed the battlefield. More and more of the undead were streaming into the square. He knew that if their numbers could not be stemmed, then victory would slip eternally from their reach.

'Kill 'at fucking sorcerer! He dies or we dae!'

The Dwarf's words rang clearly at the centre of Máher's consciousness. He knew what had to be done. Narrowing his focus, he concentrated his thoughts and projected them towards his brother.

'Beher! This situation is truly dire. We. Need. You. Now. We must kill that sorcerer. I'll send Eris to assist, and I'll do what I can from here, but I need you to lead the charge.'

Almost immediately, Máher's mind echoed with Beher's distinctively unenthusiastic response.

'Fine. But the she-elf better help. Beher can't be expected to do everything by himself.'

'Thank you.'

A rising glow of deep purple energy drew Máher's attention back to the battlefield. Eldritch tendrils roiled violently around the elven sorcerer's arms, constantly building in both size and intensity. It was an entrancingly beautiful display of power, which Máher couldn't help but to feel conflicted about. He was impressed by it, and respectively acknowledged the difficulty of the feat, but was simultaneously concerned, as he knew that such energy would be capable of killing any of his compatriots. Or, for that matter, himself.

Momentarily pushing his worry to one side, Máher sought out Eris's mind and projected his thoughts into hers.

'Leave the lesser risen be and focus your efforts on the necromancer. You'll have to get in close to do any real harm, but Beher's already on his way to engage him. Eris, that elf needs to die. As soon as possible.'

'As soon as I'm able, I'll take to the air and do as you ask.'

'Thank you.'

Máher winced in pain and clutched the side of his head as the necromancer forced his way into his mind. He tried to hold him back, but despite his efforts, the elf's vitriol filled words reverberated around his consciousness.

'You're pathetic, half-breed. Your magic is useless. Your resistance is pointless. Submit to me. Submit to the shadows. Submit to the inevitability of death!'

Thrusting out his hand, the purple energy that had built to a horrendous tempest, burst forth. Through his blurry eyes, Máher could see that he was the necromancer's intended target. Focussing his will, he conjured a small ball of fire and propelled it towards the oncoming beam of energy. He knew that he would not be able to stop the necromancer's attack, he had not the time nor the energy to do so, but perhaps, he hoped, it could be deflected.

With an aim that must have been blessed by the gods, Máher's bolt of fire careened into the side of the necromancer's beam. His own bolt ricocheted downwards, exploding harmlessly on the courtyard's cobbles. The necromancer's beam, however, was diverted towards the upper floors of the town hall, whereby it impacted, detonating spectacularly.

Máher covered his ears as an explosion, the likes of which he had never heard before, drowned all other sounds from perceptibility. A blinding flash of lavender tinged light, forced him to avert his gaze as the darkness of twilight was expelled from existence. Even though he was at what most would consider to be a safe distance, Máher felt the blast wave of the explosion wash over him, causing his exposed skin to prickle with an odd tingling sensation. Despite everything, as far as Máher was concerned, it was truly an astounding spectacle.

By the gods, so much power with so little preparation. Colour me impressed.

As shards of shattered masonry rained down alongside splintered lumber, Máher looked around. Everyone still stood, looking none the worse for wear, despite the explosion. Sighing in relief, Máher counted his blessings that his desperate gambit had succeeded.

That was too close.

*   *   *

Fixated entirely upon the elven necromancer, Thoron let the rest of the battle melt away into the background. The path to his foe was clear, so without further hesitation he lowered his head and charged.

A small cloud of fog coalesced before Thoron. Wary of magical trickery he slowed his advance. Peering into the mist, he tightened his grip upon his sword. Seeing nothing, he licked his lips, which were inexplicitly dry, and took a single tentative step forward. Nothing. Growing more confident that the fog posed no threat, he took and second step and then in rapid succession a third. Still nothing.

As he was beginning to doubt that the mist posed any threat to him at all, a singular figure apparated from within the haze before him. Over twice his own height, and almost entirely clad in blackened steel plate, the man stood immobile, resting his great sword upon his shoulder.

Ronar.

'Crikey that bloke's bloody huge! Um, you sure you can take him Thor? I don't doubt your skills mate, well maybe I do a little, but it's just that you are kind of on the small side compared to him is all. Plus, my current form is not the best suited for armour penetration. Just saying.'

'Whit dae ye mean, current form?'

'I'm glad that's what you're focussing on mate, really, I am, but it aint the time for an in-depth discussion relating to my more advanced features. I'll tell you later. Assuming you survive that is. Which of course you will. Probably.'

Quicker than what Thoron thought possible, Ronar closed the gap between the two of them, stabbing the tip of his sword at Thoron's face. Reacting on nothing more than instinct, Thoron raised his shield to block the blow, but too late realised the true intention of the attack. It was nothing more than a feint. Before he could correct his mistake, the trajectory of Ronar's sword changed from a thrust to a sweep. Searing pain burst across Thoron's chest as razor-sharp obsidian sliced through gambeson and flesh alike.

Grimacing through the pain, Thoron danced around Ronar, stabbing, and thrusting his sword towards the Goliath, but an opening in Ronar's defences never presented itself. Strike after strike was blocked, parried, or simply skirted harmlessly off of the goliath's armour. Inevitably, Thoron tired from the combination of continual exertion and blood loss, and became sloppy. Despite his training, he made what any experienced swordsman would call a rookie mistake, he overextended himself. Immediately, Ronar capitalised upon Thoron's error.

Stepping within Thoron's reach, the goliath squatted low and thrust the pommel of his sword into Thoron's chest. Despite his planted stance, Thoron's feet left the ground as he was picked up and thrown across the square.

Landing with a heavy thud, and a deep groan, Thoron rolled across the cobbles. Coming to a stop, he desperately tried to stand, but before he could, Ronar thrust his sword at him once more. Just barely, Thoron managed to dodge the blow, but he knew that it was only a matter of time before he would fall victim to the goliath's advances. He could feel his stamina wane and he could tell that his movements were slowing.

Rolling away from Ronar, Thoron lay on his back, breathing hard. Staring up at the night sky, the stars, a blanket of twinkling majesty, stirred within him a sense of personal irrelevancy. For the first time in his life, he truly felt small. Thusly inspired, he pushed all vestiges of arrogance aside and embraced humility.

'Please Rivalitas. I beg o' ye. I require yer aid.'

The air above him shimmered and the winged form of his patron apparated. Motionless, Rivalitas hovered over him with a faint glimmer of love in her eyes. Though Thoron heard Rivalitas speak, her lips never parted, a curl into the faintest of smiles was all they mustered.

'I'm sorry my child. But I cannot.'

'But how?'

Rivalitas's eyes darkened and her subtle smile turned to a contemptuous smirk.

'Because I choose not to. I find your lack of anger wanting. My champion should be a font of avenging rage, driven and fuelled by their righteous purpose. Existing only to smite those deserving of vengeance. Never accepting defeat until embraced by death, and yet you lay there pleading, nay begging for aid. Pitiful.'

Thoron's head rang with his patron's mocking laughter and he felt his heart sink as he fully began to comprehend the hopelessness of his situation. Stunned, he heard Rivalitas continue her monologue, but the words barely registered and for him imparted no meaning nor insight.

'Besides, I have found another. Now, your soul is mine.'

Rivalitas opened her arms wide just as Ronar's sword plunged through the god's incorporeal form and into Thoron's chest. Blood spluttered from Thoron's mouth as the air was forced from his lungs. Instantly, the god's visage disappeared and the entirety of Thoron's attention turned to the obsidian blade imbedded inside him. Strangely, there was no pain.

Wordlessly, the goliath twisted his blade before yanking it from Thoron's torso. A geyser of blood spurted from the wound and Thoron's body spasmed unbidden.

Internally, Thoron was panicking, trying to stand, trying to simply move, but no matter the command his body would not respond. His eyes were wild, strained wide with futile exertion. His mouth, wet from the continual stream of blood flowing from it, opened, and closed rapidly as he muttered incomprehensible pleas for mercy, or at the very least assistance. None were forthcoming.

Thoron never saw Ronar's blade rise for the second time, for his senses were overwhelmed by his own impotence and dread. Thoron never heard Ronar's sword sing as it carved its way through the air towards him, as all he could hear was his own laboured, gargling breaths. Thoron never felt the blow that severed his head from his body, for he was no longer alive to feel.

Chapter 44

The Heroes of Thered's Field

Drawing a single deep breath into her lungs, Eris launched herself towards the Crown's Guard before her. In response, the risen swung its sword at her chest. Catching the blow with her offhand dagger, she deflected the blade harmlessly away from her.

Following up with a strike of her own, Eris thrust her blink dagger through the crowns guard's throat. Black blood gurgled from the risen's mouth as it toppled over, hitting the ground with Eris's dagger still stuck firmly in its neck. Clicking her fingers, willing her blade to return, the dagger vanished in a puff of smoke, reappearing instantly in her waiting hand.

Freed from immediate danger, Eris muttered an elven phrase as she ran towards a particularly clear section of the square. Magic hummed around her heels as the enchantment within her boots activated. She continued to run, but left terra firma behind as her feet found purchase on the empty air.

Climbing above the square, Eris angled her trajectory towards the elven necromancer. Focussing her mind, she willed her conscious thoughts towards Beher.

'Beher. Do you have a plan or is it to be a head on attack?'

Almost immediately, she got a response.

'Beher will do what Beher always does. Bite bad things neck till it's dead. This has always worked for Beher before, why shouldn't it work now?'

Eris could not fault the young dragon's logic. Ripping out the necromancer's throat or breaking his neck should kill him, but Eris doubted it would be as simple as running up to the guy and just doing it.

Okay full attack it is. This cannot end badly. Nope. Nothing can go wrong at all. I can't think of a single thing.

'Understood. Let's get this done.'

Illuminated by the purple light that surrounded him, the necromancer was an easy target to detect in the night-time gloom. Gauging the distance between herself and her quarry, all the while constantly moving, Eris threw her blink dagger. Slicing cleanly through the air, the blade flew true. She knew, as soon as it left her hand, that it was going to hit its mark.

Reacting faster than what should have been possible, the necromancer's eyed narrowed. His neck twisted rapidly towards Eris and he outstretched his hand, directly into the path of the flying dagger.

Somehow, he sensed my attack. He's going to try and block it. Well, not today.

A wall of purple energy flashed into existence, interposing itself between its conjurer and the oncoming weapon. However, before her dagger struck the energy shield, Eris snapped her fingers and the dagger disappeared.

To what realm, or distant place, the dagger went to when it disappeared, Eris knew not. Nor did she care. The only thing that mattered, and this was something she did know, was that wherever it did go, its momentum was maintained. As such, when the dagger reappeared, a scant few seconds later, it had passed the necromancer's shield and immediately thudded heavily into the elf's chest.

If the necromancer felt the blow, he gave no indication, for despite its insertion, mere inches above his heart, his expression barely changed. With his off-hand, he moved to pull the weapon free, but as his hand closed around its hilt, Eris clicked her fingers once more. The weapon vanished and then immediately reappeared in her own hand. Thwarted, the necromancer grimaced, narrowing his eyes further.

I think I just pissed him off. Gods, where's Beher?

*   *   *

Many who are incapable of flight, dream of what it would feel like. To feel the air rush over their face, to leave the trials and tribulations of the ground behind, to be absolutely free. Not Beher. He held flight in no romantic esteem, for him it was just how he got around. As a dragon it was just what he did. Soaring over the village of Thered's Field, Beher made for the town hall as fast as he could.

Why Máher always seeks to do strange things Beher will never know. Why Máher has to help man-things, why not leave them be. Not Beher's problem, not Máher's problem. Beher should just leave. Máher should just leave.

Far beneath him, he could hear the screams of the innocent as they were unceremoniously slaughtered. He could see them as they ran, driven by terror and desperation. He could smell them as they voided their bowels and emptied their bladders. He could taste the blood of the freshly dead on the air. None of these things bothered him. It was the way of the world for the strong to overcome the weak. That was how it has always been, and as far as Beher was concerned, the way it should always remain. But, something about what was happening did bother Beher.

Animals wrong, strange human-things wrong, all wrong. Nothing smells right, doesn't belong, not here, not anywhere. Not natural, not normal, bad. What has Máher got Beher into this time?

Once he reached the town square, Beher circled overhead as he looked for the sorcerer Máher wanted him to kill. The first thing Beher noticed was the fiery hair of Máher, it stood out to such a large extent it was impossible to miss.

Máher's not in any immediate danger. Good. Otherwise Beher would have to save Máher. Again.

The second thing that drew his attention was an odd purple glow, emanating from a floating elf at the other side of the square.

Strange elf, glows. Different scent to wrong animals, not the same as she-elf. Must be sorcerer Máher wants dead. Unnatural, Beher should avoid. Not safe.

As soon as Beher contemplated reneging on his promise to help Eris, a second, stronger thought crossed his mind.

Beher promised Máher. Máher won't leave. Must kill strange elf or Máher dies. Father wouldn't like that. Be bad for Beher that would. Beher doesn't want to, but Beher must.

Resolute in his purpose, Beher circled high above the necromancer and waited for an opportune moment to attack. He saw Eris running in the air below him and was pleased to see her, but was also unsure as to how useful she would actually be.

Beher wonders what she-elf will do. How will the she-elf hurt strange elf from air? She-elf could distract the strange elf, Beher thinks. That would be of some use, Beher supposes.

It didn't take long for Eris to attack. Beher saw her dagger thump into the necromancer's chest, but more importantly, as far as Beher was concerned, he saw the necromancer focus the entirety of his attention upon Eris.

Strange elf looks away, focus on she-elf. Hm, she-elf useful after all. Strange elf alone. Beher thinks it good time to strike.

Tucking his wings into his side, Beher angled his body downwards. Air rushed over his face as he rapidly accelerated. A surge of adrenaline surged through his bloodstream and he smiled, as much as a dragon can smile, in joy, for he deeply enjoyed the feeling of a steep nosedive. Yet, as good as it was, he couldn't let himself become carried away by emotions, he had to remain focussed. Timing was everything.

If he were to open his wings too late, then he would crash and potentially die. If he were to open his wings too early, then he would stop before reaching his target, loose the element of surprise and leave himself vulnerable to counterattack. The outcome of which would almost certainly be his death. As far as Beher was concerned either outcome was to be avoided.

Judging it to be the opportune moment, Beher flared his wings. His muscles strained under the stresses of his rapid deceleration, but it was nothing unusual, he had done this a thousand times before.

Beher's coming to get you strange elf. Beher's going to eat you.

Apparently from nowhere, something crashed heavily into Beher. The world spun in a crazy, blurring cyclone. Crashing to the ground, Beher tumbled across the cobblestones, losing all sense of direction. Eventually, he came to a stop, battered and no doubt bruised. He leapt to his feet, lashing his neck from side to side, desperately trying to locate whatever, or whomever, had plucked him from the air.

What was that? What hit Beher?

He found the culprit almost immediately. It was a tiger. A really big tiger. At least a third larger than Beher, its muscles rippled as it paced gracefully between Beher and the necromancer. As this was the first of the necromancer's risen that

Beher had encountered in such close proximity, he noted with a concerned confusion the twin black flames that burned in its empty eye sockets.

Beher no like strange kitty cat, unnatural, wrong. Gets in Beher's way it does. Mm, Beher has never eaten giant cat before, makes Beher wonder if it tastes good. Beher should find out.

Hissing towards the tiger, teeth bared aggressively, Beher pushed off of his haunches and lumbered towards his feline adversary. In a way Beher thought impossible, the tiger sprang upwards and leapt over the entire length of Beher's body. As it flew over his head Beher snapped at the tiger's heels, but the cat was too fast for the dragon.

The tiger landed gracefully, as any feline would, behind Beher. The young dragon was already in the act of turning to face his foe, but again he was too slow. Fangs sunk into his back, penetrating his scales. Beher roared, both for the indignity of it and for the stabbing pain in his side.

Kitty cat hurt Beher. That's not how it works. Beher should be the one doing the hurting. Oh, kitty cat, now Beher mad.

Beher slapped the tiger away with his tail and spun to face his foe before it could get behind him again. He could feel his blood trickle over his scales, but he didn't let that bother him. Roaring for as second time, Beher released his frustrations and revealed his aggressive intent.

*   *   *

Once Thoron had left, Jeeves turned his attention to Neesa. Kneeling down beside the wounded infernati he checked for vital signs. She was breathing, barely, and there was a heartbeat, but it was faint, very faint.

Not good, not at all good.

As gently as he could manage, he rolled Neesa onto her back and peeled her arms away from her stomach. A brief inspection of her wound told him all he needed to know, without aid, she was going to die, and soon.

I can't help her, it's too dangerous. I don't have the proper equipment anyway. I'm going to need some help.

Glancing furtively around the square, Jeeves searched for someone, anyone, that could help. His options were rather limited.

'King John!'

Upon hearing his name, the monarch shifted his attention from Selene, who was still catatonic, onto Jeeves. He didn't respond, but the quizzical look on his face told Jeeves to keep talking.

'We need you.' Jeeves pointed to Neesa. 'She needs you. Now!'

If the King was offended by Jeeves's lack of royal decorum, he didn't show it. Instead, he just nodded, face set with a grim determination, and ran over to Jeeves and Neesa.

'Get her out of here, help her if you can. Get the elf to help as well.' Jeeves paused for a moment, remembering Selene's less-than-useful state of mind, but didn't give King John any time to interject. 'Slap her if you have to, just get her moving.'

'I'll do what I can.'

Much to his credit, the King wasted no time. He grabbed Neesa by her underarms and dragged her away.

Good, one less problem to deal with. I do hope that she'll make it. Now, back to the fray.

Most of the risen in the immediate vicinity had already been dispatched. As Jeeves stood and looked for the next foe to fight, he only saw one. Implacably marching towards him was the armour-clad goliath, Ronar.

Ok, it's you and me tin man.

Steeling himself, Jeeves sprinted towards Ronar. As he ran, he slipped a silver disc into each hand. Flicking his wrists, he hurled the projectiles at the goliath. They spun gracefully through the air, but failed to find their mark. Instead of flesh, they met hardened steel, whereby they ricocheted harmlessly away.

Damn.

Abandoning a ranged approach as a futile endeavour, Jeeves reached behind him and pulled two short swords from underneath his tuxedo jacket.

Up close and personal it is.

*   *   *

The Baron's throat constricted and he found it hard to swallow. Seeing his friend, whom he had known for the entirety of his life, in such close proximity to peril worried him. Even though he knew it was necessary, and that Jeeves had proved himself capable, the Baron found no comfort in logic.

Dash it all, you blasted old man. You best not get yourself hurt. I wouldn't know what to do if you did.

Raising Peacemaker towards Ronar, the Baron did what he always did when he needed to make a shot requiring a high level of accuracy. He breathed in and steadied himself. Gently, he squeezed Peacemaker's trigger, all the while keeping the gun's barrel fixed firmly upon the armoured goliath. For the Baron, time seemed to slow and all the pandemonium around his periphery faded to irrelevance. For him, there was only Ronar and Jeeves. Peacemaker's hammer fell.

'*Click.*'

Nothing happened.

Desperately the Baron pulled Peacemaker's trigger again.

'*Click.*'

Still nothing.

With a sick realisation, the Baron played back in his mind each of the times he had fired Peacemaker, counting his shots. Instantly, he understood what the problem with his gun was. It was empty.

You bloody moron. You should have counted your shots. You should have known you were out of bullets. You should have bloody well reloaded. Oh gods, what a fool I am.

Unlocking Peacemaker's cylinder from its frame, the Baron popped it out to one side and tilted it back. Spent brass slid easily from the cylinder and tinkled melodically against the square's cobbles. Reaching into one, of his many, coat pockets, the Baron withdrew a single fresh bullet and slid it into Peacemaker's cylinder.

Only five more to go. I really need to think of a faster way to do this. This is simply not practical, especially in a pinch.

*　　*　　*

Knowing that the battle was steadily turning against them, Máher felt that he had to do something more. A plan quickly formed in his mind. He knew that it would be dangerous. He knew that he might die. But he also knew that it was necessary and that paying for victory with his life would be a fair trade.

Closing his eyes, Máher sought out the glowing orb at his centre. Focussing on it more intently than he had ever done so before, he willed the energy it offered into every fibre of his being. Every inch of body tingled with power and grew warm. It was a pleasant heat, comforting and welcoming.

Throwing caution to the wayside, Máher drew more and more power into himself. Far faster than he had ever done so before. The welcome warmth was replaced with a burning heat, not yet painful, but fast approaching so.

Not yet. I still need more power.

*　　*　　*

Continuing to run in the air, Eris circled above the necromancer's head. She saw Beher be intercepted before he could properly engage the elf and inwardly, she cursed her luck.

Damn, looks like it's just me.

Seeing it as the only logical course of action, Eris threw her dagger at the necromancer, blinking her weapon past his defences once more. Just as before, he tried to grab her dagger and, in an exact replica of her previous manoeuvre, she blinked it back to herself before he could take it.

The necromancer remained stationary as he floated above the ground, his scowl lifting to a self-assured smirk. is winced as a lance of white-hot agony stabbed at her temples. She knew what the pain foretold and steeled the defences of her mind, but despite her focus, her head rang with a series of unwanted words.

'*Though you are nothing, you are beginning to annoy me. No more.*'

The necromancer's shield disappeared in a cyclonic blur and his hand flared in an impossibly bright shade of purple. Unable to stand it, Eris shied away, shielding her eyes from the retina burning flare.

Hidden by the glare, seven small motes of light darted from the palm of the elf's hand. Through parted fingers Eris barely saw them fly towards her, but there was nowhere to hide and no time to react.

A single word, "shit," crossed her mind as she feebly raised her arms in defence. Pointless. Undeterred, the seven balls of energy slammed into her body. Her chest, waist, back and head, they were all pummelled.

Searing pain, encompassing every part of her body, overcame her. Her body locked into place as her muscles tensed tight. The incantation that was keeping her aloft failed as she lost her focus. Immediately, she started to tumble from the sky. Eris's mind raced as she fought to speak the words, that one phrase that could stall her uncontrolled descent. However, no matter how she tried, her mouth wouldn't do as she willed, instead of discernible elvish she could only manage incomprehensible gibberish.

The single word that had just crossed her mind was joined by a second. Together they provided an excellent summary of the situation Eris was now in.

Oh shit.

With a sickening series of cracks, Eris crashed heavily onto the stone-clad ground. Instantaneously, her vision went black as she lost all worldly sensation.

*   *   *

Keeping his eyes locked with the flickering flames of his adversary, Jeeves rapidly sidestepped to his left, attempting to circle around the armoured goliath. Refusing to expose his flank, Ronar mirrored Jeeves's movements and also sidestepped to his left.

Internally, Jeeves was frustrated.

Blighter is quick, despite his armour, and he definitely knows what he's doing. I'm not sure that I can best him. Dash it all.

Externally, he let none of his doubt show.

With a calm and exacting precision, the elderly butler lunged forwards. Ronar deflected the strike with his sword, swatting it away as if it was nothing, but that was the plan. Jeeves had expected it. Hope surged in the butler's chest as he saw an opening.

There it is.

Jeeves stepped forwards, the blade in his right hand already singing as it swung towards Ronar's head.

Unbelievably fast, Ronar twisted away from Jeeves's sword, reversing the grip on his hilt. Unable to react, the great sword's heavy pommel slammed into Jeeves's abdomen. Reflexively, he dropped the sword in his left hand as an overwhelming pain surged through his body. Biting his teeth through the agony, Jeeves rolled away from Ronar before the goliath could follow his pommel strike with a lethal cut.

Standing from his roll, Jeeves raised his sword and readied his guard, but he found it difficult. His body ached and his arm wobbled under the strain.

I must say, this is less than ideal.

Effortlessly, Ronar batted away Jeeves's blade, stepped within Jeeves's guard and impaled the hapless butler upon his sword. Jeeves's eyes shot wide with surprise as a fountain of hot blood spurted from his gaping mouth. Mesmerised by the twin dancing flames, mere inches from his own eyes, Jeeves never even contemplated resisting.

*   *   *

Máher grimaced, his eyes still shut tightly. Pain burned through his flesh as every one of his atoms screamed for release. He knew he should release the energy he held, but still, he channelled more.

Almost there, but not yet. I must hold on.

Radiating with power, the air around him shimmered with heat. The ground at his feet shone brightly as his glowing skin illuminated the cobbles as though it were the midday sun. In every sense, he was a literal, and metaphorical, beacon of righteous fire.

It's time.

Máher opened his eyes. In that moment he forgot his pain. In that moment he forgot the horrors that surrounded him. In that a moment he was consumed by purpose.

Concentrating upon the elven necromancer, Máher willed his magic free. Just as an elderly star would end its life in a supernova, the pent-up energy within Máher exploded outwards. Instantly, Máher's vision went black as he keeled over, landing motionless on the ground.

For the most part the detonation of Máher's spell was harmless, a wave of warmth-tinged light that barely fought off the night's chill. But just as he had willed it to be, a trio of scorching rays of fire had been called into existence. It was these three jets that were now streaking erratically through the air towards the necromancer.

*   *   *

Beher's roar died to a low rumble in his throat. His eyed narrowed, as he stared cautiously at the tiger before him, expecting it to charge towards him at any moment. It didn't.

Kitty cat won't attack Beher head on, coward. Beher's not so craven.

Beher lowered his head, nostrils flaring. In one fluid movement, he scraped his talons across the cobbles by his feet and then charged. However, this time was wary of feline trickery.

Jump over Beher again kitty cat, Beher dares you. No, Beher double dares you.

Proving to be a creature of habit, the tiger did just as it did before, but Beher would not be caught off guard for a second time. Just as the tiger sprang off of the ground, Beher also jumped, flapping his wings to propel himself upwards. Mid-air, the pair impacted with a heavy thud, two balls of solid muscle and predatory rage colliding. For the tiger it was unexpected. For Beher it was planned.

Beher has you now, kitty cat.

Beher wrapped his legs around the tiger. Furiously, the tiger tried to paw Beher off of it. Claws, razor sharp and as hard as forged steel, scrapped against Beher's belly. He felt them carve through his soft under-scales, but he held on. No matter what he wouldn't let go.

The pair crashed back down to earth, Beher on top of the tiger. Knowing that he wouldn't be able to pin the tiger for long, Beher bit down on the back of the tiger's neck. Cold, congealed blood oozed lazily into Beher's mouth. It tasted foul, but he supressed the urge to spit it out. Instead, he shook his head from side to side, as hard and as fast as he could.

Beher thinks that tiger no good for eating. Blood tastes horrible, wrong. Like it's been dead for weeks. Bah, just Beher's luck. Beher could have used a snack.

From within his jaws, Beher felt the tiger's neck snap. Instantly, the tiger went limp. Beher shook the tiger's corpse one final time and then threw it to the ground. Panting from exhaustion, but high on the fumes of victory, he climbed atop the decaying feline. Stretching his neck as high as he could manage, he let out a roar of jubilation.

Beher is the greatest! All fear the mighty Beher!

* * *

As the Baron slid the final bullet into peacemaker's chamber, he looked up towards Jeeves and Ronar. Teeth gritted in determination; he raised Peacemaker.

All right you bugger, I'll put a hole in you this time for sure.

Wrapping his finger around Peacemaker's trigger, he caressed it softly. But before he could squeeze, the square was illuminated in a fiery red glow. Captivated, the Baron looked away from Ronar and Jeeves, watching in awe as three pillars of flame soared through the air.

They were wonderous in their brilliance, but, beauty aside, the Baron retained a modicum of his inquisitive nature and wondered as to the destination of these projectiles. Rapidly running calculations in his head, determining angles and velocities, the Baron quickly ascertained that they were headed towards the elven necromancer. Blinded by the hope that this would be enough to deal with their foe, the Baron forgot Jeeves and Ronar, transfixed by the fire, he overlooked all else around him.

Across the square, the floating elf thrust his arms towards the missiles, summoning a shimmering wall of purple light before him. Undeterred by his magical defences, each tendril of flame crashed into the necromancer. With an ill-founded satisfaction, the Baron watched as liquid fire washed over the elf, disintegrating his robes, and scorching his flesh.

Losing control over his composure, the necromancer collapsed to the ground. As he continued to burn, he huddled into a ball, desperately trying to hide from the flames. Useless. Changing tack, he writhed and rolled over the cobbles, in an attempt to snuff out the fire that consumed him. Yet, despite his efforts, the flames would not be denied their feast. As a macabre beacon of hope for those that remained, he continued to burn.

For the first time, the necromancer forewent his telepathic communication and released a verbal scream. In that scream, the Baron could feel the necromancer's agony. It turned the marrow in his bones sour, but strangely, the Baron was pleased. Usually, he was never one to wish ill upon anyone, but in this instance, he felt it appropriate. Had he the time to do so, or the necessary self-awareness, he may have recognised this newfound darkness within him and recoiled at its implications, instead all he felt was jubilation.

That's right. Burn you fiend. Burn.

'You believe yourselves victorious. Argh... You know nothing. Ah... This is just the beginning. Ahh!'

It was either foreshadowing, or an attempt at bravado, the Baron knew not which. To be honest he didn't care.

It's over for you though. Good riddance, I say.

A stiff breeze blew across the square and the charred husk of the necromancer melted away to nothingness. A shower of fine ashes, all that remained of the necromancer, fell to the cobbles, coating them black. It was in those final moments, that the Baron saw a faint cloud rise from the remnants and float hurriedly into the sky.

Lost in the jubilation of victory, he ignored this inexplicable phenomenon. All around him risen were following their master's lead and crumbling to dust. He was alive and they had won. Even if the cost was high, there was still reason to celebrate. Overcome, he pumped his fist into the air and shouted an almighty, 'Huzzah!'

Turning back towards Jeeves, to offer him congratulatory praise and share in the joy of the moment, the Baron saw the final remains of Ronar disintegrate in the breeze. He was about to shout out to his friend, but before he could Jeeves listed heavily to one side before toppling over.

The Baron felt his heart skip a beat, the euphoria within him vanished, replaced with concern. Despite everything, all he could think about was the welfare of his friend, nothing else mattered to him. As quickly as he could, the Baron sprinted over to Jeeves's immobile body.

'Hold on man! I'll fetch a healer, or a cleric, or someone, just hold on.'

Blood oozed from the butler's mouth as he struggled to speak.

'Ah... It's too late for that. Argh... Just listen. Oh Gods... There's a temple, south east of Evonium. Ah... In the mountain. Bloody hell... Find it. Speak my name.'

The Baron pushed his hand firmly against Jeeves's chest, desperately trying as hard as he could to stem the bleeding, but to no avail.

'Jeeves? What in the bloody hell will shouting "Jeeves" in some gods forsaken temple do? I need to find you a bloody healer, that's what.'

Pleadingly, Jeeves grabbed the Baron's arm.

'Listen. Argh... There's no time. Ah... Speak my true name. Ow... Speak the word J'sa'var.'

As Jeeves spoke that final word, his true name, he sighed a final sigh and surrendered to the inevitable, surrendered to death. Dismayed, the Baron watched on hopelessly as the body of his oldest friend evaporated into nothingness.

Only his tuxedo, once immaculate, but now lacerated and torn, remained. The Baron, confused, distraught and alone, clutched at the silken fabric as the sheer volume of emotions overwhelmed him. Unable to process any of it, he pulled the tuxedo to his face, acting as the smallest of comforts, and cried relentlessly as he released his grief.

Chapter 45

Eris

Sitting atop a small hill, Eris gazed absentmindedly across the rolling countryside. It was no doubt a beautiful vista, but as she had spent the entirety of her life in the claustrophobic warrens of Súthburh, she found the lack of man-made structures disconcerting. It was almost as though the sky was too big and a single misstep would be all it would take for her to fall into its nothingness.

A pair of birds sung as they flew above her head, and Eris smiled briefly at their openly displayed mirth. Yet, the joy she felt was soon lost as her thoughts rapidly returned to the events of the night before. Her body ached and her soul felt violated, but the worst of it she felt, perhaps selfishly, was that Mikael wasn't there with her.

Oh Mikael, how long must I wait for us to be as one once more?

From somewhere behind her, Eris heard a twig snap. Startled from her idle ruminations, she spun around. There, walking slowly towards her was Máher.

Caught off guard by her obvious astonishment, he raised his hands in a nonthreatening gesture.

'Sorry. I didn't mean to surprise you.'

She shrugged, 'it's fine.'

'Is it okay if I join you? I can leave if you'd prefer to be alone.'

'Sure. I don't mind. To be honest I could use the company.' Eris paused for a moment, considering how much she would be comfortable sharing. 'It's Mikael, you know, I just miss him. If I'm entirely honest, I still can't quite believe that he's gone. I feel as though he'll just show up at any moment and we'll continue our life together.'

Máher eased himself onto the ground beside her. She looked away, not wanting for him to see the hurt in her eyes, not wanting for him to see just how vulnerable she felt.

Don't you dare start to cry Eris. Don't you dare.

Máher placed a single calloused finger upon her chin. Instinctually she shivered, but did nothing to remove it or back away. She felt the pressure it exerted upon her increase. She could have fought it, refused it, but instead she yielded to it and turned back to face Máher.

Eris could see a pain in his eyes, a pain that she was certain mirrored what he could see in hers. Wordlessly, he wrapped his arms around her back and pulled her into him. With a hunger for intimacy that surprised her, Eris reciprocated Máher's hug with gusto.

Feeling not only relief, but also a heartfelt contentment Eris whispered into Máher's ear.

'Thanks. I needed this.

Although he almost always spoke softly, Eris almost couldn't hear Máher as he whispered his response to her.

'Me too.'

Eris's spine tingled and her heart skipped a beat. She had never considered Máher as a potential sexual partner, but as he held her and consoled her, she felt something deep within her, something primal, rise to the forefront of her being. For the first time, in the longest time, she entertained the thought of being with someone other than Mikael.

As soon as she thought this though she felt a deep shame. She had only just lost the love of her life. She still grieved for him. She still wanted him. She was carrying his child. How could she in good conscience legitimately think about sleeping with another man? Deep down she knew the answer.

Mikael's gone. I'm alone and I'm hurting. I just want to feel better.

Trying as hard as she could to hide her emotions, she pulled away from Máher.

'So, was there a specific reason for this visit?

'Spending time with you is reason enough.'

Petrified by shock, Eris remained silent, but noted a distinct tightening of the muscles at the pit of her stomach. It was an all too familiar feeling, and one that got her mind racing.

Calm Eris, be calm. It's too soon. You're friends, just friends. Oh gods.

'But, in this instance there is one. Apparently the infernati woman in the town hall is almost fully healed.'

Overcame by a combination of surprise and curiosity, Eris forgot her inner turmoil, forwent all decorum, and interjected loudly.

'Already? She was in awful shape. Selene must really be quite the healer.'

Máher gave her a sideways glance and Eris felt her cheeks burn red.

Oops.

'Sorry.'

Máher waved her apology away as unnecessary.

'It's fine. Anyway, as I was about to say, The King has asked for us all to meet him there. And I quote "at our earliest convenience".'

'Do you know why?'

Máher shrugged.

'To thank us for last night I suppose, or ask something more of us.' Máher shrugged again. 'I'm not certain. Either way it won't serve us well to refuse a king. Or keep him waiting.'

'Well then.' Eris leapt to her feet. 'We had best be off.'

As she left the picturesque wilderness behind, Eris was confronted by the grim aftermath of last night. Numerous tendrils of acidic smoke curled into the sky, each denoting an individual funeral pyre. Those differing faiths worked tirelessly to intern their lost loved ones into the earth. However, yet more stood idle, clustered in small groups, unable to find their loved ones and lay them to rest. In each instance, wailing mourners surrounded the silent fallen. Eris was unsure of how many citizens of Thered's Field remained, but from what she could initially see, she guessed it to be far less than half.

She was no stranger to death. She had killed more than a few civilians herself, those who were unwise enough to cross the guilds. But, death on such a large scale was alien to her. And then, there were the children. Unable to defend themselves, and unable to flee as fast as their adult brethren, they died in disproportionally higher numbers. She found it obscene. Within her chest she felt her soul break.

Máher grabbed her hand and gave it a reassuring squeeze. Although she appreciated the gesture, it ultimately did little to ease her heartache.

'I'm glad you're okay.'

Sighing deeply, Eris looked around her. As bad as it was, she found it easier than meeting Máher eye to eye.

'I'm not sure that I am.'

'That's not what I meant.' He paused. She gave him the time he needed. 'When I saw you fall, I thought the worst, I thought you had died. I'm glad you didn't.'

'That makes two of us.'

Máher said nothing, but couldn't prevent a low chuckle from escaping between his smiling lips. Glad that her impromptu attempt at humour had the desired effect, Eris squeezed Máher's hand in return. Still unable to meet his gaze, she spoke from the corner of her mouth.

'Thank you.'

Eris let go of Máher's hand. Not because she was tired of the physical contact, in fact she yearned for it. That was her primary concern. It would be all too easy for her to relent to her emotions, to give herself to Máher. But she feared that such a coupling, though pleasurable in the short term, would lead to nothing but regret and an irreparably shattered friendship.

I can't. Not yet, perhaps not ever.

As they entered Thered's Field proper, they were greeted by a myriad of collapsed or damaged buildings. Juxtaposed against the human toll, the loss of property seemed almost irrelevant. Only the crassest would argue a lost building to be as important as a lost life. However, Eris knew it to be a more complicated problem. A lost house would mean exposure to the dangers of the wild, whether it be the elements or a hungry beast. A lost business would mean a loss of income and the inability to purchase food, leading eventually to starvation and death. Amidst a tragedy such as this, there are only losers and Eris felt for them all.

Looming above them, scarred, but still standing, the town hall appeared to be in far better shape than most of the other buildings in the township. Its open doors bid them welcome. Beseeching them to enter. As they crossed the building's threshold Eris hoped that its interior would offer a reprieve from the desolation outside. Even if it just served as a distraction, as a means of forcing the worst of the situation from the forefront of her attention.

Before them stood a large oak counter, curved, and topped with a mosaic of lacquered hardwoods. Sitting behind the counter was a young human woman, beaming with a perfectly pearlescent smile.

'Good morning, sir. Good morning, madam. How can I help the pair of you today?'

Eris stepped up to the counter, meeting the receptionist's smile with a forced one of her own.

'Good morning. Which way to the infernati's room?'

'Hm, I only know of one infernati that's currently here. Does the infernati you're after happen to be blue, was almost killed last night and wears a kimono?'

Eris nodded. 'Yep, that's the one.'

Though it should not have been possible, the woman's smile intensified.

'Excellent, just thought I'd check. You never know, there might have been a second infernati around the place that I was unaware of.' The woman unleashed an unbelievably shrill giggle at a joke Eris was not party to. 'Hm, as unlikely as that would be.'

With an animated enthusiasm the woman stood and gestured with her hands as she relayed directions.

'Okay, so you want to go up the stairs to your right, all the way to the top, turn right, go to the end of the hall, turn left, then it's the door at the end of that hall.'

Feeling none of the lady's eagerness, Eris reinforced her already strained smile and nodded to the woman.

'Thank you.'

'That's what I'm here for. Have your selves a lovely day now.'

Most would have thought it strange, that a person could be so outwardly happy amidst such horrific circumstances. Eris, not so much. She knew that it was nothing more than a veneer, a perverse means of coping. Under the surface, Eris knew, the woman was hurting, perhaps even close to breaking. She knew this, for she had experienced it and, in many ways, still was.

Either that or she's a psychopath. Yes, with a laugh like that, she's definitely a psychopath.

Wordlessly, and in an almost silence, they followed the greeter's directions. The sound of their footfalls rang in her ears, loud not for their own resonance, but for the lack of any competing noise. By all appearances, both visual and auditory, the town hall was near deserted, those who would normally walk its corridors drawn away by more pressing concerns. Finding the experience utterly disconcerting, Eris suppressed the urge to leave and continued onwards.

At the end of the final hallway a dishevelled man in nobles dress, paced erratically outside of a closed door. Eris immediately recognised him.

He was in the square last night.

The man saw them and waved in their direction. Eris was about to call out a greeting, but before she could, the man opened the door and eased himself inside. Almost immediately, he leapt back into the corridor, but it was only for the briefest of instances as he quickly re-entered the room, shutting the door firmly behind him.

Stunned, Eris stopped walking. Equally perplexed, Máher stopped simultaneously beside her. Shaking her head, but still looking towards the door, Eris mumbled loud enough for only Máher to hear.

'What did we just see?'

He whispered back to her.

'A strange man. Nay, a very strange man.'

Finding Máher's statement both apt and amusing, Eris smiled.

The pair resumed their walk and just as they reached the end of the hall the door opened. Out popped the head of the strange man from before. He offered them no greeting, but bode them to enter.

'Come on in folks.'

The head withdrew and the door swung wide open. Hesitant, Eris turned to Máher, an unsure look on her face. He just shrugged and entered the room. Sighing, she followed.

Well here goes nothing I suppose.

Chapter 46

Neesa

Dreamless sleep serves as a means of teleporting us instantaneously from the present into the future. Usually when one awakes from such a slumber a modicum of disorientation is to be expected, but in most cases any discombobulation is quickly alleviated by the individual's sensory faculties.

For Neesa, this was not the case. Conscious thought had returned to her and she was aware of herself, but she could feel nothing. Surrounded by a void of darkness, she could see nothing. Lost in an ocean of nothing, she had no notion of where she was. As far as she was concerned, she should have been dead, as her final, faintly tangible memory would have her believe.

Is this the beyond? Surely this cannot be. There must be more.

Perhaps, she thought, she was dead and this was simply how her afterlife was destined to begin. Perhaps, and worryingly so, a second, darker thought took root at the centre of her mind. Maybe, this is what the entirety of her afterlife would be, an endless and empty void. However, as Neesa focussed more keenly upon herself, she noted the steady rise and fall of her chest as she breathed.

I'm not dead then.

Exerting herself, Neesa willed herself to move. At first, she focused on only the extremities, begging her fingers and toes to wiggle. Slowly, but surely, her efforts were repaid and eventually she felt her digits respond to her commands.

Moving onto her next task, Neesa begged her eyes to open. Initially obstinate, they eventually capitulated to her demands. Her vision was blurred and unfocussed, yet she gasped when she was met by a distorted, yet still clearly bovine, head. Searing pain stabbed at her abdomen and she cried out in an involuntary hiss of pain. Startled by her outburst, the young builg calf leapt off of Neesa's bed and scampered out of the room. He didn't bother closing the door.

As the minutes passed, Neesa slowly recovered her faculties. Pushing the persistent pain aside, she inspected her surroundings. She was in a small room. It's only notable features a pair of windows, neither of which offered a particularly stimulating view, and the bed that she lay in. It was a simple thing, not uncomfortable by any means, but a long way from luxurious.

At least I'm alive. By all rights I should be dead.

After an indiscernible amount of time, a builg woman, the adult version of the departed child, walked into her room.

'Hm, Edwardo tells me you're in a wee bit o' pain. Let's see what the go is hey?'

Lifting the hem of her nightshirt, the woman poked, prodded and kneaded Neesa's torso. At sporadic intervals Neesa grimaced, as the woman touched a particularly sore area, but no apology was ever offered, just a collection of hm's and mm's.

'Easy, just breathe dearie, just breathe.' Reaching into a satchel by her side the elderly woman pulled out a clay bottle, uncorked it, and handed it to Neesa. 'I may not have the gift like that elven lass does, but I knows well the ways of healing herbs. Here, drink this.'

Neesa eyed the vessel suspiciously, but did as the woman asked. Bitter herbs burned her throat, causing her eyes to water. She coughed and spluttered as she supressed the urge to vomit, but eventually she had drunk the entirety of the vile concoction.

'Good, very good. You'll be right as rain in no time at all lassie, just try to avoid anything too strenuous for a few days.'

With those final few words, the Builg wandered off, closing the door behind her, and leaving Neesa alone.

As nasty as that potion was, it has dulled the pain.

Whether from the potion, or the boredom, Neesa drifted fitfully between slumber and wakeful moments. It was during one of these wakeful moments which she heard the door to her room open. Reflexively, Neesa looked to see who it was. There, easing himself tentatively into her room, was the Baron. However, for whatever reason the man quickly backed away as he saw Neesa laying in her bed. A triad of muttered curses, none of which Neesa could make out clearly, was immediately followed by a far louder query.

'You decent my dear?'

Having no notion of what the Baron considered to be decent, Neesa pulled up her bedsheets, as high as practical, and responded with a hesitant affirmative.

'Yes?'

Having ascertained that the room was indeed safe to enter, the Baron, with infinitely more confidence this time, re-entered the room.

'Capital. I should have knocked first. You know, announced myself. I'm ashamed to say that propriety completely slipped my mind. Hope you won't think less of me because of it.'

He paused and in that moment of silence his face morphed from one of joviality to one of deep disappointment.

'Blasts and damnations, there I go again, immediately after my first faux pas I only go and step my foot in it again. Please forgive me my lady and please allow me to start over.'

Coughing to clear his throat, the Baron swept his arm to his side and bowed impossibly low in her direction.

'Good morning my dear. It's good to see you on the mend. I very much do hope you are well and will ever continue to be so.'

Overwhelmed by the hilarity of it all, Neesa couldn't help but laugh.

'Ha, ha. Thanks for coming to visit Baron, it's very kind of you.'

'Pish posh, it's nothing. Besides, I would have had to pop in regardless. King John called a meeting you see. Apparently, he wants to thank everyone that fought in the square last night and, as you're laid up and all that, he thought to have it here. Every one's already here so I imagine he'll be joining us rather soon as a matter of fact.'

'Oh, bugger it.'

The Baron held up a finger, as if asking her to wait and stuck his head out the door.

'Come on in folks.'

Immediately, Neesa recognised the two people who entered her room as those she had fought alongside last night. The tall elementarian man and the lithe elven woman. Neither said a word, but both nodded to her in a respectful greeting.

'Okay then, now we're all here.'

Neesa's brow furrowed.

'Where's Jeeves and the dwarf, Thoron, wasn't it? Shouldn't they be here too?'

The Baron bowed his head, unable to meet her eye to eye.

'What is it?

His voice quivered and Neesa's heart dropped, sensing what the Baron was about to tell her. As soon he had spoken a single word she knew for certain.

'They didn't make it I'm afraid. Um… They're both gone.'

'Oh gods. I'm so sorry. I…' Neesa trailed off unable to continue. In her mind, she ran through things she ought to say, things that would offer even a modicum of relief. But, irrespective of what she could conceive, none of it felt right. It all seemed hollow and meaningless. Dejected, she just repeated what she had already said, 'I'm sorry.'

Both the Baron and Neesa attempted to spark a meaningful conversation, but neither possessed the social grace to overcome the gloomy atmosphere. Thankfully, for the pair of them, the excruciatingly awkward situation was short lived.

King John, accompanied by Selene in a flattering ankle length dress of the most striking aquamarine, entered the room in a way that made it clear to everyone present that this would be an exchange of great importance. He glided in with a powerful stride and abided no simple small talk, only granting those who met his gaze a simple nod of recognition. He waited for no one, unilaterally initiating the conversation himself.

'Good morning, ladies and gentlemen, I wish I had time for pleasantries and to thank you all properly for what you did, and sacrificed, last night, but alas time will not allow it.'

At the word sacrificed, Neesa keenly noted the Baron stiffen and avert his attention from the King. He rested his head in his hands and she knew, though she was unable to see it, that he was doing all he could to stop himself from weeping. Barely able to contain the still raw pain of his loss, that he was feeling.

'As such, I'll just say this. Thank you. From the bottom of my heart, thank you. I am certain that without each of you I, and more importantly my family, would be dead. For this, I will forever be in your debt.'

The King paused, bowing to each of those assembled in the room in turn. When it came to her, Neesa could feel the King's sincerity in this most simple of actions. She was immediately reminded of those in The Empire and their hollow, meaningless gestures, that more often than not concealed nefarious motivations. She found the difference to be a welcome change.

If only more could say what they mean.

From his side, Selene flowed King John's lead by curtsying deeply to everyone.

'I am also deeply grateful. Thank you.'

'Capital. To that end I have written a small letter to my Seneschal, Ronald, granting each of you a large sum of coin, five thousand crowns in all to be precise. 'If you wish to collect it, all you would have to do is travel to Evonium and present him with this letter.'

Five thousand crowns. That's a lot of money. That can't be right. I must have misheard him.

'Did you say *five thousand* crowns?'

King John stopped speaking mid-word and turned towards Neesa, an incredulous look on his face. Apparently, he was not accustomed to being interrupted.

Oh gods.

'Apologies, your Majesty. I didn't mean to be rude. It's just that that's so much money, I thought you must have miss-spoke. Or something. Um…'

His eyes narrowed, as if he was examining her for the slightest of faults, but his stern demeanour quickly softened into an easy grin.

'Apology accepted. I rarely misspeak and this is definitely not one of those times. Five thousand is the sum, it would have been more if not for the imminent war with The Empire.' His voice shifted in tone, almost as though he was speaking to himself. 'Outfitting and provisioning armies is not a cheap endeavour.'

'In any case I have devoted the missive to The Heroes of Thered's Field. As your group has no formal name, I thought it fitting. When introducing yourselves to Ronald you will have to use this title, lest he think you forgers and have you imprisoned. Is that acceptable or in there another name you would prefer?'

The King looked to each of the newly dubbed Heroes, seeking their answers. Each remained silent, only shaking their heads, deeming their new moniker acceptable, if perhaps a little pretentious.

'Now, I need to move on to more important matters. Those monstrosities that we fought last night were not the first of their kind I have encountered. Before my journey here, I was assaulted by a similar foe, in my private quarters no less. I have no doubt that what occurred here is by no means an isolated incident and that a similar, if not the same, evil threatens my own people. As I am currently unable to tend to this myself, I would ask of you all one simple thing. Investigate whatever in the hells is going on and put a swift stop to it. There will of course be a suitable reward.'

Pausing, the King rubbed his chin. 'The Heroes of Thered's Field, it does have a good ring to it, doesn't it? Perhaps this will simply be the first of many titles you garner as you continue along the path of heroism.' Sighing heavily, the King shook his head. 'I digress. I must leave, but I'll send a runner with the letter within the hour. Gods speed to you all.'

As quickly as he had entered, King John swept from the room amidst the flurry of his billowing cloak. Selene, however, remained.

Sitting in an awkward quiet the five shared timid glances, each waiting for another to commence the inevitable conversation. Finding such hesitancy ludicrous, Neesa broke the silence.

'I do believe that fate has forced the five of us together, but for the most part we are still strangers. let us begin as we should, with introductions. I am Neesa and that is Baron Victor von Grumanhieser III, but just call him the Baron.'

Bowing low from the waist, the elementarian spoke in soft, barely audible tones.

'A pleasure to make your acquaintances. I am Máher and the woman is Eris. We have another companion, whom is currently enjoying a feast of lamb and piglet, that I shall introduce in good time, but for now I will simply tell you his name, Beher.'

From the corner of the room, Selene curtsied again.

'Well met. Each of you know my name, but formally I am referred to as Selene Amakiir of the Taoiseach Spire.'

'Wonderful. Good day to you all and all that, but, ah, what's the plan now?'

Selene sighed deeply.

'I know that I wasn't a great deal of help last night, but I, should you choose to take the King up on his offer, wish to join you. I, like the King, suspect that something far greater, and more sinister, than what we have thus far uncovered is at work. I would see it stopped by any means.'

Before he answered the Baron, Máher took a deep breath before exhaling slowly.

'As far as I see it, five thousand gold pieces, or one thousand each, is too much coin to refuse. I'd travel to Evonium for that alone, even without the prospect of work and future wealth. Truth be told, I was considering traveling to Evonium regardless, but I feel as you do Selene. If there is more of what we faced last night out there in the world, it must be stopped. If we are the ones fated to do that, then so be it.'

'I hate to brag, as vulgar as it is, but the coin is not so important to me as it may be to you. I'm not exactly lacking in the currency department, if you know what I mean. That said, I do believe I need to head in that rough direction for other reasons, so why not I say. I'm in.'

As she answered, Neesa could see an abundance of emotion line Eris's face.

'I have nothing and no one, but I will do all that I can to prevent what happened here to anyone else. I will join you. Until the end.'

Being the only one yet to answer, the room turned collectively towards Neesa.

'Until recently I was enslaved by The Empire. If they ever recapture me, they will kill me. I don't have a single coin to my name and know no one, except for the Baron that is. I'm confident that I could make my way in the world alone, but I'm not sure it would be wise to try.' Neesa paused, considering her next words carefully. 'For now, I will travel with you and lend you my aid in the destruction of evil.'

Even though his demeanour remained unreadably stoic, Máher nodded as though pleased.

'Well, that's decided. We go together. From memory it's not a long journey, but we'll still need some supplies and at least one horse each.'

'Don't worry yourself about transport my boy. I have a carriage that can accommodate us all quite comfortably. It might also have a few rations tucked away inside of it already to boot.' The Baron paused in thought and his expression twisted into an openly embarrassed frown that was tinged with a hint of sadness. 'That is to say as long as one of you can drive it. I've never done it myself you see and I am, um, not really sure how it's done.'

Máher, Eris and Neesa shared a glance while Máher mouthed silently 'is he serious?' towards Neesa. She just shrugged, but sensing the Baron's dejection decided to ease the man's shame.

'Don't worry about it, Baron. I'm sure that between the rest of us we'll manage just fine. We can always teach you along the way.'

Buoyed by her kindness, the Baron let his lips form into a subdued smile.

'Thank you my dear.'

'Very well, it's settled. Make your preparations, for tomorrow our adventure begins.'

*   *   *

When she awoke the next morning Neesa felt infinitely better. The searing pain that accompanied her the day before, was now nothing more than a dull ache. By the time Edwardo had delivered her a piping hot stew for her breakfast and she had taken her morning constitutional, even this was nothing more than a memory.

Spirits inspired by the tantalising possibilities that awaited her, Neesa exited the Town Hall with an insuppressible smile. However, this was quickly tempered by the piles of rubble that as of yet had still not been removed. Soul now wearied by memories of the past, she quickened her step, even more eager to leave.

As she descended the Town Hall steps, she felt a tug at the corner of her mind. Knowing not what caused her to do so, either instinct or some outside control, she turned her head towards a specific scattering of rubble. There at the centre of the debris lay Thoron's sword and shield, forgotten and abandoned by all.

How odd. It's strange that no one has scavenged them already.

With steps that were not fully her own Neesa abandoned all preconceived plans and walked towards the weapons. The citizens of Thered's Field meandered around her, intent on completing their morning tasks. Neighbours conversed loudly over their morning beverages, lamenting the weather, or remembering better times. Neesa registered none of this as the wall that was her purpose focussed and occupied the entirety of her attention.

Reaching the weapons, she bent down and, oblivious to any danger that they may or may not pose, picked them up. As she stood Neesa rapidly blinked her eyes. The fog around her consciousness lifted and her consciousness returned its focus to the present.

'Well, isn't this a fantastic turn of events, am I ever glad you heard us and decided to scooch on over and pick us up. Now, before you lose your shit and decide to throw us into next week, let me introduce ourselves. My name is Barry and that other lump of steel over there is Harry.'

Before she could stammer a response, a second, distinctively different, voice piped into her thoughts.

'Good day madam, an absolute pleasure to make your acquaintance.'

'That it is mate, that it is. Now that that's over with, let me fill you in on exactly what the fuck is going on. Fair warning though, you'd best get comfortable.'

Epilogue

When one contemplates the nature of heroes in the stories they hear, many believe that there is only one, perhaps two that are responsible for the salvation of the many. Others believe that there are many heroes, each of whom contributes to the success of the whole in meaningful, yet disparate ways. A handful of people believe that the story we choose to tell necessitates that we highlight some heroes over others, but in actuality each person is the hero of their own story.

Irrespective of which one of these schools of thought you aspire to, you are wrong.

The true nature of heroes is to be nothing more than the champion of the God that chose them as their conduit. Without the divine patronage that ignites the spark of greatness in heroes they would be irrelevant in the extreme.

Almost all would argue against this notion, clinging to the lie of free will, from fear of losing all meaning in the life they lead. This is foolish. A god's knowledge of their chosen is absolute. They know what they would do in any situation and it is this knowledge that allows them to select for elevation only those who would serve their goals. In doing so, subtlety guiding the flow of history in any way the wish.

Our only saving grace is that there are many gods. Each of whom is compelled to work against the machinations of their brethren to achieve their own objectives. I make no claim to know what these objectives are, but I know without doubt, that as long as mortals worship a broad range of deities, there will never be a consensus between all gods. This is a fortunate thing.

For if ever the House of Gods became controlled by a singular deity, or a coalition of likeminded gods, then we would be completely subject to their mercy. If benevolent we would enter a golden age, the likes of which has never been seen before. However, if malicious in nature, we would no longer need to fear the realm of damnation, for we would already occupy its halls.

Thus, I implore all who read this to continue their worship of the old Gods. Do not fall for the lies of the One God, do not bend to his ways, lest he gain dominion over the House. I know not if he would prove to be a benevolent patron, or a malicious tyrant, but I fear that once this becomes known our fate would already be sealed.

*   *   *

As the wizened man put the last full stop onto the page, he let out a satisfied sigh. His work was at last complete.

I know it's said that quality cannot be rushed, but even I will admit, that took far too long.

Leaning back in his chair he stretched his arms to the sky and his back audibly popped. Discomfort was instantly replaced with relief and the man couldn't help but release another sigh of satisfaction.

Who says getting old is without benefit?

Closing his latest manuscript, *The Ways of Gods and Heroes by Xenophanes,* the man reached for the small brass bell by his side and shook it wildly. As the bell chimed pleasantly throughout the room, as well as the house proper, the man contemplated his accomplishment and pondered what was next. Now that it was finished, all that remained was to copy and distribute his work.

Bah, Alphonso can organise that, I need some rest. Maybe a holiday.

The man gave the bell another shake. Still, no one came. After waiting briefly, he ran it yet one more time. Nothing. His manservant continued to ignore his call. Confounded by Alphonso's absence, the man rose slowly from his chair, knees straining in protest, and prepared to do battle with the stairs before him. Climbing slowly, Xenophanes called out his servant's name, but he was greeted by nothing but the echo of his own voice.

Where in the seven hells has that boy gotten himself too now?

As Xenophanes reached the top of the stairs, he was greeted by the prone form of Alphonso. Driven by worry, the man shuffled to his servant's side, still slowed by his old bones, but faster than what he had moved in years.

He ignored the blood pooling around Alphonso's body and checked his servant's neck for a pulse. Failing to find any sign of life, yet compelled by an inexplicable curiosity, Xenophanes rolled over the corpse. A large knife protruded from his chest; the wound clearly fresh. In a panic, Xenophanes stood hurriedly and rushed towards the main door, he needed to escape.

Oh gods, they're after me. Poor Alphonso, but I can't help, I can't tarry. I'll be next. Oh gods.

After he had barely taken three steps, a shadowed figure dropped from the ceiling. Silently, the stranger landed on the floor behind Xenophanes, and in a blink, grappled the aging philosopher. A hand, clad in black leather, smothered Xenophanes's mouth, preventing any outburst. Xenophanes tried to break free, but was far too weak.

All attempts at escape ended as Xenophanes felt a sharp searing pain in his side. In an instant, the assassin's blade pierced Xenophanes's flesh, driving straight through his ribs and into his heart. Losing all sensation, Xenophanes fell as his assassin released him. With the last of his will, he twisted in mid-air, turning to face his slayer. As his vision faded and his life fled, two flickering black flames ushered his soul into the next realm.

*   *   *

Elsewhere, in a long forgotten, but recently rediscovered subterranean chamber, the eyes, behind still closed eyelids, of an almost naked man twitched as though in the midst of a dream. It was only the smallest of movements and though it went unwitnessed, any who would have seen it would have questioned their sanity, for surely this man was dead, not a slumber.

Appendix

A brief detailing of some of the sentient species occupying Térrtha.

Extracted from Sir David Goodall's *Encyclopaedia of Nature*

Foreword: Before I begin properly, I feel it is important for me to make a single point of clarification. The following is by no means a complete compilation of all Térrtha's sentient species. I have deliberately omitted any reference to those sentient species typically regarded as monstrous. For example, I am aware of several instances of evidence that support the argument that 'giants' are indeed sentient[1], but I will not mention them here further. The same is true for both orcs and goblins.

Builg: The Builgs are a strange people. Averaging at nine feet tall and almost entirely covered in fur, they have the appearance of bipedal bovines, but, along with all other humanoid species, have been gifted with opposable thumbs.[2] By virtue of their size they are one of the physically strongest races[3], as such it considered by most unwise to voluntarily seek physical altercations with builgs. Fortunately, builgs are a mostly peaceful peoples that prefer peace and harmony[4] over violence.[5]

Not much in know about their culture, save for the fact that their lifestyle is founded upon tribal, family units. They worship no specific god and in fact abhor almost all deities.[6] Their knowledge of natural remedies, as well as poisons, is second to none. Many consider, by a great margin I might add, the best apothecaries to be builg.

---

[1] And I wholeheartedly believe that the evidence is sound enough to legitimately advocate for their induction to the pantheon of sentient species.

[2] Many evolutionists would contest the term 'gifted.'

[3] Only the Goliaths are on average stronger.

[4] Especially with nature.

[5] They will however defend the environment with a calculated ferocity that all whom have witnessed it describe as 'terrifying.'

[6] Save for Gaia.

Typically, builgs occupy small, remote villages that are rarely, if ever, visited by outsiders. It is uncommon, though not unheard of, for builgs to leave their village of origin, but predominantly this is for the express purpose of marriage.[7] They have no need to trade, as their villages are entirely self-sufficient, will never wage war on neighbours and never explore past the well-established borders of their territories. Those builgs found in more advanced civilisations are almost exclusively those deemed banished by their tribes for grave indiscretions[8] or the remnants of a murdered tribe.

Dragons: Dragons, in a similar fashion to elves[9], are not native to Térrtha. Old dwarven frescos were discovered in the ruins of one of their ancient cities depicting a mass of flying lizards[10] flying through a shimmering portal over a crowd of dwarven onlookers. It is unknown when this occurred, or what prompted dragon-kind to migrate to Térrtha, but such questions are academic for they are here and here to stay at that.

Having to contend with animosity towards their species, low fertility rates and a long gestation period, numbers of dragons across Térrtha are low. Many scholars estimate that they are constantly on the brink of extinction, but as of yet no one in the nobility[11] wishes to act of their behalf and implement conservation measures.

Dragons take a long time to reach maturity, but when they do, they become truly ferocious. An adult dragon is capable of slaying scores of soldiers with ease and sustaining little damage in response. Mature dragons also have the ability to morph into humanoid form at will. This is no illusion, but rather a true polymorph. This makes it almost impossible to detect a mature dragon if they wish to not be discovered. Due to the fact that dragons continue to grow indefinitely, the eldest of dragons are essentially unkillable.[12] In addition to their ability to alter their

---

[7] I use the term "marriage" as an approximation, builgs will mate with a single partner for life, but the ceremonies of their unions are a mystery.

[8] There is no record as to what may constitute a "grave indiscretion" for a builg.

[9] More on them later.

[10] Interpreted to be dragons.

[11] Rather *any* nobility.

[12] At least by regular means. Magic, on the other hand, may do the trick.

form at will, adult dragons are always powerful spell casters. For all but the most powerful to contend with a dragon is to invite death upon themselves.

Dragonkin: Dragon blood runs strong and even when a mature dragon transforms its blood runs hot with the power of dragons. Those children born from the coupling of a transformed dragon and a regular humanoid are the dragonkin.

Typically, dragonkin adopt the physical profile of their mother, with minor traits adopted from their father. As such, if a dragonkin's mother is a dragon they will be appear to be mostly a dragon, but will be much more humanoid in size and physicality. Many will be capable of walking bipedally as a humanoid would and most are incapable of flight. Dragonkin such as this mature at the same rate as their humanoid progenitor and will cease growing once they reach maturity. Unlike their dragon forebears, dragonkin will eventually die from old age.[13] All dragonkin share the same traits, but those with dragon fathers appear a lot more like their humanoid mothers. These dragonkin may have patches of scales over their skin, horns, serpentine eyes, or tails, but are almost entirely humanoid in appearance.

Due to the nature of their birthing dragonkin do not exist in large groups. They have no cities, no culture, no society. They either stay with their mother for the entirety of their life or embrace the lifestyle of a wanderer, constantly moving from place to place. The more humanoid dragonkin can integrate into society with sometimes little effort, but dragonkin that appear closer to their dragon forbears are shunned, reviled, and actively hunted. For these individuals, life is often nasty, brutal, and short.

Unlike their draconic progenitors, dragonkin do not possess any innate magical ability. Those that do have always obtained it through their mortal lineage.

Dwarves: Dwarves are rather similar to humans, albeit a much shorter and stockier version. Ranging from 4-5ft in height the often exceed the average weight of a human as their considerable bulk makes up for their vertical shortcomings.[14]

---

[13] If they are not killed before then.
[14] Pun intended.

This bulk results in dwarves being considerably stronger, physically, than humans. Even an average dwarf is considerably stronger than a 'strong' human. Naturally at home underground, dwarves have highly evolved sight and can see remarkably in low-zero light. Famous for their lustrous beards, dwarven facial hair grows rapidly, and at early ages. Amongst dwarves it is culturally taboo to trim one's beard before it has reached an appropriate length.[15]

Dwarves are the oldest race that has occupied Térrtha, but due to constant wars and other such calamities, they have lost much of their early histories. Dwarven ruins are scattered across the entirety of Ulandir and expeditions to uncover their secrets are routinely dispatched by those wishing to make (or build upon their existing) fortune.

There are two main sub-races of dwarfs, de animabus montibus[16] (colloquially referred to as mountain dwarves) and the clann nam beann[17] (colloquially referred to as hill dwarves). The mountain dwarfs are native to Iuga Quinque and its surrounding subterranean outposts. Typically, they are remarkably strong and hardy, even for a dwarf, and are known for their excellent professional soldiers.[18]

Politically the mountain dwarves are ruled by a senate of elders, composed of one chosen representative from each of the most powerful families. Once deemed worthy of having a seat on the senate the family in question holds it until there are no more living family members. New families can be inducted onto the senate, but this is rare as it requires a unanimous vote in their favour.

The hill dwarves also dwell in Iuga Quinque, but are in fact refugees. Their original homeland, roilgeadh plaidean[19], was conquered and absorbed into the Empire's territories. They have adopted the military traditions of the mountain dwarves, but still exhibit a strong tie to their own cultural heritage. In particular, their fondness for, and aptitude with, smithy tools and fine metal working.

---

[15] When it is able to be tucked into the dwarf's belt.
[16] Literally translates to souls of the mountains.
[17] Literally translates to children of the hills.
[18] Referred to as Legionaries.
[19] The Rolling Plains in their native tongue.

Historically, the hill dwarves existed as one intertwined clan, of which they were all a part. To this day, their clan hierarchy still exists. The clan is headed by the Clan Chief who has ultimate power when dealing with hill dwarf matters. This power also supersedes the senate's power whenever a hill dwarf is involved. As such, no hill dwarf can ever be punished or disciplined by the senate.

Elementarians: Elementarians are the physical embodiment of the elements.[20] Currently we know of seven distinct sub-sects of elementarians (they being the fire, water, wind, earth, ice, dusk/dark and bright/light elementarians). Some scholars suggest that other sub-species may exist, but they have yet to be discovered and no evidence of their existence currently exists.

Each of the different sub-species herald from unique city states. Each of which are entirely independent from not only each other, but every other established nation. Unsurprisingly, for beings formed from the elements, each elementarian city was founded in a relatively suitable geographic location. The fire elementarians in the Scorched Lands, the water elementarians in the Atlantean sunken city of Atlan,[21] the earth elementarians in the Geode Caverns, the air elementarians in the Floating Isles, the ice elementarians upon the World's Summit, the dusk/dark elementarians within the Twilight Dominion and the bright/light elementarians in the Drifting Plains. Each of these cities is highly developed, but are varied on how they welcome strangers. The bright/light elementarians are open and trusting of foreigners, while the ice elementarians are highly distrustful and rarely let outsiders into their city.

The defining feature of the elementarians is their ability to manipulate their associated element. Fire elementarians can bend flame to their will in particularly astounding ways, while the dusk/dark elementarians are similarly gifted in their manipulation of shadow/darkness. Fortunately, elementarians have no ability to

---

[20] Though the name is hardly original, and in my opinion entirely bland, it has stuck due to its simplicity and technical accuracy.
[21] The water elementarians took control of the city during their final war with the Atlanteans. Soon after the Atlanteans became extinct.

channel magics that are not associated with their element, if they were able to do so then they would easily be the most powerful magic casters of any realm.[22]

Elves: Elves (often referred to as the fair folk) are no taller than the average human, but are far slenderer. Typically, they have high cheekbones, large oval shaped eyes, and sharp pointed ears, which makes them appear somewhat hawkish. Depending upon ones taste they can be considered to be strikingly beautiful or hideously gaunt.[23] Elves are almost unique amongst the races of Térrtha as they are functionally immortal.[24] While each of the other races have an easily defined life span, elves will live until they are killed.

Currently, there are three distinct sub-species of elves inhabiting Térrtha.[25] They are the wood elves, high elves, and the daoi-sith (dark elves). The high elves are the most common and widely known. They have changed little since they first arrived on Térrtha and still occupy their spires, dealing with those outside their borders only when it suits them. For the most part the wood elves occupy the fae realm, sometimes they will explore wooded or forested areas, but they will never venture beyond them. Altered and twisted by the fae realm, they appear wild and animalistic, barely resembling the high elves that they once were. The daoi-sith inhabit the deep places of Térrtha. Far underground, they revel in the darkness and have grown to shun the light. Over time, their auditory senses have heightened, as their vision had diminished, and their skin has become black. Most surface races shun the daoi-sith [26] and perceive them as evil. This may or may not be the case, but the characteristic aggression and violence of the daoi-sith has done nothing to dissuade this stereotype.

---

[22] That said they are already extremely powerful spell casters as they don't seem to fatigue at the same rate as ordinary magic users and are able to manipulate their element in any way they see fit.

[23] This latter opinion is common amongst the dwarves who believe elves to be far too skinny to ever be considered attractive.

[24] Dragons being the only other race that can boast this.

[25] At one time there was a fourth, the Atlanteans, but for reasons unknow they were rendered extinct several centuries ago.

[26] In the rare event that they interact with them.

None of the elves are native to Térrtha, or indeed this reality.[27] Several thousands of years ago[28] a small cluster of spires, in which the elves resided, spontaneously popped into this reality. It is believed that at that time all elves were what we consider today to be 'high elves' and through nothing more than circumstance, elements of their society fractured away from the whole and over time were altered by their new environments. Thus, they evolved to exhibit the racial diversity we are familiar with now.

Though elves hail from a distant, unfathomable, realm, unlike dragons, they still conform to the laws of magic observed in this realm and do not possess any inherent magical abilities of their own. Woods elves are the exception to this, but their magical abilities are a direct result of their mutation from the fae realm.

Garula: The garula[29] are a particularly strange species. Almost entirely avian in appearance they only diverge slightly from their bird cousins. The primary alteration is that they have a pair of arms, though they are entirely feathered[30] and sport talons in lew of nails. In addition, their hind legs are elongated which allow the garula to walk upright almost as easily as a human.[31] In regards to their size, the garula differ widely. Where those akin to eagles can reach 4-5ft in height those related to the common starling may only reach 2ft in height.[32] Irrespective of size, all garula are capable of flight and all garula are equally intelligent.

Culturally, the garula are relatively simplistic. They typically form small clans with little to no racial diversity.[33] Almost always these clans are led by their eldest female member, save for the more war-like clans which are almost exclusively helmed by their eldest male member.

---

[27] As far as anyone can tell.
[28] No one knows exactly when.
[29] Colloquially know as bird-men.

[30] Just like the rest of their body.
[31] Though their hunched frames force them to sway from side to side as they do so.
[32] Other sub-species have been found to be even smaller.
[33] By this I mean that the entirety of a clan will be of one bird species (i.e. falcon), obviously they are all garula.

It is unknown what the garula believe spiritually and currently no evidence exists to suggest that they ascribe to a clearly defined religion.

Technologically, they are primitive, relying upon simple tools for hunting and little more than that. No evidence exists to suggest that they have the capabilities to forge complicated metal objects.

Sightings of the garula are rare as they tend to inhabit those mountain peaks and cliffsides located far from occupied habitations. Typically, they only leave their dwellings to hunt or repel intruders from their territories.

As they are expert hunters, it is recommended that their territories should be avoided by anyone not travelling in force.

Gnomes: Gnomes are small,[34] quick witted and naturally industrious. They make up for their lack in size and strength by possessing a natural aptitude for magic.[35] For those problems they encounter that magic cannot solve, they are experts at inventing solutions. The most well renowned of these inventions is the golem. A magical and mechanical hybrid, the golem is capable of completing many tasks[36]. Gnomes age far slower than humans and will not reach maturity until almost one hundred years of age. However, they tend to live for several centuries.[37]

Though they are capable of inhabiting anywhere, gnomes tend to favour either dense forests or subterranean caverns. Their cities vary in size, but each of them seems to blend with and be moulded by the environment around them. Instead of twisting nature to their will[38], gnomes accept nature and alter their designs to better coexist with it.

Amongst all the races of Térrtha, gnomes are the most technologically sophisticated. Their forged wares are considered superior to those of the dwarves[39] and their siege weapons are considered by all who have witnessed them, as

---

[34] Approximately the same height as halflings, but far skinnier.

[35] For some unknown reason the genetic trait, green eyes, that denotes magic capabilities is more prevalent amongst gnomes.

[36] From simple cleaning, to heavy labour, to full out warfare.

[37] The eldest gnome on record reached nine hundred and eighty years of age before she died.

[38] As humans are want to do.

[39] Most dwarves would disagree, but they'd be wrong.

nothing short of diabolical. Fortunately for the rest of Térrtha, gnomes are a peace-loving people who actively avoid conflict. Rumours of a new 'clockwork' based technology have permeated from one of the gnomes more industrious cities, but as to what that actually means I have no idea.

Goliaths: Goliaths are a tall and proud race. Hailing from the far south, they roam their snow coated mountain peaks in small family-orientated tribes. The leader of these tribes is always the strongest member, regardless of age or sex. At any time, a tribe member can challenge their current leader for the right to rule, but challenges are rare as they will often result in either one or both of the combatants dying.

Descendants of the now extinct yetis,[40] goliaths are on average taller than nearly all other humanoid races.[41] Their skin is a unique shade of grey and they, including the females of the species, are covered almost entirely with hair.[42]

Goliaths respect strength and reward those tribespeople who demonstrate their strength through aggressive feats.[43] Weakness is not tolerated and any tribesperson deemed to be too weak will be mercilessly banished from the tribe. These Goliaths are magically 'shaved' and rendered hairless.[44] Male outcasts are forcibly castrated and the women have their wombs surgically removed, this is to prevent the weakest of their species from reproducing and spreading the shame of their inferiority. Female exiles are incredibly rare though as most powerful male Goliaths would still enjoy them as sexual partners. However, any offspring born from such a 'weak' coupling are almost always killed by their father soon after birth.

Without their tribe to help them hunt, those banished rarely survive. Those that do tend to gravitate towards society where they sell their services as

---

[40] Commonly referred to as abominable snowmen.
[41] The average goliath is around eight feet in height and the tallest of the species can near ten.
[42] The women sport the most impressive of beards.
[43] Whether they be hunting or warfare.
[44] This is a great shame to Goliaths as they perceive 'hairless' races as inferior and weak.

mercenaries. Even these 'weak' goliaths are highly sought after as they are almost exclusively 'better' than most other humanoid mercenaries.

It is common practice amongst exiled goliaths to tattoo their skin in a variety of tribal patterns. It is unknown if these have an inherent meaning or are purely for decoration.[45]

Goliaths care not for the gods and don't actively worship any of them. They only care for power and live by the notion that 'might equals right.' Fortunately, goliaths seem content to war with each other rather than to descend their mountains to attack anyone else. To this day there has never been a major goliath incursion into the lowlands.

Half-Breeds: The term half-breeds[46] refers to those people of mixed decent. In other words, those people with parents from different races. While half-breeds are rare it is possible for any humanoid male (irrespective of species) to impregnate any humanoid female (also irrespective of species). Some pairings seem to result in more offspring than others[47], while evidence of other pairings is almost completely non-existent.[48] The reasoning for this has been theorised to primarily be due to the relative attraction levels between the two species. For example, an elf is close enough to a human in appearance to garner a romantic connection. As a garula is so physically dissimilar to every other species only under the rarest of circumstances would a romantic coupling would even be considered. In addition to attraction levels, it has been theorised that the odds of an effective impregnation are diminished as the physical differences between the parents increase. As such the odds of a garula successfully impregnating a dragonkin would be close to zero.

With regards to physicality half-breeds inherit more of the physical traits of their mother. Without question they inherit some physicality's from their father, but these are generally far more subtle.

---

[45] Knowing goliaths, it could also be that they simply like the pain.
[46] Though I am well aware of the offensiveness of this term, it is biologically accurate and used commonly. As such I will also use it in this instance.
[47] The combination of human and elf being the most common.
[48] For example, no known garula half-breed has ever been observed.

From a cultural and social perspective, a half-breed inherits the social norms of whichever parent it is raised by. If both parents play an active role in raising a half-breed child, then typically they adopt a perspective that is an amalgamation of both parents' perspectives.

Halflings: Far shorter than an average human, halflings often appear to those unfamiliar with their kind as nothing more than children. Even smaller than an average dwarf, and nowhere near as stocky, halflings are amongst the smallest of the sentient races. By virtue of their size halflings are physically weaker than nearly all other races. This disadvantage is balanced by the fact that they are phenomenally sneaky. All of the best thieves/burglars have been halflings and the greatest amongst them were never once caught in the act.[49] On top of this, halflings are a typically happy and joyful people that have extraordinary interpersonal skills that lead them to excel at mercantile and thespian pursuits.

Halflings do not own a defined territory, nor have any of their own cities.[50] During all of recorded history they have always co-existed with humankind. They have always shared humanities cities and adopted the cultural, social, religious, and legal tenants of their human 'hosts.' Seen by mankind as nothing more than smaller versions of themselves, halflings have always been tolerated, if not welcomed, and throughout their history have never suffered persecution from human hands.

Some scholars have hypothesised that the halflings trend towards 'passive assimilation' is a well-constructed survival mechanism.[51] Others believe that halflings simply gravitate towards humanity because they are so similar with it, and that there are no greater designs at play at all. A third group believes that long ago halflings were cursed by the gods to suffer eternally by being stripped of the ability to determine their own future and were instead tied to that of humankind. Whatever the reason, the fate of halflings, on Térrtha at least, is inexorably tied to that of humans.

---

[49] A halfling, named Alphonso, confessed to a multitude of robberies on his deathbed. In every instance the authorities had no witnesses or evidence against him.
[50] No evidence has ever been found that they did either of these things in the past either.
[51] The world, they argue, is a large and dangerous place for those as small as a halfling.

Humans: Compared to each of the other races inhabiting Térrtha humans have very few biological advantages. Unlike dwarves they aren't particularly strong. Compared to elves they are slow and clumsy. They aren't as physically resilient as dragonkin and are intellectually inferior to gnomes[52] All things considered they are nothing but average in every respect. That said, humans have overcome their biological inferiority to spread throughout Térrtha. Not a single continent exists that is completely devoid of their influence and the greatest of their city's rivals those of other races. Scholars have contributed the pre-eminence of humankind to the combination of their relatively short reproductive cycle, high fertility rates, ruthlessness, ingenuity, and their unshakable faith in their own superiority.[53]

Though all humans are essentially the same[54] they differ widely in their physical appearance. Some are tall, others are short. Some have fair skin, while others are dark skinned. Their language is just as diverse, and while every human society is well versed in the common tongue, they will often speak a second dialect unique to their particular civilisation.

Culturally, humans are incredibly diverse. Some, like the Akkadian Empire for example, are empires built upon slavery and warfare. Others, like the monarchy of Estmire, are founded upon honour and a benevolent legal system. Republics, dictatorships, democracies, and any other political system you care to name, all exist across Térrtha and humans of varying societies have adopted them all.

Religiously, technologically, socially, when comparing them to whatever measure you care to mention, humans are the very definition of diverse.

Infernati: In recorded history the seven hells have launched six major invasions against the mortal realms. It was during the final invasion that infernati[55] first

---

[52] On average.

[53] This view doesn't exist amongst the common man, but is the norm amongst the elite of some of humanity's larger kingdoms or empires.

[54] In so far that they are all the same species.

[55] The name is not their own. Derived by Dr Leonard the Younger from his native tongue, *inferna*, meaning 'infernal' or 'hell,' and the suffix -*nati*, meaning 'born,' he was alluding to their hells-born nature.

made their appearance on Térrtha. Bred by the daemon lords of Ratna Prabha as shock troops, infernati exhibit an extreme propensity towards violence. Able to become enraged at the slightest insult or injury, infernati would enter a berserk rage during combat. This 'berserk' state drove them to godly feats of strength and allowed them to ignore wounds that would have been fatal to those from other species. Even when not enraged, an infernati is far stronger than an ordinary human.

When the daemon invasion was thwarted and the hell portal[56] closed, many infernati were stranded on Térrtha. Those that did not fall during the infernati final stand on the barren plains of Haradeous, scattered across the world. Most were hunted down and slaughtered, but some[57] were able to escape persecution and live a simple life in the wilderness and small villages. Many of these were able to breed with the locals, and while their numbers are small, their race still exists throughout Térrtha to this day.

Though they are no longer actively persecuted, many abhor infernati and it is common for them to be vilified or shunned for nothing more than being what they are. For this reason, most infernati prefer a nomadic lifestyle avoiding major population centres in favour of societies outskirts.

Infernati have no culture specific to themselves, nor are they industrially minded, nor do they possess and magical abilities. However, the anger that was initially bred into them has persisted[58] and all infernati must be considered to be extremely dangerous. Once enraged, even an unarmed adolescent infernati is capable of tearing an armed and trained soldier to pieces.

Iasgair: When the Atlantean elves abandoned the surface in favour of a sub-aquatic life they evolved in such a manner as to lose their ability to resurface.[59] As a result they required an intermediary to act on their behalf when interactions with surface dwellers were necessary. So, the iasgair were bred.

---

[56] The gateway that daemonic forces used to enter the mortal realm.
[57] Specifically, the females of the species, who are reputed to be phenomenally alluring.
[58] Despite the many generations of breeding with the other mortal races.
[59] They lost their legs in favour of a fish-tail and their lungs for gills.

No one knows exactly how the Atlanteans managed it, but they created a truly unique being. Iasgair have both lungs and gills. They have humanoid legs and feet, but their fingers and toes are webbed. They are able to see well in low-light[60], but also have a second eyelid that protects their sensitive eyes in brightness. While they are unable to stand the absolute depths of the ocean, as its immense pressure would crush them, and their skin quickly dries upon the surface, the Atlanteans created a species to be an almost perfect bridge between themselves and the surface races.

During the current day, the iasgair are renowned for always remaining neutral. No matter the issue iasgair will not involve themselves politically with others. This is not to say the iasgair are isolationist, they are not. Anátristé, the capital city of the iasgair, is renowned for being the largest trading city on Térrtha. In addition, diplomats from every nation/people are not only welcome, but encouraged to establish embassies within Anátristé's limits.

Anátristé is by far the largest of iasgair's cities and the only one to be constructed above the waterline. Many travellers note the beauty and awe that Anátristé inspire, but many of them are unaware that the majority of Anátristé lies underwater. The surface sections of the city are almost exclusively for foreigners. All other iasgair cities are deep underwater and closed to visitors.

Though they never actively wage war on others and have no real navy, the iasgair are not defenceless. Anátristé is ringed by three outer walls[61], atop from which siege weapons equipped with eternal fire[62] stand sentinel. Also, any navy foolish enough to assault Anátristé will in all likelihood be scuttled as iasgair commandos saw out their hulls from below.

---

[60] Perfect for the darkness of the depths.
[61] The size of which are barely believable.
[62] A particularly nasty concoction that will continue to burn even when fully immersed in water.

Author's Note

My many thanks to all who took the time to read this book. As a reader from a family of readers, I understand all too well the reticence of the audience to pick up and try the work of an untested author, especially an independent one at that. That's fine.

I really do hope that you have enjoyed what you have read here, but if not, I appreciate your time no less than that of my stoutest fans. Thank you.

For those of you who have loved their time within my world, and cannot wait to return, bear with me, I've already begun working on the next instalment and it should be completed soon(ish). Sign up to the newsletter on my website, www.mjcoad.com.au, to stay informed and never miss a new release.

 I am loath to ask anything of my readers, for by reading this book you have already done more than enough and owe me nothing else, but reviews are the lifeblood of an author's success. If you enjoyed *Heroes of Thered's Field,* or any of my other works, please consider leaving a review on either Goodreads or the storefront where it was purchased.

Thank you.

About the Author

M. J. Coad was born in 1989 in a small Australian town called Seymour, which is a smidge over 100km north of Melbourne. However, during his childhood, as an army brat, he moved frequently and has never considered Seymour to be his home. From an early age, he enjoyed reading and grew up on the fantastical tales of Tolkien, Rowling, Feist, Pratchett, and Martin. To name but a few. Throughout his six years of study at the University of Tasmania, culminating in a Masters of Teaching, he never really knew what he wanted to be, just that it was not a teacher. It was by chance, that he discovered the Critical Role YouTube channel and the world of tabletop RPG's. The spark of inspiration struck. Deciding to combine his love for reading with the joy he found in playing games, and watching others play them, he began to write, crafting a world of his own.

You can find out more about M. J. Coad, and his other works, on his website, www.mjcoad.com.au, where you can also join his mailing list. Ensure that you never miss out on a future book launch.

www.ingramcontent.com/pod-product-compliance
Lightning Source LLC
Chambersburg PA
CBHW072018020726
47501CB00006B/1859